MEET THE MEN IN HOT SHOT'S LIFE . . .

SAM GAMBLE: Cocky and brash, this brazen young adventurer barges into Susannah's life on the back of a motorcycle. With quicksilver words and a breathtaking vision of the future, he sweeps her away from her safe world into a life of dazzling possibility.

MITCHELL BLAINE: A business dynamo, he thought he had won it all—until his wife and family left him. When Susannah and Sam lure him into their dream, he can't resist the challenge, for behind his starchy corporate image lives a powerful man ready to risk everything.

YANK YANKOWSKI: A brilliant inventor, Yank lives in the amazing universe of his own brain. He knows his inspired machine will start a revolution. But what about the complex human being hiding beneath his eccentric genius?

SUSANNAH AND HER MEN . . . THE REBEL, THE STUFFED SHIRT, THE GENIUS . . . TOGETHER, THEY SET OUT TO CHANGE THE WORLD!

"A crackerjack tale about the birth of high-tech industry. . . . A fascinating look at the personalities and passions that created Silicon Valley and the computer industry."

—*Rave Reviews*

"[An] unforgettable, powerful story with strong characterizations—a definite keeper."

—*Rendezvous*

"A fun and lively ⟨...⟩ d rock 'n' roll."

⟨...⟩*hers Weekly*

Books by Susan Elizabeth Phillips

Fancy Pants*
Glitter Baby
Honey Moon*
Hot Shot*
Risen Glory

*Published by POCKET BOOKS

SUSAN ELIZABETH PHILLIPS

Hot Shot

POCKET BOOKS

New York London Toronto Sydney

This book is a work of fiction. Names, characters, places and incidents are products of the author's imagination or are used fictitiously. Any resemblance to actual events or locales or persons, living or dead, is entirely coincidental.

An *Original* Publication of POCKET BOOKS

 POCKET BOOKS, a division of Simon & Schuster, Inc.
1230 Avenue of the Americas, New York, NY 10020

ISBN: 978-1-4767-3115-5

First Pocket Books printing June 1991

15 14

POCKET and colophon are registered trademarks of Simon & Schuster, Inc.

For information regarding special discounts for bulk purchases, please contact Simon & Schuster Special Sales at 1-800-456-6798 or business@simonandschuster.com

Printed in the U.S.A.

To Bill Phillips, B.E.E., M.S.E.E., who, in 1971, told me of a time when ordinary people would have computers in their homes. He told me other dreams, too.

PROLOGUE

● ● ● ● ● ● ● ● ● ● ● ● ● ● ● ● ● ●

For three terrifying days in 1958, the bride was the most famous child in America.

Eighteen years later, Susannah Faulconer once again felt like that panic-stricken seven-year-old. As she began walking at her father's side down the white runner that had been laid in a rigid path through the exact center of the Faulconer gardens, the heirloom pearl choker that encircled her throat seemed to be cutting off her breath. She knew the sensation was irrational since the choker wasn't the least bit tight and she had worn it many times, beginning with her debutante ball when she was eighteen. There was no reason for her to feel as if she couldn't breathe. No reason for her to experience such an overpowering urge to rip it from her throat and fling it into the crowd of well-dressed guests.

Not that she would actually do such a thing. Not proper Susannah Faulconer.

Although she was a redhead, people didn't tend to think of her that way, since her hair wasn't the fiery red of a slick Clairol ad, but a patrician auburn that conjured up images of a gentler time—a time of early morning fox hunts, tinkling teacups, and women who sat for Gainsborough. Beneath a Juliet cap, she wore her hair swept neatly away

1

from her face and simply arranged at the nape of her neck. The style was a bit severe for a bride, but it somehow suited her. Instead of an elaborate wedding gown, she wore a tea-length dress of antique lace. The open mandarin collar revealed a slim, aristocratic neck encircled by the lustrous five-strand heirloom pearl choker that was giving her so much difficulty. Everything about her bespoke wealth, breeding, and an old-fashioned sense of constraint out of place in a modern twenty-five-year-old woman.

A hundred years earlier, Susannah Faulconer would have been considered a great beauty, but her finely chiseled, elongated features were too subtle to compete with the bold cover-girl faces of the seventies. Her nose was thin and long but exquisitely straight; her lips narrow but beautifully arched. Only her eyes had a modern look about them. Wide-set and well-shaped, they were a light gray. They were also unfathomable, so that occasionally during a conversation, the person with whom she was speaking had the uncomfortable sense that Susannah simply wasn't there, that she had withdrawn to a place no one else was permitted to see.

For the past hour, the cream of California society had been arriving for the wedding. Limousines swept up the tree-lined drive and into the cobbled motor court that formed a crescent in front of Falcon Hill, the Faulconer family estate. Falcon Hill looked very much as if it had been part of the hills south of San Francisco for centuries, but it was barely twenty years old—built in the posh community of Atherton by Susannah's father, Joel Faulconer, not long after he had taken over control of Faulconer Business Technologies from his own father.

Despite differences of age and sex, there was a sameness about the guests who sat in the carefully laid-out rows of lacy white wrought-iron chairs. They all looked prosperous and conservative, very much like people accustomed to giving orders instead of taking them—all except the beautiful young woman who sat toward the back. In a sea of Halston and Saint Laurent, Paige Faulconer, the bride's younger sister, was conspicuous in a maroon thrift-store dress from the thirties draped at the shoulders with a funky, pink marabou boa.

2

As the music of the processional swelled, Susannah Faulconer turned her head slightly and spotted the cynical smile on her sister's pouty mouth. She resolved not to let her old conflicts with Paige spoil her wedding day. At least her sister had decided to attend the ceremony, which—after everything that had happened—was more than Susannah had expected.

Once again she was conscious of the tight pearl choker. She made herself forget about Paige and take in the beauty of the gardens instead. Marble statuary carved in Vicenza, and sparkling fountains purchased from a chateau in the Loire Valley, gave the gardens an old world look. Dozens of urns containing rose bushes heavy with white blooms had been strategically placed throughout the greenery. Gardenias floated in the fountains, and festoons of white ribbon blew gently in the June breeze. Everything was perfect, exactly as she had arranged it.

She concentrated on Cal, who was waiting for her beneath the pristine white canopy that had been constructed in front of the largest of the stone fountains. With his upper-crust good looks, Calvin Theroux reminded her of the men in magazine ads for expensive Scotch. At the age of forty-two, he was one of the most influential men in the Faulconer corporation. Despite their seventeen-year age difference, she and Cal were considered to be a perfect match. They had everything in common. Both had been raised in prosperity —she in San Francisco, he in Philadelphia. They had gone to the most exclusive private schools and moved in the best circles. Of course, Cal hadn't been kidnapped when he was seven, but then, neither had most people.

The choker tightened around her throat. She heard the distant sound of a riding mower and imagined her father's displeasure when he realized that the gardener at the neighboring estate had chosen this particular hour on a Saturday afternoon to cut the lawn. He would be annoyed that she hadn't thought to send the neighbors a note.

Cal's arm brushed against her own as she reached the altar. "You look beautiful," he whispered. The suntanned creases at the corners of his eyes deepened as he smiled.

The minister cleared his throat and began. "Dearly beloved . . ."

3

She knew she was doing the right thing by marrying Cal. She always did the right thing. Cal loved her. He was mature and thoughtful, and he would be a perfect husband. But the knot of misery that had been growing inside her refused to ease.

"Who gives this woman to be married to this man?"

"I do." Joel Faulconer's strong, handsome features were softened by the intense expression of fatherly pride that lurked about his mouth as he transferred her hand from his own arm to Cal's. He stepped away, and she could hear him taking his place in the second row of chairs.

The sound of the lawn mower grew louder.

Her maid of honor took the bridal bouquet, and Susannah's hand slipped discreetly to her neck. She looped her index finger just over the top of the Bennett family choker and eased it away from her skin. Cal was listening intently to the minister's words and didn't notice.

"I, Calvin James Theroux, take thee, Susannah Bennett Faulconer . . ."

The noise of the mower had grown so loud that others had begun to notice. Cal's nose twitched as if he had just caught a whiff of something unpleasant. Susannah stood quietly, her eyes steady, her mind unsettled.

And then she realized that the sound wasn't coming from a mower at all but from something else entirely.

She sucked in her breath and all the blood drained from her head. The minister was talking to her now. She couldn't concentrate. The noise was coming closer, moving around the side of the house and heading directly for the gardens. Cal turned to look, the minister stopped talking. Susannah could feel her skin growing damp beneath her breasts.

And then it happened. The peaceful gentility of the Faulconer gardens was shattered by the loud, vulgar roar of a big, black, twin-engine Harley-Davidson motorcycle shooting into view.

The bike barreled across the manicured lawn and cut past a statue of Andromeda. The rider's cry rang out over the noise of the engine, a primitive, atavistic cry.

"Suzie!"

With a choked exclamation, she spun around. The pulse at the side of her throat began to throb.

Her father leapt to his feet, knocking his chair askew. Cal curled his hand protectively over her wrist. The bike came to an abrupt stop at the far end of the aisle runner she had so recently walked along. Its front wheel crumpled the pristine fabric.

No, she thought. *This isn't real. It's only a nightmare. Just another nightmare.*

"Su-zie!"

He wore a black leather jacket and blue jeans that were taut across his thighs as they straddled the motorcycle. He had the dark, snapping eyes and high flat cheekbones of a full-blooded Comanche, although he was more Mediterranean than Native American. His skin was olive, his mouth thin, almost cruel. The breeze blowing off San Francisco Bay caught his shoulder-length black hair and tossed it away from his face. It blew long and free like a flag.

"What's the matter, Suzie? Forget to send me an invitation?" His voice rose over the roar of the Harley, and his dark, mesmerizing eyes speared through her skin.

A murmur went up from the guests, an expression of outrage, astonishment, and horrified delight at being present to witness such an outrageous scene. Could this *person* be one of Susannah's friends? None of them could imagine it. One of Paige's flings, perhaps, but certainly not Susannah's.

In the background, Susannah was dimly aware of her maid of honor muttering "Ohgod, ohgod, ohgod" over and over like a mantra. She found herself holding onto Cal's arm as if it were her lifeline. She tried to speak, but the proper words wouldn't form. She began to pull at the choker, and her long, aristocratic fingers shook as she attempted to free it from her neck.

"Don't do this, Suzie," the man on the bike said.

"See here!" her father shouted as he tried to disengage himself from the row of wrought-iron chairs and the rope garland that cordoned off the seats.

She was so anguished that she couldn't even think about the embarrassment she was suffering in front of her guests, the personal humiliation of what was happening. Stay in control, she told herself. No matter what happens, stay in control.

The man on the bike held out his hand toward her. "Come with me."

"Susannah?" Cal said behind her. "Susannah, who is this person?"

"Call the police!" someone else exclaimed.

The man on the Harley continued to hold out his hand. "Come on, Suzie. Climb up on the back of my bike."

The Bennett family choker gave way under Susannah's fingers, and heirloom pearls tumbled down onto the white cloth that had been laid for the ceremony, some even rolling off into the grass. It was her wedding day, she thought wildly. How could such a vulgar, untoward event happen on her wedding day? Her grandmother would have been prostrate.

His arm slashed the air in a contemptuous gesture that took in the garden and the guests. "Are you going to give cocktail parties for the rest of your life, or are you going to come with me and set the world on fire?"

She pulled away from Cal and pressed her hands over her ears—a shocking, awkward gesture from proper Susannah Faulconer. Words erupted from her throat. "Go away! I won't listen to you. I'm not listening to you." And then she began moving away from the altar, trying to separate herself from all of them.

"Follow me, babe," he crooned. "Leave all this and come with me." His eyes were hypnotizing her, calling to her. "Hop on my bike, babe. Hop on my bike and follow me."

"No." Her voice sounded choked and muffled. "No, I won't do it."

He was a ruffian, a renegade. For years she had kept her life under perfect control. She had done everything properly, followed all the rules, not stepped on a single crack. How could this have happened? How could her life have careened out of her control so quickly?

Behind her stood safe, steady Cal Theroux, her twin, the man who kept the demons away. Before her stood a street-smart hustler on a Harley-Davidson motorcycle. Impulsively, she turned away from both of them and looked toward her sister, only to see the frozen shock on her face. Paige wouldn't help her. Paige never helped.

Susannah clawed at her neck, but the pearl choker was gone. She felt the old panic grip her, and once again she found herself being drawn back to the horror of that spring day in 1958—the day when she became the most famous child in America.

The memory washed over her, threatening to paralyze her. And then she grew aware of her father freeing himself from the row of chairs, and she summoned all of her strength to shake away the past. She had only an instant, only an infinitesimal fragment of time to act before her father took control.

Calvin Theroux stood to her right, promising love, security, and comfort. A messiah on a motorcycle stood to her left, promising nothing. With a soft cry, proper Susannah Faulconer chose her destiny.

BOOK
ONE

. . . .

THE
VISION

Whatever you can do, or dream you can, begin it.
Boldness has genius, power, and magic in it.

—Goethe

BOOK
ONE

- -

THE
VISION

Whatever you can do, or dream you can, begin it.
Boldness has genius, power, and magic in it.

—Goethe

1

• •

Susannah's real father wasn't Joel Faulconer, but an Englishman named Charles Lydiard, who met Susannah's mother when he visited New York City in 1949. Katherine "Kay" Bennett was the beautiful socialite daughter of a recently deceased New York City financier. Kay spotted Lydiard on the afterdeck of a friend's yacht, where he was leaning against the mahogany rail smoking a Turkish cigarette and sipping a Gibson. Kay, always on the lookout for handsome unattached men, immediately arranged an introduction, and before the evening was over, had fallen in love with Lydiard's finely chiseled aristocratic looks and cynical world-weary manner.

Kay was never the most perceptive of women, and it wasn't until a year after their marriage that she discovered her elegant husband was even more attracted to artistic young men than he was to her own seductive body. She immediately gathered up their two-month-old daughter and left him to return to her widowed mother's Park Avenue penthouse, where she threw herself into a frantic round of socializing so she could forget the entire unsavory incident. She also did her best to forget the solemn-faced baby girl who was an unwelcome reminder of her own lack of judgment.

11

Charles Lydiard died in a boating accident in 1954. Kay was in San Francisco when it happened. She had recently married Joel Faulconer, the California industrialist, and she was much too preoccupied with keeping her virile young husband happy to dwell on the fate of a disappointing former husband. Nor did she spare any thoughts for the three-year-old daughter she had left her elderly mother to raise on the other side of the continent.

Susannah Bennett Lydiard, with her gray eyes, thin nose, and auburn hair tightly confined in two perfect plaits, grew into a solemn little mouse of a child. By the age of four, she had taught herself to read and learned to move soundlessly through the high-ceilinged rooms of her grandmother's penthouse. She slipped like a shadow past the tall windows with their heavy velvet drapes firmly drawn against the vulgar bustle of the city below. She passed like a whisper across the deep, old carpets. She existed as silently as the stuffed songbirds displayed under glass domes on the polished tables.

Her Grandmother Bennett was gradually losing her mind, but Susannah was too young to understand that. She only knew that her grandmother had very strict rules, and that breaking any one of them resulted in swift and terrible punishment. Grandmother Bennett said that she had already raised one frivolous child, and she didn't intend to raise another.

Twice a year Susannah's mother came to visit. On those days, instead of walking around the block with one of her grandmother's two elderly servants, Susannah went to tea with Kay at the Plaza. Her mother was very beautiful, and Susannah watched in tongue-tied fascination as Kay smoked one cigarette after another and checked the time on her diamond-encrusted wristwatch. As soon as tea was over, Susannah was returned to her grandmother, where Kay kissed her dutifully on the forehead and then disappeared for another six months. Grandmother Bennett said that Susannah couldn't live with her mother because Susannah was too wicked.

It was true. Susannah was a horribly wicked little girl. Sometimes she touched her nose at the dinner table. Other times she didn't sit up straight. Occasionally she forgot her pleases and thank-yous. For any of these transgressions, she was punished by being imprisoned for not less than one hour in the rear closet. This was done for her own good, her grandmother explained, but Susannah didn't understand how something so horrible could be good.

The closet was small and suffocating, but even more terrifying, it held Grandmother Bennett's old furs. For an imaginative child, the closet became a living nightmare. Dark ugly minks brushed at her pale cheeks, and gruesome sheared beaver coats rubbed against her thin arms. Worst of all was a fox boa with a real head forming its grisly clasp. Even in the dark of the closet she could feel those sly glass fox eyes watching her and she sat frozen in terror, her back pressed rigidly against the closet door, while she waited for those sharp fox teeth to eat her up.

Life took on dark, frightening hues for such a small child. By the time she was five, she had developed the careful habits of a much older person. She didn't raise her voice, seldom laughed, and never cried. She did everything within her limited powers to stay out of the terrifying feral depths of the closet, and she worked so diligently at being good that she would probably have succeeded if—late at night when she was sound asleep—her body hadn't begun to betray her.

She started to wet herself.

She never knew when it would happen. Sometimes several weeks would go by without incident, occasionally an entire month, but then she would awaken one morning and discover that she was lying in her own urine. Her grandmother's paper-thin nostrils wrinkled in distaste when Susannah was brought before her. Even Susannah's wicked mother Katherine had never done anything so odious, she said.

Susannah tried to hide the bedding, but there was too much of it and she was always discovered. When that happened, her grandmother gave her a stinging lecture and then made her wear her soiled nightgown into the closet as punishment. The acrid scent of her own urine mingled with the camphor that permeated the old furs until she couldn't breath. Furry monsters were all around her, ready to eat her up. She could feel their sharp teeth sinking into her flesh and their strong jaws snapping her tender bones. Bruises, like a string of discolored pearls, formed down the length of her spine from being pressed so hard against the closet door.

At night she struggled against sleep. She read books from her grandmother's library and pinched her legs to keep awake. But she was only five years old, and no matter how hard she tried, she eventually slipped into unconsciousness. That was when the fox-eyed monster crept into her bedroom and dug his sharp teeth into her flesh until her small bladder emptied on the bedclothes.

Each morning she awakened to fear. Afraid to move. Afraid to inhale, to touch the sheets. On those occasions when she discovered that the bed was dry, she was filled with a sense of joy so sharp it made her queasy. Everything about the day seemed brighter—the view of Park Avenue from the front windows, the shiny red apple she ate with her breakfast, the funny way her solemn little face was reflected in her grandmother's silver coffeepot. When the bed was wet, she wished she were old enough to die.

And then several days after her sixth birthday, it all changed. She was huddled in the closet with the smell of urine stinging her nostrils and fear clogging her throat. Her wet nightgown clung to her calves, and her feet were tangled in the soiled bedclothes her grandmother had ordered be put into the closet with her. She kept her eyes fixed, staring through the darkness at exactly the spot where she knew the fox head was hanging.

Her concentration was so intense she didn't hear the noise at first. Only gradually did the piercing sound of her grandmother's voice sink into her consciousness, along with a deeper male voice that was unrecognizable. She knew so few men. The doorman called her "little miss," but the voice didn't sound like it belonged to the doorman. There was a man who fixed the bathroom sink when it leaked, the doctor who had given her a shot last year. She saw men on the street when she took her walks, but she wasn't one of those dimple-cheeked little moppets who attracted the attention of adults, so few of them ever spoke to her.

Through the thick door she could hear the male voice coming closer. It was loud. Angry. She sprang back in fear and the furs caught her. The mink, the beaver—their dead skins swung against her. She cried out as the grisly fox head struck her cheek.

The door flew open, but she was sobbing in fear and she didn't notice.

"Good God!"

The angry male voice penetrated her consciousness. Panicked, she pushed herself deeper into the suffocating depths of the furs, instinctively seeking a known terror instead of an unknown one.

"Good God," the voice repeated. "This is barbaric."

She stared into the malevolent face of the fox and whimpered.

"Come here, sweetheart," the voice said, speaking more softly this time. "Come here."

Slowly she turned, blinking against the light. She turned toward that soft, crooning voice, and her eyes drank in their first sight of Joel Faulconer.

He was big and golden in the light, with powerful shoulders and a large, handsome head. Like a magic prince in one of her books, he smiled at her and held out his hand. "Come here, sweetheart. I'm not going to hurt you. I won't let anyone hurt you."

She couldn't move. She wanted to, but her feet were tangled in the wet bedcovers, and the fox head was butting against her cheek. He reached for her. She winced instinctively and drew back into the coats. He began crooning to her as he pulled her free of the furs. "It's all right. It's all right, sweetheart."

He lifted her into his strong arms and held her against his chest. She waited for him to recoil when he felt her damp nightgown and smelled her acrid scent, but he didn't. Instead, he clasped her tightly against his expensive suit coat and carried her into her bedroom, where he helped her to dress. Then he took her away from the Park Avenue penthouse forever.

"That stupid, stupid bitch," he murmured as he led her from the building.

Not until much later did she realize that he wasn't talking about her grandmother.

* * *

Joel Faulconer wasn't a sentimental man, so nothing in his experience had prepared him for the surge of emotion that had overtaken him when he had seen Susannah huddled like a frightened animal in his mother-in-law's moth-eaten furs. Now, six hours later, he glanced over at her strapped into the airplane seat at his side and his heart turned over. Her enormous gray eyes were set in a small, angular face, and her hair was skinned into braids so tight her skin seemed as if it might split over her fragile bones. She stared straight ahead. She had barely spoken since he had taken her from the closet.

Joel took a sip of the bourbon he had ordered from the stewardess and tried not to think about what would have happened to Susannah if he hadn't given in to the vague impulse that had taken him to his mother-in-law's doorstep that morning. Kay didn't like her mother, so he had only met the woman a few times in social settings and had never spoken with her long enough to realize that she was mentally ill. But Kay should have known.

As Joel thought about his wife, he felt the familiar combination of disgust and arousal she always managed to produce in him. She hadn't even disclosed that she had a daughter until several months after their wedding—about the same time he had begun to have second thoughts concerning the wisdom of his marriage. Kay had assured him that the child was better off with her mother, and not being anxious to take on the burden of another man's offspring, Joel hadn't pressed her. She went to see the child whenever she was in New York, and he had assumed that Susannah was well cared for. By the time Kay had given birth to his own child, he had nearly forgotten the existence of the other one.

He swirled the bourbon in his glass and stared blindly out the window. What kind of woman could conveniently forget she had a child? Only someone like Kay—a woman who was too silly and shallow to see what would be perfectly obvious to anyone else. He should have taken it upon himself to investigate long ago.

He turned his head to study the little girl at his side. She sat straight in the seat with her hands clasped neatly in her lap. Her head was beginning to wobble a bit, and he suspected the noise of the airplane engines would soon put her to sleep. As he watched, her eyelids, like fragile egg-shells, began to drift downward, and then they abruptly snapped back up.

"You're sleepy," he said.

She turned to look at him, and he felt another pang of sympathy as he saw that her eyes were huge and stricken, like those of a fawn caught before a hunter's gun. "I—I'm fine," she stammered.

"It's all right. We won't be in California for hours. Go ahead and take a nap."

Susannah stared helplessly at the magic, golden prince who had rescued her. It would be unthinkable to disobey him, yet if she slept, the fox-eyed monster was certain to find her. Even in this great silver airplane, he would find her and make her wet herself, and then her prince would know how bad she was.

Joel caught her hand and gave it a soft squeeze. "Just shut your eyes."

His voice was so gentle that she could barely control her tears. "I—I am unable," she said.

He gave her all his attention, as if she were an important adult instead of only a child. "Why is that?"

"Because it's unwise. Sir." She added the courteous form of address belatedly and hoped he wouldn't notice her extraordinary lapse of manners.

"I don't know very much about six-year-old little girls. I'm afraid you'll have to explain it to me."

Those blue eyes speared through her, sympathetic but demanding. He had a dent in the center of his chin, and she wished she could push the tip of her finger into it to see what it felt like. Her mind raced as she tried to find a polite way to explain. Bathroom talk was vulgar and unacceptable. There was never an excuse for it. "I rather suspect—" she said. "It's quite possible—"

He chuckled.

Alarmed, she looked at him. He gave her hand another squeeze. "What a queer little bird you are."

"Yes, sir."

"I don't think you can keep calling me 'sir.'"

"No, sir. What would you like me to call you?"

He was thoughtful. "How about 'Dad'?" And then he smiled. "On second thought, let's make it 'Father' for the time being. Somehow I think you'd be more comfortable with that."

"Father?" Her heart soared. What a wondrous word! Her own father was dead, and she desperately wanted to ask this golden prince if that meant she would now be his little girl. But it was dreadfully impolite to ask personal questions, so she held her tongue.

"Now that we have that settled, why don't you tell me why you can't fall asleep?"

She stared ahead miserably. "I'm rather a-afraid that I might—not on purpose, of course—purely by accident . . . I might commit an unfortunate mishap on the airplane seat."

"Mishap?"

She nodded her head miserably. How could she explain something so terrible to this shining man?

He didn't say anything for a moment. She was afraid to look at him, afraid of the revulsion she would see on his face. She stared at the woven back of the airplane seat ahead of her.

"I see," he finally replied. "It's an interesting problem. How do you think we could solve it?"

She didn't move her eyes from the back of the seat ahead of her. He seemed to expect her to say something, so she made a tentative offering. "You could pinch my arm, perhaps, if I began to fall asleep."

"Uhm. Yes, I suppose I could do that. Except I might fall asleep, too, and then I wouldn't notice. I think I have a better idea."

She cautiously turned her head to look at him. His fingertips were pressed together and his forehead knitted in concentration.

"What if . . ." he said. "What if we both just shut our eyes and took a small nap. Then, if you woke up and found out you'd had an unfortunate, uh, mishap, you could nudge me in the arm. I'd ask the stewardess for a glass of water, and when she gave it to me, I'd accidentally spill it over your skirt and onto the seat."

It took Susannah's quick mind only a few seconds to

absorb the staggering brilliance of his plan. "Oh, yes," she whispered on a rush of expelled breath. "Oh, yes, please."

She slept for hours. When she awoke, she was dry, rested, and happier than she could ever remember.

Her happiness carried her through those first few California days in the place called Falcon Hill. The house was as big as a castle and full of sunshine. She had a pretty, pink three-year-old baby sister named Paige who let Susannah play with her, and she saw her beautiful mother every day, not just for tea at the Plaza. Every night her new father came into her bedroom and left a glass of water for her so she could spill it on the sheets if she had a mishap. Susannah loved him so fiercely it hurt.

From the time he was fifteen, Joel Faulconer had fed on the lore of Tom Watson, the founder of IBM. He had watched avidly as Watson had molded his company into one of the most successful corporations in the world. He wanted the same to happen with Falcon Typewriter, the company his father Ben and his uncle Lewis had founded in 1913. Being good wasn't enough for Joel Faulconer. He had to be the best.

Returning from World War II with big dreams, Joel presented his father and his uncle with audacious strategies for expanding the company. Selling typewriters was small-time, he told them. They needed to attack IBM in its own territory by expanding their product line to include accounting machinery. They should be going after government contracts and upgrading their sales force.

His uncle, Lewis Faulconer, with his flashy suits, Havana cigars, and two-toned shoes, dismissed all of his nephew's suggestions. "Your father and me made ourselves millionaires a couple of times over, buddy boy. What do we need more money for?"

"To be the best," Joel replied, tight-lipped and seething with frustration. "To give Watson and IBM a run for their money."

Lewis's gaze slithered from Joel's well-cut hair to his Stanford class ring. "Shit, boy. You're not even wet behind the ears and you're trying to tell your daddy and me how to run the company we founded."

Ben Faulconer, who had gained more social polish over the years than his brother, was intrigued by Joel's ideas, but still cautious about making the sweeping changes his son insisted the postwar economy mandated. Still, Joel was certain he could manage his father, if only he could get rid of his uncle Lewis.

In a move that was to prove prophetic, Joel snatched up patents from the infant computer industry. At the same time, he began a systematic courtship of the high-ranking officers of the company, and with very little effort maneuvered his uncle into an escalating series of blunders. It took two years, but he finally succeeded in uprooting Lewis Faulconer.

On Lewis's last day with the company he had helped found, he confronted his brother in Ben's comfortable, paneled office. "You let a fox in the hen house, Benny," he warned, his words slurred because he no longer had any reason to wait until noon to take his first drink of the day. "Watch your ass, boy, because he'll be after you next."

Nonsense, Ben had thought to himself, secretly proud of Joel's cunning in ridding the company of a man who had become an embarrassment. The very idea of worrying about the security of his own position seemed ridiculous to Ben. He was chairman of the corporation—an untouchable. Besides, Joel was his son.

One year later, at the age of thirty, Joel Faulconer had forced his father into early retirement and taken over the helm of the newly renamed Falcon Business Technologies—or FBT, as it was being called. The company immediately began to prosper beyond anyone's imagination.

Two weeks after Susannah's arrival in California, FBT was marking the eighth anniversary of Joel's ascendancy to the chairmanship with the dedication of their new corporate headquarters near Palo Alto. Officially named the FBT Center of Corporate Activities, it had already become known simply as the Castle. Joel was secretly pleased with the nickname. After all, what better place for a king to live than a castle?

Not that he actually thought of himself as a king. But in the kingdom of Falcon Business Technologies, he certainly had unlimited power. Even the President of the United

States was answerable to the people, but Joel was only answerable to himself and a handpicked Board of Directors. He was proud to have accomplished so much at such a young age. At thirty-eight, he was one of the most influential men in American industry. If only he had as much control over his own household.

As he shot a pair of onyx cuff links into the sleeves of his dress shirt, he glanced impatiently at his wife. She was sitting at her dressing table and applying lipstick to the full mouth that had ministered so effectively to his body such a short time before. At thirty-three, she was just entering the prime of her beauty. Her breasts strained seductively against the bodice of her slip whenever she leaned toward the mirror. She worked with utter concentration, as if the simple act of applying lipstick took every ounce of her intelligence—which wasn't far from the mark, he thought.

"You're going to be late again, Kay," he snapped. "You know how important tonight's affair is. You promised me you'd be on time."

"Did I?" she said vaguely. She screwed the lipstick down into its tube and then began looking about for the jeweled cap. Wisps of light brown hair from her short Italian cut feathered her cheekbones, softening features that were already pleasantly blurred. Her mouth was too full for fashion, but he had always liked it. Too much, perhaps. It was more a trollop's mouth than the sort of mouth that belonged on the wife of a powerful man.

"Don't be angry, darling," she said. "Ever since you got back from New York, you've been so angry with me."

"Do you blame me? I knew you were stupid, but I never imagined that even you could have been this stupid."

Kay reached for a cigarette and smoothed the thin arch of her eyebrow with her little finger. "Don't start shouting at me again, Joel. I've explained that it wasn't my fault. Whenever I went to see Susannah, she was well-dressed. How was I to know anything was wrong?"

Joel bit back a retort, knowing that he would only end up making his feather-headed wife later than she already was. What a terrible marriage he had saddled himself with. Still, he refused to dwell too critically on the sensual side of his nature that drew him to women like Kay—seductive high-born kittens who were marvels in bed but inept at the business of daily living. After all, powerful men were allowed a few weaknesses of the flesh. He had toyed with the idea of divorcing her, but that sort of scandal was dangerous for someone in his position. Instead, he blamed her for not becoming the efficient sort of wife a man of his stature needed.

"Have you seen my earrings, darling? The sapphires?" She poked ineffectively at the clutter on her dressing table in hopes her expensive jewels might be lurking among the Max Factor bottles and cubes of Ayds diet candy.

"God, Kay, if you've misplaced those sapphires again, I'm going to take them away from you. Do you have any idea how much they cost?"

She absentmindedly picked up her lipstick tube again. "A fortune, I'm sure. I remember now. I took them off in the living room and tucked them in a drawer of the secretary so I wouldn't lose them. Be a darling and get them for me."

He stalked from their bedroom and went downstairs. As he walked into the living room, he didn't see Susannah sitting like a quiet little mouse in the corner chair, her legs drawn up under the skirt of her new calico nightgown, her eyes bright with adoration as she caught sight of him.

"Damn!" The drawers of the walnut secretary held the usual clutter of Kay's possessions, but no earrings. He banged them shut one by one. "Dammit to hell. Where could she have put them?"

"Can I help you, Father?" Susannah slipped from the chair and walked toward him, her voice quietly deferential. Joel had forbidden anyone to braid her hair, so it hung loose and bone-straight. As she stood before him, she looked so anxious that his heart turned over in his chest. Because he was so powerful himself, he felt her absolute helplessness and total dependence on him even more acutely. She was so solemn, so quiet, so overly polite with her old woman's vocabulary and desperate obsequiousness. He could not ever remember feeling so protective of another human being—not even his own daughter. Baby Paige had an army of caretakers to watch out for her well-being. This ancient little girl had no one but himself.

"Your mother left some earrings here."

"Earrings? Might they be blue?"

"Yes. They're sapphires. Why? Have you seen them?"

"Yesterday I saw Mother put some earrings in that bowl on the mantel."

Joel went over to the bowl and pulled out the sapphires. He smiled at her. Her lips curled in response. It was a trembling, uncertain attempt at a smile, but it was a smile nonetheless.

"What a good girl you are," he said softly. "What a very good girl." And then he hugged her.

Without either of them realizing it, six-year-old Susannah had taken the first step toward becoming the efficient wife that Joel Faulconer so badly needed.

2

The next year was magical. Joel legally adopted her so that she was now his real daughter—no longer Susannah Lydiard, but Susannah Faulconer. She went to school for the first time, and the teacher praised her because she was the smartest student in the class. She stopped wetting the bed and began to smile more. Everyone except her mother seemed to like her.

Although Susannah tried hard to please her mother, nothing seemed to work. She kept herself as neat as a shiny new penny and did everything that was asked of her, but Kay still complained.

"Don't sneak up behind me like that!" Kay shrieked at least once a day. "I've told you a hundred times! It gives me the creeps!"

Susannah perfected a quiet little cough when her mother was around so Kay would always know she was there.

Kay liked Paige much more than she liked Susannah—not that Susannah could really blame her. Paige was so adorable that Susannah immediately made herself a willing slave to her baby half sister. She fetched toys for her, entertained her when she was bored, and placated her when she had a temper tantrum. The sight of her sister's chubby

24

pink face crumpled in tears was more than she could bear.

"You're spoiling her," Kay complained one afternoon as she looked up from the society pages and flicked her cigarette ash. "You shouldn't give her everything she wants."

Susannah reluctantly withdrew her new Barbie doll from Paige's destructive grasp. Paige's blue eyes darkened and she began to howl in protest. The howls grew louder as she ignored all of Susannah's attempts to distract her with other toys. Finally, the newspaper snapped closed.

"For God's sake!" Kay screeched. "Let her play with your Barbie. If she breaks it, I'll buy you another one."

Only her father remained immune to Paige's charms. "Paige has to learn that she can't have everything she wants," he told Susannah in his most severe voice after observing several of these exchanges. "You need to start exercising some judgment. God knows your mother won't."

Susannah promised him she would try to do better, and the very next day she walked out of the room when Paige threw a temper tantrum, even though it nearly broke her heart.

By the time Susannah had finished first grade, the wounds inside her were beginning to mend. Ironically, Kay's criticism proved to be nearly as healing as Joel's affection. From Kay Susannah learned that she wouldn't be shoved in a closet simply because her mother didn't like her. As the world became a safer place that summer, she gradually began to relax her diligence and behave like a normal child.

It was a terrible mistake.

Falcon Hill was set at the end of a long tree-bordered drive sealed off at the entrance with iron gates. In the late afternoon when the adults gathered on the terrace behind the house for martinis, Susannah developed the habit of wandering down the drive to the gates where she played with a doll or climbed up on the filigreed ironwork to extend her view. After having spent so many years being restricted to prescribed walks around the same city block, she found her new freedom dazzling.

She was jumping rope at the bottom of the drive one June afternoon when the balloon man appeared. Even though she was seven years old, jumping rope was a new skill for her—one requiring all her concentration—so at first she didn't see him. The soles of her leather sandals scuffed on the blacktop as she counted softly under her breath. Her fine auburn hair, neatly secured back from her face with a pair of barrettes shaped like cocker spaniels, lifted off her shoulders each time the rope snapped.

When she finally looked up and saw the balloon man, she didn't find his presence along the narrow residential road unusual. A magician had entertained at Paige's birthday party, and an Easter Bunny had personally delivered their baskets. California was an enchanted place where all sorts of magical things could happen.

Tossing down her jump rope, she stepped up on the bottom rung of the gate and watched his approach.

"Balloons for free!" the man called as he came nearer.

He was wearing dusty brown shoes along with a workman's gray pants and gray shirt. Unlike a workman, however, his face was covered by a merry clown mask with a cherry nose and fuzzy purple hair.

"Balloons for free! They never pop, they never stop. Best balloons around."

Balloons that didn't pop? Susannah's eyes widened in amazement. She hated the angry noise balloons made when they broke, and she was entranced with the idea of possessing one that wouldn't frighten her.

As the man approached, she pushed a small hand through the fence and, gathering her courage, said, "Could I please have one of your free balloons, sir?"

He didn't seem to hear her. "Balloons for free. They never pop, they never stop. All my balloons for free."

"Excuse me," she repeated politely. "Might I have a balloon."

He still didn't look at her. Maybe he couldn't see her through his clown mask, she thought.

"All my balloons for free," he chanted. "Come and follow me."

Follow him? Although no one had ever spoken to her

26

about it, she wasn't certain she was permitted beyond the gates. She gazed longingly at the multicolored bundle of balloons dancing on their strings, and their beauty made her feel giddy.

"All my balloons for free. Come and follow me."

The balloon man's chant seemed to sing in her blood. Her parents were drinking martinis on the terrace, and by the time she ran back to ask for permission, the balloon man would be gone. It seemed silly to lose her chance to own one of these magical balloons, especially since she was certain her father wouldn't mind. He kept telling her to have fun and not to worry so much.

"All my balloons for free. Come and follow me."

She pulled the gate key from its hiding place in a little tin box tucked inside one of the stone urns. Precious seconds elapsed while she fit it into the lock. "Wait," she called out, afraid the balloon man would disappear. She caught her bottom lip between her teeth and concentrated on making the lock work. The key finally turned. Planting the heels of her sandals firmly on the blacktop, she dragged open the gate far enough to slip through.

She felt enormously pleased with herself as she began running beside the high row of hedges that had been planted next to the fence to give the estate privacy from the road. "Please wait for me!" she cried.

It was a warm June day. The hem of her bright yellow sundress slapped her legs and her hair skipped out behind her head. In the distance the balloons bobbed on their strings, gay splashes of color spangled against the open sky. She laughed at the beauty of them, at the distant music of the balloon man's cries, at the joyous feeling of being a child and running free along the narrow road. Her laughter sounded strange and wonderful to her ears. Although she was too young to articulate it, the heavy weight of her past no longer seemed so burdensome. She felt happy, secure, and wonderfully carefree.

She was still laughing when a strange man jumped out from a stand of sycamores and grabbed her.

Fear coagulated in her throat, and she made a horrible animal sound as his fingers dug into her arms. He had a big, fleshy nose and a bad smell. She tried to scream for her father, but before she could utter a sound, another man—the balloon man—came up beside her and pressed his hand over her mouth. Just before he covered her with a blanket, he yanked off his mask and she caught a glimpse of his face, as thin and sly as the head of a fox.

They shoved her down on the floor of a paneled van. One of them kicked her and told her to be quiet. The heavy weave of the blanket snagged a cocker spaniel barrette and pulled a clump of her fine hair from its roots. She bit through her bottom lip to keep from crying out. The heat inside the blanket was suffocating and her cramped position agonizing. But it was fear rather than pain that finally forced her into unconsciousness.

Hours later, the harsh jolting of the van awakened her. She tasted the rusty blood in her mouth and knew she was going to die, but she didn't make a sound. The van jerked to a stop. Her body began to tremble. She curled tighter, instinctively protecting the fragile organs that supported her life. The hinges of the rear doors squealed like a dying animal as they opened. The blanket was snatched away and she squeezed her eyes shut, too young to look bravely at what she feared.

They dragged her from the van. The cold night air hit her skin, and she gazed hopelessly at the flat desert landscape around her. The darkness was as thick as the inside of her grandmother's closet, its blackness penetrated only by a thin icing of stars and the dim glow of the van's interior light.

The sly-faced balloon man had her in his grasp. As he carried her toward a wooden shack, her instinct for survival took over and she tried to free herself. She screamed over and over again, but the emptiness of the desert absorbed her little girl's cries as if they were nothing more significant than the whisper of a few grains of blowing sand.

The man with the fleshy nose unfastened a padlock on the door of the shack and thrust her inside. The interior smelled like dust and rust and oil. Neither man spoke. The only sounds were her own broken whimpers. They wrapped a heavy chain around her neck as if she were a dog and bolted the other end to the wall. Just before they left her alone, one of them thrust the bundle of balloons inside. But the balloon man had lied. By the second day the heat in the shed had popped every one of them.

Newspapers all over the country carried the story of the kidnapping of little Susannah Faulconer. The police guards found a ransom demand for a million dollars in the mailbox. Kay sealed herself in her bedroom with Paige and refused to go near the windows, even though the draperies were tightly closed. Joel was wild with fear for the small, solemn stepdaughter he had grown to love so deeply. As he paced the rooms of Falcon Hill, he asked himself how something like this could have happened. He was an important man. A powerful man. What had he done wrong? She meant more to him than any person on earth, but he had not been powerful enough, he had not been *ruthless* enough, to protect her.

On the third day of the kidnapping, the FBI received an anonymous tip that led them to the shack on the edge of the Mojave Desert. The agents found Susannah chained to the wall. She was curled on the floor in her soiled yellow sundress, too weak to lift her head or to realize that these men were friends instead of enemies. Her arms and legs were raw with scrapes, and the strings of a dozen broken balloons were wrapped through her dirty fingers.

Susannah was so severely dehydrated that there was some concern among her doctors about brain damage. "She's a fighter," Joel said over and over again, as if repetition would make it true. "She'll make it. She's a fighter." Holding her hand, he willed his strength to pass into her small body.

The men who had kidnapped Susannah were betrayed by a former cellmate, and less than a week after Susannah's rescue, they were caught at a roadblock. The balloon man pulled a gun and was killed instantly. The other man hung himself in his cell with a length of twisted bed sheet.

To Joel's joy and Kay's relief, Susannah's body gradually grew stronger. But her spirit didn't heal as quickly. There had been too much evil in her young life, too many battles to fight. Weeks passed before she would speak, another month before Joel coaxed a smile from her. If she had been kidnapped when she had been living with her grandmother, the effect might not have been as devastating. But kidnapping a child who had finally begun to feel secure enough to behave like a child left permanent scars.

Every school morning for the next ten years, she was driven in a securely locked limousine from Falcon Hill to the portals of one of San Francisco's most exclusive girls' academies. She grew tall and coltish. The other girls respected her because she was always willing to help them out of whatever scrape they might have gotten themselves into, and she never spoke badly of anyone. But she was too reserved to make easy friendships, and so serious that she sometimes reminded them uncomfortably of their mothers.

Kay found Susannah's quiet efficiency and perpetual composure irritating, but Susannah spared her so many tedious burdens that she developed a detached affection for her oldest daughter. Still, she couldn't understand how it was possible for Joel to favor his adopted daughter over his own flesh and blood. Unfortunately, the more he criticized Paige, the more rebellious her second daughter became. Without Susannah to act as a shield, Kay knew that her beautiful child would have constantly been at the mercy of her father's displeasure.

By the time Susannah was seventeen, she had become as indispensable to Joel as one of his senior vice-presidents. She kept track of his social schedule, dealt with his servants, and was the perfect hostess—never making her mother's mistake of greeting someone with the wrong name. With Susannah sitting capably at the helm of his household, Joel was spared the more disastrous effects of Kay's incompetence.

As Joel's kingdom grew, so did his arrogance. Not even Susannah escaped the chill of his displeasure when something wasn't arranged to his satisfaction, but this only made her try harder. She pleased him by becoming the most successful debutante San Francisco had seen in years—at least in the eyes of the social matrons who arranged the events. They were enraptured by her reserve and graciousness. The old ways weren't dying, they agreed—not with a young woman like Susannah Faulconer to carry forth the torch.

Susannah loved mathematics, and her excellent academic record would have guaranteed her admittance to any university in the country, but she enrolled in a local college so she could continue to manage the household at Falcon Hill. From the beginning her grades suffered because she missed so many classes while taking business trips with her father and tending to her ever-increasing responsibilities at home. But she owed Joel Faulconer everything, and the glow of living in the warmth of his approval more than compensated for setting aside her own vague dreams of independence.

When she was twenty, she fell in love with a thirty-year-old investment analyst and they began to discuss marriage. Free love floated in the air of the early seventies like oxygen molecules, but the man was so intimidated by her father that he attempted no more than chaste kisses. When she finally gathered enough courage to tell him that she wasn't averse to deepening their relationship, he said he had too much respect for her to sleep with her and she would only hate herself afterward. Several months later she discovered that he was sleeping with one of Paige's friends, and she ended their relationship.

She tried to accept the fact that she was the sort of woman to inspire respect rather than passion, but as she lay in bed at night, she lost herself in sexual fantasies. Not proper fantasies with soft music and romantic candlelight, but raunchy scenarios involving swarthy desert sheiks and brutally handsome white slavers.

And then Kay developed lung cancer, and nothing else mattered. Susannah dropped out of college to care for her mother and tend to her father's increasing demands. Kay died in 1972, when Susannah was twenty-one. As she watched her mother's coffin being lowered into the ground, she experienced both grief and the terrible foreboding that her own young life had just ended with as much finality as Kay's.

On a sunny April day in 1976, two months before her wedding to Calvin Theroux, Susannah met her sister Paige at a small, weathered restaurant tucked away from the city's tourists on one of San Francisco's commercial fishing piers. It was an unusually busy day for her, but she didn't appear either rushed or flustered. Her sage-green suit looked as fresh as if she had just put it on minutes before, instead of at seven that morning. She wore simple gold clips at her ears, and her auburn hair was pulled back into a soft French twist that was a bit severe for a woman who had only the month before turned twenty-five.

Although Paige was already ten minutes late, Susannah didn't fidget as she waited. She gazed at Russian Hill in the distance and mentally rearranged her schedule.

Paige's voice interrupted her reverie. "I've got a million things to do, so this had better not take long."

As she looked up at her sister, Susannah firmly repressed her irritation. Paige was prickly at best, and it would do no good to antagonize her before they'd even had a chance to talk. Her mind flashed back to the time when they were young children, and she had smuggled Paige small toys and chocolate-covered cherries after Joel had punished her. But then one day Paige had told him what Susannah was doing, and Joel had put a stop to any more errands of mercy. Susannah still didn't understand why her sister had tattled.

Paige tossed her knapsack on the floor and took the opposite chair. While she was getting settled, Susannah studied her sister's appearance. Even in worn blue jeans and a faded Mexican cotton top, Paige was extraordinarily beautiful. Her nose was petite, her lips as pouty as Kay's had been. She had Joel's blue eyes, and lush blond hair that fell halfway down her back and always managed to look as if some lusty young man had just rumpled it with vigorous lovemaking.

At the age of twenty-two, Paige was as modern as Susannah was old-fashioned. She was tough and cocky, with a longshoreman's mouth and apparently unlimited self-confidence. Susannah ignored the familiar stab of envy that always passed through her when she was with her sister. She gestured toward the menu. "The abalone is really wonderful here. Or you might enjoy the avocado stuffed with crab."

"I'll have a hamburger," Paige replied indifferently.

Susannah placed her own order for mahi mahi, a fish she'd grown fond of during her frequent trips with Joel to

Hawaii. As the waiter moved away, she broached the subject of their meeting.

"Did you think about what I said on the phone? Tonight is Father's fifty-eighth birthday party. I know it would please him if you were there."

"Did King Joel tell you that?"

"He didn't have to. I'm certain of it." Susannah was certain of no such thing, but she had to end this estrangement between them. Right now her sister was living in a shabby one-bedroom apartment with a would-be rock singer named Conti Dove.

Paige impatiently pushed her hair away from her face. "Don't you ever get tired of running around playing Miss Goody-Two-Shoes? Fuck off, will you?"

Susannah's impassive expression gave no hint of how much she disliked hearing those tough, ugly words coming from her sister's lovely mouth. At the same time, she thought how exciting it would be if, just once in her life, she could toss those rude words at somebody. What would it be like to be so free? What would it be like to have life stretching ahead like a blank canvas—unplanned and waiting to be filled with bold, exciting strokes from one's very own brush.

"He's your father," Susannah said reasonably, "and this estrangement has gone on long enough."

"Exactly twenty-two years."

"That's not what I mean. I'm talking about your leaving home."

"I didn't leave, Susannah. His Highness kicked me out. Not that I wasn't getting ready to split anyway, so you can wipe that pitying look off your face. The best thing that ever happened to me was getting out of that mausoleum." Paige pulled a cigarette from a pack she had tossed on the table and lit it with a cheap plastic lighter. Susannah looked away. Cigarettes had killed their mother, and she hated seeing Paige smoke.

"Look, you can stay around and play Queen of the Castle to Daddy's King if you want—waiting on him hand and foot, giving him birthday parties, taking all the shit he hands out—but that's not my scene."

Definitely not, Susannah thought. Within the space of

eighteen months, Paige had flunked out of college and had an abortion. Joel had finally lost patience and told her she wasn't welcome in the house until she was ready to start acting like a responsible adult.

The waiter arrived with their food—broiled mahi mahi for Susannah, a burger and fries for Paige. Paige sank her teeth into her hamburger. As she chewed, she refused to look at the creamy amandine sauce that covered Susannah's fish, refused to think about how wonderful the mahi mahi must taste. Since her father had ordered her out of Falcon Hill, Paige couldn't remember having eaten anything more exotic than an anchovy pizza. The bite of hamburger she had just swallowed settled heavily in a stomach already churning with years of resentment from growing up in the shadow of an older sister who was perfect—an outsider who had taken her place in her own father's heart when she had been too young to defend herself.

Paige watched as Susannah delicately set her fork on her plate. Susannah had begun to remind her of those nineteenth century portraits she had studied in her art history class before she'd flunked out of college—portraits of thin, juiceless women who spent their lives languishing on chaise longues after giving birth to small blue-lipped infants. A deceptive image, Paige admitted to herself, since Susannah seemed to have an endless supply of energy, especially for good works such as saving her younger sister from a life of rock 'n' roll and sexual debauchery.

Paige could barely resist the urge to reach across the table and rumple that always-tidy auburn hair, rip away that carefully tailored suit. If only Susannah would scream or yell once in a while, Paige might have been able to get along with her better. But Susannah never lost control. She was always calm and cool, Daddy's paragon of a daughter. Susannah always said the right thing, did the right thing, and now she was capping her accomplishments by marrying exactly the right man—Mr. Calvin Stick-Up-His-Ass Theroux.

Paige was absolutely certain that Susannah was still a virgin. A virgin at twenty-five! What a joke. An image flashed through her mind of the bride and groom climbing

34

into bed the night of their wedding. She saw Cal Theroux flashing that spectacular smile of his and easing up Susannah's nightgown just to the top of her thighs.

"Pardon me, darling, but this won't take a second."

Paige imagined Susannah picking up her reading glasses along with the latest issue of *Town and Country* from the bedside table and speaking in that quiet, carefully articulated voice of hers. "But, of course, dear. Just tap me on the shoulder when you're finished."

Across the table Susannah spotted the cynical smile on her sister's face but decided to ignore it. "The party starts at eight," she told Paige. "All his old friends will be there, and I know they'll think it's strange if you don't show up."

"Tough shit," Paige snapped. "Get off my ass, will you?"

"Paige—"

"Look, you're not my mother, so stop acting like you are."

Susannah hesitated. "I know you still miss her. I don't mean to nag."

"He won't even notice that I'm not there." Paige tossed down her half-eaten hamburger and stood. "Listen, I've got to go. See you around sometime." She snatched up her knapsack from the floor and made her way through the dining room. Her swaying blond hair, along with her tight-fitting jeans, attracted the attention of most of the male diners. She favored several of them with a seductive smile before she walked out the door.

As Susannah watched Paige disappear, she wished for the thousandth time that the two of them could have the close loving relationship other sisters shared. It would be so wonderful to have someone to confide in—to be silly with.

But then Susannah was never silly with anyone. For her the daily business of living required great seriousness. As she paid the check, she remembered how often she had listened to Paige giggling with her friends, and she felt another stab of envy toward her rebellious sister.

"I hope everything was satisfactory, Miss Faulconer?"

"Excellent as always, Paul. Thank you."

Susannah slipped her credit card back into her purse and

got up from her chair. As she left the restaurant, her posture was perfect, her movements contained and graceful. She bore no resemblance at all to the little girl who had once been so enchanted with a bundle of dancing balloons that she had unlocked the protected gates of her own life and—for a few glorious moments—run free.

3

・・・・・・・・・・・・・・・・・・・・・・・

Falcon Hill had been built in the style of an opulent French manor house. In addition to marble bathrooms and polished teak floors, it contained five fireplaces with Louis XV mantels, an oval-shaped morning room, and a well-stocked European wine cellar. Susannah paused inside the arched entryway to the dining room to check the last-minute arrangements for her father's birthday celebration. The handpainted wallpaper was softly illuminated by a matching pair of antique chandeliers sparkling with a waterfall of crystal prisms. Sprays of white flowers spilled from the low Georgian silver bowls. The antique linen tablecloth and twenty matching napkins had been purchased at auction in London a decade earlier. Each piece bore the gold-embroidered crest of Czar Nicholas I.

Susannah had just finished adjusting one of the floral arrangements when she heard Cal's voice in the foyer. She went out to greet him and to straighten his tie, just as she had straightened her father's tie a short time before. Cal and her father were alike in so many ways. Both were commanding presences, both utterly self-assured.

"You look lovely, darling," Cal said, openly admiring her black evening gown. It had an off-the-shoulder neckline surrounded by a wide white organdy ruffle. When she'd put it on, she had thought the combination of the frothy neckline and her bare shoulders made her look as if she had just climbed naked out of a vat of whipped vanilla nougat.

He chucked her under the chin. "You look like a beautiful, graceful swan."

Just her luck, she thought. Cal ate vanilla nougat, but she had never known him to eat a swan.

She turned away abruptly and led Cal toward the living room. He kissed her again—a neat kiss, precisely on target, as neat as the crease in his trousers, as exact as the part in his hair.

"Do you remember me telling you about the problems I was having with Harrison's region?"

He kept his voice low in case there were any eavesdroppers lurking about, and without waiting for her answer, launched into a detailed account of his latest success at work. She needed to speak to the cook, but she listened patiently. Serving as Cal's audience wasn't something she minded. In public, her fiancé was both discreet and modest to a fault, and it was only when he was with her that he dropped his natural caution. Sometimes she thought he didn't really enjoy his triumphs until he had spread them out before her.

After the guests arrived, dinner progressed agreeably. She had seated Cal and her father close together. Although only forty-two, Cal was a senior vice-president, and insiders considered him Joel's probable successor, especially in light of his upcoming marriage to Susannah.

She noticed how handsome the two men looked sitting at the other end of the table. At fifty-eight, Joel was nearly as lean and fit as her fiancé, and his ice-blue eyes hadn't lost a bit of their sharpness. Age had given his face more character than it had possessed on the day he pulled her from her grandmother's closet. The cleft in his chin had deepened, and his square jaw was sharper. Although his blond hair had darkened at the top and grayed at the temples, it hadn't thinned, and he was still vain about it.

Cal's triangular face was much narrower than her father's, broad at the forehead but tapering from the cheekbones down to the jaw. A gray streak, like a lightning bolt, cut a dashing path through the center. He was always tan from sitting behind the helm of his French-made racing sloop, and he had a ready smile that flashed white teeth and oozed confidence.

"Wonderful dinner, Susannah," Joel said, lifting his glass in her direction. "You've outdone yourself." He gave her their private smile, and she felt as if someone had tossed a shower of gold stars over her head. Her father could be difficult and autocratic sometimes, but she loved him deeply.

The plump, aging Italian countess at her side finished a generous wedge of chocolate truffle cake. "You thin girls are so lucky," she said in heavily accented English as she gazed at the barely touched piece of cake on Susannah's plate. "I have to watch every bite I put in my mouth."

"No one would ever know it," Susannah replied graciously. "You have a wonderful figure. Tell me about your gown? It's Italian, isn't it?" Skillfully, she deflected her guest from worries about her waistline to a rapturous description of Valentino's last collection.

She heard her father's laughter at the other end of the table. By tilting her head ever so slightly, she could observe Joel sharing a joke with Cal. She nodded agreeably at the countess's description of a two-piece dinner ensemble, and at the same time noted Cal's hand resting lightly on the stem of his wineglass. His fingers looked sun-browned and strong. She could see the starched edge of his shirt cuff showing beneath the sleeve of his dinner jacket. He was wearing the monogrammed gold cuff links she had given him, and his fingers were sliding up and down the stem of the wineglass. She felt a hot rush of sexual excitement.

"You're absolutely right, Countess," she said. "The Italian designers have been so much stronger this year."

She remembered the first time she and Cal had made love. She had been so excited, so pitifully grateful that she had finally found a man who would relieve her of her burdensome virginity. But it had been over with quickly and wasn't nearly as thrilling as she had thought it would be. It was her fault, of course. After indulging in so many lewd fantasies, was it any wonder that Cal's all too human touch had seemed vaguely antiseptic and somehow perfunctory?

She remembered her embarrassment afterward.

"You nearly poked my eye out, darling," he had said. "I didn't imagine you would be quite so . . . athletic." And then he'd smiled, as if a smile could take the sting out of his words. "Not that I'm complaining, mind you. Just rather surprised, that's all."

He had made her feel as if her passion were a breach of etiquette, and she'd been more restrained ever since. Now the bedroom was one more place where she had to mind her manners.

She took a small bite of truffle cake and nodded at the countess. While she chewed she envisioned herself licking a line from the hollow at the base of Cal's throat down his chest and over his hard belly. She saw herself using the tip of her tongue as a sharp, pointed dart, making little stabs at his skin and then softening her tongue to dip lower and lick again.

"More sherry, Countess?" she inquired.

"That would be lovely, dear."

With the barest tilt of her head, Susannah caught the attention of one of the waiters she had hired for the evening to supplement her regular staff. The glow of the candles glimmering in her fine auburn hair touched the strands with gold just as candlelight had illuminated the gracious heads of women of wealth and privilege for centuries.

Another burst of laughter rang out from the head of the table, and Cal called down to her, "Susannah, your father is telling lies about you."

She smiled. "My father never lies. He just colors the truth to suit his purpose."

Joel chuckled and gazed at her fondly. "Not this time, Susannah. I was telling Cal about your hippie period."

Her fingers clenched in her lap, but no trace of agitation was evident in her voice or in the calm, smooth line of her brow. "Be careful what you say, Daddy. You'll scare poor Cal away before we get him to the altar."

"He's made of stronger stuff. He won't be frightened by a little mushy-headed liberalism."

Susannah took a sip from her wineglass, maintaining her

cool, careful smile even though she was having difficulty swallowing.

"I can't imagine Susannah going through a hippie period," Paul Clemens said. He was FBT's Vice-Chairman of the Board and Joel's oldest friend.

"She wasn't wearing beads and living in a commune," Joel quickly interjected. "But when she was twenty, she came to me and—with great solemnity, mind you—announced that she was thinking about joining the Peace Corps."

There was a momentary silence, and then the sound of several chuckles. *Please don't do this, Daddy,* Susannah silently pleaded. *Please don't trot out my confidences for dinner party conversation.*

She touched her napkin to the corner of her lips, smearing her lipstick on the gold crest of Czar Nicholas I. "I'm certain no one wants to hear about my boring youth," she said.

The flicker of a frown passed briefly over Joel's features, and she knew her interjection had displeased him. He disliked it enormously when anyone interrupted one of his stories.

Madge Clemens, Paul Clemens's wife, turned toward Susannah. "Why on earth did you want to join the Peace Corps? It's so—I don't know—*bacterial* or something."

"I was young," Susannah replied with a trace of a smile and a casual shrug. "Young and idealistic." Her fingers tightened in her lap.

"You little rebel." Cal winked at her as if she were a mischievous ten-year-old.

Joel leaned back in his chair, the worldly-wise patriarch protecting foolish females from their silly little mistakes. "A stern lecture on the political facts of life from Old Dad put an end to it, of course. But I haven't stopped teasing her about it."

The smile never left Susannah's face. No one watching her could guess at the humiliation she felt.

"If everyone has finished," she said smoothly, "let's have our after-dinner drinks in the living room."

Everyone was finished, and the party moved on.

An hour later one of the waiters came up behind her as she stood chatting with several of the FBT wives while a string quartet from the San Francisco Symphony played discreetly in the background. The waiter whispered, "There's a man who wants to see Mr. Faulconer. He wouldn't leave, so we put him in the library."

What now? she wondered. She excused herself from the group before her father became aware that there was a problem and headed for the library. As soon as she opened the doors she saw the worn soles of a pair of motorcycle boots propped on top of Joel Faulconer's massive walnut desk.

"Un-fucking-believable," a male voice murmured.

For a fraction of a second she thought he was talking about her, and then she realized his head was turned upward toward the hand-embossed copper ceiling that had come from an old French tavern.

"May I help you?" she asked, her voice cool and distinctly unhelpful.

Somewhat to her surprise, he didn't jump up in embarrassment when she spoke. Although he swung his boots to the carpet, he remained seated as he studied her.

He was so obviously foreign to her world that she felt a combination of unease and fascination. He wore an old leather motorcycle jacket over a black T-shirt, and his hair was long. It wasn't the fashionable length of a young executive's hair, but Apache-long, falling straight as the blade of a knife until it curled up on the shoulders of his jacket. He was perhaps a year or so younger than she was, and brash—she saw that, too. His cheekbones were high and flat, his mouth thin. But it was his eyes that ultimately held her attention. They were hard black marbles flecked with amber. And they were incredibly vulgar.

It wasn't a lecherous vulgarity she saw there. He didn't try to undress her visually or make an exploratory trip down her body. Instead, she saw the vulgarity of too much intensity of expression for too short an acquaintance.

"I'm going to have to ask you to leave," she said.

"I want to see Joel Faulconer."

"He's unavailable."

"I don't believe that."

Why did he keep looking at her as if she were some sort of

42

exotic species on exhibit at the zoo? "If you'd like to meet with him, I suggest you call his office for an appointment."

"I did that. The bitch who answers his phone keeps brushing me off."

Her voice passed from cool to cold. "I'm sorry, but there's nothing I can do."

"That's bullshit."

A small pulse began to throb in her throat as he slowly rose from the chair. She knew she should call for help, but she had grown so very tired of talking to overweight countesses and gouty vice-presidents. Would it be so terrible —not to mention dangerous—to wait just a few more minutes and see what the outspoken stranger who had invaded her father's library had in mind?

"Saying you can't do anything is bullshit," he repeated.

"I'm asking you to leave."

"You're what—his wife, his daughter? You can do anything you want." He snapped his fingers in the air in front of her eyes. "Just like that, you can arrange for me to see him."

She raised her head ever so slightly, so that she was looking down the length of her nose at him in the deliberately hostile fashion her father employed so effectively. "I'm his daughter Susannah, and he's entertaining tonight." Why had she told him her name? Whatever had possessed her?

"Okay. Tomorrow, then. I'll meet him tomorrow."

"I'm afraid that won't be possible."

"Christ." He looked at her with disgust and shook his head. "When I first saw you—those first few seconds—I had this feeling about you."

He fell silent.

It was as if he'd tapped out the initial seven notes of Beethoven's Fifth, but left off the eighth. She waited. The white organdy ruffle rose and fell over her breasts. She was frightened so badly that her palms had begun to perspire. Frightened, but excited, too, and that frightened her even more. She knew all too well that disaster could appear from nowhere—on the sunniest of June days, from behind the merry mask of a clown. Still, she couldn't seem to force herself to break away from him and go for help. Perhaps it was the aftereffect of her meeting with Paige, perhaps it was simply a reaction to spending too many evenings with people who were so much older than herself.

"What kind of feeling?" The words seemed to have left her mouth of their own volition—she who never spoke impulsively.

He walked around to the front of the desk, those dark, amber-flecked eyes never moving from hers. When he spoke, his voice was low and intense, barely more than a whisper. "A feeling like maybe you'd understand."

She heard the sounds of the string quartet playing another world away. Her mouth felt dry. "Understand what?"

Now his eyes did roam over her, suggestively, unapologetically, as if he alone could see the red-hot wanton who was hidden beneath her composed exterior. An erotic image flickered unbidden through her mind of his hand reaching out and lowering the bodice of her dress. The image lasted only a second, but the effect was almost unbearable—flooding her body first with heat and then with self-disgust.

He grinned—as if he had read her mind—and his brash young lips parted. She became aware of a tapping sound and followed the noise with her eyes. He was bumping the toe of one of his motorcycle boots against an old leather sample case that was leaning against the side of her father's desk.

"Do you know what I've got in here?" he asked, still tapping his toe. His voice was intense; his eyes blazed like an Apache warrior about to take a scalp. Unable to draw her gaze away from him, she shook her head.

"I've got the key to a new society in here."

"I—I don't understand." The stammer was back. She hadn't stammered since those first few years after her kidnapping. It was as if her unconscious were sending her danger signals.

Unexpectedly, his face shattered into a grin that was charming, boyish, and completely disarming. He whipped the sample case from the floor and laid it on the highly polished surface of Joel's desk, paying no heed at all to the neat stacks of papers he sent flying. He patted the case with the flat of his hand. "I've got the invention of the wheel in here. The discovery of fire. The first steam engine. The cotton gin. I've got the genius of Edison and the Wright

Brothers, Einstein and Galileo. I've got the entire fucking future of the world in here."

His casual obscenity barely registered as he mysteriously telegraphed his fervor to her.

"This is the last frontier," he said quietly. "We've built condos in Alaska and McDonald's in Africa. China sells Pepsi. Blue-haired old ladies book weekend trips to Antarctica. There's only one frontier left, and I've got it."

She tried to keep her expression cool and guarded—revealing nothing of what she was thinking—but for the first time in as long as she could remember, she couldn't quite pull it off.

He came closer until they stood nearly eye to eye. She felt the vitality of his breath on her cheek and wanted to trap it in her own lungs for just a few moments to see what all that energy would feel like.

"The frontiers of the mind," he whispered. "There's nothing else left. And that's what I've got in this case."

For a moment she didn't move, and then his words gradually penetrated the cool, logical part of her brain. At that moment she finally realized he was making a fool of her, and she felt both cheated and angry. "You're a salesman," she said, overwhelmed with the irrational notion that a bright, shining star had been snatched from her fingers. He was only a salesman. All this time she had stood here and let herself be conned by the Electrolux man.

He laughed. It had a youthful sound to it, rich and full, much different from the subdued masculine chuckles she had grown accustomed to. "I guess you could say that. I'm selling a dream, an adventure, a whole new way of life."

"My father doesn't need any more life insurance." The sarcastic bite to her words felt good. She was hardly ever sarcastic. Her father didn't approve.

He rested his hips against the front edge of the desk, crossed his ankles and smiled at her. "Are you married?"

The question took her by surprise. "No, I—I'm engaged. That's really none of your business, is it?" There was no reason for her to be stammering. She had been handling difficult social situations for as long as she could remember, and her awkwardness unsettled her. She hid her discomfort behind cool hostility. "Let me give you some advice, Mister . . ."

"Gamble. Sam Gamble."

A perfect name for a con artist, she thought. "It will be nearly impossible for you to get to my father. He keeps himself well insulated. There are, however, other people at FBT—"

"I've already seen them. They're turkeys. Real three-piece suit deadheads. That's why I decided to crash your party tonight. I have to talk to your old man in person."

"He's entertaining guests."

"How about setting up an appointment for me on Monday, then? Would you do that?"

"Of course not. He'd be quite angry—"

"You know, you're really starting to piss me off." His mouth tightened with irritation and his hand flattened on the leather sample case. "I don't know whether I'm going to show you this or not, even if that's the only way I can get to your old man. I'm just not comfortable with who you are."

His brashness dumfounded her. "*You're* not comfortable with who *I* am?"

"I mean, it's bad enough that I have to come to a reactionary company like FBT with my hat in my hands."

Heresy was being uttered in Joel Faulconer's library. It should have made her furious, but instead it gave her a strange thrill of excitement. She beat the emotion away and paid penance for her disloyalty. "FBT is one of the most progressive and influential corporations in the world," she said, sounding nearly as pompous as her father.

"If it's so progressive, how come I can't get anybody in the whole, deadhead organization to talk to me?"

"Mr. Gamble, your obvious lack of credentials might explain the difficulty." Along with your leather jacket, she thought. And your motorcycle boots and long hair. And those jeans that show off far too much.

"Credentials are crap." He picked up his sample case and, looking edgy and restless, ran his hand through his hair. "Listen, I've got to sleep on this. You're sending me mixed signals, and I'm still not sure about you. I'll tell you what. If I decide you're okay, I'll meet you in the rotunda at the

Palace of Fine Arts tomorrow around noon. If I don't show, you'll know I changed my mind." And he began to walk toward the library door.

She stared in astonishment at the back of his leather jacket. "I'm not going to meet you anywhere."

He stopped walking and slowly turned to her, one corner of his mouth lifting in an engaging grin. "Sure you are, Suzie. You wouldn't miss it for the world. And you know why? Because underneath that pretty upper-class poker face of yours, you think I'm sexy as hell. And guess what? I think you are, too."

She stood without moving as the door closed behind him. The skin on her scalp felt as if it were burning. The mounds of her breasts were hot. No one had ever called her sexy. No one—not even Cal, her lover.

And then she was filled with self-disgust for having been taken in—even for a moment—by macho swagger. Did Sam Gamble actually imagine she would meet him tomorrow? A feeling of satisfaction shot through her as she pictured him arriving at the Palace of Fine Arts only to discover that he had been stood up.

With her posture so erect she might have been wearing a whalebone corset from another century, she returned to her guests. For the rest of the evening, she determinedly ignored the faint echo of a long ago chant ringing in her head.

All my balloons for free. Come and follow me.

When Sam Gamble got home, he saw that the lights in the garage were still on. That wasn't unusual. Sometimes the lights didn't go off until five or six in the morning. He set the sample case on the kitchen table. It was an old table—gray Formica with curved chrome legs. There was a sad-looking spider plant hanging in the window. An empty can of Pringles sat on the counter next to an ugly ceramic cookie jar. He lifted the jar's lid and tossed in the small electronic device that he had used to trigger those fancy iron gates at Falcon Hill. She had been so shaken up, she hadn't even asked him how he'd gotten past them.

Walking over to the refrigerator, he opened the door and propped one hand on the top as he bent down to look inside.

"Shit. The spaghetti's gone." He pulled out a can of Coke instead and opened it. After he took a swig, he picked up the sample case and walked outside to the garage.

A man was standing at a lighted workbench with his back to the door. He didn't turn as Sam came in.

"I just met the most incredible woman I've ever met in my life." Sam sprawled down on a dirty floral couch. "You should have seen her. She looks like that actress I was telling you about who did that play on PBS a couple of weeks ago—Mary Streep or somebody—except she's prettier. And cool. Christ, is she cool. Snooty on the surface. High-class. But there was something about her eyes . . . I don't know. She pulled this bitch routine, so I knew it wouldn't do any good to show it to her right then. But I wanted to. Damn, I really wanted to blow her mind."

Breathing in the pleasant smell of hot solder, Sam lay back on the couch and propped the can of Coke on his chest. "I never saw anybody move like she does. She's *still*, you know what I mean? A still person, even when she's in motion. You can't imagine her ever raising her voice, even though I could tell I was really pissing her off."

He sipped his Coke for a while and then got up and wandered over to the workbench. "I have to talk to her old man—show him what we've got—but every time I try to get to him, somebody stands in my way. I think if I could catch her interest—get her on my side—she might arrange a meeting. I hate the idea of selling out to FBT, but we don't seem to have any other choice. I don't know. She might not show up. I'll have to think about it."

He watched the other man's hands—the precision of his touch, the sureness of his movements—and shook his head in admiration. "You're a genius, you know that, Yank. An honest-to-shit genius."

And then he threw his arm around the man's shoulders and gave him a wet kiss on the cheek.

The man named Yank jerked around indignantly, splashing a trail of hot solder on the surface of the workbench. "What the heck's wrong with you?" He hunched his shoulder to his cheek, wiping off the kiss. "Why the heck did you do that?"

"Because I love you," Sam said with a grin. "Because you're a goddamned genius."

"Well, heck, you don't have to kiss me." Again, he wiped at his cheek with his shoulder. Finally, calming, he looked around the garage, studying it as if he'd been gone for a very long time. "When did you get back? I didn't hear you come in."

Sam's grin broadened. "I just got here, Yank. Just this second."

4

. . . .

Conti Dove, born Constantine Dovido, was dumb, sweet, and sexy as hell. A few months earlier a girl had told him that he looked like John Travolta, and he had been talking to Paige about it ever since. Conti had dark hair and a Jersey accent, but as far as Paige could see, the resemblance ended there.

Paige almost loved Conti. He treated her well and he wasn't astute enough to see what a fake she was.

"Does that feel good, doll?" he asked, using his fingers on her like he used them on the strings of his Gibson.

"Uhm, yes. Oh, yes." She moaned and writhed, putting on a top-notch, first-class, all-star performance so Conti would never suspect that his hot little mama could barely stand to have him touch her.

Nothing was specifically wrong with Conti's lovemaking. He pushed all the right buttons and didn't fall asleep the minute he was done. It was just that Paige found sex to be a drag. She did it, of course, because everybody did, and she liked being held. But most of the time she didn't enjoy it very much. Sometimes she really hated it.

When she was sixteen, she had been raped by a college boy she had met at a rock concert in Golden Gate Park. She had never told anybody about it. Either people would feel sorry for her or they'd say she had it coming.

While she waited for Conti's lovemaking to be over, she clutched his bare arms, cupping the biceps he had developed so spectacularly by working out with the weights they kept in the corner of their bedroom. The bedroom was as clean as she could make it because she hated dirt, but it was painfully ugly. It had a cracked ceiling, mismatched furniture, and a double mattress on the floor. Paige wouldn't sleep on the mattress unless Conti was beside her, because she was always afraid a mouse would run over her head and get tangled in her hair.

"Tell me how good it feels," he crooned in her ear. "Tell me it's good."

"It's good, Conti. It's good."

"Doll . . . doll . . . God, I love you. I love you so much." He pushed himself inside her and began pumping away to the rhythm of "I Can't Get No Satisfaction" that kept playing over and over in her head.

It was the song that the Doves did best. Paige sang backup, Jason was on bass, Benny at the drums. Mike played the keyboard while Conti sang lead, banging his Gibson and thrusting his hips to the rhythm.

I can't . . . get no . . . satis . . . faction

Conti dug his fingers into her buttocks, tilting them higher to receive him, plunging deeper. She let her mind slip away from what was happening, to a beautiful, pure place—a country garden with hollyhocks and larkspur and an old iron pump in the center. She imagined the sound of birds and the scent of honeysuckle. She saw herself lying back on a homemade quilt under a shady old tree. And at her side a plump, rosy-cheeked baby kicked happily and batted the air with its fists. Her baby. The baby she had lost when she'd had her abortion.

I can't . . . get no . . .
I can't . . . get no . . .

Conti let out a low, strangled moan and buried his mouth in her neck. As he shuddered, he seemed so vulnerable to her that she felt a foolish need to protect him. She stroked his back, giving him a sad kind of comfort. How many men had shuddered over her like this? More than a dozen. A lot more. Her friend Roxie said a girl wasn't really promiscuous until she'd hit triple digits, but Paige had felt promiscuous ever since she'd been raped.

When Conti had calmed, he drew back and gazed down at her. "I love you so much, doll."

Tears glistened in his eyes, and to her surprise she felt her own eyes fill. "I love you, too," she replied, even though she knew she didn't. But it seemed unspeakably cruel to say anything else.

Their bedroom romp had made them late, and they had to hurry. All five members of the Doves waited tables at a club called Taffy Too, named after the original owner's dog, who presumably had been Taffy One. They received no salary and only half their tips, but the Doves put up with it because the owner let them play a one-hour set at eleven o'clock each evening.

Taffy's was a third-rate club located in the heart of one of San Francisco's less picturesque neighborhoods, but occasionally some big shots slumming it would end up sitting at a front table. Conti thought the Doves might get discovered that way. In Paige's more depressed moments she thought that perhaps Conti was the only member of the Doves talented enough to perform any place better than Taffy Too's, but generally she repressed such thoughts. She might not be the world's best singer, but somehow she was going to make a success of herself and rub it in her father's face.

They had almost reached the alley that led to the back entrance of Taffy's when Conti lifted his arm and yelled out, "Yo, Ben, my man!"

Paige winced at the loudness of Conti's voice. Benny Smith, their drummer, approached. He was small and thin, with a short Afro and light brown skin.

"Hey, Conti. What's happenin'?"

Conti slid his hand up under her hair and wrapped his fingers around the back of her neck like a high school jock with his cheerleader girlfriend. "Nothin' much. You hear anything more about that dude from Dee-troit Mike was telling us about?"

"Dude's disappeared," Benny replied. "But I hear some dudes from Azday Records showed up at Bonzo's last night."

"No kidding? Maybe they'll come over to Taffy's."

Paige didn't think that was too likely. Unlike Taffy's, Bonzo's was a semirespectable club that booked better acts. She listened as Benny and Conti continued to trade rumors, acting as if each day held a golden key that would open the door to their success. She no longer remembered what that sort of optimism felt like.

They had a thinner crowd at Taffy's that night than normal, so the latecomers who arrived in the middle of the Doves' third Stones number were even more noticeable. Paige, wearing a cheap blue sateen jumpsuit with flashy metal studs, was beating her tambourine against her thigh when the two men took their place at the front table. One of the men was in his early fifties, the other younger. They both looked prosperous. Their suits bore the unmistakable sheen of silk and she caught the glint of expensive watches at their wrists.

Benny nearly knocked over his drums when he spotted them. As they finished "Heart of Stone," he whispered, "Those are the dudes from Azday records. I recognize the old guy—he's Mo Geller. Come on, everybody. Don't fuck up! This is it!"

Conti looked over at her, a panicked expression on his face. She felt surprisingly calm, given the importance of the event, and she gave him a reassuring smile. Benny hit the downbeat and the band kicked in. As she felt the beat of the song, she whipped her head to the side, letting her hair fly. It caught the lights so that it looked as if shimmering golden flames were leaping up from her head. She shook it again. Conti turned toward her as he sang. A wildness seemed to hit him, and he laughed at her—a sexual dare. She caught his mood as he picked up the beat. His hips moved and she laughed back at him—then stuck out her lip in a sexy, taunting pout. He came over to her, not missing a beat of the music, and leaned into her. She whipped him with her hair. They did a frenzied, dirty dance while the other band members called out encouragement. When the number ended, they got more applause than they had received in months.

The two men stayed through the rest of the set, and afterward bought them all drinks. "You kids generate a lot of excitement," Mo Geller said, clinking the ice cubes in his glass. "Got any material of your own?"

Benny assured him that they did, and the Doves took the stage again, performing two songs that their bass player had written. When they were done, Mo handed them one of his cards. "It's early to be talking about a contract, but I'm definitely impressed. We'll be in touch."

All of the Doves went to Conti and Paige's place afterward to celebrate. They smoked grass, told stupid jokes, and drank cheap wine. Conti started to talk about how much all of them meant to him and dissolved into sentimental tears. They were giddy and silly, high on pot and their first brush with success. By the time dawn lightened the sky, the men had curled into various corners of the apartment and fallen asleep. Paige, however, was sitting wide awake in a chair by the window.

At six o'clock she slipped out of the apartment and made her way down the littered hallway to the pay phone that hung near the front door. Digging a coin from the pocket of her jeans, she pushed it into the slot and, after a few moment's hesitation, dialed. Susannah would still be in bed, and the housekeeper shouldn't be in until eight. Unless her father was out of town, he would pick up the phone himself.

"Yes?" He answered brusquely, as if he were speaking into his office intercom.

She tangled the dirty, stretched-out telephone cord through her fingers. "Daddy, it's Paige."

There was a moment's silence. "It's six o'clock, Paige. I'm just getting dressed. What do you want?"

"Look, I'm sorry I couldn't make it to your birthday party. I—something came up."

"I wasn't aware that you'd been invited."

Her mouth twisted bitterly. She should have known that Saint Susannah was responsible for the invitation. "Yeah, well, I was."

"I see."

She turned to face the grimy wall. Her words came quickly, fiercely. "Listen, I just thought you might like to know that a man from Azday Records came to hear us play last night, and he wants to talk to us about a contract."

She squeezed her eyes shut, barely breathing as she waited

for his response. She wanted to frame the words for him so he would say what she needed to hear—words of enthusiasm, of praise.

"I see," he repeated.

Leaning her forehead against the wall, she gripped the receiver so tightly that her knuckles turned pale. "It's no big deal or anything. Azday is an important company. They listen to a lot of bands, and it might fall through."

Joel sighed. "I don't know why you've called to tell me this, Paige. You surely don't expect my blessing. When are you going to start acting like an adult?"

She winced and set her jaw. "Hey, Joel, I'm having fun. Life's too short for all that shit." Silent tears began to slide down her cheeks.

His reply was stiff with disapproval. "I have to dress, Paige. When you're willing to start acting responsibly like your sister, I'll be more than willing to talk to you."

A harsh click traveled over the line as he ended the conversation.

Paige stood perfectly still, holding the receiver to her ear. Her wet cheek lay pressed against the wall where her tears smeared the carelessly scrawled obscenities and abandoned phone numbers of a decade. "Don't go," she whispered. "I never meant to cause you so much trouble. I just wanted you to notice me, to be proud of me. Please, Daddy. Just once be proud of me."

A door slammed and a kid in his early twenties came out into the hallway on his way to work. She banged the receiver down and straightened so quickly that her spine might have been shot through with an injection of liquid steel. Lifting her chin, she swept past him, her hips swaying in an easy, carefree manner.

A long, low wolf whistle sounded from behind her. She tossed her hair. "Fuck you, shithead."

Susannah pulled the silver Mercedes sedan her father had given her for her birthday into the parking lot at the Palace of Fine Arts. The rotunda rose like a Baroque wedding cake over the other buildings in San Francisco's Marina District. A light drizzle had begun falling when she'd reached the city. Her hand trembled as she turned off the windshield wipers and the ignition. There was still time to go back, she told herself. She nervously touched her neatly coiled hair, then she slipped the keys into her small leather shoulder bag.

As she got out of the car, she felt as if a stranger had taken over her body—a restless, rebellious stranger. Why was she doing something so out of character? Guilt gnawed at her. She was getting ready to commit exactly the sort of irresponsible act she criticized her sister for.

She walked across the parking lot toward the main building, thinking about the Palace's history so she wouldn't have to think about her own behavior. The Palace of Fine Arts had been constructed in 1913 as part of the Pan-Pacific Exposition to celebrate the opening of the Panama Canal. It had been restored from near ruin in the late 1950s and now held the Exploritorium, a hands-on science museum that was a favorite of the city's children. Joel had served on the Board of Directors until recently, when she had taken his place.

Bypassing the Exploritorium, she walked along the path that took her to the rotunda, which was set next to a small lagoon. The rotunda, open to the elements, had massive columns and a dome that was circumscribed by a classical frieze. It was raining harder now and the building was damp, chilly, and deserted.

As she stared through the columns out toward the dreary, rain-pocked lagoon, she crossed her arms over her chest and hugged herself. Although she had on wool slacks and a cable-knit sweater, she wished she had chosen a warmer blazer. Nervously, she fingered her engagement ring. With the exception of a thin gold watch, it was her only piece of jewelry. "Less is more," her grandmother used to say. "Remember, Susannah. Less is always more." Sometimes, though, Susannah thought that less was less.

Misery settled over her. She shouldn't be here. She was uneasy and guilt-ridden. She wanted to believe that she had come today only because she was curious about what Sam Gamble carried in his leather case, but she didn't think that was true.

"I was right about you."

Startled, she spun around and saw him walking into the rotunda. Drops of rainwater beaded on his jacket and something silver glimmered through his dark hair. With a jolt she realized that he was wearing an earring. Her stomach knotted. What kind of woman slipped away from her father and her fiancé to meet a man who wore an earring?

He set the leather sample case next to a sawhorse and some wooden crates being used for repair work. She could smell the rain in his hair as he came close. Her eyes fastened on a few dark strands that were sticking to his cheek, then moved to his silver earring, which was shaped like one of the primitive heads on Easter Island. It swayed back and forth like a hypnotist's watch as he spoke. "I usually expect too much from people, and then I'm disappointed."

She slipped her hands into the pockets of her blazer and prepared to keep silent, as she frequently did when she was uneasy. Ironically, these silences had earned her the reputation of being totally self-possessed. And then—as if she had fallen under the spell of that hypnotically swaying earring—she heard herself saying exactly what she was thinking. "Sometimes I don't think I expect enough from people."

For her, it was an uncharacteristically bold piece of self-revelation, but he merely shrugged. "I'm not surprised." His eyes moved over her face with an intensity that further unnerved her. And then his lips curved into a cocky grin. "You want to take a ride on my Harley later?"

She looked at him for a moment and, amazingly, felt herself beginning to smile. His question was so unexpected, so wonderfully startling. No one had ever asked her such a thing.

"I'm not exactly the motorcycle type."

"So what? Have you ever ridden one?"

For a moment she actually considered the idea. Then she realized how ridiculous it was. Motorcycles were dirty and unsafe. She shook her head.

"It's great," he said. "Incredible. Straddling the bike. Feeling all that power between your thighs—the vibration, the surge of the engine." His voice dropped and once again his eyes caressed her face. "It's almost as good as sex."

She was a world champion at hiding her feelings, and not by a flicker of an eyelash did she betray the effect his words had on her. All too clearly, she saw what a mistake she had made by coming to meet him. Something about him fed those inappropriate erotic fantasies that plagued her. "I was under the impression that you asked me to come here today to discuss business, Mr. Gamble."

"I thought redheads were supposed to have hot tempers. You don't look like you ever get mad."

She felt strangely defensive. "Of course I do."

"Have you ever gotten royally pissed off?"

"I get angry like everyone else."

"Have you ever thrown anything?"

"No."

"Hit anybody?"

"Of course not."

A mischievous smile tilted the corner of his mouth. "Have you ever called anybody an asshole?"

She started to make a properly stuffy response, only to feel that treacherous smile once again tugging at the corners of her mouth. "I've been much too well brought up for that sort of thing."

He lifted his arm and, without warning, gently scraped the backs of his knuckles over her cheek. "You're really something, Suzie. You know that?"

Her smile faded. His hand felt slightly rough, as if the skin were chapped. Cal's hands were so smooth that she sometimes didn't realize he'd touched her. She eased her head away from him. "My name is Susannah. No one ever calls me Suzie."

"Good."

Discomfited, she slid her fingers along the leather shoulder strap of her purse. "Perhaps you should tell me why you wanted to meet me here today?"

He laughed and lowered his arm. "Other than a couple of English professors I had in college, you're the only person I know who can use a word like 'perhaps' and not sound like a phony."

"You went to college?" Somehow, it didn't fit his wild biker's image.

"For a couple of years, and then I got bored."

"I can't imagine anyone getting bored with college."

"Yeah, well, I'm pretty restless." Without asking permission, he clasped her arm and led her over to one of the wooden crates the workers had left. "Sit down here. I want to show you something." She sat and crossed her hands in her lap as he lifted his case to the spot beside her.

"I like challenges, Suzie. Adventure. Maybe you'll understand who I am when you see this."

She found herself holding her breath as he pressed the latches. What secrets did this biker medicine-show man carry with him? Her imagination conjured up a panoply of ridiculously romantic images—yellowed treasure maps, precious jewels bearing ancient curses, sacred scrolls from the caves by the Dead Sea.

With a dramatic flourish, he flipped open the lid.

For a moment he was silent. When he finally spoke, his voice held the whispered awe of someone in church. "Did you ever see anything so beautiful in your life?"

She stared down into the contents of the case and was overwhelmed with disappointment.

"The design is so elegant, so damned efficient, it makes you want to cry. This is it, Suzie. You're looking at the vanguard of a whole new way of life."

All she saw was an uninteresting collection of electronic parts mounted on a circuit board.

"It's a computer, Suzie. A computer small enough and cheap enough to change the world."

Her feeling of letdown was almost palpable. This was what she got for sneaking around like a cat burglar. It must be the pressure of the wedding that had made her act so irresponsibly. She twisted her engagement ring so the diamond was straight and slipped back into her polite, cool shell. "I really don't know why you're showing me this." She began to rise, only to have a hard hand settle on her shoulder and push her firmly back down. It startled her so much she made a small exclamation.

"I know what you're thinking. You're thinking this is too small to be a computer."

She wasn't thinking any such thing, but perhaps it was better to pretend she was than to let him suspect how jumbled her real thoughts were. "FBT has been a pioneer in computers since the 1950s," she said evenly. "I've been around them most of my life, and they're much larger than this."

"Exactly. Even the so-called 'mini' computers are nearly as big as a refrigerator. But this is still a computer, Suzie. The heart and guts of one. A *micro* computer. And Yank's improving it every day."

"Yank?"

"He's an electronic genius—a born hacker. We met when we were kids, and we've been friends ever since. He can design the sweetest pieces of integrated circuitry you've ever seen. It's a point of pride with him to come up with a design that uses one less chip than anybody else's. With an established company behind this computer, it could be on the market before the end of the year."

By "an established company," he meant FBT, she thought. How could she have lost sight of the fact that he wanted to use her to get to her father?

He had made her feel foolish, so she was deliberately unkind. It wasn't like her, but then, neither was slipping away from home to meet a street-smart biker. She gestured dismissively toward the unimpressive batch of electronic parts that obviously meant so much to him. "I can't imagine anybody wanting to buy something like this."

"You're kidding, aren't you?"

"I never kid."

She saw his impatience and once again found herself staring at him, almost mesmerized as she watched him try unsuccessfully to contain his emotions. Unlike her, he didn't seem to conceal anything. What would it feel like to be so free?

"You don't get it, do you?" he said.

"Get what?"

"Think about it, Suzie. Most of the computers in this country are million-dollar machines locked up in concrete rooms where only guys in three-piece suits can get to them—guys with ID cards and plastic badges with photos on them. Companies like FBT and IBM make these computers for big business, for government, for universities, for the military. They're made by fat cats to serve fat cats. Computers are knowledge, Suzie. They're power. And right now the government and big business have all that power locked up for themselves."

She tilted her head toward the collection of electronic circuits. "This is going to change that?"

"Not right away. But eventually, yes, especially with a company like FBT marketing it. The board needs expanding. Everything has to be self-contained. We need a terminal, a video monitor. It needs more memory. But Yank is coming up with new hacks all the time. The guy's a genius."

"You don't seem to have much respect for FBT. Why are you offering them your design?"

"I don't have enough money to manufacture it myself. Yank and I could make a few of these and sell them to our friends, but that's not good enough. Don't you see? A giant like FBT can make it happen. With FBT behind Yank's design, the world will have a computer that's small enough and—even more important—one that's *cheap* enough so that people can buy it for their homes. A person's computer. A home computer. Something to stick on top of a desk and hack around on. In the next couple of years, we're going to turn those big fat cat computers into dinosaurs."

There was something so charismatic about the fire in his eyes, the energy charging through his body, that for a few moments she actually found herself caught up. "How does it work?"

"I can't show you here. It has to be hooked up. You need a power supply. The memory has to be loaded in. You have to have a terminal—like a typewriter keyboard. A television for video display."

"In other words, this doesn't do anything."

"It's a computer, for chrissake!"

"But it can't do anything unless you attach all these other things to it?"

"That's right."

"I think you're wasting your time, Sam. My father won't be interested in something like this. I can't imagine anyone wanting to buy it."

"Everyone in the entire frigging world is going to want to buy it! Before too many years have passed, a home computer will be another everyday appliance—like a toaster or a stereo. Why can't you see that?"

His antagonism jarred her, but she forced her voice to

remain smooth yet strong, just as it was when she needed to make a point at a hospital auxiliary meeting. "Maybe in the twenty-first century, but not in 1976. Who would actually buy something like this—a machine that doesn't do anything until you hook up a dozen other things to it?"

"For the next few years, mainly hobbyists and electronics junkies. But by the 1980s—"

"There can't be enough hobbyists to make something like this profitable." She forced herself to glance at her watch so he could see that she had more important things to do than sit here chatting about his quixotic vision of computer-filled households.

He shook his head and regarded her with thinly disguised hostility. "For someone who looks intelligent, you're really out of touch. Do you spend so much time planning dinner parties that you can't see what's happening all around you? This is California, for chrissake. You're living on top of Silicon Valley. The electronics capital of the world is right at your feet. There's a whole universe of people out there who've been waiting all their lives for something like this."

As Joel Faulconer's daughter, she had spent most of her life in a world where high technology was served right along with the soup course. She wasn't ignorant, and she didn't like his condescension. "I'm sorry, Sam," she said stiffly, "but all I see is a briefcase full of electronic parts that don't do anything. I'm certain you're wasting your time. My father won't agree to see you, and—even if he did—he would never be interested in anything this impractical."

"Talk to him for me, Suzie. Convince him to see me. I'll take care of the rest."

Her gaze took in the leather jacket, the length of his hair, the earring. "I'm sorry, but I can't do that."

His thin lips twisted and he looked past her toward the lagoon. It had begun to rain harder and the surface of the water was gray and rippled. He shoved his hands in the pockets of his jacket, making the leather rustle. "Okay, then here's something you *can* do. Come to a meeting with me next week."

She was alarmed. Meeting him once was bad enough— twice would be unforgivable. "That's impossible."

"You just think it's impossible. Loosen up a little. Take a risk for a change."

"You don't seem to understand. I'm engaged. It would be unseemly for me to meet you again."

"Unseemly?" His eyebrows shot up. "I'm not asking you to sleep with me. I just want you to meet some people I know. Do it, Suzie. Throw away your etiquette book for a change."

She tried not to let him see how badly he had shaken her. Gathering up her purse, she stood—straitlaced Susannah Faulconer wrapping propriety around her like a maiden aunt's crocheted shawl. She opened the catch on her purse and pulled her car keys from one of the neatly arranged compartments. "What kind of people do you want me to meet?" She asked the question coolly, as if a guest list were the only really important thing on her mind.

Sam Gamble smiled. "Hackers, honey. I want you to meet some hackers."

5

They were the nerdiest of the nerds—bespectacled California boys of the sixties, who grew up in the suburbs of the Santa Clara Valley south of San Francisco.

In other parts of America, baseball and football reigned unchallenged, but in the Santa Clara Valley electronics permeated the air. The Valley harbored Stanford and Hewlett-Packard, Ames Research Laboratory and Fairchild Semiconductor. From the moment they woke up to the moment they fell asleep, the boys of the Valley breathed in the wonders of transistors and semiconductors.

Instead of Wilt Chamberlain and Johnny Unitas, these boys of the sixties found their heroes in the electrical engineers who lived next door, the men who toiled in the laboratories at Lockhead and Sylvania. Electronics permeated the air of the Santa Clara Valley, and to the bespectacled boys of the suburbs, the engineers with their slide rules and plastic pocket protectors were modern-day Marco Polos, adventurers who had unlocked the exotic mysteries of electron flows and sine waves.

The boys grew adept at barter. They did odd jobs in exchange for the surplus parts the men culled from the storerooms of the companies for which they worked. The boys washed cars for boxes of capacitors, painted garages for circuit boards, and every spare penny they earned went into buying parts for the transistor circuits and ham radio receivers they were building in their bedrooms.

In actuality, there wasn't much else for these boys to do with their money. Most of them were still too young to drive, and the older ones had no need to save their money for dates because no self-respecting California schoolgirl would have been caught dead with any one of them. They were the nerdiest of the nerds. Some were so overweight that their stomachs bulged from beneath their belts, others so underweight their Adam's apples seemed larger than their necks. They were pimply, myopic, and stoop-shouldered.

As they grew older, they went to college. Despite their impressive IQ's, some of the most talented never graduated. They were too busy having fun hacking around in their university's computer lab to go to their thermodynamics class or study for an exam in quantum mechanics. They programmed the big mainframes to play games they invented—games with galaxies exploding in dazzling patterns of starbursts and jets streaking across screens spattered with constellations that actually moved. They could only get time on the machines at night, so they slept during the day and hacked until the graduate assistants kicked them out in the morning. They ate junk food to the point of malnutrition and lived their lives under the blue flicker of fluorescent lighting. Like vampires, their skin turned pasty and white.

They were always horny. When they weren't hunched over a terminal, they were dreaming of feelable, kissable, suckable breasts and sweet little miniskirted asses. But they lived at night, it was hard for them to meet women, and when they did, they ran into trouble. How could anyone talk to a person who didn't understand the joy of spending an evening with a DEC PDP-8 writing a subroutine to solve quadratic functions?

They were the nerdiest of the nerds, and their encounters with women frequently didn't go well.

Most of them were too caught up in the excitement of an interesting hack to think about the fact that they might hold the keys to a new society in their heads. Although they yearned for small, inexpensive machines they could use freely at any time of night or day instead of having to sneak into a computer lab at three in the morning, most of them didn't let their thoughts go much further than ephemeral daydreams. They were having too much fun writing elaborate sine-cosine routines that would make the games they had invented run better. They were hackers, not visionaries, and they didn't think too much about the future.

But the visionaries were around. With rebellious young eyes uncorrupted by old knowledge, they saw what was happening at places where the nerds got together, places like the Homebrew Computer Club. The visionaries saw, and they understood.

Sam Gamble impatiently paced along the walkway leading to SLAC, the Stanford Linear Accelerator Center. Susannah was late. Maybe she wouldn't come. He pushed his hands in the back pockets of his jeans and encountered his wallet. It was thicker than normal because he'd gotten paid that day. He'd bought two books—Clarke's *Profiles of the Future* and Minsky's *The Society of Mind*—along with a new Eagles tape.

Sam hated his job. He worked as a technician at a small semiconductor company in Sunnyvale. He was competent at what he did, but since he didn't have a degree, it was basically dead-end work. Yank didn't have a degree either, but Yank was an electronics genius and he had a good job at Atari. A job that would probably end soon, Sam reminded himself. Yank tended to be chronically unemployed because he would get involved in some incredible hack and forget to go to work. Sam had come to the conclusion that the modern corporation—even one as freewheeling as Atari—wasn't designed for guys like Yank. In his opinion, time clocks were one of a million things wrong with the way businesses were run in this country.

After Sam had dropped out of college, he'd bummed around the country for a while on his bike. It was fun. He'd met a lot of people, slept with a lot of women, but he'd finally gotten tired of the aimlessness of it all. When he'd come home, he'd fallen in with Yank Yankowski, who'd just flunked out of Cal Tech. He and Yank had known each other since they were kids, but Yank was a year older and they'd run in different crowds. Sam had been a hell raiser, while Yank was almost invisible—this weird skinny kid who hid away in his family's garage and built strange gadgets.

The sound of a well-tuned German engine caught Sam's attention. He watched the silver Mercedes pull into the parking lot, and the efficient, no-nonsense design of the car gave him a visceral rush of pleasure. There wasn't any reason in the world Detroit couldn't build a car like that—no reason except greed and a lack of imagination.

As Susannah came up the walk, she looked like all the women in the world he'd ever wanted but had never been able to have. It wasn't either her money or her looks that primarily attracted him. He'd slept with rich women before, and he'd certainly slept with prettier ones. But Susannah was different. He took in the way she moved, that discreet mouth, the simple design of her belted cashmere coat. It was classic, just like the car she drove. Just like Susannah Faulconer.

Susannah walked toward him, her spine as straight as the yardstick her grandmother had strapped to her back when she was a child. All day she had been telling herself she wouldn't come here tonight, but then she had been on the phone with Madge Clemens, discussing a luncheon program for the wives of the FBT regional presidents. Madge was debating whether Susannah should invite someone to do the women's colors, which was the very latest thing, or whether they should have a guest speaker. Madge had been going on about how nice it would be to have a personalized packet of fabric swatches when she'd suddenly changed her mind and told Susannah that they simply had to invite this wonderful doctor her sister had heard speak.

"He's marvelous, Susannah," Madge had said. "I know everyone will get a lot out of his presentation. He brings slides and everything. And all of us are interested in menopause."

Susannah hadn't said a word. For a moment she had sat without moving, and then she found herself slowly lowering the receiver to the cradle and hanging up right in the middle of Madge's sentence. It was unforgivably rude, but her arm had seemed to move of its own volition. Ten minutes later she was on her way to Palo Alto.

"I—I'm sorry I'm late," she said to Sam. "There was a lot of traffic and I—"

"You lost your guts?" He ambled toward her, his walk slightly bow-legged, as if he were still riding his Harley.

"Of course not," she replied stiffly. "I just didn't leave myself enough time."

"Sure." He stopped in front of her and his gaze was openly admiring as it traveled over her coat, although what he found so fascinating about her old cashmere wrap-around, she couldn't imagine. "How old are you?" he asked.

Fifty years old. Fifty-five. Ready for menopause; ripe for estrogen supplements. "I was just twenty-five last month," she replied.

He smiled. "That's great. I'm twenty-four. I knew if you were too much older than me, you'd have all kinds of hang-ups about the two of us. You look closer to thirty." He took her arm and began drawing her toward the building, apparently unaware of how rude his comment was. He must have felt her resistance because he stopped. At first he looked puzzled, and then he scowled.

"You're not used to people who say what they're thinking, are you, Suzie? Well, I don't go for any dishonest bullshit. I'm real. That's one thing you have to learn about me."

"I'm real, too," she countered, which was a perfectly ridiculous thing to say. She unsettled herself even further by adding, "Nobody seems to understand that." She was appalled. Why did she keep making these personal revelations to a man she barely knew?

He studied her with his intense dark eyes. "You're something, do you know that? Classic, elegant, efficient—like a great piece of design."

She took a shaky breath, forcing herself to speak lightly so she had time to pull back into her shell. "I don't know if I like the idea of being compared to a piece of design."

"I appreciate quality. I may not have any money, but I've always appreciated the best."

And then, unexpectedly, he slipped his arm around her

shoulders and pulled her body close to his. The contact dazed her. He stared down into her face, his eyes touching her forehead, her nose, her mouth.

"Please," she whispered. "I don't think—"

"Don't think," he said, leaning forward to nuzzle her neck with his lips. "Just feel."

He was a seducer, a tempter, a peddler of patent medicines hawking his wares from the back of a Harley-Davidson, a tent-show evangelist delivering the promise of eternal life, a salesman in a sharkskin suit selling shares in the Brooklyn Bridge. He was a *hustler*. She knew all that. She knew it without question. But still she couldn't make herself draw away.

He tilted his head, and his mouth settled on hers. His lips were moist and warm, alive with activity. He was so lusty, so young, his skin so fresh and rough. Her hand crept upward until she rested her open palm on his jacket. She felt starved for the touch and taste of him. Her fingers constricted, grasping at the leather, and her lips parted involuntarily.

Their tongues tangled—hers tentative at first, his quicksilver and full of magical promises. She forgot about good manners, about reserve and dignity. She even forgot about being afraid as youth churned in her veins—springtime green and callow. Her blood was young and abundantly fed. She felt its surge. She grew weak beneath the spurt of rich new hormones flowing through her veins. He opened her mouth farther, slipped his hands inside her coat, pushed them under her sweater to touch her skin. He made love to her with his tongue. She moaned and leaned toward him.

It was he who finally pulled away.

"Christ," he muttered.

Appalled, she pressed her wrist over her lips. She had lost control again—just like the first time she and Cal had made love. Just like that long-ago June day when she'd slipped through the safe iron gates of Falcon Hill to chase a bundle of balloons.

"Relax, Suzie." His voice was soothing as he observed her consternation. "Don't get so uptight about everything. Take it easy."

"I can't take it easy. I'm not like you." With shaking

fingers she reached into her coat pocket for her car keys. "I can't do this anymore, Sam. I'll—I'll talk to my father and ask him to meet with you. I can't do anything more."

And then, because she was frightened and couldn't think clearly, she did something incredibly stupid. It was a reflex, the involuntary response of someone who has attended too many formal receptions. Before she turned to leave, she extended her hand to him.

He looked down at it and laughed. She started to snatch her hand back, but he caught it, lifted it to his mouth and bit down hard on the ends of her fingers.

She gave a small exclamation of pain.

He sucked where he had bitten, and then kissed the tips of her fingers. "You crack me up," he said huskily. "You really do."

She wanted to bolt, but before she could get away, he caught her arm in a firm grip. "Not yet, honey. I'm not letting you leave yet."

Holding her tightly, he steered her up the steps and into the breezeway that led to the building. "I really have to go," she protested.

"You don't have to do anything you don't want to. And right now, you want to stay with me."

He led her across the lobby to the auditorium doors. Without giving her time to recover, he pulled them open and thrust her into the very epicenter of nerddom—the Homebrew Computer Club.

Her thoughts still weren't coherent, and it took her a few moments to calm her breathing pattern enough so she could adjust to the activity taking place around her. She saw several hundred people gathered in clusters about the auditorium and vaguely noted that they were an odd mixture. As her head cleared, she saw that almost all of them were male—most of them in their twenties, although some were obviously teenagers. A few wore the shirts and ties of respectable businessmen, but the majority were scruffy—many of them leftovers from the counterculture. She saw unshaven cheeks and long ponytails draping the backs of faded blue work shirts. Groups huddled around electronic equipment set up on card tables placed near the stage and across the back wall of the auditorium. Directly in front of her, a pimply-faced boy who couldn't have been more than fourteen or fifteen was engaged in a hot argument with a group of men who were twice his age.

An obese character with polyester pants belted above his protruding stomach passed in front of her. "Who's got an oscilloscope?" he called out. "I need to borrow a 'scope for a couple of days."

"You can borrow mine if you've got a logic probe."

Electronic parts were being passed back and forth. Schematic drawings exchanged hands. Sam gestured toward an unkempt-looking man with a sharp nose and tangled hair. "That's John Draper. He's Captain Crunch—probably the most famous phone phreak in the world."

"Phone phreak?"

"He discovered that the toy whistles packed in Captain Crunch cereal produced the same 2600 Hertz tone that the telephone company was using to move long distance calls over its lines. He dialed a number, blew the whistle into the mouthpiece, and the call went through free. Then he started mapping telephone access codes, bouncing from one trunk line to another—hitting communications satellites all over the world. He got a kick out of taking the longest possible route to call himself—sending the call through Tokyo, India, South Africa, about four or five other places—all to make a second phone ring on the table right next to him. With the time delay, he could actually talk to himself."

Susannah couldn't help but wonder what he had to say.

"Captain Crunch knows more about building illegal blue boxes to make free telephone calls than anybody here. Just mention his name and the phone company goes nuts."

"I can imagine."

"He's on probation now."

She smiled, although she shouldn't have, because she was on close terms with several members of the Bell System's Board of Directors.

"A lot of these guys really get off on exploring the telephone system."

"Because of its elegant design?" she inquired, feeling as if she was starting to catch on.

"The best. Fantastic."

"Your design's shit," an acne-scarred kid told a man in a wheelchair. "A bucket of noise."

"I worked on that design for six months," the other man protested.

"It's still a bucket of noise," the kid replied.

Sam steered her toward one of the card tables where a group of onlookers was gathered around an untidy-looking man in his early twenties with a beard and thick-lensed glasses. He was peering intently at a moving pattern on a television screen. "That's Steve Wozniak. He's the only engineer I know who's as good as Yank. He works as a technician for Hewlett-Packard, and he and a buddy of his—a guy named Steve Jobs—are putting together a single-board computer, sort of like the one Yank and I have made. They've named theirs Apple. Pretty weird name, huh?"

Weird wasn't the word for it, she thought as she looked around at the strange assortment of people clamoring for information. Despite the fact that she didn't understand most of the technical references flying around her, she felt their excitement just as Sam had said she would.

"Everything is open here. Everybody shares whatever they know. It's part of the hacker heritage from the early 1960s—free exchange of information." He pointed toward the young kid arguing with three older men. "At Homebrew, people are judged by what they know, not how old they are or how much money they make. A lot different from big corporations like FBT, isn't it?"

A shadow passed across his face, and she knew that even while he urged her to set up an appointment with her father, he was regretting the necessity of dealing with FBT. His prejudice rankled.

"Let me introduce you to Yank."

As he led her toward the front of the auditorium, he called out greetings to various club members. Just like Steve Wozniak at the back of the room, Yank Yankowski was at the center of a group gazing down at a television set hooked up to a circuit board that looked like the one Sam had been carrying around in his case.

"It'll take me a few minutes to get his attention. Sometimes when he gets involved, he's—" Sam broke off as he stepped in front of her and spotted the design flashing across the television screen. "Holy shit," he said, his voice full of wonder. "Yank's got color! He did it. He actually got color." He immediately forgot about her and pushed through the men clustered around the card table so he could make his way to Joseph "Yank" Yankowski.

Yank was one of the more noticeable figures in the room, Susannah decided. Probably four or five inches over six feet, he stood half a head taller than Sam. He wore thick-lensed glasses with black plastic frames and sported a short dark brown crew cut. Thin almost to the point of emaciation, he had a high sloping forehead, prominent cheekbones, and a long nose. His spare torso ended in a pair of pipe-stem legs. With twenty extra pounds of flesh, a decent haircut, contact lenses, and some clothes that didn't look as if they'd been slept in, he might have been moderately attractive. But as it was, he reminded her of someone Paige would have dismissed as a complete nerd.

Susannah watched as the demonstration continued. Sam had apparently forgotten she was there. He kept throwing questions at Yank and studying the machine on the card table. She took one of the aisle seats and watched the way his hair curled up on the shoulders of his jacket. Her father wouldn't listen to a word Sam had to say once he caught sight of that hair, not to mention the Easter Island earring. Why had she promised Sam that she would try to set up an appointment?

She didn't want to think about her father, so she concentrated on the lively chaos in the auditorium. The confusion made her remember tours she had taken through the research and development labs at the Castle. Everything was always orderly in the FBT labs. Men with neat hair and necktie knots showing at the top of their white lab coats stood at well-defined work spaces. They spoke to each other respectfully. No one shouted. Certainly no one ever called a coworker's design "a monumental piece of shit."

What she saw in front of her now verged on anarchy. Vehement arguments were still breaking out. People were climbing up on chair arms and calling out the name of a piece of equipment they wanted to borrow. She remembered the plastic ID badges she had seen on those white FBT lab coats, the special pass even her father had to display. She remembered the locked doors, the uniformed security guards, and she thought about what Sam had said concerning the hacker heritage. Here in the environment of the Homebrew Computer Club, no one seemed to have any secrets. Everywhere she looked, she saw a free exchange of information. Apparently, none of them thought about holding back what they knew for personal profit.

Sam appeared in the aisle at her side. "Susannah, come on over and meet Yank. That crazy son of a bitch got color without adding any more chips. At the last meeting, he and Wozniak talked about running it off the CPU, but nobody really believed either one of them could do it."

"Incredible," she said, although she had only the vaguest idea what Sam was talking about.

"It might take me a minute to get his attention." Sam led her forward. "Yank, this is Susannah. The one I was talking about."

Yank didn't look up from his screen.

"Yank?"

"The son of a gun still won't synch up." Yank's eyes remained glued to what he was doing.

Sam looked over at her and shrugged. "He gets pretty involved when he's working."

"I can see that."

Sam tried again. "Yank?"

"Why the heck won't it synch up?"

"Maybe we should save introductions for another time," Susannah suggested.

"Yeah, I guess so."

As they began walking toward the back of the auditorium, she wished she hadn't spoken as if they had a future. There wouldn't be another time. After what had happened between them outside, she couldn't possibly see him again.

"So what do you think?" he asked.

"It's definitely an interesting group."

"It's not the only one, either. There are others all around the country—hundreds of hardware hackers getting together to build small computers." He studied her face for a moment. "Can't you see what's happening here? This is the

74

vanguard of the future. That's why it's so important for me to talk to your father. Did you mean it when you said you'd set up that appointment?"

"I'll try," she said reluctantly, "but he may not agree."

"I'll give you my phone number. Call me when you arrange it."

"*If* I arrange it." She hesitated, knowing he would probably laugh at her, but also knowing her father too well. "There's one thing more . . ."

"What's that?"

"If I can make the appointment, you'll—you'll be careful how you dress, won't you?"

"Afraid I'll show up like this?"

She hastily denied the truth. "Oh, no. Of course not."

"Well, you're right. I will."

Her forehead creased with alarm. "Oh, no. I'm afraid that would be a terrible mistake. My father's from another generation. He doesn't understand people who don't wear a business suit. Or men who wear earrings. And you'll need to get your hair cut." Even as she spoke the words, she felt a stab of regret. She loved his hair. It seemed a part of him—free and wild.

"I told you, Suzie. I don't go in for any bullshit. This is who I am."

"If you want to do business with my father, you'll have to learn to compromise."

"No!" He spoke the word so loudly that even in the chaos of the Homebrew Computer Club, people turned to look. "No. I don't make compromises."

"Please, not so loud."

He grabbed her arm, his fingers digging through her sleeve. "No compromises. Don't you see, Suzie? That's why people fail. It's why this country is so fucked up—why businesses are so fucked up. That's what I love about computers. They're as close as we can get to a perfect world. There aren't any compromises with computers. Something is either black or white. Octal code is absolute order. Three bits of ones or zeros. Either a bit *is* or it *isn't.*"

"Life's not like that," she replied softly, thinking of all the compromises she had to make.

"That's because you won't let it be. You're a chickenshit, Suzie, you know that? You're afraid to get passionate about anything."

"That's not true."

"You pull this class A con job trying to keep anybody from seeing how scared you really are. Well, it's a waste of time when you're with me, so don't bother."

He glared at her for a moment, and then his expression softened. "Look, stop worrying about business suits and haircuts. Just get your old man to talk to me. He was a pioneer in the fifties when he whipped up those early computer patents. I know I can make him understand. I'll make him see the magic. Damn, I'll make him understand if it's the last thing I do!"

As Susannah watched the fire of his vision burn in Sam Gamble's young eyes, she almost thought he would succeed.

6

● ●

As Sam drove north toward the FBT Castle, he didn't need to remind himself how important today's interview was. For months, doors had been closing all over Silicon Valley.

At Hewlett-Packard Steve Wozniak had shown his bosses the Apple motherboard he had designed and asked if they were interested. Hewlett-Packard had said no.

At Sam's insistence Yank had approached Nolan Bushnell at Atari with his board, but the company was too busy trying to stay on top of the video-game market. Atari had passed.

On the East Coast Kenneth Olsen, president of Digital Equipment Corporation, the leading minicomputer company in the world, couldn't understand why anyone would want a computer at home. DEC had passed.

And in Armonk, New York, mighty IBM dismissed the microcomputer as a toy with no business application. IBM saw no market. IBM passed.

One by one, all of the Big Boys had shaken their heads. All but FBT. Today, Sam was determined to make certain recent history didn't repeat itself.

The engine was pinging on the Plymouth Duster he had borrowed from Yank, and the muffler needed to be replaced, resulting in a combination of noises that was driving Sam crazy. How could Yank tolerate owning a car that was such a total piece of garbage? Sam hated the way Detroit had given up quality for the fast buck.

The upholstery on the seat next to him was torn, fast-food wrappers were scattered everywhere, and several old motors were tossed in the backseat, along with the guts from a Zenith television set. Most mysterious of all, a shoe box full of vacuum tubes lay like excavated dinosaur bones on the floor next to him. Sam couldn't imagine why Yank was carrying around a box of vacuum tubes. They'd been obsolete for two decades, ever since Bardeen, Brattain, and Shockley had taken advantage of the semiconducting qualities of silicon and invented the transistor. That invention had changed both the history of the Santa Clara Valley and Sam's life forever.

By the sixties, electronic circuits microscopically etched on tiny chips of silicon had pushed the cattle and the fruit orchards out of one of the most perfect agricultural climates in the world. Now electronics was the cash crop. Sam frequently heard the adults clucking their tongues over how the Valley used to be, but he liked living in a place that harvested semiconductors instead of apricots. He loved being part of the age of electronic miniaturization—an age where a computer circuit that would once have filled an entire room with thousands of inefficient, heat-producing vacuum tubes could now be contained on a silicon chip no larger than one of those soapy little Sen-Sen's he used to pop into his mouth when he was a kid.

He jammed the Duster's reluctant accelerator to the floor and switched lanes. It didn't take a crystal ball to see that the continuous miniaturization of electronics would inevitably lead to a small computer, so why were the established companies so apathetic? Not after today, he told himself. Thanks to Susannah's intercession, he had his audience with Joel Faulconer.

He rubbed his thumb along the steering wheel as he thought about Susannah. When he'd walked into that Homebrew meeting with her, he'd felt like a goddamned prince. But being with her wasn't just an ego trip. There was something else. When he was with her, he heard this click in his head. It was weird. This weird *click*. Like maybe some of his missing parts had just slipped into place.

The idea was odd, and he shook it off as he exited the freeway just west of Palo Alto and drove into the hills. It wasn't long before he spotted the entrance to the Castle. The FBT complex occupied 125 acres of land. Sam turned into the palm-lined drive and approached the central building. His lip curled in distaste. If he had built the place, he would have done the whole thing differently. That phony Greek revival style belonged on Wall Street, not in Northern California. And there were too many columns, too much marble. Total crap.

After a hassle with the security people over the sample case containing the computer motherboard, Sam was escorted across the lobby to the elevators. His aesthete's eye gave high marks to the paintings on exhibit in the lobby at the same time that his idealist's heart attempted to ignore the plastic visitor's badge that protruded from the pocket of his leather jacket. Once again he found himself torn between his determination to give Yank's beautiful design to the world by selling it to FBT and his distaste at the idea of turning it over to such a huge, impersonal corporation.

The receptionist on the top floor was young and attractive. Her mouth tightened at his appearance, so he let his eyes slide insolently to her breasts. Fuck her. He didn't have any use for women like her—phony sophisticates who thought that class was something they could buy at a high-priced boutique. After he gave her his name, she checked an appointment book, then led him down a corridor. He grew increasingly contemptuous. The interior decor might be first-class, but the atmosphere at the FBT offended him—the guard-dog secretaries, the elitism of the closed doors, the sterile, hushed silence. With every step, he yearned for the rowdy openness of the Homebrew Computer Club. If only he and Yank had enough money to start their own company. If only they had more options.

Susannah was sitting in a wing chair in the reception area outside Faulconer's office. As he spotted her, he heard that click in his head again. That strange, comforting click. Her auburn hair was neatly brushed back from her face and arranged in a French twist. She looked composed and costly in a beige wool dress with a single strand of pearls at her throat. The sight of her gave him a rush. He wanted to touch her, to hear the soft tones of that expensive private-school voice.

Susannah lifted her head as Sam approached. Her heart plummeted to her stomach and then catapulted back into her throat. She felt breathless and disoriented. The effect he had on her was so strong that several seconds passed before she could take in his appearance, and then she was barely able to hide her consternation. Despite what he'd said, she hadn't actually imagined that he would show up in jeans and a leather jacket for his meeting with her father. Her gaze lingered on those jeans and the intimate way they cupped him.

The secretary disappeared. She remembered how displeased Joel had been when she'd asked him to meet with Sam. He had insisted she be present for the meeting, and she suspected it was a subtle form of punishment for imposing on him. With a sinking dread and an awful exhilaration, she rose and stepped forward.

"Hello, Sam."

His eyes swept over her appreciatively, and he nodded.

She tucked her purse under her arm. As she spoke, she tried to hide the fact that her pulse was racing out of control. "My father's not pleased about this, I'm afraid. He doesn't approve of family interference in business, and he probably won't be very receptive to you."

"I'll make him receptive."

His arrogance maddened her. How could someone who was only twenty-four have so much self-confidence? "I told him you were a friend of one of the new board members at the Exploritorium." It wasn't entirely untrue. *She* was a new board member.

"I won't lie to him about us."

She gripped her hands together. Why was he being so unbending? He had catapulted into her life without invitation and upset everything. "There isn't any *us,*" she said stiffly. "And sometimes lies are a kindness."

He looked at her for a moment, and then the hard lines of

80

his mouth softened. "Trust yourself, Suzie. Don't be so afraid of everything."

No other person had ever accused her of being afraid. Even when she was a child, people had told her how brave she was for surviving her kidnapping. How could Sam know these things about her?

Joel's secretary appeared and led them through paneled doors into her father's private office. He rose from behind his massive desk with its polished malachite top. Not by a flicker of an eyelash did he betray any reaction to Sam's long hair and informal attire. Yet even as he graciously extended his hand, Susannah felt as if she could hear his contemptuous, unvoiced scorn.

Sam took his time moving forward to return Joel's handshake. Susannah experienced an uneasy combination of dread and admiration. What kind of man wasn't intimidated by Joel Faulconer?

"Thanks for agreeing to see me," Sam said. "You won't be sorry."

Susannah inwardly winced.

"My pleasure," Joel replied.

Not waiting for an invitation, Sam began talking about Yank's design and the future of the microcomputer at the same time that he was tossing his sample case onto a chair and flipping open the latches. "I'd like to have been able to give you a full demonstration of the machine in operation, but apparently you didn't have the time." Did he linger on the last word deliberately, she wondered, or was that vaguely insulting emphasis accidental?

Susannah turned toward the wall of windows that overlooked the manmade lake outside. A series of seven stone fountains shaped like obelisks rose from the water. They represented the seven continents of the world, all of them part of the FBT empire. As she watched their spray shoot high into the sky, she wished she were anyplace but in her father's office. She hated being in a tension-ridden atmosphere. She always thought it was her responsibility to somehow make things better.

Sam took out the motherboard and pushed aside a neat stack of reports to set it on the desktop in front of Joel.

"This is the wave of the future. The heart and guts of a revolution. This machine will shift the balance of power from institutions to individuals."

Without waiting for an invitation, he launched into a technical explanation of the efficiency of the design. Her father asked a number of quietly uttered, overly polite questions. She retreated to a leather chair on the far side of the room.

"FBT has never been inclined to enter the consumer products market," Joel said mildly.

Sam dismissed this with a disdainful wave of his hand. "Haven't you been following the Altair 8800?"

"Perhaps you should fill me in."

Sam began pacing in front of the desk, filling the office with his restless energy. Even from her safe perch at the side of the room, she could feel his intensity. "A year and a half ago, *Popular Mechanics* ran a picture on its cover of the Altair 8800, this small computer about half the size of an air conditioner that can be built from a kit. The only way to get information out of it is by reading a panel of lights flashing octal code. The machine doesn't have any memory, so it can't do much, and all anybody gets for his money is a bag of parts that have to be assembled. But within three weeks the company that was manufacturing it went from near bankruptcy to having $250,000 in the bank."

Joel's eyebrows lifted, but Sam was so wrapped up in his enthusiasm that he didn't notice. "Two hundred and fifty thousand dollars! They got more orders than they could fill. People were sending money for add-on equipment that was only in the talking stages. One guy drove all the way to Albuquerque and lived in a trailer outside the company's offices while he waited for his machine."

"My, my," Joel said, shaking his head. And then he looked thoughtful. "Two hundred and fifty thousand dollars, you say?"

Sam planted his hands on the edge of Joel's desk, then leaned forward eagerly. "In only three weeks. There's an incredible market, especially when you consider the fact that the Altair is primitive compared to what Yank has designed."

Joel gazed down at the motherboard in front of him with admiration. "Yes, I can see that. And how much are you and Mister—is it 'Yankowski'? How much are the two of you asking for this design?"

Sam sat down, hesitating. "We'd want some assurance that FBT would aggressively market the machine."

"I understand."

"And we'd like to be involved with the process."

"Ah, yes. Heading up the project team, perhaps? Something like that?"

Sam looked a bit surprised, but then he nodded.

"And the price tag?" Joel inquired.

Sam leaned back in his chair and crossed one ankle over his knee. Susannah could almost see him pulling the number from the top of his head. "Fifty thousand dollars."

"I see." Joel picked up a stainless-steel letter opener. "And how much yearly revenue do you think your computer could generate for FBT once the product was established?"

"A few million, I'd guess," Sam said cautiously.

"Ah." Joel looked thoughtful. "Could you be more specific?"

"Maybe two and a half million."

"Two and a half million? Are you sure about that number?"

Sam had begun to grow wary. "I haven't done any research, if that's what you mean."

"Could it be less?"

"I suppose."

"More? Perhaps three million?"

"Possibly."

"Two point eight million?"

Sam stared at Joel for a few seconds and then slowly stood. "You're jerking me off, aren't you?"

Susannah made a soft, barely audible gasp and rose from her chair.

"Jerking you off?" Joel looked puzzled, as if he were trying to understand the meaning of the expression. "Now why would you think that?"

Sam's jaw jutted forward. "Just answer my question."

Joel scoffed. "Why would I be jerking someone off who wants to make this company two million dollars a year? That's nearly what FBT pays to have its garbage collected."

Sam's complexion turned chalky.

"You don't have the slightest idea what you're talking about, Mr. Gamble. You have no idea of the value of what you're selling or of its worth to this corporation. It's obvious that you haven't done your homework, because if you had, you certainly wouldn't be wasting my time with this meeting."

Joel had been toying with a panel of switches set into the top of his desk, and now he began to press them. Slowly he turned his head to look out the window. Sam followed the direction of his eyes and watched as the seven columns of water rising from the stone fountains outside began to still, one by one. Like God, Joel Faulconer could command the forces of the universe. The show of power wasn't lost on Sam.

As the last column of water disappeared and the lake grew still, Joel resumed speaking. "I have no interest at all in someone who comes to me with a story about a bankrupt company making a profit of $250,000. I'm not even interested in a profit of two million dollars. Now if you had said you were going to make me a hundred million, I might have listened."

"You son of a bitch."

Joel's hand moved and all seven fountains once again sprang to life. "I'm not turning you down because you're crude and arrogant. I'm not even turning you down because you didn't have the common courtesy to get a haircut before you came to see me. I'm turning you down because you don't think big enough. Good day, Mr. Gamble."

For a few seconds Sam didn't move. Then he snatched up the motherboard and began walking toward the door. Before he got there, however, he stopped and turned back to Joel. "I almost feel sorry for you, Faulconer. You're even stupider than I thought you'd be." Then he left the office.

The blood had drained from Susannah's face and her skin was ashen. As Joel turned to her, he could clearly see her distress, but he didn't take pity on her. "I don't care how many favors you owe your friends. Don't ever impose on me like this again."

"I—I didn't mean to impose," she said shakily. "I know he was unforgivably rude, but—" Joel's eyes gave her a look so imperious that she faltered. How could she defend Sam after what he'd said? But her father had been rude, too—deliberately baiting Sam.

"It's just—you were rather hard on him," she finished lamely.

"Are you actually defending him?"

"No, I—"

He tilted back his head so that he seemed to be looking at her from a great distance, and the acute hostility in his expression made her feel ill. She'd had the audacity to question her father's authority, and now she would be punished.

Without saying another word, he punched a button on his intercom. "My daughter is leaving now. Would you please see her out."

The endless winter of Joel Faulconer's disapproval had begun.

Susannah had watched others endure her father's icy silences, but she had seldom had to endure one herself—and never one of this duration. As the weeks passed and the time for the wedding drew nearer, Susannah began to feel as if someone had placed a curse on her. Despite her repeated apologies and her attempts to restore her father's good mood, he remained silent and condemning.

Cal had to be in Europe for several weeks on business, so he wasn't around to act as a buffer, and each day seemed to bring another last-minute crisis with the wedding arrangements. Twice she picked up the phone to call Sam Gamble and tell him how she felt about the way he had behaved, but both times she hung up before she dialed. It was infinitely better not to talk to him again. Infinitely better not to think about either his rudeness or his crazy enthusiasm for putting computers in people's houses right along with their stereos and television sets.

Her father finally forgave her, but only after he delivered a stinging lecture about imposition and disrespect. A newly cynical voice inside her whispered that he wouldn't have relented so quickly if he hadn't needed her to accompany him on a week-long trip to Paris. It would inconvenience him to entertain French cabinet members without an official hostess at his side.

In Paris they stayed at Joel's favorite hotel, the Crillon, an imposing graystone edifice on the northwest corner of the Place de la Concorde. The evening they arrived, Cal appeared at their suite to escort them to a reception at the American embassy, located nearby on the Avenue Gabriel. Since Joel was present along with several of his aides, her reunion with Cal was warm but restrained. They had little time to talk during the reception at the embassy, but as they were leaving, Cal gave her a mischievous I've-got-a-secret smile.

"We have some celebrating to do tonight," he said. "I've made dinner reservations for us at the Tour."

Tour l'Argent was one of the most famous restaurants in the world, but as Susannah settled into the limousine, she felt restless and suggested they go someplace that wasn't quite so formal. Her mind drifted back to a rainy afternoon she had spent in Paris some years ago.

"Would you mind going to La Coupole in Montparnasse? I know it's just a brasserie and we're overdressed, but it'll be fun."

He gave her one of those skeptically indulgent looks she sometimes received from her father. "You're not in one of those crazy Montparnasse sort of moods, are you?" The creases at the corners of his splendid blue eyes deepened as he teased her.

She sensed that he was excited about something, and she smiled back. He undoubtedly had a story he'd been saving for her about some brilliant maneuver he had pulled off in his negotiations with the French manufacturers. He was so handsome, so perfect. Despite the difference in their ages, he was everything she could possibly want in a husband. They had common interests, similar backgrounds.

Impulsively, she leaned over and pressed her lips to his in a fierce, possessive kiss. He returned the kiss for only a moment before he drew away and gave her a meaningful glance toward the back of the driver's head. Patting her on the knee, he began to speak about an incident that had happened at the reception.

His rejection hurt her. Cal was a stickler about appearances, and most of the time she didn't mind. But they were in Paris. Couldn't he let down his guard just for the evening? As the neon sign of La Coupole came into view and Cal chatted about the embassy reception, she envisioned Sam Gamble sitting beside her in the limo. Sam—pushing her down on the plush seat and slipping his hands up under the skirt of her gown. Sam, discovering that she was naked beneath—naked, open, ready to receive him. With Sam, she could be another sort of woman, someone sexy and sultry, loose and wild.

She firmly pushed the image from her mind. A few minutes later, as they walked into La Coupole, the conversation that floated between them was as light and aimless as a cloud of soap bubbles.

For half a century La Coupole had attracted a diverse group of artists, intellectuals, students, and assorted eccentrics. Henry Miller had played chess with Anaïs Nin beneath its lofty ceiling. Jean-Paul Sartre had eaten a late lunch with Simone de Beauvoir at the same corner table nearly every day. Chagall and Picasso had dined there, as had Hemingway and Fitzgerald. But as Susannah took her seat across from Cal, she thought of the legends she had heard of the brasserie's nascent days during the 1920s, when Kiki de Montparnasse, Paris's premier playgirl, had stuck a rose between her teeth and cavorted nearly naked in the fountain that sat in the center of the dining room.

"The fountain was turned into a giant flower vase decades ago," she said. Cal looked up from the menu he had been studying. She smiled self-consciously and nodded toward the center of the room. "That giant flower vase was originally a fountain, but the restaurant had to drain it because the patrons kept swimming in it."

He nodded politely and asked her if she would prefer lamb curry or fish. "Honestly, Susannah, I can't believe we're giving up duck at the Tour for such ordinary food."

"The lamb curry will be fine," she replied quickly. As they waited for their order to arrive, she gazed around her, but the magic was gone and she could no longer recapture La Coupole of her imagination. Now she saw only a noisy dining room full of ordinary people. There was no sign of a Modigliani or a Camus. No one who resembled Josephine Baker was walking through the door leading a pet lion cub on a diamond-studded leash. Where are you, Kiki de Montparnasse? she thought. I wish I could see a woman free enough to jump into a fountain without thinking about what people would say.

Cal reached across the table to take her hand. "I had planned a more romantic setting to tell you this, but I may not have another chance." With his thumb, he covered the diamond on her engagement ring. It was exactly one carat because both of them had agreed that a larger stone would be ostentatious. Less is always more.

"It's actually your father's surprise, and you're going to have to pretend to hear it for the first time when he announces it, but it's so extraordinary that I wanted to give you a chance to prepare yourself."

"Our mysterious wedding present?" she asked. He nodded and his smile broadened.

Ever since the engagement, Joel had been hinting at a spectacular gift. She had overheard part of a telephone conversation he'd had with one of his attorneys, and told Cal that she suspected Joel was deeding them the charming vacation house he owned on Maui. It was a valuable piece of property, and both of them had been moved by the possibility of such generosity.

"You were right about the house," he told her.

"I thought so."

"Except you picked the wrong one."

"Oh?" She took a sip from her wineglass. "It can't be London. He needs that for business. It must be the house at Pebble Beach, although it's hard to imagine him parting with it. He loves living on the golf course."

"It's not Pebble Beach." Cal clasped her hand between both of his. She could not remember seeing him look so pleased. He chuckled and his blue eyes gleamed with triumph.

"Susannah, Joel is giving us Falcon Hill."

7

• •

The next evening over thin stalks of white asparagus and
glasses of finely aged Vouvray, Joel made the announcement
that he was deeding them Falcon Hill as a wedding gift. He
told them that he wanted to spend more time at Pebble
Beach, that he no longer needed such a large house. And
then, casually, he suggested that Susannah convert the guest
house at Falcon Hill into something comfortable for him
when he was in town.

She had barely slept the night before, and now her heart
felt as if it were shrinking in her chest. He was trapping her.
Until that moment she hadn't realized how much she had
been looking forward to living independently from her
father. Why hadn't she guessed that he would want to
continue to have her at his beck and call? Now, by giving
them Falcon Hill as a wedding gift, he had made certain that
her marriage wouldn't inconvenience him, that she would
still be available to do his bidding.

And then she was filled with guilt at her selfishness. Joel
Faulconer had given her everything. He was the shining
prince who had rescued her. How could she be so ungrateful? Throughout the rest of the meal she found herself
thinking about debts of love and wondering how they were

ever repaid. She loved her father very much, but did she owe him her life?

Later that evening, when Cal took her to her suite, she tried to discuss her feelings with him. He drew her into his arms and rubbed her back as if he were comforting a child. "I think you're overreacting, darling. I know he can sometimes be domineering, but I'll be there to make certain he doesn't take advantage of you. Let's not cast a shadow over such an extraordinary gift. Falcon Hill is worth millions."

"Is that all you can think about? How much Falcon Hill is worth?"

He stepped away from her, his face mirroring his surprise at her outburst. And then his eyes grew as chilly as the silver streak that shot through his hair. "You've deliberately chosen to misunderstand me. I don't appreciate being snarled at."

She pressed her fingertips to her temple. "I'm sorry. I guess I'm just tired."

"I'm tired, too, but I don't snap at you."

"You're right. It was unforgivable."

But Cal refused to accept her apology. Giving her a stony look, he stalked from her suite. Susannah felt the familiar tightness in her stomach as one more male chose to punish her with silence.

She returned to San Francisco feeling as if something hard and cold had taken up permanent lodging inside her.

After his confrontation with Joel Faulconer, Sam had jumped on his bike and headed for San Diego. Although he had a couple of friends there, he made no effort to contact any of them because he didn't want company. Instead, he played Breakout in the arcades, slept on the beach, and woke up at night with the cold sweats. All he could think about was what a prick Faulconer was. No matter how hard he tried, he couldn't blot out the image of Susannah standing there watching her father make an asshole out of him.

Day after day he got angrier with Yank. This was Yank's problem, not his. Sam was tired of playing father and mother to a guy who couldn't drive three blocks without getting lost. Yank should be out hustling his own design. But

Yank couldn't see any further than his next hack, and Sam knew that his friend didn't have the most rudimentary understanding of the significance of what he was doing. And then one night while Sam was playing his dozenth game of Breakout, he saw Yank's hands in his mind—the incredible genius of those hands—and his anger dissolved.

That was when he realized that Joel Faulconer was right about him. He hadn't even started to think big enough. He'd been so wrapped up in the idea of selling Yank's design to somebody else that he hadn't listened to the voice inside him telling him that handing Yank's genius over to a fat-cat company went against everything he believed in.

He got on his bike that same night and headed north. He was going to start his own company. No matter what it took, no matter what sacrifices he had to make, he was going to do it.

And the closer he got to San Francisco, the more he found himself thinking about Susannah. He kept remembering all those leggy San Diego girls with their short shorts and those skimpy halter tops that outlined their nipples. Wherever he went, they had given him sexy come-ons, but even though many of them were more beautiful than Susannah, he kept thinking about how cheap they looked.

He hated imitations. All of his life he had been surrounded by inferiority—the shoddy little house he had grown up in, the incompetent public school teachers with no tolerance for a sullen, gifted rebel who had asked all the wrong questions, the father who spent every evening staring at the television screen and telling his son that he was a loser. For as long as he could remember, Sam had dreamed of surrounding himself with beautiful objects and exceptional people. And now, making the best microcomputer had become inexorably linked in his mind with having the best woman. By the time he reached the Valley, he was convinced that if he could have Susannah Faulconer, he could also have everything else that was missing from his life.

The next day he quit his job and packed up the computer board, the television—everything he needed to demonstrate Yank's machine. That same afternoon he began to make the rounds of Silicon Valley electronics shops. No one was interested.

By the second day, he was seething with frustration. "Just let me set it up," he told a Santa Clara store owner. "Let me give you a demo. It'll only take a few minutes."

"I don't have a few minutes. Sorry. Another time maybe."

The following day he had his first piece of luck. One of the store managers agreed to watch Sam's demonstration and even marveled over the elegance of Yank's design. Then he shook his head. "It's a neat little machine, no doubt about it. But who'd buy it? People aren't interested in a little computer. What are they going to do with one?"

The question drove Sam crazy. People figured out what to do with a computer—that was all. How could he explain something so rudimentary? "Hack around," he said. "Play some games."

"Sorry. Not interested."

On the fourth day the machine never made it out of the trunk of Yank's Duster because Sam couldn't find one store owner who would agree to see it. "Let me just show you what it can do," he pleaded. "Look, it'll only take a few minutes."

"Listen, kid. I'm busy. I got customers."

In an electronics store near Menlo Park, Sam finally lost his temper. He slapped his hand down on the countertop so hard he knocked a box of switches to the floor. "I've got a machine here that's going to change the future of the world, but you're telling me that you're too goddamn busy to spare a few lousy minutes to look at it!"

The owner took a quick step backward. "Get out of here before I call the cops!"

Sam drew back his boot and kicked a hole through the side of the counter. "I don't give a fuck! Call them! Let's see if you're smart enough to dial the fucking telephone!"

Then he stalked out.

Two weeks before Susannah's wedding, some of the FBT executive wives gave her a shower. It was nearly midnight when she got home. She swung the Mercedes around the east wing of the house toward the garage. The trunk was loaded with bridal lingerie and monogrammed towels. With the exception of a nymphet third wife, Susannah had been the youngest person there, yet they had all treated her as if she were their contemporary. Several of them had started talking about the movie stars they'd had crushes on when they were young—Clark Gable, Alan Ladd, Charles Boyer. They'd all looked at her strangely when she'd mentioned Paul McCartney.

As she reached up to punch the garage door control that was attached to the visor, she found herself longing for the days when her fantasies had starred a chubby-cheeked Beatle instead of a long-haired biker. She jabbed the control again. The garage door refused to budge, and she remembered that it had stopped working the day before and been disconnected. Her head was aching, and she rubbed her temples. If only she were sleeping better, she wouldn't be so edgy. But instead of sleeping, she kept staring at the ceiling and replaying every encounter she'd had with Sam. She reconstructed from memory exactly what he'd said to her and what she'd said in return. But most of all, she remembered the way he had kissed her.

Sagging back into the seat, she pressed her eyes shut and let that forbidden image wash over her. Once again she felt his brash young mouth settling over her own. Her bottom lip grew slack as she relived the moment his tongue had entered her mouth. She expanded the memory from what had happened to what had not, and imagined the feel of his naked chest against her bare breasts. Her breath made a soft rasping sound in the quiet interior of the car.

With a great strength of will, she forced her eyes open and fumbled for the door handle. She had to quit doing this. She was becoming obsessed with him, and she had to pull herself together. As she got out of the car and walked toward the garage door, she promised herself that she would stop dwelling on what had happened. She would stop thinking about him at all.

A rustling noise in the trees penetrated her thoughts. She glanced uneasily over her shoulder, but the outside lights hadn't been left on and she couldn't see anything. Walking a little faster, she stepped into the path of the Mercedes headlights and reached for the garage door handle.

"Enjoy your party?"

She gasped, and spun around in time to see Sam coming out of the shadows, both thumbs tucked into the side pockets of his jeans. Blood coursed through her veins at the sight of him. She pressed her hand to her throat and took a deep breath. "What are you doing here? You scared me."

"Good."

"How did you get through the gates?"

"Gadgets are a hobby of mine," he said sarcastically. "Or have you forgotten?"

"Sam, I—I'm tired. I don't want any confrontations."

He scowled at her. "How was your wedding shower? I've been reading about all the festivities in the papers. Why the hell haven't you put a stop to it?"

"Put a stop to it?" It was as if he had suggested she grow another head. Didn't he understand that once something like this was set in motion, there was no turning back? She was trapped. No, not trapped. Of course she wasn't trapped. She wanted to marry Cal. Cal was perfect for her.

"It's not right," he exclaimed. "You're locking the door on the two of us before we've had any chance at all. God, you're a chickenshit. If my own guts weren't aching so bad, I'd almost feel sorry for you."

"There isn't any two of us," she said fiercely. "You asked me to help arrange a meeting with my father. I did. That's all."

"You're a liar." He walked over to the Mercedes, then ducked his head inside and turned off the ignition. His hand lingered for a moment on the leather upholstery before he straightened to face her. She thought uneasily of her father. His bedroom was in the far wing of the house, but what if he heard them?

"I'm going to start my own company, Suzie, and I want you with me."

"What?"

"Any day now I'll get the first order. It's starting. Everything's starting right now."

"I'm glad for you, but—"

"It's starting. *Right now!*" Each part of his face had gone rigid with intensity. "Stop being so scared. Build my dream with me. Forget about your wedding. We can change the world. You and me. We can do it together."

"What are you talking about? I want you to leave. Don't you see? We're not anything alike. We don't understand each other." Even as she said it, she knew the words were a lie. He could read her mind. He saw inside her when no one else could.

"Don't you think I'm good enough for you? Is that it?"

"No! I'm not a snob. I'm just—"

"I need you. I need you to help me get my company started."

He speared her with his dark, exacting eyes. She wanted to weave her fingers through his hair, touch his silver tongue with her own. Desperately, she tried to make him understand. "I'm getting married. And I don't know anything about starting a company. Why would you want my help?"

He could barely explain it to himself, let alone her. "I feel good when you're around. You remind me of what it's all about. Quality, elegance, classic design."

"Is that all I am to you? A piece of design?"

"That's only part of it. There's something between us—something strong and right. Get rid of that deadhead you're engaged to. If you loved him so much, you wouldn't have turned into a firecracker when I kissed you. There's a whole world out there. Don't you want a little bit of it?"

"You don't know anything about my life."

"I know that you want a hell of a lot more from it than you're getting."

"I'm getting a lot," she retorted, determined to hurt him. "Like that Mercedes that you keep touching. And Falcon Hill. My father is giving us this house as a wedding gift."

"Is the house going to make good love to you at night?" Stunned, she stared at him.

"Is it, Suzie?" His voice dropped, grew low and husky. He walked closer to her, and she took an involuntary step back, only to bump into the garage door behind her. "Both of us know how much you want that, don't we? Will the house love you real good? Will it hold you at night and fill you up and make you moan?" Reaching out, he pushed his hand inside her jacket and rubbed the skin at her waist through the soft knit of her dress. "Will the house make you cry out real deep in your throat? Have you ever cried out like that for a man? Fast little pants? Whimpers?"

"Stop. Please don't."

"I could make you cry out like that for me."

96

He pushed his hips into hers and pressed her against the garage door. She saw the flicker of the silver earring through the strands of his hair and felt that he was hard. The dark eroticism she no longer seemed able to control swept through her like wildfire. "Don't," she whispered. "Don't do that."

He leaned forward to brush his lips along her neck. She turned her head to the side, moaning softly. His hand moved upward over her rib cage and cupped her breast through the dress. He laughed softly and touched the nipple. "Can that house make you come?"

It was too much. With a cry that came from the deepest part of her, she pushed away from him. "Don't do this to me! Leave me alone!" And then she fled into the house.

She moved through the next few days in a daze. Her father and Cal seemed to attribute her distraction to bridal nerves, and both were exceptionally considerate. One morning as her father was leaving for an overnight business trip, he hugged her and said, "You know how much I appreciate all the ways you help me, don't you? I know I don't say it often enough, but I love you, sweetheart."

Her eyes misted at the tenderness in his voice. She thought of her secret meetings with Sam, the way she had deceived him, and was overwhelmed with guilt. At that moment, she silently vowed to be the best daughter in the world.

But the vow was easier made than kept. With only a week left until her wedding, Susannah lay in the darkness and watched the illuminated numbers on her digital clock flip to 2:18. She couldn't eat, she couldn't sleep. Her chest felt heavy, as if a great weight were pressing down on her.

Without warning, the phone on her bedside table jangled. She snatched it up and held it to her chest for a moment. Then she cradled it to her ear. "Hi," she whispered, grateful to have a partner in insomnia. "You couldn't sleep either?"

But it wasn't Cal. It was Conti Dove—Conti, Paige's lover, calling to tell Susannah that Paige had been arrested several hours before at an all-night grocery store and he didn't have enough money to bail her out of jail. Susannah pressed her eyes shut for a moment, trying to imagine what else could go wrong. Then, being careful not to wake her father, she threw on the first clothes she could grab and left the house.

Paige was being held at a downtown police station on the fringes of San Francisco's crime-infested Western Addition. Conti was waiting by the front door. Susannah had only met him once before, but she had no trouble recognizing him. Low-slung chinos, sleepy bedroom eyes with lids at half mast, wiry dark hair. He didn't look like a candidate for Mensa, but he was definitely sexy in an earthy sort of way.

He slipped his hands from the pockets of a red Forty-Niners' windbreaker and walked toward her. "Uh, yeah—listen, I'm sorry I had to bother you. Paige'll probably kill me when she finds out, but I couldn't leave her in jail."

"Of course you couldn't." Shouldering her purse, Susannah followed him into the station, where she posted Paige's bond, handling everything as efficiently as if she did this kind of thing all the time. She was courteous to the police officers and did what she could to keep the arrest from ending up in the newspapers. She made polite conversation with Conti, but all the time she wanted to cry from a combination of exhaustion and rage. Her sister had been arrested for shoplifting. Her beautiful sister, child of one of the wealthiest men in California, had been caught slipping two cans of cat food into her purse.

"Why, Conti?" she asked, as they took their seats on a scratched wooden bench that lined one wall of a claustrophobically narrow hallway. "Why would Paige do something like this?"

"I dunno."

Normally, Susannah would have let it go at that, but something had happened to her in these past two months that had made her impatient with polite social evasions, so she pressed him. "If she needed money, I would have given it to her."

He looked embarrassed. "She doesn't like to take money from you." Shifting his weight on the bench, he crossed his ankle over his knee and then uncrossed it. "I dunno. We thought we was going to get this contract with Azday Records. Paige was all excited. And then a couple of weeks ago, this guy, this Mo Geller, backed out. He heard another group play and he said they had a better sound. Paige took it pretty hard."

Susannah asked several more questions, but Conti was uncommunicative. Finally, they lapsed into silence. Fifteen minutes passed. Conti got up and wandered over to a water cooler. Half an hour went by. Susannah had to go to the bathroom, but she was afraid to leave the hallway. Conti bummed a cigarette from an empty-faced teenager.

"I'm not supposed to smoke, you know," he finally said. "My voice."

"Yes. I understand."

"They got her in this holding cell."

"I know."

"You don't think there would be, like, guys or anything in there with her? Givin' her trouble."

"I don't think so. I'm sure they separate men and women." Why was she so sure? She had never been in a police station.

"She stole cat food," he said suddenly. "She's in jail because she stole two cans of cat food."

"Yes. That's what they said."

He dropped his cigarette and ground it into the linoleum with the toe of a leather sneaker. When he lifted his head, he looked as baffled and unhappy as a child. "See, the thing of it is—we don't have a cat."

At that moment, Paige came through the door. Her jeans were ripped at the knee. Her pretty blond hair hung in tangles around her face. She looked tired, young, and scared. Conti rushed toward her, but before he got there she spotted Susannah. Paige's shoulders stiffened. She lifted her head defiantly. "What's *she* doing here?"

"I'm sorry, hon," Conti said. "I—I couldn't pay the bond."

"You shouldn't have called her. I told you never to call her."

As Susannah stood, she found herself remembering the chocolate-covered cherries she had tried to smuggle to Paige when she got in trouble as a child.

"I don't need you here," Paige said belligerently. "Go back where you came from."

The hostility in her sister's face made Susannah feel ill.

Why did Paige hate her so much? What did everyone want from her? She tried so hard to please them all, but whatever she did never seemed to be enough. She slipped her hand into the pocket of her trench coat and squeezed hard, digging the nails into her palm so she wouldn't lose control. "Paige, come home with me tonight," she said calmly. "Let me put you to bed. We can talk in the morning."

"I don't want to talk. I want to get laid. Come on, Conti. Let's get out of here."

"Sure, honey. Sure." He looped his arm around her shoulders and pulled her protectively to him. With her upper body turned into Conti's chest, she walked awkwardly.

Susannah stepped forward. She meant to tell Paige that they had to talk, that they couldn't just forget something like this had happened. She would be logical, reasonable, choose her words carefully. But the soft words that came from her mouth weren't the ones she had planned at all.

"Paige, I don't know if you remember, but I'm getting married on Saturday. It would mean a lot to me if you were there." At first Susannah didn't think Paige had heard. But then, just before Conti led her through the door, her sister gave a nearly imperceptible nod.

The electronics shop was located in Cupertino just off Stevens Creek Boulevard. Sam thought he knew every shop in the Valley, but Z.B. Electronics was new. As he pulled up outside, he spotted a group of three teenage boys approaching the shop. He immediately tagged them as "wireheads" —the name high school kids gave to the boys who spend all their time in the school electronics lab. When Sam was in high school, he had hung out with both the "wireheads" and "freaks," the kids who were caught up in the counterculture. The fact that he didn't stick to one group had confused everybody.

Acting on impulse, Sam got out of the car and opened the trunk of the Duster. He called out to the boys, "Hey, help me carry this stuff inside, will you?"

A pudgy, long-haired kid detached himself from the group and walked forward. "What do you have?"

"A microcomputer," Sam replied casually, as if everybody in the Valley drove around with a microcomputer in the trunk.

"No shit! Hey, guys, he's got a micro in his trunk." The kid turned to Sam and his face was alive with excitement. "Did you build it?"

Sam handed him one of the boxes of equipment and picked up the heavy television himself. Another boy slammed the trunk lid. "I helped a friend of mine design it. He's the best."

As they walked toward the shop, the boys began peppering him with questions.

"What kind of microprocessor did you use?"

"A 7319 from Cortron."

"That's shit," one of them protested. "Why aren't you running it off an Intel 8008 like the Altair?"

"The 8008 is old news. The 7319 is more powerful."

"What do you think of the IMSAI 8080?" the pudgy kid asked, referring to a new microcomputer that was rapidly challenging the Altair's supremacy.

"IMSAI's nothing more than a rip-off of the Altair," Sam said derisively. "Same old stuff. Have you ever taken one apart? Total shit. A bucket of noise."

One of the boys rushed in front of Sam to open the door. "But if you're using another microprocessor, none of the Altair equipment will work with it."

"Who cares? We've done everything better."

As they walked inside Z.B. Electronics, an enormously obese man with yellow hair and pink watery eyes glanced up at them from behind the counter. Sam stopped in his tracks. As he looked past the man, his stomach did a flip-flop, and the television in his arms suddenly seemed as light as a box of microchips. No wonder the kids were attracted to this store. On two rows of shelving directly behind the man's head rested a dozen Altair microcomputers.

Sam Gamble had hit pay dirt.

"Chamber of Commerce weather," Joel kept saying the morning of the wedding. "It's Chamber of Commerce weather."

Susannah forced herself to take a bite of dry toast while she stared through the dining room window at the sun-spangled June day and watched the gardeners tying the last of the white ribbon festoons in the trees.

Her father glanced up from his newspaper, a man in complete command of his world. "Could I have more coffee, dear?"

As she refilled his cup, she felt tired and worn, like an old lady with all the drama of life behind her.

The woman who was coordinating the wedding arrived shortly before noon, and for the next few hours she and Susannah busied themselves double-checking arrangements that had already been triple-checked. She sat for the hairdresser who arrived at two, but the style he arranged was too fussy. After he left, she brushed it out and made a simple coil at the nape of her neck. At three o'clock she put on her antique lace dress and fastened a little Juliet cap to her head. While she secured the Bennett family choker around her neck, she watched through the window as the guests arrived. And then, when it was time, she went downstairs.

"My little girl," Joel whispered as she approached. "My perfect little girl."

Moments later the trumpets sounded, heralding the beginning of the ceremony.

Cal was smiling at her as she approached. The minister began to speak, and she tugged surreptitiously on the pearls. Why couldn't she breathe? Why was the choker so tight?

The ceremony continued, and the noise of the lawn mower that had been bothering her grew louder. People were turning their heads and Cal's eyebrows drew together. The minister had just begun to address her when she finally recognized the sound for what it was. Her gasp was drowned out by the noise of the Harley shooting into the garden.

"Suzie!"

She spun around and saw his black hair flying in the breeze like a pirate's flag. He looked magnificent and appallingly dangerous—a dark angel, a wicked messiah.

"What's the matter?" he called out. "Forget to send me an invitation?"

As he taunted her from the seat of his Harley, the long-ago chant of the balloon man began to beat in her ears.

"Come on, Suzie. Climb up on the back of my bike."

She pulled away from Cal and pressed her hands over her

ears. "Go away! I won't listen to you! I'm not listening to you!"

But Sam was a man with a vision, a child of the middle class, immune to the rules of upper-class propriety, and he paid no attention to her entreaty. She stumbled away from the altar, trying to distance herself from all of them.

"Follow me, babe. Leave all this and come with me."

She wouldn't do it. She wouldn't go to the end of the drive. She wouldn't unlock the iron gates. She was a good girl. Always a good girl. She wouldn't ever, ever again run off with a clown-faced balloon man.

All my balloons for free. Come and follow me.

Her father was untangling himself from the rope garland that cordoned off the end of his row, coming to rescue her, to protect her and keep her. To keep her at Falcon Hill. To keep her with Cal. She saw Paige's shocked face, Cal's appalled one. She clawed at her neck so she could breathe, but the choker was no longer there. A sprinkling of pearls had scattered over the toes of her wedding pumps.

"Hop on my bike, babe. Hop on my bike and follow me."

She felt the pull of his sun, the light of his vision, the blazing glory of his challenge. A yearning for freedom burst inside her like a rocket-born rainbow. She heard the rage of proper angels in the outbursts of the people around her, but the call of a leather-clad devil spurred her on. No more. No less is more. Not ever. From now on more is more.

She began racing toward him, flying along the pristine white runner and crumpling it beneath her feet. One of her shoes came off. She kicked off the other. The little Juliet cap blew away, tugging free her careful hair.

Paige's voice rang out over all the rest. Paige—proper Paige—calling out in horror at the unforgivable act her sister was committing. "Susannah!"

Joel shouted her name and rushed forward. Paige cried out again.

Sam Gamble threw back his head and laughed at them all. A strand of black hair blew in front of his mouth and stuck to his bottom lip. He gunned the Harley. Held out his hand. Come on, babe. Come-on, come-on, come-on.

She lifted the lace skirt of her dress high up on her thighs, revealing long thin legs and a flash of garter blue. Her auburn hair flew out behind her. She reached for him. Reached for her destiny and felt his tight grip pulling her into the future as she straddled the Harley.

She wrapped her arms around his waist and pressed her breasts against his jacket. The Harley roared to life between her thighs, its vibrations shooting high up inside her, filling her full to bursting with new life.

At that moment she didn't care if all the balloons in the world would someday burst around her. She only cared that she was finally free.

8

For several moments the wedding guests stood frozen like well-dressed figures in a modern *tableau vivant*. Cal Theroux was the first to move. White-faced and humiliated, he shoved a path through the crowd and disappeared. Joel, looking neither right nor left, made his way to the house with rigid dignity.

Paige was too stunned to move. The breeze picked up a cluster of feathers from her boa and blew them against her cheek, but she didn't feel anything. Her world had tilted, shifting everything it contained so that it could never resettle in the same position.

She shook her head slightly as she tried to reconcile all that she knew about her cool, perfect sister with the woman who had just fled her wedding on the back of a Harley. As she stared at the crumpled aisle runner and the place where the grass had been trampled down, she realized that she hadn't known her sister at all.

The idea terrified her. She immediately shoved it away and let a clean, pure surge of anger take its place.

Susannah had lied to all of them. She had a secret life, a secret self that none of them had ever suspected. That image of cool perfection had been a sham. How clever her sister was, how deceitful. She had manipulated them so that she remained the favored daughter while her younger sister was the outcast.

Paige nurtured her anger, clasping it to her breast and hugging it close. She let it fill every pore so that there was no room left for fear, so that no place remained inside her where she might hide other lies—lies about herself.

Sounds began to work their way into her consciousness—exclamations, muted conversation. The guests had formed animated groups, and at any moment they would begin to descend on her. They would ply her with questions she couldn't answer and pour buckets full of pity over her head. She couldn't bear it. She had to get away.

Her battered VW was parked in the motorcourt among the Jags and Rollses, and she wove her way along the perimeter of the garden toward it. But before she slipped around the corner of the back wing, she slowed and looked back.

The groups were still huddled together. Heads were moving back and forth as everyone offered an interpretation of what had just happened. She waited for the men to reach for their pens so they could calculate the effect that this might have on the price of FBT stock.

As she watched them, she could feel the blood rushing through her veins like a river on a rampage. Her ears were ringing. This was it! This was what she'd been waiting for. All her life she'd been waiting for this chance.

Hesitantly, she slipped her tawdry boa from her shoulders and let it fall behind an urn of roses. Then, with her heart in her throat, she began moving toward the guests. When she reached the nearest group, she gathered her strength and spoke.

"It seems a shame for all this food to go to waste. Why don't we move toward the reception tent?"

Everyone turned to her, surprised.

"Why, Paige!" one of the women exclaimed. "Poor dear. What an awful thing."

"None of us can believe it," another interjected. "Susannah, of all people."

Paige heard herself replying in a smooth, careful voice that sounded a bit like her sister's. "She's been under a lot of pressure lately. I— We can only hope she gets the professional help she needs."

An hour later, with the small of her back aching from the tension of fielding their questions, she said good-bye to the last of the guests and entered Falcon Hill. The house enveloped her—comforting and suffocating at the same time. She walked through the deserted rooms on the first floor in search of her father and then climbed the stairs. The door to her old bedroom was shut. Nothing was there for her and she felt no temptation to go in.

Susannah's room was neat as always. The suitcases for the honeymoon waited by the door like abandoned children. Paige stepped into the adjoining bath. The marble tub and sink were immaculate. No auburn strands of hair clung to the sides, no smears of makeup spoiled the ebony surface. It was as if her sister never used the room, as if she somehow managed to emerge into the world clean and perfect— without any effort on her part.

Her father's bedroom was as orderly as Susannah's and just as empty. She found him in a small study at the back of the house, which overlooked the gardens. He was standing at the window, staring down on the shambles of his daughter's wedding.

Her stomach pitched. "Daddy?"

He turned his head and gave her a calm inquisitive stare, as if nothing of any import had happened. "Yes, Paige?"

Her fragile self-confidence deserted her. "I—I just— wanted to see if you were—were all right."

"Of course. Why wouldn't I be?"

But as she looked more closely, she could see his pallid complexion and the harsh brackets at the corners of his mouth. His weakness gave her a sudden spurt of strength. "Would you like me to fix you a drink?"

He gazed at her for a moment as if he were making up his mind about something, and then he nodded stiffly. "Yes, why don't you do that?"

She turned to leave, only to have him speak again.

"And Paige. That dress is quite ugly. Would you mind changing it?"

Her first reaction to his criticism was the familiar defensive surge of anger, but almost immediately the anger faded. He wasn't sending her away. He wanted her to stay. Now that Susannah was gone, she wasn't an outcast anymore.

It took her only seconds to make her decision. Slipping out into the hallway, she went to Susannah's room and removed the thrift-shop dress. Five minutes later she descended the stairs wearing one of her sister's soft Italian knits.

The world flew past Susannah's eyes like a carousel spinning out of control. The wind tore at her hair, snarling it around her head, whipping it against Sam's cheeks. Her dress had ridden up, and the tops of her legs chafed against the rough denim of his jeans, but she didn't notice. She had moved to a point beyond simple sensation. As she clung to his waist, she prayed the wild ride would never end. The motorcycle was a magic chariot that held time at bay. As long as the machine kept moving, there was no yesterday, no today, no tomorrow.

Sam seemed to understand her need to fly. He did not take them due south, but zigzagged across the peninsula, showing her a familiar world from a different perspective. The San Andreas Reservoir flashed by, and later the bay. They roared through quiet neighborhoods and ran with the wind along the highway. Eighteen-wheelers sped by them, tossing grit and belching blast-furnace gusts of air that stole her breath. Car horns blared at the lace-clad runaway bride perched so incongruously on the back of a Harley-Davidson. She wanted to ride forever. She wanted to race through time into a different dimension—a world where she had no name. A world where actions bore no consequences.

South of Moffet Field, Sam pulled off the highway. Before long, they were passing industrial parks and strip malls. Then he began to slow. She pressed her cheek against the back of his shoulder and closed her eyes. Don't stop, she prayed. Don't ever stop.

But he did. He kicked off the engine, and the bike became still between her thighs. Turning, he pulled her close against him. "Time to get a move on, biker lady," he whispered. "Your man is hungry."

She made a breathless, frightened sound. Was he her man? Oh, God, what had she done? What was going to happen to her?

He let her go as he got off the bike, and then he held out his hand. She grasped it as if his touch could save her.

"It's a new world," he said. "We're walking into a new world."

More accurately, they were walking into a Burger King.

Susannah's eyes flew open as she became aware of where they were. The asphalt of the parking lot was warm beneath her stockinged feet. She was barefoot. Oh, God, she was barefoot in front of a Burger King! A hole had formed in her silk stockings over one knee, and a small circle of skin pushed through like a bubble on bread dough. Sam pulled her forward, and she saw faces gaping at them from the window.

Her frightened reflection stared back at her—rumpled lace wedding dress, auburn hair hanging in rowdy tangles, thin nose red from the wind. Panicked, she grabbed at his arm. "Sam, I can't—"

"You already have."

With a tug on her hand, he thrust her through the door into the burger-scented heart of middle America.

A gaggle of teenage boys interrupted a burping contest to stare at them from an orange booth. She heard laughter at the spectacle she was making of herself. The soles of her stockings clung to a sticky spot on the tiled floor. A group of six-year-olds celebrating a birthday party looked up from beneath crooked cardboard crowns. One of them pointed. Throughout the restaurant, patrons abandoned their french fries and Whoppers to stare at Susannah Faulconer. She stood there and tried not to let the enormity of what was happening sink in.

Good girls didn't get themselves kidnapped. A society bride didn't flee her wedding on the back of a Harley-Davidson. What was wrong with her? What was she going to do? She had humiliated Cal. He'd never forgive her. And her father . . .

But what she had done was too monstrous, and she couldn't think about her father. Not now. Not yet.

Sam had stopped at the counter. He turned to her and studied her for a moment. "You're not going to cry, are you?"

She shook her head, not able to speak because her throat had closed tight. He didn't know her well enough to know that she never cried, although at that moment she very much wanted to.

"You look great," he whispered, his eyes sweeping over her. "Loose and sexy."

A thrill shot through her, the sensation so intense that she forgot for a moment where she was. No one had ever called her such a thing. She drank in the sight of his face and wondered if she would ever get her fill of looking at him.

He gave her a crooked grin and glanced up at the menu board. "What're you going to have?"

Abruptly, she remembered where she was. She tried to take courage from his complete disinterest in the opinions of the people watching them. He had called her loose and sexy, and with those words she wanted to become a new person, the person he was describing. But words weren't enough to make her into someone else. She was still Susannah Faulconer, and she hated the spectacle she was making.

He ordered and picked up their food. Numbly, she followed him to a table by the window. Her appetite had deserted her, and after a few bites she abandoned any pretense of eating. Sam reached for her hamburger.

As she watched his strong white teeth rip through the bun, she tried to tell herself that no matter how frightened she was, anything was better than dying a slow death of old age at twenty-five.

Susannah had somehow imagined Sam living in a small bachelor apartment, and she wasn't prepared for the fact that he still lived with his mother. The house was one of the small mass-produced ranches that had sprung up in the Valley during the late fifties to house the workers who had flooded to Lockheed following the launching of Sputnik. The front was faced with green aluminum siding, the sides and back with dingy white stucco. Tarpaper topped with fine gravel covered the roof. It sparkled faintly in the fading sunlight.

"The light's not on," Sam said, gesturing toward the garage that sat off to the side along with a ragged palm. "Yank must not be here."

"Does he live here, too?" she asked, growing more nervous by the minute. Why couldn't Sam have lived by himself? What was she going to say to his mother?

"Yank has an apartment on the other side of town. Mom's in Las Vegas with a girlfriend for the next couple of weeks. We have the place to ourselves."

That, at least, was a relief. She walked behind him to the front of the house. Next to the door stretched a long opaque window with vertically ridged glass. The caulking around it had loosened and cracked. Sam unlocked the door and went inside. She followed, stepping across the threshold and directly into the living room. She caught her breath.

The decor was a monument to bad taste. Ugly gold shag carpeting covered the floor. An aquarium filled with iridescent gravel sat next to a Spanish sofa with dark wood trim, brass nail heads, and red velvet upholstery. Sam flipped a wall switch, turning on a lamp made up of a wire bird cage filled with plastic philodendrons. Nearby, occupying what was obviously a place of honor, hung a full-length oil painting of Elvis Presley wearing one of his white-satin Las Vegas outfits and clutching a microphone with ring-encrusted fingers.

Susannah looked over at Sam and waited for him to say something. He returned her stare, his expression belligerent as he waited for her to make a comment. The look of challenge in his eyes and the stubborn set to his jaw touched her. She wanted to go to him and lay her head against his shoulder and tell him she understood. A man with so much passion for elegant design must find it unbearable to live in such a place.

She asked to use the bathroom. Decals of fat fish were stuck to tangerine tiles. She took off her torn stockings and stuffed them into a plastic wastebasket. A smaller painting of Elvis done on black velvet regarded her from the wall behind the toilet. LOVE ME TENDER was written in glitter script across the bottom, except some of the letters had worn off so that it read LOVE ME TEN. Not one, she thought as she washed her hands, avoiding her reflection in the mirror. Don't love me two or three. Love me *ten*.

She found Sam in the kitchen. He offered her a can of Coke and a pair of gold sandals with a plastic daisy at the apex of each thong. "They're my mother's," he said. "She won't mind."

She slipped into the sandals but politely refused the Coke. He studied her for a moment, then picked up a handful of hair next to her cheek and closed it in his fist. She felt dizzy with his closeness, as if she were racing toward the edge of a cliff.

"You have beautiful hair," he whispered. He brushed his thumb over her lips. Her breath quickened. The amber flecks in his eyes glowed like the fireflies she had once trapped in a jar as a child. When Susannah wasn't looking, Paige had opened the lid and dumped the insects on the ground, then squashed them with the soles of her sneakers so that their crushed bodies left a yellow phosphorescent streak in the grass. Afterward, Paige had cried so hard that Susannah had thought she would never stop.

The expression in Sam's eyes told Susannah that he wanted to make love to her, and the tissues in her body began to feel loose and fluid, as if she'd had too much wine. There had been so much emotion that day, so many feelings rushing through her. She wanted to live out all her fantasies, but she was frightened. This was the final step in her emancipation, and she wasn't ready.

She pulled abruptly away from him and walked back into the living room. Elvis, soul-eyed and sullen, looked down at her from the wall. Did she love Sam ten? she wondered frantically. She didn't even know what love was anymore. Was this love or was it simply lust? She loved her father, and look what she'd done. She'd been pretending to love Cal, and that had resulted in disaster. And Sam? Had she gone crazy succumbing to the sexual fantasies this amber-eyed renegade aroused in her? Had she thrown away everything familiar for sex?

"Come on out to the garage with me," he said from behind her.

She whirled around and saw him standing in the archway between the kitchen and living room.

"I want you to see what we're doing," he said. "You're going to be part of it now."

He led her toward the back door, talking all the time. "I told you it was starting for us, Suzie, and I meant it. Last week I got an order for forty circuit boards from this guy named Pinky at Z.B. Electronics. Forty! And this is just the beginning."

As Joel Faulconer's daughter, it was difficult for her to work up much excitement for such small numbers, but she tried to respond enthusiastically. "That's wonderful."

She felt the plastic petals on the daisies of her sandals scratch at her toes as she crossed the backyard. Sam pointed toward the garage with his can of Coke. She studied his hand as it curled around the can. It was a working man's hand. His fingernails were clean but uneven, and an untidy white scar marred his thumb.

"Garages are good luck in the Valley. Bill Hewlett and David Packard started Hewlett-Packard in a garage in Palo Alto, and we're going to start our company in this one. Right now, half the guys in Homebrew have projects going in garages. Do you remember Steve Wozniak from the Homebrew meeting? I pointed him out to you."

"He and his friend are the ones building that single-board computer with some sort of fruit name."

Sam nodded and stopped in front of the side entrance to the garage. "They're working out of Steve Jobs's parents' garage in Los Altos. I heard that Mrs. Jobs is driving Woz crazy by running in and out all the time to use her washer and dryer." Sam grinned and opened the door. "Yank has it even worse."

Susannah didn't understand what he meant until she stepped inside the Gamble garage. It was roughly divided into two sections. The back section held shelves of electronic equipment, a long lighted workbench, and a faded floral sofa. The front of the garage was partitioned off with blond paneling. Susannah walked through a narrow doorway set in the paneling and saw a shampoo bowl, a beauty-shop chair, and several hair dryers. Where the garage door should have been stood a wall of gold-flecked mirrored tiles.

At that moment a phone sitting on a small desk next to an appointment book began to ring. An answering machine clicked on and a woman's voice announced, "This is Angela at Pretty Please Salon. I'm closed for the next two weeks while I try my luck in Vegas. Leave a message and I'll get back to you."

There was a pause and then a beep. "Hi, Angela. It's Harry Davis at Longacres Funeral. Old Mrs. Cooney passed away during the night. I wanted you to do her before the first viewing on Monday, but since you're not going to be around, I'll get Barb. I'll call you with the next one."

The answering machine gave its final beep. Susannah turned to Sam and said weakly, "Your mother does the hair on corpses?"

"She does them when they're alive, too, for chrissake," he retorted belligerently. "She works with one of the nursing homes. When the old ladies finally croak, the funeral home calls her. It drives Yank crazy."

"The funeral home?"

"The old ladies. The nursing home buses them over here to get their hair done. Sometimes when he's working, they peek through the door and start asking him questions." He took a swig of his Coke and gestured with his thumb toward the other side of the partition. "Come on. Let me show you what we're doing."

She left the Pretty Please Salon to follow him into the other section of the garage. The guts of a Sylvania television along with the computer circuit board, a keyboard, and a cassette tape recorder sat on a workbench. He flipped on the overhead work light and began to fuss with the equipment. In front of her, the picture tube started to glow. He put a tape in the cassette recorder, and before long a message appeared in block letters on the screen.

WHAT IS YOUR NAME?

"Go on," Sam said. "Talk to it."

She walked forward and hesitantly typed, "Susannah."

"Now push this key." She did as Sam directed, and another message appeared.

HI, SUSANNAH. I'M HAPPY TO MEET YOU. I DON'T HAVE A NAME OF MY OWN YET. DO YOU HAVE ANY IDEAS?

She was struck by the oddity of having a machine address her by name. "No," she typed.

THAT'S TOO BAD. LET ME TELL YOU ABOUT MYSELF. I AM BEING RUN OFF A 7319 MICROPROCESSOR FROM CORTRON. I HAVE 8K BYTES OF MEMORY. WOULD YOU LIKE TO KNOW MORE?

"Yes," she typed.

The machine responded with more technical information and then, to her surprise, flashed the question, ARE YOU MALE OR FEMALE, SUSANNAH?

"Female," she typed.

ARE YOU PRETTY? it asked.

Sam reached around her and typed, "Yes."

ARE YOU STACKED?

She smiled for the first time that day. "This machine has a naughty mind."

"Don't blame me. I didn't program it."

She entered the word no on the keyboard.

THAT'S TOO BAD. WOULD YOU GO TO BED WITH ME ANYWAY?

She chuckled and entered the word no.

DARN. I NEVER HAVE ANY LUCK WITH WOMEN. I THINK MY MICROPROCESSOR IS TOO SMALL.

She laughed. "What would the machine have done if I'd said yes?"

Sam's hand slid up along her spine. "It would have told you to stand in front of the screen and take off your clothes."

She shivered. His fingers rose above the mandarin collar of her wedding dress and touched the skin at the back of her neck. She didn't move as he held his hand there. He rubbed the skin lightly with his thumb while he pointed out other features on the small computer. She was barely listening.

She wanted to lean back into his chest and press so tightly against him that her body dissolved into his. She envisioned her spine slipping through his skin, her ribs locking with his. And once he had absorbed every part of her flesh and sinew and bone, she would be able to feed from the very source of his spirit. His energy would become her own. She would feast on his brashness and arrogance, on his daring and certainty, on all of those qualities that were missing in her but that he possessed in abundance. By absorbing Sam's spirit, she would make herself complete. And reborn, she would finally be able to march boldly into the world, fully armed against all of the boogeymen, protected against evil, so that nothing bad could ever happen to her again.

He took her hand and led her from the garage. They walked back across the small yard to the house. The scent of someone's backyard barbecue was heavy in the evening air, and a group of kids were playing flashlight tag in the next yard.

When they got inside, Sam gestured toward the kitchen table. "Have a seat. I'll take care of dinner tonight. You can do it tomorrow."

Her stomach was no more ready to handle food now than it had been earlier. "We just ate a couple of hours ago."

"Yeah, I know, but I'm hungry again." He went over to the refrigerator and looked inside. "I'm funny about food. I'll go for a couple of days without eating much of anything, and then I'll eat everything in sight." He pulled another Coke from the refrigerator, shut the door and leaned back against it, apparently not having found anything else that suited him.

He took a swig. The expression in his eyes was so piercing that she had to look away. "You seem to drink a lot of Coke," she said nervously.

"I'm addicted. I got hooked on Coke when I stopped smoking pot." He wandered over to a sliding pantry door, opened it with his foot, and after contemplating the shelves for a few moments, pulled out half a loaf of white bread, a jar of Jif peanut butter, and a plastic squeeze bottle of honey. He grabbed some utensils and sat down next to her.

"Gourmet fare," she said lightly, trying to relieve the awful tension that had taken hold of her.

He didn't smile. "I've got other things on my mind besides food."

"Such as what?" Oh, God. What a stupid question. What an incredibly stupid question. He had sex on his mind. Sex with her.

He squeezed a drop of honey through the bright yellow nozzle onto his index finger. His eyes never left hers as he sucked it off. "Can't you guess?"

A wave of desire curled through her, starting in the center of her chest and moving down through her body into her legs. She tried to tell herself to get up and move away, but she felt as if she were paralyzed. What if sex was all that he wanted from her? She knew that he was a daredevil. What if he was only interested in the challenge that she presented? She realized that she could not let anything else happen between them until they had talked. They needed to understand each other better before they did something that could never be taken back.

He tilted his head, and the ends of his hair formed a dark pool on top of his left shoulder. She snatched up the jar of peanut butter as if she were suddenly ravenous and began clumsily unscrewing the top while she framed the words that needed to be spoken.

He gave her a slow smile and took the jar from her. "I said I'd do the cooking."

She watched as he spread peanut butter on a piece of bread, set it down on the table, and picked up the honey bottle. He gazed at her for a moment. She realized she was holding her breath. His arm seemed to move in slow motion as he reached for the silk-covered buttons on the front of her wedding dress. She needed to tell him to stop, but she couldn't speak.

He paused only when he reached a point well below her breasts. The dress was fully lined, so she wore no slip. He brushed the bodice aside to reveal her bra. It was filmy, part of a bra and panty set she had bought to light a fire in the stodgy soul of Cal Theroux.

He hooked his finger over the front clasp and tugged on it but made no real effort to open it. "Scared?"

She was terrified. Staring at the honey bottle he still held in his hand, she felt her mouth go dry with fear. If only she could reach through his skin and draw out his brashness. "Of—of course not," she stammered. "Don't be ridiculous."

He moved his thumb roughly over the top curve of her breast. "Maybe you should be scared. Because, baby, you can't imagine what I'm thinking about doing to you."

Rockets went off inside her. The edges of her fear evaporated in the strength of her desire. *Do it!* she wanted to scream. *Do it! Please!* She gripped her hands tightly in her lap to keep herself under control. Despite the fact that she had run away from her wedding on the back of a motorcycle, despite the fact that she wore sandals with a plastic daisy stuck between her toes and had gone to the toilet in front of a portrait of Elvis Presley, she was still Susannah Faulconer. And a well-bred young woman didn't scream *Do it*, not even to a man who set her on fire.

He let go of her bra clasp and squeezed a honey spiral over the surface of the peanut butter he had spread for her. Then he lifted the bread to her mouth. She looked at it. Her jaw wouldn't move.

"Open up," he whispered.

She was accustomed to obeying a man's orders, and she did what he said. After she had taken a small bite, he bit into the other side. "Is it good?" he said.

She nodded. He pushed the bread toward her for another bite. They ate without speaking, chewing slowly, looking into each other's eyes.

He picked up the honey bottle and lifted the yellow plastic nozzle to her mouth. For a moment, she thought he was going to feed it to her like a baby's bottle. Instead, he squeezed a curl of honey on her narrow bottom lip. She felt it hanging there, lush and heavy. Before it could drop, he leaned forward and sucked it off himself.

"I love honey," he murmured against her mouth.

His tongue stroked her lip. She whimpered and closed her eyes, knowing she was losing the battle for control of her body. He kissed along the curve of her throat, leaving a sticky trail. "Do you love honey?" he whispered.

"Yes. Oh, yes."

He pulled open her bra and pushed the fabric out of his way. The cool air feathered her skin; his fingers brushed against her. She could barely keep from crying out. She felt a rough scrape. Her eyes flew open in time to see him deliberately rubbing the yellow plastic nozzle back and forth over her nipple. As she watched, he squeezed a droplet of honey onto her pebbled flesh.

She cried out as his head descended and his mouth closed over her, sucking her clean.

The cry released her. She could no longer hold herself in check. She could no longer be a good girl—a pristine princess with deadened breasts and tightly seamed legs. She caught his hair in her fists and crumpled it, then she brought her fists to her mouth and tasted the long rough strands. She wanted to eat him, to devour his hair, his strength, his audacious courage.

With a wicked laugh, he lifted her from the table and pressed her against the ugly wallpaper. She caught the back of his head in her hands and pulled his mouth to hers. Opening wide, she took him in. The kiss was hot and bold, rich with peanut butter and honey.

He pulled the bodice of her dress farther down over her shoulders, so that she had to lower her arms. She reached for his buttocks and clutched him through the seat of his jeans, pushing the heels of her hands into the caves formed in the sides of his hard, young man's cheeks.

He began to murmur naughty words, dirty little phrases, what he would do to her, what she would do to him, crude, filthy, fabulously inventive sonnets of obscenity. As he talked, he pushed up her dress and tugged at her silk panties. Her bad-mannered hands rushed to his zipper. Because he was so hard, she had to struggle with it.

"I'm going to . . ."

"I'll make you . . ."

"Before I'm done, you'll . . ."

To everything he suggested, she cried yes.

And then he had her on her back. The ugly kitchen spun around her as she splayed her legs to act out her naughty girl dreams. His long bad boy's hair tickled the insides of her thighs just as she had imagined it would. His mouth encompassed her. She couldn't breathe. She was going to die. Only the smallest fragment of time passed before she shattered. She heard her voice as if it belonged to someone else, moaning and crying out again and again.

As she settled back to earth, she knew that this was what she had been missing. But her feeling of completion dissolved as she remembered the abandonment of her behavior. Whatever would he think of her? She would have to apologize, try to explain.

He kissed the soft flesh on the inside of her thigh. "You're starved, aren't you?" he said. "Poor starved baby."

A feeling of lassitude stole through her as he began to croon, "I'll take care of you, poor baby. I'll feed you." And then he pressed his mouth to her and did it again.

She had barely finished crying out the second time when he shifted his weight. "I want it like this," he said to her or to himself—she wasn't sure which. "I want you like this."

And then he thrust inside her. He was young and randy, fundamentally selfish, dangerously impatient. He plunged himself between her well-bred thighs and took her with all the vigor of a brash, blue-skies thinker for whom no part of life—not even sex—would ever be enough.

She cried out with every thrust, digging her hands into his flesh and begging for more. They rolled over and over on the hard floor, knocking away a chair and banging up against the cupboards. Her hair tangled with his, her long thin legs clutched his darker ones. When he spilled himself within her, he let out a roar of satisfaction.

Afterward, he let her rest for a while. She played with his hair and took the silver Easter Island earring into her mouth so she could avoid talking.

He made her get up to take off the rest of her clothes. She glanced nervously toward the kitchen window. He laughed at her as she pulled away from him and slid the café curtain closed on its phony wooden rod.

"There's nobody back there," he said, brushing his brown hand over his pale, flat stomach. "No one can see."

"Better safe than sorry," she said inanely.

He emitted a bark of laughter and consumed what remained of their peanut butter sandwich in one bite. With his mouth stuffed full, he said, "You crack me up. You really do."

Then he picked up the plastic honey bottle and came toward her again.

9

● ●

In contrast with the rest of the house, Sam's bedroom was almost monastic in its simplicity. It contained a sturdy antique chest and a simple bookcase holding a top-quality stereo system. The walls were painted stark white and were unadorned, and the top of the chest was swept clean of any knickknacks.

Susannah tossed restlessly in the double bed. Her hair, still damp from the shower she and Sam had shared a few hours before, tangled around her throat. The world she lived in had been turned upside down, and she was dizzy with the upheaval. Her logical brain—the brain that had made her excel at science and mathematics when she was in school—refused to let her sleep. It kept ticking off the crises that she faced.

She had no clothes and no money. Her bank accounts would be closed by morning. She loved her father, and how could she ever make him understand what she had done? How could she ever make him forgive her? She turned her head toward the man for whom she had given up everything. Even in sleep he looked driven. His forehead was furrowed, his lips compressed. She should never have let him make love to her until they'd had a chance to get to know each other better.

But even the logical part of her brain couldn't make her regret what had happened between them. Their joining was everything she had imagined lovemaking should be. For the first time in her life, a man had praised her passion so that she felt joy in her sexuality instead of shame. It was a gift so precious she could barely absorb it.

He stirred at her side and reached out—lusty, insatiable, just like all the demon lovers she had ever imagined. He whispered her name. His eyes drifted open and he smiled at her.

She knew then that she loved him. It was more than lust that had made her turn her back on her family for this man. When she met him, she had been dying inside. Her attraction to him was as primal as a drought-starved plant drinking in a summer rain shower. She needed his wildness, his youth, his delirious optimism. She needed his freedom from fear.

Turning to him, she touched the earring that lay against his jaw. Within minutes, they were making love again.

The bed was empty when Susannah awakened. She found one of his T-shirts lying across the footboard along with a wraparound denim skirt he must have appropriated from his mother's closet. She lifted the T-shirt to her nose for a moment before she put it on, but it held the scent of laundry detergent instead of his skin.

After she had dressed, she went into the kitchen to look for him. No one was there, but through the window she could see into the garage. The side door was open, and she spotted him standing at the workbench. Part of her wanted to race across the yard just so she could touch him for a moment. Instead, she went over to the kitchen telephone. Her hands shook as she dialed the number for Falcon Hill. The line was busy. She hung up, grateful for her reprieve. She told herself that she had to try to reach Cal and offer some sort of apology. But she simply couldn't bring herself to call him.

After drinking a small glass of orange juice, she headed out to the garage. As she crossed the yard, she heard the distant sound of Sunday morning church bells and watched as a beat-up Plymouth Duster pulled into the drive. The engine ground to a stop and Yank Yankowski got out. He came toward her, all knobby wrists and bony face, rather like a stork wearing eyeglasses. His hair looked even worse than she remembered. He didn't have one of those tough, Marine Corps, go-to-hell crew cuts, but something that looked more like David and Ricky Nelson permanently trapped in the fifties.

His forehead was knotted in concentration. As he came nearer, she could make out his eyes through the lenses of his glasses. They were light brown and vague. She hadn't known until that moment that a pair of eyes could appear so completely unfocused.

"Hello." She held out her hand politely. "I don't believe we were ever formally introduced. I'm Susannah Faulconer."

He walked right past her.

Startled, she watched him disappear through the garage door. One of his socks was navy, the other white. What a curious person, she thought.

A few seconds later she entered the garage. He and Sam were engaged in a technical discussion. She waited for Sam to turn and catch sight of her. When he finally did, she searched his face for some sign that last night had changed him. He looked no different, but in the seconds that flashed by before he spoke, she imagined that he was remembering what had passed between them.

"Yank's invented a new game, Suzie. Come on over here. It's great! You've got to play."

She needed no prodding to move closer to him, and she soon found herself shooting at speeding targets while the men called out instructions. She was so absorbed in Sam's nearness that she barely noticed Yank. His comments were all impersonal, directed toward the game. Despite the fact that he was actually speaking to her, she had the sense that he still didn't really see her. She was only a disembodied pair of hands manipulating his precious machine.

"The other way," Yank said. "Go to the left!"

"There!" she cried. "I got one!"

"Watch out! You're going to get hit."

It really was fun, she decided, but that was all. Nothing more than a few hours' clever entertainment. She couldn't understand Sam's obsession with this impractical little toy.

"Come on, give me a turn," Sam said.

She waved him off. "In a minute. Let me play one more game."

Yank finally took the game away from them so he could do some troubleshooting on the circuit board. While he worked, Sam gave her a lesson in basic electronics. He pointed out components of the single-board computer to her—integrated circuits and multicolored resistors, tubular capacitors, a power transistor with a heat sink. He talked about miniaturization, and painted a picture for her of a future in which today's tiny microchips would be viewed as large and cumbersome. Some of it she already knew, much of it she didn't. It was a fascinating world, made beautiful by Sam's gift for creating word pictures.

When Yank asked for Sam's help, she watched them work for a while and then reluctantly slipped back into the house to try to call Falcon Hill. The line was still busy, and after several more tries, she concluded that the phone had been left off the hook. She thought about her father's battles with Paige and felt a wrenching inside her as she tried to imagine living without his love. In some families love was given unconditionally, but not in hers.

She called Cal but got no answer. Eventually she sat down and wrote him a letter, asking forgiveness for the unforgivable.

Sam came inside for her and announced that he was taking her to a Chinese restaurant for dinner. Susannah was about to say that she needed a few minutes to change her clothes, but then she remembered that she had nothing to change into.

As they walked out the back door, she spotted a dark blue Ford Pinto that had pulled in behind Yank's Duster. "Shit," Sam said.

"What's wrong?" Had Angela Gamble returned ahead of schedule? What was she going to say to Sam's mother?

Sam didn't answer her question. Instead, he stalked toward the garage like a man with a deadly mission. Reluctantly, Susannah followed him.

To Susannah's relief, the woman standing next to the workbench was about her own age—certainly not old enough to be Sam's mother, although her polyester blouse and navy skirt combined with a bad permanent made her look older. She had a pear-shaped build—narrow shoulders, small bust, plump hips. Her skin was beautiful—pale and unblemished—but the faintest shadow of a mustache hovered above her top lip. It wasn't a gross mustache, merely the sort of thing that a stylish woman would have taken care of with a monthly application of depilatory.

". . . all the food groups, Yank. I left you my three-bean salad, but did you eat any? No you didn't. Not one bite. Kidney beans are a wonderful source of protein, but all you eat are chocolate chip cookies. Well, I'll tell you something, mister, I'm not making you any more chocolate chip cookies. No, sir. Not until you start eating right."

"Leave him alone, Roberta."

The woman had been so engrossed in her lecture to Yank that she hadn't heard them come in, and she jumped when Sam spoke. Susannah watched as her face filled with color. "Sam. I—I didn't— That is—"

He walked slowly forward. With his low-slung jeans and bow-legged biker's gait, his advance bore more than a trace of menace, and Susannah didn't blame Roberta for moving back a few steps. He tucked one of his thumbs into a belt loop, and she felt a primitive sexual thrill at the expense of the hapless Roberta.

"I guess I wasn't clear enough when we had that little chat a few days ago," he said.

"Now, Sam. I—I just stopped by for a minute."

"I don't want you here, Roberta. I don't like the way you nag him."

Roberta attempted to gather herself together. "I can come here if I want. Yank likes to have me around. Don't you, Yank?"

Yank picked up a roll of solder and bent over the circuit board.

Sam leaned against the side of the bench. "Like I said. Stay away from here. If Yank wants to sleep with you, that's his business, but keep away from him when he's working."

Roberta glared at Sam, obviously trying to summon her

courage to argue with him, and just as obviously failing. With dismay, Susannah saw the woman's chin start to tremble. She hated unpleasant scenes and couldn't help but do her best to put an end to this one.

"Hello, I'm Susannah." The Faulconer name was well-known, and she instinctively withheld it.

The woman, obviously grateful for the intercession, came toward her with awkward haste to return the greeting. "I'm Roberta Pestacola. Like Pepsi Cola, but with a 'pesta' instead."

"You're Italian."

Roberta nodded. "On both sides of my family—not just one side like Sam."

Until that moment Susannah hadn't known that Sam was Italian.

"I'm Yank's girlfriend," Roberta went on. "We're practically engaged." She told Susannah that she was a hospital dietitian and that she did ceramics as a hobby. When she finally paused, it was obvious that she was waiting for Susannah to offer some information about herself and her relationship to Sam.

"How fascinating," Susannah replied.

Sam stepped forward and took Roberta's arm. "I'll walk you to your car, Roberta. I'm sure you've got some food groups that you need to go balance."

Roberta's hand shot out and she gripped the vise on the end of the workbench, less from a desire to stay, Susannah suspected, than from uneasiness at the thought of being alone with Sam. Once again, her distress won Susannah's sympathy.

"I'll walk to the car with you."

But Sam wasn't having any of it. "Stay out of this, Susannah. Roberta and I need to have a little chat all by ourselves."

A soft voice pierced through the tension. "Roberta, get that trouble light for me, will you?" Yank lifted his head and blinked a few times as if he had just awakened from a long slumber. "Hold it so I can see what I'm doing."

Roberta dashed eagerly forward, breaking Sam's grip as she snapped up the light.

Sam looked at Yank with disgust and turned his attention back to Roberta. "You'd better not start nagging him. I mean it, Roberta. We've got an order for some boards, and Yank has to work out the last of the bugs. I don't want you here when I get back."

Sam stalked out of the garage with Susannah following him. "God," he said. "That's the worst case of sexual desperation I ever saw in my life."

Susannah wasn't exactly certain whether he was talking about Yank or Roberta, since neither of them struck her as any kind of prize.

"I know it's practically impossible for Yank to get a woman to go to bed with him, but I can't imagine being desperate enough to stick it to old Roberta. I'll bet you anything she makes him disinfect it first."

Their intimacy was still new, and his comment flustered her. "Yank doesn't seem like the sort of person who would be very interested in sex."

"He's interested, all right. He's the one who wrote that raunchy computer program. But Yank's a lot better with machines than he is with women." Sam threw his leg over the Harley and gave her his cockiest grin. "I—on the other hand—am fantastic with both."

They ate at a seedy Chinese restaurant where Sam consumed all of his cashew chicken and three quarters of hers. Then they munched on fortune cookies and he felt her under the table. She grew so aroused, she had to beg him to stop.

On the way home he wheeled the Harley into a deserted school playground. As they dismounted, he held out his hand for her. "Tonight's going to be the last vacation either of us has for a while. We might as well make the most of it."

He led her over to a free-form structure made of tractor tires and she sat on top of one of them. The area was lit by a pair of floodlights that threw exaggerated shadows of the equipment across the playground. It was chilly, and she zipped the windbreaker Sam had given her. As she looked up, she saw that the stars were obscured by either clouds or smog, she wasn't sure which.

Sam saw something quite different in the night sky.

"We're going to unlock the power of the universe, Suzie. You and me. Not just for the big honchos in their ivory towers, but for everybody. We're going to give ordinary people the power of the gods."

She shivered. "I don't know if I want that kind of power."

"That's because you're still afraid of your own shadow." His voice grew quiet. "Do you know what Yank's machine is going to give you? Do you know?" He gazed at her so searchingly, she felt as if she had no secrets left. "It's going to give you courage."

She gave a shaky laugh. "Just like the cowardly lion in *The Wizard of Oz*."

"Just like that."

"I don't think you can get courage from a machine."

"You can from this one. If you want it. But you've got to want it bad, Suzie." He leaned back against one of the tractor tires. "The order for the forty boards doesn't just mean we're in business, you know that, don't you? It gives us a chance to put ourselves to the test. Not many people get that kind of chance. We have to get more orders, run some ads. And we're not going to make the same mistake MITS is making with the Altair. We're not offering any kits. Every board we sell is going to be fully assembled and top quality."

His plans were so unrealistic that she was deeply disturbed. It was all very well to talk about the power of the gods, but the truth of the matter was that he had a machine nobody knew they wanted, and it was being built in the garage of a woman who did the hair on corpses. How could he stake his future on something like that? How could she stake *her* future?

"Parts are expensive," she said noncommittally. "What will it cost to build forty boards?"

"With discounts, price shopping—I figure around twelve thousand. Then we have to have cases made. Something plain, but sturdy. I've already got a guy working on a printed circuit board to make the assembly easier. Have you ever seen one?"

"I think so. I'm not certain."

"It's a fiberglass board covered with a thin layer of copper. The copper gets etched away until only narrow paths of it are left on the fiberglass—like tiny wires."

"Copper conducts electricity," she said. "At least I know that much."

"Right. And fiberglass doesn't. The components fit into slots on the board. The right components, elegant design, and you've got a single-board computer. I figure we should be able to complete each board for around three hundred dollars. Pinky's going to pay us five and sell them for seven. We'll plow the profits into more boards, and before long we'll be able to produce a self-contained computer—terminal, monitor, the works. One of these days we're going to blow FBT right out of the water."

"Do you have twelve thousand dollars?"

"Yank and I have about two thousand between us, but I had to use some of that as a deposit for the printed circuit boards. A guy I know offered me eight fifty for my stereo system. That's about it."

With three thousand dollars, Sam thought he could take on FBT. She loved him, and so she concealed her dismay. "Did you try the banks?"

"The banks are run by morons. They don't have any vision. They're fossils. Monumental dinosaurs."

He had obviously tried the banks.

She lifted up her sandal and let the sand that had collected under her toes drift out. "What are you going to do?"

He gave her a searching look. "It's what are *we* going to do, isn't it? You're part of this. Or are you planning to run home to daddy and Calvin?"

The schoolyard lights caught the amber flecks in his eyes. She shivered. "That isn't fair."

"I don't give a shit about fair. I want to know. Are you in or out?"

"I want to be with you, Sam."

"That's not what I'm asking."

He was backing her into a corner, and she was frightened. Awkwardly, she slid down off the tire and looked beyond him to the dark borders of the playground. "I don't have any money. In case you were counting on it, you should know that I can't help you. My father controls everything."

"I don't expect money from you," he said angrily. "That's not why I want you with me. Goddammit! Is that what you think I want from you?"

"No, of course not." But just for a moment, she had thought exactly that. "I don't have anything, Sam—no clothes, no money, no place to stay."

"I didn't ask for a frigging dowry! We'll get you some clothes and you're staying with me. Are you in or out, Suzie?"

He was so certain, always so certain. The darkness at the edge of the playground suddenly seemed to be full of menace. "I told you. I want to be with you."

"You can't be with me and not be part of this."

What was she going to say? She was a practical person. The only impractical thing she had ever done in her adult life was fall in love with Sam Gamble. "It's not that simple." She turned away from him, but he came right up behind her.

"Bullshit. I want to know!"

"Don't bully me!"

"I want to know, dammit! Don't keep throwing up all these artificial barriers. Do you have the guts to go through with this or not? Do you have the guts to put yourself to the test?"

She spoke rapidly, pushing out the words before he could stop them. "It's not just a matter of guts. I have to be practical. I need to support myself."

"That's not the most important thing! Supporting yourself isn't the most important thing. You don't need money or clothes. Those are just excuses. It's your soul. That's what's important. That's all anybody really has. Don't you see? If you want your soul to survive—if you want it to grow and thrive instead of shriveling up and drying out like it was doing in that mausoleum at Falcon Hill, you have to dare. You have to give the world the finger, and you have to dare."

How he could talk. How this man could talk. She hugged herself against the night and the chill and the menace at the edge of the playground.

He caught her arm. His eyes blazed. "Suzie, listen to me. We're living on the threshold of a new society—a whole new way of doing everything. Can't you feel it? The old ways don't work anymore. People want information. They want control. They want power! When you look at Yank's circuit board, all you see is a collection of electronic parts. But what you should be seeing is a wave—this little wave way out in the water, far away from shore. This little hump of water that's just starting to form. But this little hump of water keeps coming closer. And the closer it comes, the more it starts to pick up speed. And then, pretty soon you look up and—Christ!—its not a little hump any longer but a great big wall of water that's risen up so high you can see it looming against the sky. You can see a white crest starting to form on the top like a crown. And that white crest is getting bigger and it's starting to churn and curl over at the top. And then you hear the noise. This tidal wave of water is picking up speed and it's starting to roar. And before long it's gotten so loud you have to hold your hands over your ears. That's when you start stepping backward. You don't want the wave to knock you down, and you're stepping backward faster and faster. And then—that's when you realize it. That's when you realize that no matter how fast you run, that motherfucker is going to slam right down on top of you. It's going to slam right down on top of everybody in the world. That wave is the future, babe. It's the future, and it's Yank's machine. And once that wave hits, none of us will ever be the same again."

He was filling her with his words just as earlier he had filled her with his sex. He was filling up her body and taking it over. The words caught her, heaved her about in their undertow and made it hard for her to breathe. But for all his talk, Sam didn't really understand what it meant to dare. He had nothing to lose. He lived in an ugly little house with a painting of Elvis Presley on the wall. He owned a stereo system and a Harley-Davidson. When Sam talked about not being afraid to dare, he wasn't risking anything. She—on the other hand—was risking it all.

He touched her. He cupped her face in his hands and stroked her cheeks with his thumbs. The wave washed her up on shore, and she experienced that helpless feeling women throughout the centuries have known when they realize that loving a man means loving his vision as well, that it means traveling across oceans, across continents, that it means being uprooted from family and giving up the safe for the unknown. "I—I need to think about this. Tomorrow, while you're at work, I'll think about it."

"I'm not going to work tomorrow."

"Why not?"

"I quit. I'm *in*, Suzie. I'm in all the way."

"You quit your job?" she said weakly.

"Last week. Now how about you? Are you in or out?"

"I—I don't know."

"Not good enough."

"I need time."

"There isn't any."

"Don't do this, Sam. Please don't badger me like this."

"I want to know, Suzie. Right now. Make up your mind. Are you in or out?"

She felt as if she were eons older than he was instead of only a year—millennia older in experience. A lifetime of dinner-table conversations drifted back to her. She saw hurdles he couldn't imagine, difficulties his visionary's eyes hadn't begun to glimpse. Everything she had learned from the day she was born urged her to tell him she couldn't help him and then to run back to Falcon Hill and beg her father's forgiveness.

But she loved him, and she loved the new spark he had ignited inside her—a spark that had been lit by his reckless energy, a spark that wanted to grow brighter and become stronger. A spark that was urging her to follow this restless young man she had so unwisely fallen in love with right off the edge of the earth.

When she finally spoke, her voice was shaky and barely audible. "I'm in."

10

∙∙∙∙∙∙∙∙∙∙∙∙∙∙∙∙∙∙∙∙∙∙∙∙∙∙∙∙∙∙∙

Yank's Duster coughed like an emphysema victim as Susannah drove north to Falcon Hill several days later. She had owned high-performance automobiles all her life, and until this moment she hadn't realized a car could behave like this one. She thought about using the car as an excuse to go back, but then imagined how Sam would scoff at her if she returned without getting the things she needed.

Each day it had grown more difficult for her to live without her possessions. Sam had given her money to get a new prescription filled for her birth control pills, and although that had been her most pressing need, it was only one of them. She needed her reading glasses and her driver's license. She needed clothes to replenish her borrowed wardrobe. No matter how much she wanted to avoid it, she hadn't been able to postpone going home any longer.

The gates loomed ahead of her. Sam had given her the small electronic gadget he had used to release the locks, but she didn't need it. It was Thursday morning and the gates were open for a grocery delivery. As she turned into the drive, she remembered the newspaper gossip column from last Sunday's paper that she had stumbled upon. It had contained a sly account of what had happened at her wedding and was accompanied by a picture of herself and

133

Cal "in happier times." Sick at her stomach, she had tried once again to reach her father, this time at his office. His secretary had pretended not to know who she was and informed her that Mr. Faulconer was currently out of the country.

Her trepidation grew as she parked the Duster in the motorcourt and climbed the front steps to the house. While she waited for someone to answer the bell, she wished a familiar household retainer would appear—one of those mythic housekeepers of fiction who would welcome her home with a tart scolding and a warm plate of cookies. In reality, Falcon Hill's current housekeeper had a small tattoo on the back of her hand and had only been with them a few months.

The slim hand that opened the door, however, bore no tattoo.

"Paige?"

"Well, well, the runaway bride returns."

Susannah was astonished to see her sister, but even more surprised to see that Paige was wearing one of Susannah's own silk dresses instead of her customary blue jeans. Antique gold earrings glimmered through her hair. They were the ones Joel had bought Susannah as a high school graduation present.

A smirk distorted Paige's pretty mouth. "I can't believe you have the nerve to come back."

"What are you doing here?"

Paige's eyes skimmed Susannah's tidy hair and untidy outfit, then flicked to the battered Duster in the driveway. "Falcon Hill is my home, too. Or have you forgotten that?"

There was an expression of such smugness on her sister's face that Susannah felt sick. "I'm just surprised, that's all. Is Father home?"

"Luckily for you, no. You've been declared persona non grata for the rest of your natural life. He's left orders that your name is no longer to be spoken in this house. You're being disinherited, spurned—I actually think he's trying to find a way to un-adopt you. Right out of the Old Testament."

Susannah had known it would be bad, but not this bad.

Like someone deliberately probing a sore tooth, she inquired, "What about Cal? How is he?"

"Oh, he's just peachy—considering the fact that he's been publicly humiliated. It's a miracle the newspaper story hasn't gotten bigger play, but you've still managed to make him look like the Bay Area's biggest asshole."

Susannah didn't want to think about what a terrible thing she had done to Cal. She couldn't bear any more guilt.

"Actually, it's been pretty interesting around here. It's starting to feel as if you never existed. As if you never came into our lives."

Susannah didn't want to hear any more. She moved forward, ready to slip past Paige and get what she needed, but Paige sidestepped, blocking the way. "You can't come in, Susannah. Daddy's forbidden it."

"But that's ridiculous. I need to get some of my things."

Triumph glittered in Paige's eyes. "Maybe you should have thought of that before you ran off with your stud."

"He's not a—"

"I thought you were a virgin. Isn't that a hoot? If you had to have a toy boy, Susannah, you could at least have been nice enough not to wave him in Daddy's face."

Susannah mustered her dignity. "I didn't mean to hurt anyone. I just couldn't help it."

"Don't tell me you couldn't help it!" Paige's smugness dropped away, and for a few moments she looked as befuddled as a child. "I thought I knew you, but that's not true at all. The person I knew wouldn't have run off like that. God, Susannah . . ." And then her hostility slipped back into place like the click of a lock. "Not that I care."

Susannah tried to make her understand. "I couldn't stand it any longer. I love Father, but I felt as if he was choking me to death. And Cal was becoming an extension of him. They were making me feel old. I'm only twenty-five, but I felt like an old lady. I didn't really expect either of them to understand, but I thought you would."

"I don't understand any of it. All I know is that perfect Susannah isn't so perfect anymore. For the first time in my life, Daddy has stopped waving all those unlimited virtues of yours in my face. Do you know how long I've waited for this? He talks to me at dinner now. He tells me about his day. He doesn't even miss you, Susannah!"

Susannah felt weak under the strength of Paige's antipathy. A bittersweet image passed through her mind of a crayon picture Paige had drawn when she was in kindergarten. The two of them had been holding hands and standing together under a rainbow. Whatever had happened to those two little girls?

"We're sisters," Susannah said. "I've tried to watch out for you."

"Half sisters. And you're not the only one who knows how to play Lady Bountiful. Wait for me here. I'll put some of your things together and bring them out to you."

Before Susannah could react, the door to Falcon Hill had been firmly slammed in her face.

Paige delivered Susannah's possessions in two shopping bags from Gump's. She had included the reading glasses and driver's license as well as miscellaneous pieces of clothing, none of it Susannah's best. There was no jewelry, nothing of monetary value. When Susannah returned to the Gamble house, she put the clothes neatly away in Sam's closet and tried not to dwell on Paige's vindictiveness.

While the printed circuit boards were being finished, Sam had been trying to raise money to buy the parts they needed. He brought his former coworkers to the garage and enveloped them with his rhetoric, speaking of a new society in which ordinary people would have the power of the universe at their fingertips. Exactly what they were to do with that power, he never defined. Gradually Susannah realized that he had only the vaguest idea himself what ordinary people would really do with a computer.

Even as she stood mesmerized at his side, she found herself growing increasingly uneasy. Not only didn't they have a definable market for their product—they couldn't even tell future customers what to use it for. By the weekend he had raised less than eight hundred dollars. It was only a fraction of what they needed.

She spent all of her spare time at the local library reading everything she could find about starting a small business.

She wanted to learn as much as possible so that she could set her discoveries before him as small gifts of her love. But it didn't take her long to discover that they weren't doing anything right. They had no money, no defined market for their product, no experience. None of them were college graduates. Every piece of evidence pointed to the fact that they could not possibly succeed.

She read about venture capitalists—that unique breed who made fortunes from financing risky new businesses. But she couldn't imagine interesting any reputable venture capitalist in backing a three-person operation being run out of a garage that was partially occupied by the Pretty Please Beauty Salon.

In the evenings while the men worked, she curled up on the old floral sofa in the garage and made her way through one business- or economics-related book after another. Occasionally they needed an extra set of hands and she was called upon to fetch a part or hold a light. When Yank wanted something from her, he tended to call her Sam.

"Hand me that jumper, Sam," he would say. Or, "Sam, how about a little more light."

The first few times she had corrected him, but he had looked at her so blankly that she had finally given up. He couldn't seem to comprehend the simple fact that she existed, let alone that she had become a fixture in his life. He was the strangest person she had ever met—so absorbed in his work that he seemed to inhabit an entirely different dimension of reality from everyone else.

Another week slipped by. The printed circuit boards were to be ready the next day. They had enough money to pay for them, but that was all. Where were they going to find the thousands of dollars they needed to purchase parts for forty boards? Without collateral, Sam couldn't get credit from any of the suppliers, and none of the banks would talk to him.

"They're all morons," he complained to Susannah as he paced back and forth across the garage, growing more agitated by the minute. "They wouldn't know a good idea if it hit them on the head."

It was past midnight and she was tired. Still, she tried to

make him see the situation realistically. "Sam," she said gently, "you can't really expect them to lend you money. Setting aside the issue of collateral, all they see when they look at you is a wild-eyed biker."

He shoved his hand impatiently through his hair. "Don't start with all your uptight crap again, all right? I'm not in the mood."

His attack was unfair and it hurt, but she had no idea how to defend herself, so she retreated like a turtle ducking into its shell. As she picked up the book on production efficiency that she had been reading, she tried to make excuses for him. He had been working hard. He hadn't meant to attack her. But the words on the page in front of her wouldn't focus. She kept remembering the night at the playground when Sam had asked her if she had the guts to put herself to the test. Did she have the courage to stand up for herself or was she going to spend the rest of her life nodding her head in agreement to the opinions of every man she met?

Hesitantly, she closed the book. "I think it's important for us to deal with reality. The world as it actually is—not as you think it should be." Her voice sounded tentative instead of assertive, as she had intended.

He spun on her. "What's that supposed to mean?"

"It means that appearances are important. I love the way you look and the way you dress. I love your hair. It's part of you. But hard-headed businessmen don't tend to have much patience with nonconformists."

His lips tightened scornfully, the lips that had kissed her so passionately that morning. "Appearances are shit, Susannah. They don't mean anything. Quality means something. Ideas. Hard work. That's all that counts."

Her brain was calling out alarms and her stomach had begun to twist into its familiar knots, but still she forced herself to press on. "Appearances mean something in the business world."

"Maybe in that phony FBT world, but that's not what I'm about. I want success, but I goddamn well won't sell my soul for it. That's your territory, not mine."

Failure pressed in on her. Some people were good at confrontation, but she wasn't one of them. Her fingers crept toward her book and her lips began to frame a retraction. But Sam hadn't finished with her.

"You know, you're really starting to piss me off. You're a goddamn snob. If you want to go around looking at the labels in people's clothes before you talk to them, that's your business, but don't expect me to buy into it. And another thing—"

"These decoder chips are out of tolerance, Sam," Yank said from the workbench.

Susannah felt a rush of gratitude for the timeliness of Yank's interruption. Although he had been standing right in front of them all evening, she had once again forgotten he was there. As Sam went to help him, she quickly gathered up her book and retreated to the house. She would pretend to be asleep when he came in so she wouldn't have to deal with any more conflict. She had tried to hold her ground, but Sam was like a steamroller mowing her down.

Ever since she had moved in with him, she had slept nude, but now she found an ugly cotton nightgown Paige had packed for her and she slipped into it. As she went into the bathroom to brush her teeth, she thought of her father's icy silences and Cal's cold withdrawal. She tried to find comfort in the fact that at least Sam expressed his anger openly.

The bathroom door banged open. "What the hell happened to you?" he inquired angrily.

She spun around, her hand flying to her throat. "I—I was tired. I decided to go to bed."

"The hell you did. We were in the middle of a goddamn fight, and you ran away." He pushed himself into the small room. She waited for the tiled walls to bulge outward from the strain of trying to contain all the energy that he brought with him.

"Arguing never solves anything."

"Who says? Who comes up with shit like that?"

"I don't want to fight."

"Why not?" He glared at her belligerently. "Are you afraid you won't win?"

"I'm not a fighter. I don't enjoy conflict."

"You're an asshole."

She was stunned by his attack. Nothing in her life had

prepared her for this kind of overt hostility. A surge of anger, dark and ugly, began to creep through her. She didn't deserve this. She loved him, and he had no right to say these things to her. Her anger frightened her as much as his attack, and she realized that she couldn't deal with either one. She had to get away from him. She had to escape before something terrible happened. Rushing to the door, she tried to push past him.

He caught her arm and pulled her around. His lips had narrowed into a hard line, and his expression was tight with anger. "You're a real chickenshit, you know that? A little mouse afraid of her own shadow."

"Let me go!" Her own anger was growing bigger and stronger, taking over her body like a foreign virus.

"No. I don't like scared little rabbits."

"Stop it! Let me go!"

"Make me."

"Don't do this!" she shouted. "Don't you treat me like this. I don't deserve this and I won't stand for it, and you can just go to hell!"

He laughed and dropped his head to her mouth. "Better. That's lots better." Her lips were already parted in indignation and he slammed his teeth against hers.

She couldn't breathe. She tried to shove him away, but he pinned her against the vanity. She struggled, pushing at his chest with the heels of her hands. And then something strange began to happen inside her. A heat was building there, a dark excitement. She parted her lips and thrust her tongue into his mouth.

The heat turned to fire. He pushed up her cotton nightgown. It bunched around her waist as he lifted her onto the edge of the vanity. He opened her legs and stepped between them. She felt him fumbling with the front of his jeans, and she began pressing hard against him. He grabbed her knees from behind and lifted them higher. She cried out as he thrust inside her, then she locked her legs around his waist so she could take him all.

Their lovemaking was wretchedly uncomfortable and she didn't have an orgasm, but she reveled in the ferocity of it. Afterward he took her to bed and made love to her all over again. That night she lay spent next to him, exhausted from an outpouring of so much emotion, and yet filled with triumph. She had gotten angry, and her world hadn't come to an end.

Her mind churned with so much activity that she couldn't fall asleep. The light patterns shifted on the ceiling. She repositioned her pillow, but it didn't help. Taking care not to wake Sam, she slipped out of bed and headed toward the kitchen so she could get a drink of water. As she passed naked beneath Elvis's full-length portrait in the living room, she glanced uncomfortably at the singer's image. She should have put on a robe, but all her robes were back at Falcon Hill.

The fluorescent stove light in the kitchen was on, emitting a blue-white glow. Her bare feet padded across the floor. She crossed to the cupboard and reached for a glass. At that exact moment she heard a thump.

She spun around, all her senses alert, and watched in horror as the back door began to swing open.

A dark form loomed on the threshold. It took her only a few seconds to recognize the tall, thin figure as Yank Yankowski's. What was he doing here? she thought wildly. It was nearly three in the morning and she was stark naked. What was she going to say?

The chill night air he had brought with him raised goose bumps on her bare skin. Her nipples were puckered, the hair on her arms standing up. He still hadn't seen her. As he pushed the door shut, she glanced desperately around for a place to hide. She wanted to vanish into the walls, get swallowed up by the floor. If she tried to make a dash for the living room, he would see her.

He crossed directly in front of her, passing not more than five feet away but still not looking at her. The edge of the kitchen counter dug into the small of her back as she tried to smear herself into a film as thin as the aluminum coating on a wafer of silicon. The rubber soles of his sneakers squeaked on the floor. He stopped in front of the refrigerator with his back toward her. Her hand snaked along the counter, frantically groping for something to cover her nakedness.

At that moment the kitchen was flooded with light. In her

imagination, it seemed as if thousands of watts of electricity had been let loose, but in reality Yank had only pulled open the refrigerator door and activated the small appliance bulb.

She made an audible gasp and then froze, afraid he had heard her. But he didn't turn. He stood in front of the refrigerator staring inside. Seconds passed. Half a minute. The tips of her fingers bumped against a pot holder lying on the counter. She clutched it like a fig leaf in front of her, feeling more embarrassed, more ridiculous by the minute.

Why didn't he move? For one wild moment she thought that maybe she was still asleep, that this was all a silly dream like the ones where she was presiding naked over a committee meeting.

He kept one hand clamped to the refrigerator handle, the other hung at his side. What was wrong with him? Why didn't he move? He was dead, she thought frantically. He had died standing up.

She inched to her right and stepped out of the direct path of the refrigerator light into the glow from the stove light. Maybe she could get to the back door and slip outside. She could hide behind the house until he left. But what if she got locked out?

He turned so abruptly that she made a small, startled sound. It reverberated in the quiet of the kitchen. Finally, he was facing her.

She froze like an animal caught in the beam of a car's headlights. His torso was silhouetted against the open refrigerator, and the stove light had silvered the lenses of his glasses so that she couldn't see his eyes clearly. But there was no doubt about the direction in which he was looking. Those glasses were pointed right at her.

Her hand was clammy around the pot holder. She hunched her shoulders forward, trying to cover her breasts with her upper arms. Her upbringing had prepared her for every conceivable social situation, but she couldn't imagine what to say in this one.

Yank continued to stare at her. She had to do something! Without taking her eyes from him, she began inching toward the living room door, the pot holder clutched over her pudendum so that she looked like Eve fleeing the

Garden. As she passed in front of the stove, her body temporarily blocked the stove light and the reflection in his glasses disappeared. For the first time, she could see his eyes.

They were completely blank.

She was so surprised that she stopped moving and looked at him more closely. She had never seen eyes so vague, so unfocused. She took another step to the side. His head didn't move; his gaze remained firmly fixed on some mysterious point to her right. She couldn't believe it. What kind of man was he? Slowly she lowered the pot holder.

She almost laughed. *He didn't see her!* Once again, Joseph "Yank" Yankowski was too enmeshed in some complex internal electronics problem to be aware of what was happening around him. He was so lost in thought that he didn't see a naked auburn-haired woman standing directly in front of him.

She slipped from the kitchen and made a dash for the bathroom, where she locked the door and indulged in the first honest laughter she could remember in weeks.

Meanwhile, in Angela Gamble's kitchen, Joseph "Yank" Yankowski remained just as Susannah had left him. The refrigerator door was still open and he hadn't moved from his position. Only his eyes were different. Beneath the lenses of his glasses, the lids were squeezed tight while inside his skull billions of interconnected nerve cells churned with activity. Thalamus, hypothalamus, the fissured moonscape of cerebrum and cerebellum—all the parts of Yank Yankowski's genius brain were at work, accurately reconstructing from memory each separate micron of Susannah Faulconer's pale naked flesh.

Even though she hadn't slept well, Susannah awakened early the next morning refreshed and full of energy. The encounter with Yank had amused her, and the confrontation with Sam had given her courage. She decided that a woman who could stand her ground in an argument with Sam Gamble was capable of anything. Even while she slept, her mind had been working, and as she stepped into the shower, she once again heard the voice that had whispered to her in her dreams. *Appearances. Appearances are everything.*

Sam came into the kitchen a little after eight o'clock. She had already dressed and she was standing at the sink drying the dishes from the night before. Normally, he teased her about her tidiness, but this morning he didn't seem to have the heart for it. She didn't need to ask why he was so quiet. They were due to pick up the printed circuit boards in an hour. But what good were circuit boards when they didn't have the money to buy the components that went on them?

He walked over to the refrigerator and pulled out a carton of orange juice. Without bothering to fetch a glass, he tilted the container to his lips. She wiped off the counter with the dish towel and then hung it away neatly. Appearances, she told herself. Appearances were everything.

He turned, really seeing her for the first time. "What are you all dressed up for?"

She wore square-heeled leather pumps and a black and white checked suit that was several years old and had never been one of her favorites. Still, it was good quality, and it was the only professional-looking outfit Paige had included. Her hair was neatly coiled at her neck with the pins she had borrowed from the Pretty Please Salon. She stepped forward. Sam had said that Yank's machine could give her courage. It was time to find out if that was true.

"We've tried it your way," she said. "Now I want to try it mine."

Spectra Electronics Warehouse was exactly the sort of place most women hated. It was a vast electronics junkyard of a building with concrete floors and towering shelves filled with cardboard cartons reinforced by wire strapping. An open ceiling supported a network of pipes and jaundiced neon lights. Thick parts catalogues with dog-eared pages were mounted next to a long wooden counter plastered with Fly Navy bumper stickers. The place felt cold and smelled like metal, plastics, and old cigarettes. It was so different from the sorts of places Susannah normally patronized that she might actually have liked it if she hadn't been paralyzed with fright.

"Hey, Sam. Howzitgoin'?" The man behind the counter looked up from a pile of invoices.

Sam swaggered forward. "Not too bad, Carl. How about you?"

"All right. No complaints." Carl pulled a pen from an ink-stained plastic pocket protector and returned his attention to the invoices. Sam was obviously not regarded as a customer important enough to warrant any more of his time.

Sam looked at her and shrugged, telling her without words that this had been her idea and she was the one who could see it through. The piece of toast she had eaten for breakfast clumped in her stomach.

When Sam saw that she wasn't moving forward, he came to the proper conclusion that she had lost her nerve and gave her a look of disgust. She wanted to show him that he was wrong—that a socialite could teach a silver-tongued hustler a few things, that she was good for something more than planning cocktail parties. But her feet felt as if they were glued to the floor and she couldn't seem to unstick them. He wandered over to thumb through a parts catalogue, separating himself from her.

Without quite knowing how it had happened, she found herself moving forward. Carl looked up. He seemed vaguely perplexed. Women in Chanel suits—even suits that were five years old—weren't frequent patrons of Spectra Electronics.

She extended her arm for a handshake, then tightened her grip when she realized it wasn't firm enough. "Faulconer," she said, introducing herself with her last name for the first time in her life. "I'm Susannah Faulconer. Sam's business partner."

Her hand was clammy. She withdrew it before he noticed and gave him a bright red business card with SysVAL boldly printed in black. As she passed it over, she prayed that the ink was dry.

SysVal stood for "Sam Yank and Susannah in the Valley," the name she and Sam had been arguing over all morning, right up to the time they stood at the counter of a print shop that guaranteed business cards in an hour. Sam had wanted to give the company an antiestablishment name like General Egocentric or Hewlett-Hacker, but she had stubbornly resisted. He had yelled at her right in front of the clerk at the print shop, but their confrontation the night before had stiffened her resolve not to let him have his way when she knew he was wrong. She still could barely believe that the name on the card was the one she had chosen.

"Faulconer?" Carl said as he eyed the card, which had her name written in the bottom corner incongruously placed in front of Sam's and Yank's and—even more incongruously— with the bold title "President" printed after it. "You have anything to do with FBT?"

"Joel Faulconer is my father," she said, "but I'm currently on sabbatical from FBT." That was vaguely true.

She turned her head as if she were knowledgeably surveying her surroundings, when actually she was just trying to slow down her heartbeat. From Sam's briefing, she knew Carl was the person they had to deal with, but what did she know about someone who owned an electronics warehouse? The building was cool but she was perspiring. She would never be able to carry this off. She was a socialite, not a businesswoman.

And then she saw the respect in his eyes generated by hearing her last name, and she found the courage to plunge ahead. "Sam tells me that you're the best dealer in the area. He's a severe judge, and I'm impressed."

Carl was pleased by her praise. "We try," he said. "We've been here for ten years. In the Valley that's a long time." He began telling her in some detail about his business.

"Interesting," she said as he wound to a close.

He gestured toward a cloudy Pyrex pot sitting on a hot plate. "Can I get you a cup of coffee, Miss Faulconer?"

He seemed to have forgotten Sam's existence, and for the moment that was fine. Off to the side, she could see Sam thumbing through the catalogues, but she knew that he was taking in every word of this exchange.

"Thanks, but I'm afraid I don't have time. I have another appointment." She gave her wrist a brisk glance only to remember, too late, that she wasn't wearing a watch. All of her watches were in her dresser drawer at Falcon Hill—or on her sister's wrist. She surreptitiously tugged down the sleeve of her jacket before Carl could notice.

"You're obviously competent at what you do. Reliability is important to me." Her knees were starting to feel weak, but she plunged on before she lost her nerve. "For some time I've been interested in helping develop small companies outside the FBT umbrella. I've been looking for ventures that excite me—new products, new concepts, fresh people. When Sam showed me the computer that he and his associate had designed, I knew I'd found exactly what I'd been looking for."

"Sam's a good guy," Carl said, belatedly remembering who had brought her here. "He's got good instincts."

"I think so, and I'm not easily impressed." She couldn't believe the man wasn't seeing right through her, but he continued to listen. "We're lining up suppliers now, which is why I'm here. We think this new computer marks the wave of the future. I've made the decision to commit myself and all my resources to SysVal." That was true anyway. Carl didn't have to know just how nonexistent those resources were.

"I'll be happy to help you in any way I can."

"Good. I want to make certain you'll give Sam everything he needs."

"He's got it," Carl replied enthusiastically.

"And time is important. We need reliable parts and we need them quickly."

"I understand."

She put out her hand and shook his, her grip much stronger this time. "I know you're busy, and I won't take up any more of your time. You have my business card." She hesitated at the exact moment when she wanted to appear most in control. Hoping she hadn't already betrayed herself, she said firmly, "Use that address for billing. Thirty days, normal terms."

For the first time, Carl looked doubtful. She had expected this to happen, but now that it had, she couldn't remember what she had planned to do about it.

"If we're dealing with a new company," he said, "we generally ask for payment in advance."

Out of the corner of her eye, she saw Sam's head lift from the parts catalogue. This was it. Now the socialite had to turn into a hustler. Whatever had made her think she could pull this off? She raised her eyebrow, hoping she looked vaguely annoyed instead of sick to her stomach. "In advance? How odd. That's really going to drive my accountants wild."

"Nothing personal, Miss Faulconer. It's normal procedure."

"Of course. I understand. I should have realized this would be a problem. FBT is accustomed to working with much larger suppliers."

Deliberately, she turned her back on him and walked over to Sam. "I know that you want to get your parts here, Sam, but I'm afraid it's not possible. You have to see that this is going to cause all sorts of difficulties for me."

Sam looked properly annoyed. "The prices are better here at Spectra," he said. "You'll end up paying more somewhere else."

She managed a stiff shrug. "Cost is relative. The larger suppliers can accommodate themselves better to our accounting system. From my perspective, this is a relatively small order—"

"Now, Miss Faulconer—" Carl practically leaped around the counter. "I'm sure we can work something out."

The blood had started to roar so loudly in her ears that she was surprised he couldn't hear it. She risked glancing at her wrist again. Two hairs past a freckle. She remembered that saying from her childhood. What time is it? Two hairs past a freckle. "I'm quite late already. I really don't—"

"We'll take care of it," Carl insisted. "Don't worry. Thirty days will be fine."

It took all her self-control not to break out in a huge smile. "Are you certain? I don't want to inconvenience you."

"No inconvenience at all," Carl replied. "Now you go on to your appointment. Sam and I'll get started on your order."

She could barely restrain herself from leaping into the air like a child. She wanted to jump and shout and scream with joy at how clever she had been, how brave, how absolutely unconventional! Instead, she smiled at Carl and began walking toward the door.

As she stepped outside, she promised herself that she would do whatever she must to pay him back. She might have hustled him, but she wouldn't cheat him.

11
●●●●●●●●●●●●●●●●●●●●●●●●●●

That evening Angela Gamble burst into the garage like the rhythm section of a street band—charm bracelets jangling, stiletto heels tapping, Gypsy coin earrings tintinnabulating.

"Sammy Bammy! I'm back!" She stretched out her arms and dashed forward—a hot pink flash in a gauze jumpsuit cinched at the waist with a metallic fish-scale belt. Her shoulder-length cloud of black, sprayed hair barely moved.

"Hi, Mom." His smile didn't quite reach his eyes as he half-heartedly returned her hug.

She gave him a loud kiss on the chin and smacked his face with the flat of her hand. "That's for all the trouble you probably got into while I was away." Without stopping to catch her breath, she raced toward Yank, grabbed his rear end in both hands and squeezed hard. "Gotcha, hot cheeks. Miss me?"

Yank turned and blinked. Susannah, who had been unpacking a box of parts when Sam's mother had burst in, watched in astonishment as a smile slowly spread over his face. "Hi, Angela."

At the age of forty-two, Angela Gamble was slim and small. Only an inch over five feet tall, she was pretty despite her gaudiness, and fiercely engaged in a battle against encroaching middle age. She stretched up onto her tiptoes

150

and planted a solid kiss on Yank's mouth. Then she slapped him across the face even harder than she had slapped her son. "That's for all the trouble you *didn't* get into while I was gone."

Yank rubbed his cheek absent-mindedly, gave her another smile—this one a bit vague—and reached for his logic probe.

She turned to Susannah. "Hi, honey. I'm Angela Gamble. You Sammy's new girlfriend?"

Susannah stepped forward and introduced herself.

Angela gazed at her curiously. "You look so familiar to me. Sammy, why does she look so familiar?"

Sam, busy sorting capacitors, said offhandedly, "She looks like that actress we saw on PBS a couple of months ago."

"I never watch PBS. I can't stand foreign accents. It's your hair. I don't ever forget a hairstyle. Not too many women still wear it in a bun like that."

Susannah felt vaguely apologetic. "I don't always wear it like this. Sometimes I wear it down."

"I'd take some of that weight out of it if I were you. Cut it just below your jaw line. Soften it with long layers so it stays full but isn't fussy. You don't look like the fussy type."

Her suggestions were delivered so good-naturedly, Susannah couldn't take offense. "I'll consider it."

Angela's scrutiny continued. "What did you say your last name was again?"

"Faulconer," she said hesitantly.

Angela looked thoughtful for a moment and then she let out a squeal. "I don't believe it! I read a story about you in the newspaper, didn't I? You're the daughter of that big shot. You're the one who ran away from her wedding! Ohmygod! Sammy, do you know who this is? This is Susannah Faulconer. She was getting married to this guy, and then right in the middle of this swank society wedding this other guy shows up on a Harley and—" She stopped in mid-sentence. Her jaw dropped as her eyes flew from Susannah to Sam. "Oh my God," she said breathlessly. "Oh my God! It was you!"

Without warning, she began to squeal in delight and pound her heels up and down on the concrete floor like a pint-sized flamenco dancer. "Sammy! I should have known. When I read that story, I got this shiver up my spine. I should have known right then. You're just like your old man! God, if he could only hear about this one."

Sam stiffened. Then he stepped forward. "Susannah is staying with me for a while."

"That's great! Oh, that's just great! If I'd known about this, I would have come back last week. Vegas was dead anyway. The town just isn't the same when Elvis isn't headlining. And then I had to listen to Audrey going on and on about how fat he's gotten. Fat or not, the King is still the King."

Sam interrupted abruptly. "You feel like making some spaghetti or something? I know it's late, but we're all pretty hungry."

Susannah looked at him curiously. She had just offered to make him something to eat, but he had refused.

"Sure, baby." Angela gave him another slap on the jaw and hugged Susannah. "You stay as long as you like, honey. And if Sammy gives you any trouble, you tell me about it. Between the two of us, we'll keep him in line." She jingled-jangled as she left the garage.

Susannah moved into Angela's sewing room that same night, despite the fact that Sam's mother had made it more than clear that she wasn't a prude. Susannah's desertion upset Sam, and he gave her another lecture about how uptight she was, but she was incapable of sharing his bed while his mother slept on the other side of the hall. They weren't married. They weren't engaged. They hadn't even discussed the possibility.

The next morning Angela caught her in the kitchen before Sam was awake. "Come on, honey," she said. "We're going to do something about that bun."

Ignoring Susannah's protests, Angela propelled her out to the garage and pushed her down in the shampoo chair.

For the next twenty minutes, Angela chattered as her silver scissors snipped, snipped, snipped. She cut Susannah's hair in long, fluffy layers, lifting the length so that the ends no longer quite touched her shoulders. She could still put her hair in a French twist or pile it on top of her head, but now feathery tendrils softened the angular lines of her face and curled along her neck. The style wasn't so different that she felt uncomfortable, but much looser and more untidy than anything she had ever worn. She knew that Cal Theroux wouldn't have approved of the change, but she felt as if she had been freed from an old, burdensome weight.

Sam rolled over in bed and reached out for Susannah. He frowned as he realized she wasn't there. He didn't like it when she slipped out of bed before he got up, before he could enjoy the feeling of her bottom pressed into his stomach and inhale the light floral scent of her hair. Sometimes he propped himself next to her and watched her sleep. She was always tightly curled, with her knees drawn up and her clasped hands pressed beneath her chin. There was something sad about the way she slept, as if she were trying to compress herself into a target so small that the demons of the world would fail to notice her.

He got out of bed and, after a quick shower, went to the garage, where he found her in the beauty shop with his mother. Both were so engrossed in studying Susannah's new hairstyle in the mirror that they didn't see him standing in the doorway. As he watched them, he wished that some of Susannah's class would rub off on his mother.

As usual, being near Angela made him tense. Why couldn't she be like other mothers? Why did she have to dress like a hooker and decorate her house like the world's worst garage sale? When he was a teenager, she had flirted with all of his friends, humiliating him in a way that he still couldn't forgive. She had no taste, no class, and no interest in acquiring either one. On the other hand, she had been his relentless defender through all the battles of his childhood. When the world seemed to be crashing around him, she had stood up to his father, to school officials, and to anyone else she believed was harming her son.

Susannah lifted her head and caught sight of him in the mirror. His chest expanded with pride. He had wanted this elegant woman, and now she was his. The thrill of conquest beat like a drum in his brain. She was going to make all the difference in his life. Her stillness would calm him and help him focus his energy. Her breeding would soften his rough edges. Her grace and timeless beauty would expand him in the eyes of others. With Susannah at his side, life no longer held any limits for him.

Her eyebrows drew together, and he realized that she was waiting for his reaction to her new haircut. He loved the way his opinion mattered to her. Just as he opened his mouth to tell her how terrific she looked, Angela interrupted.

"What do you think, Sammy? I haven't lost my touch, have I?"

Without a word he turned away from his mother and went back into the garage. As he reached the workbench, Susannah came through the doorway, her gray eyes regarding him with solemn intensity. Jeezus, it was sweet to have a woman like her look at him that way.

She frowned, and he realized that his failure to comment on her hair had made her mad. She pushed back her shoulders and set her jaw, practically daring him to make a derogatory remark. He almost laughed. She was learning. All he'd had to do was point the way, and she'd caught on real fast.

He reached out and took her into his arms. "It looks great."

Her annoyance fell away, and she beamed with pleasure. "You really like it?"

"Yeah, I really do." He kissed her fiercely. She leaned into him just like always and moaned softly against his mouth. Reluctantly, he drew away.

She sighed and looked over at the boxes of parts. "You're going to put me to work now, aren't you?"

"I promise you can take a coffee break sometime next week."

She laughed, and then, together, they settled down to begin the laborious process of assembling forty single-board computers.

The task involved "stuffing" every one of the printed circuit boards by hand. Sam showed her how to insert the wires on each of the small components through tiny holes in the copper pathways that ran through the circuit board. After all the components were in position, each wire had to be permanently soldered to the board and clipped. The job was both monotonous and demanding. If everything wasn't done exactly to specifications, he made her do it again.

When Susannah had finished assembling a board, Sam tested it and then put it in a long wooden "burn-in" box where it would be left on for forty-eight hours. Parts generally failed within a short period of time or not at all.

Susannah's fingers were sore at the end of the first hour, but she didn't complain. She was too conscious of the ticking of the clock and the fact that they had only thirty days to repay Spectra Electronics.

Joel dreamed that a dog was chewing on his shoulder. He was trying to get to Susannah, to save her from something horrible, but a wild dog had sunk its teeth into his shoulder and he couldn't move.

He awoke with a gasp. The dream was so vivid that he could still feel the pain. And then he realized the pain was real. As he clumsily lifted his hand to his chest he felt his pajamas soaked with sweat.

He would never forgive Susannah for doing this to him. He had given her everything, and look how she had repaid him.

The pain in his shoulder began to ease and his breathing steadied. It wasn't the first time he had experienced this tight, cramping ache. Perhaps he should see a doctor, but the idea of revealing his personal problems to anyone, even a medical professional, repelled him. He simply needed to get a grip on himself. He hadn't worked out since all of this had happened. He should get back into his old routine, set up a golf game. There was nothing wrong with him that some old-fashioned self-discipline wouldn't fix. Self-discipline and getting his daughter back.

Unaccountably, his heart began to pound again. Two weeks had passed. She should have returned long ago. The awful thought that she might not come back was never far from his mind. What would he do without her? She meant everything to him.

The darkness in the room grew oppressive. His hand trembled as he reached out for the lamp at the side of his bed. He bumped against a vase of garden flowers that Paige had left on the table and knocked it over. He swore as he flipped on the light. Dirty flower water had soaked his papers as well as the cookies that had been lying on a china plate next to the vase. Every night Paige left a snack by his bedside, like a child putting out a treat for Santa Claus. He never ate the snack—food before bedtime didn't agree with him—but still she put it out.

Joel stared down at the sodden cookies and wondered why he couldn't love the child of his own flesh as much as he loved his adopted daughter. But emotional introspection made him uncomfortable, so he got out of bed and crossed the floor to the window. Facts were all that mattered, and he acknowledged the simple, indisputable fact that Susannah had long ago become the most important person in the world to him. He had to get her back.

As he gazed out into the darkness, he chided himself for not having taken her last telephone call. She must have realized by now what a horrible mistake she had made, and he should have given her the opportunity to beg his forgiveness.

His hand closed over the edge of the windowsill. He had always been a man of action, and it wasn't in his nature to let events slip so far from his control. He had been patient long enough. Tomorrow he was going to see her. He would point out how reprehensibly she had behaved, and after he had laid out a few conditions of his own, he would relent and let her come back to Falcon Hill.

For the first time since the afternoon of her wedding, some of the darkness inside him lifted. He walked from one window to the next, envisioning their meeting. She would cry, of course, but he mustn't give into any emotional manipulation on her part. After everything she had put him through, he wouldn't make it easy for her. He would be tough, but he wouldn't be unreasonable. Eventually, Susannah would thank him for treating her so compassionately. Years from now they might even be able to smile about what had happened.

Feeling much more like himself, Joel returned to his bed. As he sank back into his pillow, a sigh of satisfaction slipped from his lips. He had been too emotional about all of this.

By this time tomorrow night, he would have his daughter back. And then everything would be all right.

The afternoon was unusually hot for Northern California. Susannah had propped the garage door open, but only an occasional breeze managed to make its way inside. Even though she had pulled her shorter hair into a ponytail with a red rubber band from the morning newspaper, her neck was damp. She looked up from the board she was stuffing to study Sam. He had a bandanna wrapped around his forehead so he didn't drip sweat onto the boards. For a moment she let her gaze linger on the muscles bunched beneath his T-shirt.

"I sure as hell hope Pinky doesn't decide to renege on the deal," he said abruptly. "I've met guys like him before. They're hardware freaks—seduced by the last piece of equipment they set eyes on. Half the guys in Homebrew must have discovered his place by now, and I'll bet some of them are trying to sell him their boards. If we don't get ours to him fast, he might strike a deal with someone else and then back out on us."

Susannah rubbed the small of her back where it was aching from having been bent over the assembly table for so long. "It seems to me that we have enough real problems without inventing unlikely ones." She stretched, trying to work out the kinks. "Remember that we have a contract and the others don't."

The muscles she had been admiring beneath his T-shirt grew unnaturally still. Slowly, she laid down her soldering iron. "Sam?"

He didn't say anything.

A warning bell went off in the corners of her mind, and she pushed herself up from the table. "Sam, you do have a written contract with the man, don't you?"

He became unbelievably busy with the board he was putting into the burn-in box.

"Sam?"

He turned on her belligerently. "I didn't think about it, all right? I was excited. I just didn't think about it."

She pulled off her reading glasses and rubbed her temples.

Suddenly she felt very tired. Her love for him kept blinding her to the fact that he was only a kid. A wild kid with a silver tongue. And she was an uptight socialite, and Yank was a hopeless nerd, and none of them knew what they were doing. They were goofing around, playing at being grown-ups. Why was she even surprised that he hadn't thought to draw up a contract? At that moment, she realized how insurmountable their problems really were. They were deeply in debt. It was only a matter of time before this house of cards they were building came crashing down around them.

"Look, don't worry, okay?" he said. "I told you the guy's a hardware freak, and we've got the best piece of hardware in the whole Valley."

She wanted to yell at him and tell him that it was time to grow up. Instead, she said wearily, "No more oral agreements, Sam. From now on everything has to be in writing. We can't ever let this happen again."

"Since when did you start giving orders?" he retorted. "You're sounding like a real bitch, you know that?"

Perhaps it was the effect of the heat, or the ache in her muscles, but her customary patience deserted her. A surge of righteous anger swept through her, and she slapped the flat of her hand down on the table. The sound reverberated through the garage, startling her as much as it did Sam. For a few seconds she stared down at her hand as if it belonged to someone else, and then, incredibly, she found herself slapping it down again.

"You're the one who made the mistake, Sam. Don't you dare attack me. You're the one who messed up! Not me."

He looked at her for a moment and then wiped the back of his forearm over his sweat band. "Yeah, you're right. Okay."

She stared at him. Was that all there was to it? Had she actually won an argument with him?

He grinned at the expression of surprise on her face and began to amble toward her, running deliberately lecherous eyes over her body. Susannah experienced a moment of deep pleasure, a sense of the strength of her own womanhood that was new and wonderful. Without thinking about what she was doing, she hooked her index finger over the snap on his jeans and tugged. When he came up against her, she gave him a trashy kiss, open-mouthed and deep.

"Would you be a doll baby and do a shampoo for me? I hate to interrupt, but I'm really backed up."

Susannah pulled abruptly away as Angela came through the beauty shop door. Sam whirled around. "She's not your shampoo girl, for chrissake!"

Susannah interceded. "My back hurts and I need to stretch for a few minutes. I don't mind. Yank will be here before long, and Roberta's coming over this evening to help."

Sam's lips tightened at the mention of Roberta, but since he was the one who had called her and told her she had to help assemble the boards, he couldn't really protest. Susannah suspected he would have made the elderly women in Angela's beauty shop stuff boards if they had better eyesight.

A blast of cool air from the window air conditioner hit her as she stepped through the door of the beauty parlor. One elderly woman was under a hair dryer, and Angela was giving another a perm. Susannah ushered the third to the shampoo bowl and supported her as she leaned back. She didn't mind helping Angela. Sam's mother was so good-natured it was impossible not to like her. Besides, when Susannah was helping out, she felt less guilty about the fact that she wasn't contributing anything toward her room and board.

As she gently worked the lather through the elderly woman's thin hair, she thought about how badly she needed money. All her life she had been dependent on her father, and now she was dependent on Sam and Angela. She had even been forced to ask Sam for money to buy a box of Tampax. He had given it to her without comment, but she still found the experience demeaning.

"Well, h-e-l-l-o there." Angela's voice, flirtatious and sassy, rose over the sound of the water running in the shampoo basin. Susannah glanced up, then sucked in her breath as the walls of the small shop seemed to tilt in crazy directions.

Joel Faulconer stood in the doorway, aloof and out of

place in a hunter-green polo shirt and crisply creased khaki slacks. He had put on some unneeded weight since she had last seen him, and his golfer's tan had faded. It was probably only her imagination, but he seemed older than she remembered.

He gazed around him without saying anything. In the past few weeks, Susannah had grown accustomed to her surroundings, but now she saw it all again through his eyes—the garish mirrored tiles, the plastic plants and ugly photographs of overly elaborate hairstyles. She saw herself—cheap and common in a man's T-shirt and a pair of threadbare slacks she had once worn for gardening. She could almost read his mind as he watched her shampoo the hair of a woman who was wearing blue bedroom slippers with slits cut in the sides to accommodate her bunions.

Susannah heard a cry of pain and realized she had dug her fingers into the poor woman's scalp. "I'm sorry," she apologized, releasing her. Her hands shaking, she finished rinsing out the woman and wrapped her head in a towel. Then she went over to her father. Angela looked on, making no attempt to hide her curiosity.

"I—I tried to call you," Susannah said.

"So I understand." Joel's eyes flicked over her clothing, revealing nothing except distaste.

Angela's charm bracelets had stilled, and Susannah could feel the curious eyes of her customers. Making an awkward gesture with her hand, she indicated that Joel should follow her into the workshop. It was empty. Sam must have gone to see someone about the cases to house the computer boards.

The burn-in box gave off a warm plastic smell that mingled with the sharp scent of perm solution. The garage seemed unbearably hot and airless. She hugged herself. "Would you like me to get you some iced tea? There's a pitcher in the kitchen. It'll only take a moment."

Ignoring her, he wandered over to the workbench and looked at the board that was sitting on it. He snorted contemptuously.

"I can fix you a drink if you'd rather," she said quickly.

He turned and stared at her so coldly, she couldn't believe that he had ever regarded her with tenderness. She couldn't bear it. Her throat tightened as she gazed at the man she had loved for nearly as long as she could remember, the golden prince of her childhood who had slain her dragons and loved her when no one else would. "Don't hate me," she whispered. "Please."

"Surely you didn't expect me to forget all the pain you've caused."

"Let me try to explain. Let me explain how I felt."

"*Now* you want to tell me how you felt," he scoffed. "Fascinating. Now that it's all over, and hideous damage has been done, you decide you want to settle in for a cozy father-daughter chat."

He was so cold, so accusing. "I just want you to understand that I never meant to hurt you."

"I'm afraid the time for confidences has long passed. Why didn't you talk to me before that debacle of a wedding? Tell me, Susannah, when did I turn into such a monster? Did I beat you when you were a child and you came to me with your troubles?"

"No," she said miserably. "No, of course not."

"Did I lock you in a closet every time you did something wrong?"

"No, it's not—"

"When you wanted to confide in me, did I push you aside and tell you I couldn't spare the time?"

"No. You were wonderful. You never did any of those things. It's just—" She struggled to find the words. "When I displeased you, you were always so cold to me."

His eyebrows shot up. "I was *cold* to you. Well, of course. Why didn't I think of that? In the face of such terrible parental abuse, who in the world could fault you for what you've done."

She bit her lip. "Please. I didn't mean to hurt you." The words seemed to be squeezing through a microscopically tiny passageway in her throat. "I didn't mean to hurt Cal. I just couldn't stand—I just couldn't stand being perfect any longer."

"Is that what this is about?" he said scathingly. "Your perfection? I wish you'd told me, so I could have disabused you of the notion long ago. You were never perfect, Susannah."

"I know that. It's just—I felt as if I had to be perfect or

you wouldn't love me. I felt as if I always had to do what everyone expected of me."

"You certainly chose a dramatic way to prove otherwise, didn't you?" he said contemptuously. Walking over to the assembly table, he gazed down at the assorted parts with distaste. When he looked back up at her, his features were rigid. "Now that you've had a taste of real life, I suppose you're going to beg me to let you come back to Falcon Hill?"

His statement caught her unaware. "You're my father. I—I don't want to be cut off from you."

"I'm supposed to forget everything that has happened and take you back? It's not going to be that easy, Susannah. You've hurt too many people. You can't just return to your old life and expect everything to be the way it was."

"I don't want my old life back," she whispered.

"If you expect Cal to be waiting with open arms, you'll be sadly disappointed," he went on, not hearing her. "He'll never forgive you."

Cold was seeping through her skin into her bones. "Daddy, I don't want Cal. I want to help Sam build his computer. I want to stay here."

Joel's entire body stiffened and his face grew ashen. For a moment he seemed to be fighting to catch his breath, and when he finally spoke, his voice was hoarse. "Are you telling me that you would rather live in this sordid place with that hooligan than come back to your family?"

"Why does it have to be one or the other?" she cried. "Daddy, I love you! But I love Sam, too."

"I don't think this is about love," he retorted. "Your relationship with that man—it's about sex."

"No, it's not—"

"Cal was a decent man, but apparently he wasn't *hot* enough for you."

Susannah wanted to cover her ears against Joel's venom. "Don't talk to me like this. I won't listen."

"I can only guess what your particular fetish is," he lashed out. "Leather? Motorcycles?"

His expression had grown so ugly, she hardly recognized it. Was this vindictive, hateful man really her father? In the background she heard the hum of a hair dryer and Angela's chatter. She clasped her arms around her body and tried to hold herself together.

Joel's complexion looked gray and unhealthy beneath his fading tan. "What do you get from your stud? Does he beat you? Are you that sort of woman?"

A sneering voice came from the outside doorway. "Naw, Faulconer, you got it all wrong, man. She's the one who beats me. Don't you, Suzie?"

Sam swaggered forward, every step insolent. One thumb was tucked in the waistband of his jeans, the other in his pocket. His blade-straight hair fell from beneath his sweatband and pooled on his shoulders. The silver earring glimmered through the black strands.

He stopped just behind her and slipped his hand possessively around her waist. "Your little girl is a wild cat with a whip."

Joel made a choked exclamation and took a menacing step forward. "You insolent—"

"That's right," Sam drawled. "I'm insolent, I'm crude, I'm stupid. I'm so stupid that I stole your precious daughter from right under your nose." He pulled Susannah tighter against his body, her back to his chest. Then he deliberately slid his thumb up onto her breast. "Does this give you any idea what I plan to do to your company?"

"Stop it, Sam!" Susannah couldn't bear it. He had no sense of caution. No sense at all. She pulled away from him and stepped toward her father. "I didn't mean to hurt anybody. I'm sorry for that. I just— I just couldn't help it."

Joel turned away as if he could no longer bear looking at her. His eyes returned to the workbench and the cluttered assembly table. When he spoke, his voice was frigid. "You've made a poor bargain, Susannah. You've tied your future to a hoodlum and a toy that no one will ever want. If you hadn't betrayed me, I could almost feel sorry for you."

"I didn't betray you. I—I love you."

"You've turned into a tramp. An ungrateful, cheap little tramp."

His words struck her like small, deadly pellets. She wanted to protect herself against them, but she had no defenses left. A deafening silence filled the small garage.

They all stood without moving, as if they had nowhere else to go.

"Don't you think you might be getting a little carried away here, Mr. Faulconer?" The jingle-jangle of charm bracelets came from the doorway of the Pretty Please Salon.

As Angela came into the garage, Joel gave her a look so malevolent that most women would have retreated. But Angela was a sucker for great-looking men, no matter how foul their dispositions, and Joel Faulconer was great-looking, even if he was a son of a bitch—a fact she intended to point out.

"Your daughter is one of the finest young ladies it's ever been my pleasure to meet. And as for what you said about my son—calling him a hoodlum—I want you to know that I don't appreciate that one bit."

Sam took a step toward his mother. "Stay out of this. This doesn't have anything to do with you."

Angela held out her hand. "Just one minute, Sammy. I haven't had my say yet."

Joel stared at Angela as if she were a particularly loathsome reptile, and then his eyes made a path from her swaying plastic earrings to her gold-lamé sandals. "By all means let your mother speak. She's obviously a woman whose opinion deserves to be heard."

Sam's arm shot back and his breath released in a hiss. Susannah leaped forward to put herself between him and her father. "No, Sam! You're only going to make it worse." She spun on Joel. "The problems between us don't have anything to do with Mrs. Gamble."

Angela planted her hand on her hip. "Let me just tell you one thing before you go, Mr. Faulconer—"

"Mom! Don't say any more."

Angela waved Sam off and concentrated all her attention on Joel. "Let me just tell you that you might want to think twice about casting aspersions at my son, since you don't know who he really is."

The threatening tone in Sam's voice grew stronger. "Don't do this, Mom. I'm telling you."

Angela lifted her chin, more than willing to take on the chairman of FBT. "My son—the one you called a hoodlum —the one you think isn't good enough for your daughter—"

"Stop it, Mom!"

"My son happens to be the only male child of Mr. Elvis Presley!"

The garage went completely still. Sam's face looked as if it had been carved from stone. Susannah's lips parted in astonishment. For several moments Joel Faulconer didn't move. When he finally turned to Susannah, his expression was haggard.

"I will never forgive you for this," he hissed. And then he left.

Susannah started to run after him, but Sam caught her arm and hauled her up short before she could take a step. "Don't you dare," he snarled, pushing her down at the assembly table. "You stay right here! Godammit, don't you even think about going after that bastard."

Without a word of explanation, Angela returned to her elderly ladies. Sam waited for Joel's car to leave, and then he stormed from the garage. Susannah rubbed her arm where he had grabbed her and reached out to pick up the soldering iron. But her hand was shaking so badly that she couldn't manage it. She sat in silence for some time while she waited for the pain to go away.

Sam still hadn't returned by dinner time, although Yank and Roberta had shown up several hours earlier. Roberta's mindless chatter coupled with Yank's unrelenting silence strained Susannah's frazzled nerves to the breaking point. When she couldn't stand her thoughts anymore, she retreated into the kitchen and began assembling ingredients for a salad. As she tore apart a head of lettuce, Angela came inside.

"It'll probably just be you and me for dinner, Susannah. I wouldn't count on Sammy showing up for a while." Angela squirted some dishwashing liquid into her hands and washed them under the kitchen faucet. "Let me cut up some cheese and salami and we can have ourselves a big chef salad—ladies' night special."

"All right."

Angela's bracelets clinked against the refrigerator door as she opened it to pull out several deli packages. "You like olives?"

"Olives are fine." Susannah fumbled for the paring knife.

"I'm really sorry about that awful scene with my father. It's bad enough that I'm mooching off you all the time without putting you through something like that."

Angela waved away her apology. "You're not responsible for your father. And I like having you here. You're a real lady. You're good for Sammy. The two of us—you might have noticed—we don't get along too well. He's ashamed of me."

A polite denial sprang to Susannah's lips, but she bit it back. If Angela had the courage to be honest, she wouldn't insult her with well-meaning evasions. "He's still young," she said.

Angela's face softened. "Young and a rebel. What a time I've had with him."

The pain of her confrontation with Joel had overridden her curiosity about Angela's strange revelation. Now she remembered it. "His father . . . ?"

"Frank Gamble was a decent man, I guess. But he didn't have any imagination."

Susannah's hand stilled on the lettuce. She hadn't expected to hear about Frank Gamble. What about Elvis?

Angela began unwrapping the deli packages. "I had to marry him because I was a good Italian girl who had gotten herself in trouble, if you understand what I mean. But we didn't have too much in common. And when Sammy was a teenager, Frank was always screaming at him about being a hippie and a bum, and Sammy kept running away. It was terrible. I loved Sammy a lot more than I ever loved Frank. When Frank left me for another woman a few years ago, I was actually relieved, although whenever I went to Altar Society meetings, I pretended I was broken up about it since I'm Catholic."

"I see." Susannah quartered a cucumber as she tried to put it all together.

"Of course, it was hard having Frank run off with somebody in her twenties, especially when my boobs were starting to sag and my face didn't look as good as it used to. I was so pretty when I was in my twenties," she said dreamily. And then she gave a self-conscious laugh. "Listen to me. You'd think I was ready for the grave instead of just hitting my prime. You want to know about Elvis, don't you?"

"Not if you don't want to tell me."

"I don't mind. It's just— Sammy hates it when I talk about him. I know I should have kept my mouth shut out there in the garage, but your father was—pardon my French—acting like a real bastard."

"He's not like that all the time. I'm afraid I've hurt him pretty badly."

"Sammy hurts me all the time, but I don't ever go after him like that."

Tears welled in Susannah's eyes. She blinked them away and briskly rinsed off a tomato. "When did you meet Mister—uhm, Elvis?"

"Every once in a while during the fifties, I used to drive down to L.A. and work as an extra. I got a job on *Love Me Tender*. It was Elvis's first starring role, and every female extra in the world wanted to work on that film. Luckily, I had this friend in the business who had a friend. Anyway, it all worked out." She nibbled absentmindedly on a sliver of Swiss cheese. "All I have to do is shut my eyes and I can see him right now singing the title song." She began humming "Love Me Tender."

Something didn't seem right to Susannah. Sam was twenty-four. He had been born in 1952. Surely Elvis wasn't starring in movies that early. "When was that film made?"

"I'm not too good with dates. I met him for the first time much earlier than that anyway. In—I guess—'fifty-one. I went to Nashville with a girlfriend. Elvis was called the Hillbilly Cat then, and he was getting ready to sign his first record contract. You should have seen him. Young and sexy, with those eyelids drooping down and his hair all greased back. Don't get me wrong, Susannah. I was a good girl. I always went to mass. I even thought about being a nun for a while. But with Elvis, it was sort of holy anyway. Do you want hard-boiled egg in your salad?"

"Fine—anything," Susannah said distractedly.

"You really love him, don't you?"

For a second Susannah thought Angela was talking about Elvis, and then she realized the subject had shifted back to Sam.

"Yes. Yes, I do."

"You're not too much alike."

"I know."

"Suzie, be careful with Sammy. He's different. He doesn't see the world the same way as everybody else. You're really a nice girl, and I don't want him to hurt you."

Angela's warning made Susannah uneasy, but when she went out to the garage a few hours later and found Sam hard at work, she was so glad to see him that she pushed it to the back of her mind. They worked side by side for a while. Finally, she asked him about Angela's claim that he was Elvis Presley's son.

"It's a lie," he said brusquely. "Something she invented around the time she got divorced. Whenever she talks about it, her story changes. The dates never match up. Just forget about it, will you? I don't want to talk about it anymore."

She didn't press him, and sometime around midnight, he pulled her into the deserted interior of the Pretty Please Beauty Salon, where they made love in the shampoo chair. Afterwards, Susannah realized that neither of them had thought to lock the door, but since Angela had gone to bed hours before, she supposed it didn't really matter much. Yank was still in the garage, of course, but Yank didn't count. He wouldn't have noticed if they had made love right on top of his workbench.

12

T he old man's playing with his toys again."

The two FBT grounds keepers, one plump and soft, the other thin and wiry, leaned on their shovels and gazed over at the seven obelisk-shaped fountains in the reflecting pond at the Castle. One by one, they stopped sending their silvery streamers of water into the air. But before the ripples in the pond had stilled, the columns of water began flowing again, rising systematically from the first fountain to the last.

"Man, I'd like to have his job," the heavier of the two men commented as he watched the water catch the light, recede, and then catch the light again. "Sit around in an air-conditioned office all day, play with a bunch of fountains, and pull in a couple million a year."

They began digging again, only to stop and look curiously back at the reflecting pond. Instead of the systematic ebb and flow they were accustomed to, the fountains had begun going on and off in a quirky, random fashion neither had witnessed before. The effect was eerie and vaguely disquieting, turning the smooth pond water choppy and gray.

"The old man must be having a bad day."

"What's he got to feel bad about? Shit, man. If I had his money, I'd be dancin' in the streets."

The center four fountains abruptly stopped, as if someone had slammed a fist in the middle of the panel of control switches. The grounds keepers watched for a moment and then went back to their shovels.

Joel swiveled his desk chair so that he was no longer looking through the window at the reflecting pond. He had once been so proud of the FBT fountains. When he had controlled the switches, he had felt as if he were somehow controlling the continent each fountain represented: Europe brought to life with a flick of his hand, South America firmly under his rule, North America beating at the heart of his mighty kingdom. Even Asia had seemed to fall under his power. He had felt like a king in command of the world.

Now he merely felt tired.

The nagging pain in his chest was back. He could barely comprehend what had happened in that squalid little garage. She should have been repentant. She should have begged him to take her back. Instead she had asked him to *understand*. As if he could understand something so sordid.

The buzz of the intercom interrupted his thoughts, and his secretary announced Cal. Joel straightened in his chair at the same time that he pretended to turn his attention to the papers on his desk. It wouldn't do for Cal to see that anything was wrong. Not that Joel didn't trust Cal. He did. Cal was like the son he'd never had—smart, ambitious, and just as ruthless as he had been himself at that age. But the basic rule of maintaining power was not to let anyone, no matter how close he might be, see your weakness.

"I need to go to Rio next week," Cal said after they had exchanged greetings. He took a cup of coffee from Joel's secretary and, settling into a comfortable leather wing chair across from the desk, began to fill Joel in on their negotiations with the Brazilians.

As Joel listened, he was acutely conscious of Cal's appearance. The younger man was professionally attired in the FBT uniform: a dark blue suit, custom-made white shirt, and silk rep tie. His wing tips were polished to a sheen, his hair neatly trimmed. Joel had always found the white streak that ran through the center of Cal's hair too flamboyant, but he couldn't really blame Cal for that. All in all, he couldn't help comparing him to the long-haired thug who had carried off his daughter on the back of a motorcycle, a man who was purported to be the illegitimate offspring of Elvis Presley. He raged against the humiliation of Susannah keeping company with a person like that.

The discussion came to an end. Joel toyed with the edge of one of the binders on his desk. "I had our security people make some inquiries about Susannah," he said carefully, "and then I went to see her yesterday." He couldn't bring himself to mention that she had been shampooing hair.

Cal's jaw tightened, but other than that he showed no reaction. His self-control made Joel uneasy, perhaps because he no longer felt as much in command of himself as he used to. But his uneasiness might have been caused by something else, some wayward sense of protectiveness toward his ungrateful daughter, which Cal's barely repressed hostility was triggering. The thought infuriated him, and his voice hardened.

"She and that hoodlum she's living with have actually found someone naive enough to order that ridiculous machine they're working on—an electronics dealer in the Valley. It's a small business with shaky credit."

"I see." The room grew quiet. Cal's cup clinked delicately against his saucer. "From what you've told me, they don't sound much more professional than kids running a Kool-Aid stand." The leather seat cushion of the chair wheezed softly as he shifted his weight. "Amateurs run into so many catastrophes when they do business with each other."

It was exactly the tack Joel had expected Cal to take, but he still couldn't suppress a growing feeling of uneasiness.

Cal went on. "If their operation is that tenuous, the smallest setback will finish them. This fellow who ordered their little toy, for example. If he backed out, they would find it impossible to recover."

"*If* he backed out."

"It's difficult to imagine what someone like that might not be prepared to give up for a chance to do business with FBT."

Cal had finally made his point—one that Joel had already considered. He was surprised at the vehemence of his response. "No. I don't want any interference. None, do you understand?"

A muscle ticked just beneath Cal's cheekbone. "I'm a bit surprised."

"That's because you're not quite as perceptive as I thought you were. You didn't understand how unhappy Susannah was, for example."

Cal's expression grew wooden. Joel's attack had obviously surprised him, but not nearly as much as it surprised Joel. Was he actually making excuses for Susannah? He immediately backstepped. "Not that I'm blaming you, of course. Still, I don't want any interference."

For the first time, Cal let his bitterness show. "You're obviously more forgiving than I. I suppose that isn't surprising. You're her father, after all."

Joel thought of the way Susannah had let Gamble put his hand on her breast, and a rush of righteous outrage hit him anew. "Forgiveness has nothing to do with it. By God, Susannah is going to suffer the consequences of what she's done! Judging by what I saw yesterday, it's only a matter of time before they fail. But when it happens, I want her to know she did it to herself. Do you understand me? We do this my way, Cal. I won't give her a convenient scapegoat. I don't want her to be able to believe for one minute that she could have succeeded if we hadn't interfered."

Some of Joel's tension eased. Susannah just needed more time, that was all. It had only been a few weeks. By going to see her yesterday, he had rushed things. Once the reality of her sordid new life set in, her desire to rebel would fade and she would come running back to him.

He saw that Cal still looked wary. Did Cal sense his ambivalence where Susannah was concerned? He returned Cal's gaze steadily and steered the conversation into safer waters.

"Paige said you invited her to dinner at the yacht club on Saturday."

"Yes," Cal replied smoothly. "I'm enjoying her company very much."

I can't . . . get no . . . sa tis . . . fac tion . . .

Paige kept her eyes shut, waiting for it to be over. It was creepy being in bed with Cal. She didn't even know why she had let it get this far, except Conti had called her today to tell her he was going back East, and he had cried on the phone.

Cal stiffened, then relaxed. For a moment, she wondered what was wrong, then she realized that small spasm had marked his orgasm. He had made no sound—he had barely inconvenienced her. Apparently Cal was always well-behaved, even when he came.

As she eased herself out of bed and went into his bronze and gold bathroom, she was grateful that he had gotten it over with quickly. Maybe Cal didn't enjoy sex any more than she did. It was a tantalizing idea, and later, when they were dressed and he was driving her home, she decided to test it.

"I don't think it's a good idea for us to sleep together again, Cal. It's a little too weird."

The headlights from an approaching car caused an angular pattern to pass over his face. "You're quite sensitive, Paige. I never realized that until tonight." Incredibly, he reached over and patted her knee. The gesture was comforting rather than sexual. "I don't want to speak out of turn, but I know it can't be entirely easy for you at Falcon Hill. I respect Joel more than any man in the world, but he's not the easiest man to please."

His sympathy and understanding touched her. "No, he's not." Then she said bitterly, "Especially since I'm not his precious Susannah."

His expression stiffened as it always did when she mentioned her sister's name. Sometimes she did it deliberately, just so she could watch the way his lips tightened.

"Susannah manipulated him," he said. "But then, she manipulated all of us, didn't she? When I think how she used to talk about you . . . the lies and distortions she spouted behind your back. The worst of it is, I believed her." He glanced over at her. "I'm sorry for that, Paige. I feel as if I owe you something. If we're not going to be lovers, at least I'd like for us to be friends. Do you think that's possible?"

Paige was cynical about men. She knew that Cal wanted to stay close to Joel, and from his viewpoint, one daughter was probably as good as another. But he had been so kind, so sympathetic, and she needed someone to care about her. "What about—sex?" she asked. "You're not mad?"

Once again, he patted her knee. "I've never been particularly interested in carving notches on my bedpost. Don't misunderstand me. I enjoy sex, but it's not the most important thing in my life. Right now I need a friend more than a lover." He extended his hand. "Friends?"

He was so sincere that she let her guard down. "Friends," she repeated as she took his hand.

They chatted easily the rest of the way to Falcon Hill. Gradually, she found herself relaxing. Cal understood how unfair Joel had always been to her, and for the first time since her mother had died, she had someone on her side. By the time they reached home, she felt better than she had in ages—like a battered ship that had just sailed into a safe harbor.

Sam delivered the forty computers to Pinky at Z.B. Electronics precisely on schedule. Each machine was neatly encased in a wooden box with the words SysVal and the Roman numeral I visible on the front in gold rub-on letters that Susannah had finished applying just before dawn that morning.

To her relief, Pinky paid his bill on time and she was able to settle up with Spectra. But they were only out of debt for a day before Sam ordered more parts on credit and the cycle began all over again. Only this time they didn't have a committed buyer for the new boards.

During the next few weeks, Pinky sold several of their single-board computers to hardware freaks like himself, but the machines weren't flying off the shelves, and she was frantic with worry. They had taken out several ads in hobbyists' magazines and a few orders had trickled in, but not many. Yank had already started work on the prototype of the self-contained computer they wanted to build, but if they hoped to survive long enough to begin manufacturing it, they needed to buy themselves time. And they needed money. Big money. Susannah decided to swallow her pride and see if she could find it.

Every day for a week, she put on her old Chanel suit and, borrowing either Yank's Duster or Angela's Toyota, went to see acquaintances from what she had begun to think of as her former life. She didn't waste time trying to contact Joel's friends or any FBT people. Instead, she phoned members of Kay's old social circle and people who had sat with her on the boards of charitable organizations. Almost all of them agreed to see her, but she quickly discovered that they were far more interested in confirming the gossip they had heard about her than in investing in SysVal. When the subject of money came up, they shifted uncomfortably in their seats and remembered urgent appointments.

Each day, she returned tired and discouraged. At the end of the week, she went out to the garage and told Sam that she had run out of names. He pressed the half-empty can of Coke he had been drinking into her hand and said, "We need to find a venture capitalist who's willing to pump a few hundred thousand into the company. Then we could get serious about moving beyond the hobbyists' market and building the computer we really want to build." He lifted a board from the burn-in box and began putting it in its wooden case.

She rolled the lukewarm Coke can between her hands. "No respectable venture capitalist will pay any attention to us. We don't look *serious*."

At that moment the buzzer that Yank had rigged over the workbench went off. She sighed, set down the can, and rushed from the garage and across the yard toward the kitchen door.

Generally she made it to the phone on its fifth ring, but today she stumbled on the step and lost time. As she lifted the receiver to her ear, she yearned for the day they could afford to have a separate telephone line in the garage instead of being forced to use the kitchen phone. She knew that it sounded more professional to have a woman answer, but sometimes she resented the fact that she was the one who always had to make the dash across the yard.

"SysVal. May I help you?"

"Yeah. I got a question about the voltage levels at the I/O interface."

At least this phone call was from a customer instead of one of Angela's friends. "I'm sure we can answer that for you. Let me put you on hold while I connect you with our Support Services Department." She flipped on the portable radio they kept tuned to a rock station and set the receiver in

175

front of it, then she rushed back outside and gestured for Sam, who was watching at the garage window. He hurried across the yard to take the call.

Appearances, Susannah kept repeating to herself. *Appearances are everything.*

That same night she and Sam enjoyed the luxury of being able to sleep together, since Angela had taken an overnight trip to visit a friend in Sacramento. But even lovemaking couldn't push their business problems far from their minds.

"I've been thinking," Sam said, his lips resting against her forehead. "We need to take on one more partner. Someone who understands electronics and knows about marketing. A person with a sharp mind, who hasn't bought into the system." He rolled over on his back. "Someone inventive. And he can't be an asshole. We need to hire somebody like Nolan Bushnell at Atari."

"I think he already has a job," Susannah said dryly. She twirled a strand of his hair through her fingers.

"Or—this would be great—one of the big guys at Hewlett-Packard."

Susannah rolled her eyes. Hewlett-Packard, with its progressive management style, seemed to be the only American corporation that Sam admired. "Why would anyone leave H-P to come work with us in a garage for no money?"

"If they had vision they would. Hell, yes. We wouldn't even want them if they didn't have vision."

This was what she both loved about him and despaired over. "It would be impossible for us to attract anyone with an important name to this company."

"Will you stop telling me what's impossible? You do that all the time. Start telling me what's possible for a change."

"I'm just being practical."

"You're just being negative. I'm getting sick of it. I can't work like that." He pushed himself from the bed and went out into the kitchen.

Her stomach churned, but she forced herself not to go after him. She was determined not to settle back into her old patterns of conciliation. Sam's anger burned hot and fierce, but it was over quickly. Still, she didn't fall asleep until several hours later, when he slipped back into bed.

Not long after their conversation, Sam began cornering

Hewlett-Packard vice-presidents in the company parking lot. Several of them thought they were being mugged and locked themselves in their cars, but a few of them actually came to the garage to see their operation and to offer advice. On one rainy evening, Sam even managed to corner Bill Hewlett himself.

Hewlett was pleasant but firm. He wasn't quite ready to leave the billion-dollar company he had helped found and follow Sam Gamble's silver tongue to the land of small computer nirvana.

After that, Sam lost all respect for Hewlett-Packard.

Labor Day weekend marked the first small computer trade show. It was being held in Atlantic City, and Sam announced that they were going. "We need to establish ourselves as a national company instead of a local one," he said.

Susannah agreed with him philosophically, but felt that the expense of the trip for a company that hadn't sold even all forty of its original single-board computers made it impossible. He rode roughshod over every one of her objections, and when she saw she couldn't change his mind, she made a condition of her own. If they were going to exhibit at the trade show, they would do it her way.

Atlantic City, by the summer of 1976, was a faded hooker about to succumb to a variety of social diseases. Legislation was afoot in Trenton to allow legalized gambling, but until that happened, the city that had once been the gayest spot on the Atlantic seaboard had lost all vestiges of its former beauty. The boardwalk was decaying and their hotel seedy. By the time they had checked in, Susannah was convinced the trip was doomed, but she still hustled her partners over to the convention hall to set up their booth.

To her relief, the worst of her nightmares hadn't come true—the crates that held what Sam called "Susannah's Goddamn Folly" were undamaged, and he began unpacking.

She concentrated on how great his rear end looked when he bent over instead of on what he was saying. The booth had ended up costing nearly a thousand dollars—far more than they could afford. But she had wanted them to look like a much larger company than they were, and so, over Sam's strident objections, she had ordered it built. If she was wrong, she would have to shoulder the blame alone.

But as it turned out, she wasn't wrong. By noon the next day, several hundred people were wandering through the exhibits, and all of them were drawn to the SysVal booth. While the companies surrounding them displayed their products on crudely draped card tables bearing identical white tagboard signs printed with the company's name, SysVal showed off its machine in a brightly colored booth with dramatically angled walls and the company name spelled out in illuminated crimson letters. Only MITS, the manufacturers of the Altair, and IMSAI, their closest competitor, had more elaborate displays. Without a word being spoken, Susannah's booth made SysVal look like the third largest single-board computer company exhibiting, when in fact they were one of the smallest. Her triumph made her feel wonderfully cocky and full of herself.

Toward the end of the first day, she glanced up and saw Steve Jobs standing in front of their machine. Since their situations were similar, she had been interested in watching the two Steves—Wozniak and Jobs—as they tried to stir up interest in their Apple single-board computer.

Jobs was only twenty-one and Woz twenty-five, and like her own partners, neither was a college graduate. Compared to Steve Jobs, however, Sam was a fashion plate of respectability. Jobs was unkempt and unwashed, with dirty jeans and battered Birkenstock sandals. Sam had told her that he was a vegetarian and a Zen Buddhist who had traveled to India in search of enlightenment. He was still thinking about returning to become a monk.

Instead of looking at the computer they had on display, Jobs was studying Susannah's booth. He and Woz were selling their Apples from a card table on the other side of the convention hall. She watched Jobs as his alert eyes took in the multicolored backdrop and the brightly lit name. He knew the SysVal operation was just as small and eccentric as his own, but he could see that they had made themselves appear bigger and more important. He looked at Susannah, and she felt a moment of recognition pass between them—a moment that leaped across the barriers separating a San

Francisco socialite and an unkempt Silicon Valley hippie. Jobs understood what she had done. She suspected that the little Apple Computer Company—if it survived—would never again make the mistake of showing up at a trade show with their wares displayed on a card table.

Late Monday night, after the trade show had closed, Susannah, Sam, and Yank left Atlantic City and headed for the Philadelphia airport with fifty-two new orders in their pockets. Their success had even made Yank talkative, and they boarded their flight with a sense of celebration.

As Sam slid into his seat, he pulled a copy of the *Wall Street Journal* from the seat pocket in front of him. "Now that I'm going to be a tycoon, I'll have to change my reading habits," he joked. He made a great play out of opening the newspaper and busily arranging it in front of him. He was trying to be funny, but Susannah couldn't manage much more than a polite smile. She had seen her father's head buried in the same newspaper too many times.

An array of feelings, bittersweet and painful, swept over her. Several moments passed before she realized that Sam had fallen silent next to her. She glanced over and saw that his face had grown rigid.

"Sam?"

He abruptly folded the paper and stuffed it under his arm. "We've got to get off the plane."

"What?"

"Come on."

"Sam?"

"Hurry. They're getting ready to close the door."

His air of urgency alarmed her, and she found herself rising from her seat. He planted his hand in the small of her back and pushed her ahead of him. "Sam? What are you doing? Where are we going?"

He directed her past a stewardess. "We've got to get off. Hurry up."

She glanced over her shoulder at their partner, who was still seated, his eyes vaguely puzzled beneath his glasses. "What about Yank?"

"Somebody'll take care of him."

Within minutes, Susannah found herself standing in the boarding area while her few remaining clothes took off for

San Francisco. Three hours later, she and Sam were on their way to Boston in search of a man named Mitchell Blaine.

Blaine lived in an expensive English Tudor located in Weston, one of Boston's more prestigious suburbs. The afternoon sun filtered through the maple trees and sparkled on the ivy that climbed the walls of the house. As Susannah and Sam walked up the antique brick pathway toward the front door, she found herself hoping that the owner was on vacation in Alaska someplace. Although that certainly wouldn't stop Sam. He would probably insist they board the next plane to Fairbanks.

On the flight to Boston, she had studied the article in the *Wall Street Journal* that had caught Sam's attention, and she'd learned as much as she could about the man they had come to see. Mitchell Blaine was one of the wunderkinds of Route 128, the high-tech area that had formed around Boston and was the East Coast counterpart to California's Silicon Valley. A midwesterner by birth, he had a Bachelor's degree in Electrical Engineering from Ohio State, a Master's Degree from MIT, and an MBA from Harvard. But it was his ability to combine technological know-how with a wizardry for marketing that had made him a multimillionaire.

During the late sixties and early seventies, he had quickly risen through the ranks of several of Boston's most aggressive young high-tech companies and at the same time wisely taken advantage of their early public stock issues to begin amassing his personal fortune. By 1976 he had a reported net worth nearing five million dollars—insignificant compared to the world's great fortunes, but respectable money for someone who'd been orphaned at the age of seven. Business analysts had targeted him as one of the bright new leaders who would direct the course of high-tech industry as it moved into the 1980s.

And then, four days earlier, his meteoric career had come to an end. In a tersely worded one-paragraph press release that had sent industry analysts reeling, he had announced his retirement from the business world. He was only thirty-one years old.

The article had given no explanation for his decision, but that hadn't stopped Sam, who had immediately invented his own. "The man's bored, Susannah. He's only thirty-one. He wants a challenge. SysVal is going to be just what he needs."

Try as she might, she could find no evidence in the article to support Sam's conclusion. The article told the facts about Blaine's life but nothing about the man himself.

She caught his arm as they approached the front steps of the house. "Sam, this is awful. We have to call first."

"And give him an opportunity to brush us off? Not a chance. Besides, you don't think we can just ring up information and get Mitchell Blaine's private phone number, do you? It was hard enough for you to find out where he lived."

She didn't want to think about how embarrassed she had been to rouse one of FBT's Boston executives out of bed at six-thirty in the morning with a preposterous story about needing Blaine's address for her father's social calendar. "We can't just show up on his doorstep," she insisted. "It simply isn't done."

Sam jabbed the door bell. "If you're afraid you'll get kicked off the Social Register, it's too late. Our little escapade on your wedding day took care of that."

"Damn it, Sam!"

"Wow. Miss Goody-Goody is swearing. She's going to have to sit in the corner." He punched the door bell a second time.

He was being unbearably nasty, but she understood him well enough to suspect he was merely trying to distract her from the fact that he knew she was right.

"What are you going to say to him? How are you going to explain our presence?"

"I'm not. You tell him who you are and get us in the door. After that, I'll do all the talking."

That was what she had been afraid of.

He rang the bell several more times, but nothing happened. "No one's here, Sam. Let's forget—"

"Just keep ringing, damn it!" He disappeared around the side of the house.

She violated every rule of etiquette she had ever learned by ringing two more times. Just as she was turning away, Sam reappeared. "There's a television on in the rear of the house. Let's go."

"No, Sam! It might be the maid."

"He's here. I know it."

She stumbled over a sprinkler head as he dragged her through a hedge of yews. A shaded flagstone patio lay directly in front of them. As they stepped up on it, a security alarm went off.

"We're going to get arrested!"

"Not until we've seen Blaine." Without releasing his grip on her, Sam steered her across the patio to the back door and began to pound it with his fist.

"Hey, Blaine!" he shouted. "I know you're in there! I want to talk to you. I've got Susannah Faulconer here. FBT Faulconer. Joel Faulconer's daughter. She doesn't like being left on the goddamn doorstep. Let us in."

"Shhhh!" she hissed. "Be quiet! Will you be quiet!" She imagined Blaine huddled inside his house in terror while he waited for the police to rescue him from the madman who was storming his house. "He's going to think we're here to murder him!"

No sooner had the words left her mouth than one of the patio doors slid open and they had their first sight of their quarry.

In those initial few seconds, Susannah came to the rapid conclusion that Mitchell Blaine probably didn't care whether he was about to be murdered or not. As Boston's young high-tech marketing whiz stumbled out onto the patio, she realized that he was too drunk to care much about anything.

Even drunk, he was formidable. She had been around the exclusive brotherhood of powerful corporate men all her life, and although Blaine was only thirty-one and obviously not at his best, she knew at once that he was a member in good standing. But if she had been pressed to define exactly why she was so certain, she would have had difficulty. Members of the brotherhood reveled in their power too much to drink to the point of oblivion, as Blaine had done. And although he was wearing the proper uniform—a custom-tailored white dress shirt and well-cut gray trousers —the garments looked as if they had been slept in.

His straight, sandy hair was conservatively cut by a barber who had been well-trained to meet the precise requirements of the brotherhood. But the regulatory side part was uneven, and instead of being combed neatly back from his forehead, the hair at the front tumbled forward in a manner acceptable only after a set of tennis.

His body wasn't quite right, either. Although he was imposingly tall, his build was a bit too muscular for a member of the corporate elite and his abdomen a little too taut. But the directness in those wide-spaced, light blue eyes was familiar, as well as the chilling contempt in his blunt, slightly irregular features.

She caught her breath as Blaine came toward Sam. "Get the hell off my property."

Sam formed the peace sign, a gesture that would have amused Susannah if she hadn't been so appalled at the rudeness of their intrusion. "We just want to talk," Sam said, refusing to back off by so much as an inch. "We've come a long way to talk to you."

"I don't care how far you've come. You're trespassing, and I want you out of here!" Blaine took an uneven step forward.

Sam was starting to get angry, managing by some incredible sleight-of-mind to turn himself into the wronged party. "Listen. We've busted our asses finding you, and the least you can do is hear us out."

"The least I can do is kick you out of here."

Gathering her nerve, Susannah pushed herself between Sam and the formidable Mr. Blaine. "Let's go inside and I'll fix you a cup of coffee, Mr. Blaine. You look like you could use it."

"I don't want any coffee," he said with angry precision. "I want another drink."

"All right," she replied stubbornly. "I'll fix you some coffee to go along with your drink."

Fortunately, the relentless whine of the security alarm had begun to bother him even more than their presence. He turned back toward the house, and at that moment she knew why she had recognized him as one of the elite brotherhood of the powerful. Even though he was staggeringly drunk, he had been able to dismiss them with cruel accuracy as persons of no consequence to him.

He moved with surprising grace for a man in his condition, although he did manage to stub the toe of his expensive black leather wing tips on the step. Sam refused to wait for an invitation that he knew wouldn't be forthcoming. Grabbing Susannah, he pulled her through the patio door after him.

They walked into a family room complete with timbered ceiling and a soaring Old English fireplace that looked large enough to roast an ox. The green and red plaid design in the carpet held indentations showing that couches and tables had been in place quite recently, but many of the items themselves were missing. The few pieces of furniture that remained were obviously expensive, but dark and heavy.

When Blaine finally realized they had followed him, he looked annoyed, but not alarmed. She spotted the glass that he had been drinking from. Ignoring her conscience, she snatched it up and handed it to him. While Sam studied their surroundings, she adopted the deferential manner of one of Joel Faulconer's secretaries and managed to convince Blaine to deactivate the alarm and call off his security company.

When the house was finally quiet, Sam spoke. "I've got a proposition for you, Blaine . . ."

She went into the kitchen to make coffee. While she was waiting for the water to boil, she spotted a nursery school calendar hanging crookedly by a magnetic clip on the side of the refrigerator along with a collection of crayoned art work. Children had obviously occupied this house until fairly recently, but where were they now?

As she returned to the family room with the coffee, she saw that Blaine had refreshed his glass with three fingers of something that looked like straight scotch. Sam was waving a can of Coke in the air and talking, talking, talking. ". . . is the most incredible, extraordinary machine you've ever seen. Simple, elegant—it'll blow you away."

Blaine turned as he spotted Susannah. "So you're Joel Faulconer's daughter?" His consonants were slightly blurred at the edges.

"Yes, I am."

"He's a son of a bitch."

She shrugged noncommittally and held out a coffee mug, which he ignored. Taking a mug for herself, she sat in one of the remaining chairs. Something poked her in the hip. As

Sam resumed speaking, she reached behind her and pulled out a toy truck. For a moment she studied it, and then she quickly pushed it back where it had come from. The fresh indentations in the carpet and the evidence of the recent presence of children all pointed to the fact that Mitchell Blaine had marital problems, probably fairly recent ones, if she were to judge by his intoxicated condition.

Sam had been nervously passing his Coke can from one hand to the other while he spoke, and now he turned to her. "Mitch agreed to fly to San Francisco with us this afternoon."

"I did?"

"That's what you told me, Mitch," Sam replied. "Remember how anxious you are to see our computer."

Susannah rose quickly to her feet. Sam was lying. This was another one of his monumental bluffs. "Sam, I don't think—"

"Call the airlines and make certain the tickets are taken care of, will you? I want to leave as soon as possible."

Blaine drained his glass. "I'm not going anywhere until I have another drink."

Susannah was normally impatient with drunks, but something about Blaine touched her. Maybe when Sam realized that this man was in pain, he would leave him alone. She studied the fresh dents in the carpet and asked softly, "Has your wife been gone long?"

Blaine's expression closed up tight. "That's none of your business."

"I'm sorry. I'm sure this is a difficult time for you."

He reached for the scotch bottle. She realized that he was determined to drink himself into oblivion, and was equally determined that it be a solitary journey. As she watched the care with which he was performing each simple movement, she felt an unexplainable sense of protectiveness toward him. Even blindly drunk, he hadn't lost a shred of dignity.

She could tell that Sam was growing impatient, but for the first time that summer, the needs of a man other than Sam Gamble had caught her attention. "I don't think drinking is going to help," she said. "Perhaps I could call one of your friends."

Sam shot her a warning glance. Then he pushed her out of

the way and took the bottle of scotch from Blaine's hand. "You don't want to see any of your friends right now, do you, Mitch? Bunch of stiffs. The California climate will fix you right up. And once you see our computer, you won't even think about your wife anymore."

Susannah began to protest, but Sam gave her a look so murderous that she fell silent.

Two hours later they were on their way back to San Francisco with a nearly comatose Mitchell Blaine slumped in the seat between them. Every time he began to wake up, Sam ignored her protests and poured another drink for him. Long before they reached San Francisco, a terrible foreboding had taken hold of Susannah. Drunk, Mitchell Blaine was formidable. She couldn't imagine what he would be like when he was sober.

13

Blaine was not a happy man when he woke up the next morning. He staggered from Sam's bedroom into the hallway, where he bumped into Angela Gamble, who was wearing only a fluffy bath towel and nail polish. Angela was so startled that her towel slipped, which didn't bother her nearly as much as the fact that she hadn't had time to do her hair.

Blaine groaned and slumped into the wall, his solid body making a noisy thwack. In the kitchen, Susannah heard the sound and snatched up a water glass along with three aspirin before she raced back to the hallway.

He was still in the rumpled clothes he'd been wearing the day before. His jaw was covered with rusty stubble, his eyes bloodshot. Angela's towel was once again anchored under her arms, and she looked at Susannah quizzically. Since she had been asleep last night when Sam and Susannah had returned, she had no idea who her newest house guest was. Susannah gave her an I'll-tell-you-later-look and extended the aspirin and the water glass toward Blaine. He fumbled for them.

"Good morning," she whispered. As soon as he had swallowed, she gestured toward the bathroom. "I'll put some clean clothes out for you while you take a shower. There's a razor on the sink."

He gave her a bleary, hostile look. "Who *are* you?"

"We'll talk as soon as you've had your shower."

She gently steered him toward the bathroom and quietly shut the door. She wondered what he would think of Elvis.

After giving Angela a brief summary of the events of the last few days, she laid out a set of clean clothes from Blaine's overnight bag, which she had packed herself before they had ushered him out of his house the afternoon before. Then she returned to the kitchen, where she began frying bacon. She and Sam had decided it would be best if she fed Blaine to help him over the initial pain of his hangover and then brought him out to the garage. At the time, their plan had seemed logical, but now she dreaded the idea of dealing with Blaine by herself. Unfortunately, both Sam and Yank were busy setting up a crude version of the prototype of the self-contained computer that Yank had been working on, and she didn't have any choice.

Very little time passed before Blaine walked into the kitchen. A distinct feeling of dread settled over her at the difference in his appearance. All those liquor-softened edges had hardened. His jaw was smoothly shaven and rigidly set. Although his sandy hair was still damp from the shower, it had been precisely parted and combed into unquestioning obedience. His clothing was impeccable. Even after spending the night in a suitcase, neither his pale yellow sport shirt nor his expensively casual trousers had the nerve to retain a single wrinkle. His hangover had to be deadly, but he gave no sign that he was suffering. He was stiff and starchy, sternly correct, and coldly furious.

"How do you like your coffee?" she asked nervously, as she filled a mug.

"Black." He bit the word out, snapped it off, tossed it away.

She handed him a full mug and arranged the food she had prepared for him on a plate. She wasn't much of a cook and the eggs were a little too brown at the edges, but he didn't comment. Once again, she thought about fleeing to the safety of the garage, but she forced herself to pour a cup of coffee and carry it over to the table. To her astonishment,

Blaine stood and pulled out her chair. Instead of easing her mind, the display of courtesy was so chillingly correct that she grew even more uncomfortable.

She nervously sipped her coffee and observed his impeccable table manners. When Blaine was drunk, she had felt some sympathy for him, but now that he was sober, he reminded her too much of the men she had run away from.

He showed no inclination to speak, so she carefully reintroduced herself. He studied her for a moment, and she received the definite impression that he disliked everything he saw. Turning his attention away from her, he gazed intently out the dinette window. She could almost feel the effort of his self-control, and she braced herself for the inevitable.

"What is that, Miss Faulconer?" he asked coldly.

She followed his gaze. "Where?"

"In the corner of the yard."

"Do you mean the palm?"

"Palm?" He pressed his thumb against his temple and said sarcastically, "Palms don't grow in the state of Massachusetts, do they, Miss Faulconer?"

"No. No, they don't."

"Where *do* they grow, Miss Faulconer?"

She shifted uncomfortably in her seat and silently swore at Sam for abandoning her like this. "In California. You're near Menlo Park, south of San Francisco."

"Silicon Valley?" Each syllable was laced with hostility.

At that inauspicious moment, Angela came tripping into the kitchen, her heels clattering on the linoleum, her silver bangle bracelets jangling so loudly that he winced. She greeted Blaine and turned to Susannah. "Mrs. Albertson died yesterday, and I need to tint her hair before the viewing. Be a dear, will you? If Mrs. Leonetti croaks this morning, too, call me right away at the funeral home so I don't have to make an extra trip. They use the same color."

No sooner had she left the kitchen than the back door opened and Yank ambled in. He was holding a voltmeter in one hand and his shoe in the other. "The interface card," he announced to no one in particular. He limped past them and went into the living room.

Susannah didn't have to meet Blaine's eyes to read his

reaction. He was not the sort of man to tolerate personal eccentricities. She quickly rose from her chair. "Let me take you out to the garage so you can meet my partner. Actually, you met him yesterday, but—"

"I'm not going anywhere with you, Miss Faulconer." Blaine stood, his square, blunt features hard-edged and rigid. "I don't know what you did to me yesterday, and I'm not staying around this loony bin long enough to find out." He walked over to the telephone and snatched the receiver off the hook. His movements were relentlessly efficient as he dialed information, pulled a credit card from his wallet and called the airlines. While he was on hold, Susannah tried to explain to him as professionally as possible what they were doing. He ignored her.

Yank reappeared while Blaine was making arrangements for a limousine. She grabbed his arm and pushed him back into the living room. "Tell Sam I need him right away."

Yank looked blank.

She dug her fingers into his arm, barely restraining herself from rapping him on the head with her knuckles. "Get Sam. Do you understand what I'm saying, Yank? I need Sam. Do you understand me?"

"I'm not retarded, Susannah," he said quietly. "Of course I understand you." He went back outside.

Blaine had gone to fetch his suitcase. She followed him to the bedroom. "Please, Mr. Blaine, at least take a few minutes to see our computer. You won't regret it. I promise you."

"You're the one who's going to regret it, Miss Faulconer. I'm just beginning to realize that I have a legal case for breaking and entering and probably a few dozen other felonies." He snapped the lock on the suitcase she had packed for him the day before. "I don't know what sort of games you're playing, but you picked the wrong man. I've never liked your father and I don't like you."

"I don't like her old man, either," Sam said from the doorway, "but Suzie's okay."

Okay? She was only *okay?*

Sam sauntered into the room and leaned against the doorjamb. In comparison to Blaine's starchy demeanor, he looked wonderfully free and uninhibited.

"Look, Blaine," he said, "I know you're pissed, and if I was you, I would be, too. But the fact is, you don't have a damn thing waiting for you back in Boston except a bottle of scotch and a houseful of self-pity, so why don't you hear me out."

Every muscle in Blaine's body went rigid. He whipped the suitcase from the bed and stalked to the door, only to find that Sam had blocked it.

"Get out of my way."

Sam's eyes narrowed. "I've got the adventure of a lifetime out in that garage. A chance to change the world, to put your mark on the future, to paint your name across the sky in indelible ink. What you've done up till now is small-time compared with what I've got waiting for you. We're adventurers, Blaine. Soldiers of fortune and missionaries rolled into one. We're taking a joy ride into the future. A rocket-propelled rainbow right through the stars."

Blaine was not a man with a poet's soul, and his jaw clenched. "What in the hell are you talking about?"

"I'm talking about the fact that we've got a mission here. Maybe the final mission. A handful of American adventurers have been carving their names in the history books since the middle of the nineteenth century—the railroad barons, the oil men, the industrialists. They were renegade capitalists, and they weren't afraid of hard work, of risk, of daring. Men like Carnegie, Ford, Rockefeller. And do you know what, Blaine? We're going to be the last of them. Yank, Suzie, and me. We're going to be the last buccaneers of America's twentieth century."

Susannah wanted to press her hands to her head to keep it on her neck. She felt as if parts of herself were spinning. Where did Sam get these ideas? Where did he find the words?

Blaine seemed stunned. "You're nuts."

Sam bristled with hostility, then jerked back from the door. "Get the fuck out of my house."

"Sam . . ." she said warningly.

His lips thinned with contempt. "We're looking for somebody with guts and vision. I thought you might be that man, but I was obviously wrong."

She realized that Sam wasn't bluffing. Mitchell Blaine

hadn't lived up to his expectations, and—just like that—Sam was finished with him. She watched with consternation as Sam turned on his heel and left the room. Panic bolted through her—a panic that had little to do with their current situation. What a dangerously impatient man she had chosen to fall in love with—quick to judge, quick to dismiss. The kitchen door banged.

Blaine pushed past her and headed for the living room. "I'll wait for my limo outside," he said brusquely.

At that moment Yank stepped forward. Susannah hadn't seen him standing across the room near Elvis's portrait. Had he been listening to them all along, or was he merely caught up in the midst of some complex internal calculation? As she tried to think of what to say to Blaine, Yank walked over to him and took his suitcase. "I'll carry it for you," he muttered.

"You don't have to."

Yank paid no attention. He opened the front door. She followed them both outside, still frantically searching for some last-minute argument that would save the situation. Yank bumped into one of Angela's green ceramic frogs as he went down the front step. She saw the flash of a brown sock and then a blue one. He turned right and cut across the grass. Blaine made an inarticulate exclamation as Yank and his suitcase headed up the drive toward the garage.

"Hey!"

Yank didn't seem to hear. The corner of the suitcase hit the Duster.

Blaine turned to look at her, his expression incredulous. "Are all of you crazy?"

Susannah thought for a moment and then reluctantly nodded.

"Christ," he muttered. "Hey, you! Bring that back."

Yank continued toward the garage, his forward motion as immutable as the laws of physics. He and the suitcase disappeared inside.

Sam was standing by the workbench staring at the crude prototype when she and Blaine entered. Yank set down the suitcase, picked up a tattered manual and began looking through it as if he were all alone.

Blaine bent to reclaim his suitcase. "I don't know where

you people get your gall, but—" His words snapped off as he spotted the dazzling color patterns spreading across the screen. His fingers relaxed on the handle of the suitcase, and he slowly straightened.

"I thought you told me you were building a single-board computer," he said gruffly.

Sam didn't respond for a moment. He seemed to be making up his mind whether or not he would acknowledge the comment. Finally he replied, "We are."

Blaine gazed at the screen intently. "You can't get color like that on a single-board computer."

"We're running it off the CPU," Sam explained.

His suitcase forgotten, Blaine walked toward the workbench, every part of him focused on the machine in front of him. "I don't believe you. Open it up."

Sam gave Blaine a long, searching gaze, and then reached for a screwdriver. As he removed the case, Blaine began bombarding him with questions. Sam answered him tersely at first, and then became more animated as he warmed to the subject. The conversation quickly grew so technical that Susannah lost the thread, and before long even Sam began to have trouble providing the specific answers Blaine wanted. Yank stepped in, giving quiet, measured responses.

Susannah heard a horn honking, but none of the rest of them noticed. She hesitated for only a moment before she slipped outside and dismissed the limousine.

For the rest of the day, she sat at the assembly table stuffing the boards for the new orders they had picked up in Atlantic City and listening to the men talk. At one point she fetched drinks for them, and later she made sandwiches. By early afternoon, Blaine had a logic probe in his hand. As she set aside the board she had just completed, she looked over at the activity at the workbench and shook her head in bewilderment. Starchy, conservative Mitchell Blaine was a hardware freak just like her partners.

By seven o'clock Sam and Blaine were awash in male camaraderie. "Do you like pizza, Mitch?" Sam asked. "Or do we have to take you someplace with tablecloths?"

Blaine smiled good-naturedly. "I like pizza just fine."

Sam pointed his Coke can at Blaine, challenging him with it as if he held a six-gun. "How about rock and roll?"

"To tell you the truth, I'm more a country western man."

"You're kidding."

"A little tolerance for us old folks, Sam. We all have our foibles."

"Yeah, but country western is really pushing it."

Ten minutes later they were backing out of the driveway with Sam behind the wheel of the Duster and Blaine in the passenger seat. In the back Susannah held a spool of coaxial cable on her lap while Yank straddled an oscilloscope. They drove to Mom & Pop's, a pizza and burger place located in a strip mall between a dry cleaners and a Hallmark shop. The restaurant served beer by the pitcher and had video games, which made it a favorite of Sam's and Yank's. As they went inside, the uneasiness that had been building inside Susannah all afternoon grew stronger. She felt like an outsider, someone whose only function was fetching food and caring for the creature comforts of men.

They piled into the largest of the circular green vinyl booths, leaving her the place at the end and then steadfastly ignoring her. As Sam spoke, his dark eyes glittered with excitement. Even as her resentment toward him grew, she could feel that familiar core of warmth building up in the deepest parts of her body.

Just as the waitress arrived with their pizzas, Roberta slipped into the seat next to her. "I don't know why Yank and Sam like this place," she whispered, dabbing at the top of the nearest pizza with a paper napkin. "Everything is so greasy."

While the men talked electronics, Susannah listened to Roberta detailing her latest sinus infection. Her resentment fed on itself until she couldn't stand it any longer. Sam and Mitchell Blaine were acting as if they had known each other for years instead of two days. She decided she wasn't going to let them shut her out any longer, and when the next lull occurred in the conversation, she addressed Blaine. "Could you tell us what you know about attracting venture capital?"

Once again she received the impression of a chilling dislike. What had she done to this man? Why was he behaving so warmly toward Sam and treating her with such antipathy?

To her astonishment, Blaine turned to Sam as if her question had come from him. "Venture capital is tricky, Sam. You don't want to go after it until you absolutely have to. If you're not careful, you'll end up giving away the store."

"Does that happen very often?" she asked, refusing to be ignored.

Again he addressed Sam. "When Ken Olson and Harlan Anderson founded Digital Equipment Corporation in 1957, they gave up seventy percent of the business for a $100,000 investment. DEC is projecting a billion dollars in sales next year, so nobody's hurting, but it was still a lousy deal. Do you have a business plan?"

"I'm working on it," Sam replied.

Susannah stiffened. She was the one working on the business plan.

Using the information she had painstakingly gathered, Sam began discussing the specifics. Only when he forgot a statistic or some important fact did he turn to her. But as soon as she had supplied the information he needed, she ceased to exist.

"Come on, Susannah, let's go to the little girl's room." Roberta caught her arm in a death grip and began pulling her from the booth. Susannah had no choice but to accompany her, but she fumed inwardly as Roberta maintained a steady stream of chatter all the way to the rest room. Yank's girlfriend was a college graduate. Couldn't she, just once, make it to the rest room by herself?

As they walked through the swinging door, Roberta said, "Mr. Blaine seems really interested in SysVal. He's just what the guys have been looking for."

"Not just the guys," Susannah replied sharply. "I'm part of SysVal, too."

"Well, sure you are, Susannah. So am I. But it's different with us. We're in it because of them. I mean, I'm in it because of Yank and you're in it because of Sam. Right?" Roberta slipped into the stall. "Although to tell you the truth, I'm starting to get a little impatient with Yank. I'm not getting any younger, and I think it's about time we got married."

As Roberta babbled on, Susannah stared at herself in the

mirror. Was it true? Was she only part of SysVal because of Sam? Would she still want to pursue this impossible crusade if she weren't so desperately in love with him?

Her hand spun the faucet and water splashed from the bowl onto the front of her slacks. SysVal was hers, too, dammit! She had bought into Sam's dream. Somehow, along the way, she had begun to believe that it could happen. Sam had called them the last buccaneers of America's twentieth century. She wanted it to be true, and she wasn't going to let them take it away from her.

Leaving Roberta still chattering in the stall, she went back out to the booth, determined to make some sort of stand, but only Yank was there, scribbling a diagram on the back of a napkin. Blaine and Sam were playing video games. She watched as Sam let out a whoop and Blaine slapped him on the back, the uptight millionaire executive suddenly as carefree as a teenager. She could almost feel the affinity developing between them, that mysterious attraction of opposites as Mr. Establishment met Easy Rider.

She planned to talk to Sam when they got home—to tell him how she felt about being closed out—but he and Blaine sat up until dawn weaving futuristic fantasies of how everyday life might be reshaped by a small, affordable computer. They were still talking when she finally excused herself to go to bed.

The next day Blaine rented a car and moved into a hotel, but except for a few hours of sleep at night, he spent all his time with Sam. The kinship they had developed continued to exclude her. Although they argued frequently, and Blaine steadfastly resisted all of Sam's efforts to get him to commit to SysVal, the bond between the men grew daily. Each seemed to provide something the other lacked. Sam was attracted to Blaine's greater knowledge and breadth of experience—Blaine to Sam's vision and poetry.

When she was finally able to corner Sam alone, she tried to talk to him about how she felt, but he shrugged her off. "He's used to working with men, that's all. He's not ignoring you. You're making a big deal out of nothing."

But she didn't think so. Blaine's aversion to her seemed to run deeper than a general prejudice against women.

The next afternoon, while she was doing a shampoo for

Angela, she heard Blaine and Sam on the other side of the partition discussing the prototype. "The SysVal I is only a toy for hobbyists, Sam. If you want to build a company, you're going to have to base it on that self-contained computer. Ordinary people aren't going to want to hook up a television set and all sorts of other equipment to make their computer work. Everything has to be in one piece, and it has to be simple. As soon as you get the funding lined up, you have to get that machine on the market."

They talked about possible markets for the computer, and then Sam asked Blaine what he thought they should name it.

"The most obvious name is the SysVal II," Blaine replied.

"Yeah, I suppose. I just wish we could come up with something more dramatic."

Sam had never asked *her* about a name for the new computer. Her resentment gnawed deeper. She went to the library for a few hours to get away from both of them, but only ended up reading everything she could find about Mitchell Blaine. What she discovered depressed her further. In addition to being an outstanding engineer, he was considered a brilliant marketing strategist, respected by some of the most important business analysts in the country. He was everything they could have hoped for and more. Except there was no "they" as far as Blaine was concerned —only Sam and Yank.

"You can't go back to Boston," Sam told Blaine the day before he was planning to leave. "Boston's old history, man."

But the change of environment seemed to have healed some of Blaine's personal wounds, so that he was thinking more clearly. "I don't mean to insult you, Sam, but I can get a top position in just about any corporation in America. No matter how much fun I'm having, I'd be crazy to give that up to work with a couple of kids trying to run a company out of a garage. And I'm definitely not crazy."

Sam continued to badger Blaine all the way to the airport. Susannah sat in the backseat and listened as Sam asked Blaine the same question he had once asked her. "Are you in or out? I want to know."

Blaine gave Sam a good-natured slap on the back. "I'm out, Sam. I've told you that from the beginning. Do you have any idea what I was getting paid before I resigned? I was making almost a million dollars a year, plus stock options and more perks than you can imagine. You can't touch a package like that."

"Money's not everything, for chrissake. It's the challenge. Can't you see that? Besides, the money will come. It's just a matter of time."

Blaine shrugged him off. "I'm thinking about moving back to the Midwest. Chicago, probably. But I want to keep in touch. You helped me over a pretty bad time, and I won't forget it. I'll give you as much advice as I can on an informal basis."

"Not good enough," Sam persisted. "I want one hundred percent. And if you don't give it to me, you're going to regret it for the rest of your life."

But Mitchell Blaine didn't prove as easy to badger as Susannah had been. "No sale," he said.

198

14

Blaine was a fast reader with an almost photographic memory, and he devoured the printed word like other people consumed junk food. But he had been looking at the same page in *Business Week* since he had left San Francisco on the Boston-bound 747, and he didn't have the slightest idea what he had read.

He kept thinking about Sam and Yank and what they were doing in the garage. He couldn't remember being so excited by anything in years. They were doomed to fail, of course. Still, he couldn't help but admire them for making the attempt.

The flight attendant serving the first-class passengers was covertly studying him. She bent forward to speak to a passenger in the row across from him and her straight skirt tightened across her hips. As a married man, he had always been scrupulously faithful, but his days of being Mr. Straight Arrow were over, and he imagined those hips beneath his own.

She turned toward him and asked him if he needed anything. The whiff of her perfume killed his arousal as effectively as a cold shower. She was wearing an old-fashioned floral scent reminiscent of his aunts' bathpowder.

He had smelled like that bathpowder himself for years—not because he had used it, but because the scent clung to everything in that rambling old house in Clearbrook, Ohio.

He shut his eyes, remembering the bathpowder and his aunts, and the oppressive, cloying softness of his upbringing.

"Mi-*chull!* Mi-*chull!*" Every afternoon at four-thirty one of his aunts stood on the front porch of the house on Cherry Street and called him inside for piano practice.

Their names were Theodora and Amity. They were his father's relatives, and the only ones willing to take on the responsibility of raising an asthmatic seven-year-old boy after his parents were killed in a fiery automobile accident one Easter Sunday.

They were maiden ladies. Although they insisted they were unmarried by choice, not because they disliked men, in actuality there were only three males in the town of Clearbrook of whom they entirely approved—their pastor, their assistant pastor, and Mr. Leroy Jackson, their handyman. From the moment they set eyes on the small boy who had come to live with them, they were determined to make little Mitchell Blaine the fourth male in Clearbrook to receive their unqualified approval.

It was all a matter of civility.

"Mi-*chull!*"

He dragged his eleven-year-old feet reluctantly up the sidewalk. Behind him, he heard Charlie and Jerry calling out taunts just loudly enough so that he could hear, but Miss Amity Blaine couldn't.

"Sissy boy. Sissy boy. Run home and get your diapers changed."

They always said that about the diapers. They knew he couldn't play sports because of his asthma, and they knew that he had to go home to practice the piano, but they always said he was going home to get his diaper changed. He wanted to curl up his fists and smash their faces, but he wasn't allowed to fight. Fighting might make him wheeze, and the aunts got scared when he started to wheeze. Sometimes, though, he thought that his aunts might be using the wheezing as an excuse to keep him clean, because more than anything in the world, they hated dirt. They also hated name-calling, dogs, sweat, scabby knees, sports, television, curses, and everything else that went along with being a boy growing up in Clearbrook, Ohio, in the 1950s.

His aunts loved books and music, church bazaars and crochet. They loved flowers and beautiful manners. And they loved him.

The hinge on the gate squeaked as he opened it. Everything in the old house squeaked, rattled, and clucked.

"Mi-*chull*, Mi-*chull*."

Aunt Amity reached out for him as he hit the steps. He tried to make a fast dodge to the side before she grabbed him, but she was too quick. She blocked the doorway with her bony, birdlike body and drew him into her arms. While Jerry and Charlie watched in the distance, she planted a kiss on the top of his head. He could hear their derisive hoots in the background.

"You've been running again, haven't you?" she said, tidying his already tidy hair, straightening his pristine white shirt collar, fussing over him, always fussing. "Dear, dear, Mitchell. I can hear that wheezing. When Theodora discovers that you've been running, I'm afraid she won't let you go out to play tomorrow after school."

That was the way they disciplined him. One of them would catch him in a misdemeanor and blame the punishment on the other. The punishments were always gentle and unimaginative—no play after school, sentences to be written fifty times. They thought it was the effectiveness of their methods that had turned him into the best-behaved boy in Clearbrook. They didn't understand that he tried desperately to please them because he loved them so much. He had already lost the mother and father he adored. In the deepest part of him, he was afraid that if he wasn't very, very good, he might lose his aunts, too.

He washed his hands without being prompted and settled himself behind the piano, where he stared at the keyboard with loathing. He had no musical ability. He hated the songs that he had to practice about sunshiny days and good little Indians. He wanted to be out with the other guys playing ball.

But he wasn't allowed to play ball because of his asthma. The wheezing didn't bother him much anymore—not like when he was a real little kid—but he couldn't convince the aunts of that. And so, while the other guys were out playing ball, he was playing scales.

But the scales weren't the worst. Saturday mornings were the worst.

The Misses Amity and Theodora Blaine supported themselves by teaching piano and giving deportment lessons. Every Saturday morning at eleven o'clock, the daughters of Clearbrook's best families dressed in their Sunday frocks and donned white gloves to knock politely on the Misses Blaines' front door.

Wearing a suit and tie, Mitchell stood miserably in the hallway next to his aunts and watched the girls enter. One by one they dropped a small curtsy and said, "How do you do, Miss Blaine, Miss Blaine, Mitchell. Thank you so much for inviting me."

He was required to bend neatly from the waist in front of girls like fat little Cissy Potts, who sat behind him in his sixth-grade class and wiped her boogers on the back of his seat. He had to say things like, "How delightful to see you again, Miss Potts."

And then he had to take her hand.

The girls settled in the living room, where they were instructed in such skills as the proper method of performing an introduction, accepting an invitation to dance, and pouring tea. He was their guinea pig.

"Thank you, Miss Baker, I'd love a cup of tea," he said.

Snotty little Penelope Baker would pass him his cup of watered-down tea and stick her tongue out at him when the aunts weren't looking.

The girls hated the Misses Blaines' deportment class, and they hated him in turn.

He spent his Saturday mornings gracefully balancing thin china saucers on his knee and taking himself to faraway places where no females were allowed. Places where a man could spit in the dirt, scratch himself, and own a dog. While he took Mary Jane Simmons's hand and led her to the center of the living room rug for a dance, he dreamed of feeling his legs fly out from under him and his hip hitting hard against the dirt as he slid into home plate. He dreamed of going up for a slam dunk and hanging off the hoop. He dreamed of hunting rifles, fishing rods, soft flannel shirts, and blue jeans. But the aunts' cluckings and warnings and sighings held him in gentle, unbreakable bondage.

Only in the classroom was it possible to let himself go, and no matter how much the other boys taunted him, he refused to rein in his quick mind. He answered questions in class, did extra-credit projects, and got the best marks in sixth grade.

Teacher's pet. Teacher's pet. Diaper Boy is teacher's pet.

When he was fourteen, his voice dropped and his muscles thickened. Almost overnight, he shot up until he towered over his aunts' small, birdlike bodies. His wheezing disappeared, but they continued to pet him. They made him wear a white shirt and tie for his first day of high school. Freshman year brought academic brilliance and gut-wrenching, aching loneliness.

The summer before his sophomore year, he was walking home from helping his aunts teach Vacation Bible School when a moving van and a paneled station wagon pulled up to the white clapboard house next to his own. The doors of the station wagon opened, and a man and a woman got out. Then a pair of long, suntanned legs emerged, followed by frayed denim cutoffs. He held his breath and watched as a beautiful girl close to his own age appeared before him. Her hair was arranged in a sprayed blond bubble kept neatly back from her face with a madras headband. She had a pert nose and soft mouth. A man's blue work shirt clung to a pair of high pointy breasts.

She turned to study the neighborhood and her eyes fell on him. He waited for the condescending sneer, the look of superiority, and could barely believe it when she gave him a shy smile. He walked closer, wishing the bible and curriculum book he was holding at his side would become invisible.

"Hi," she said.

"How do you do?" he replied, and immediately cursed himself for not being more casual. But he didn't know how to be easy like the other guys.

She looked down at the sidewalk. He spotted a little speck of dandelion fluff caught in the top of her blond bubble, and had to fight back a nearly irresistible urge to brush it away. As she continued to stare at the sidewalk, he realized that she was shy, and he felt a great surge of protectiveness toward her.

"I'm Mitchell Blaine," he said, using the skills that had become second nature to him after nearly a decade of deportment classes. "I live next door. Welcome to the neighborhood."

She looked back up at him. Only a dab of soft pink lipstick remained at the bow of her upper lip. She had eaten the rest away. "Mitch?" she inquired.

No one had ever called him Mitch except the parents he barely remembered. He was Mitchell. Mitchell—Mitchell—Diaper Boy.

"Yes," he said. "My name is Mitch."

"I'm Candy Fuller."

They stood on the front sidewalk and talked awkwardly. Candy and her family were from Chillicothe, and she would be a sophomore at Clearbrook High that September, part of the class of '64, just like he was. Candy had been a junior varsity cheerleader at her old school, and she wanted to cheer for Clearbrook this year. When they finally parted, Mitch felt as if his life had begun all over again.

For the rest of that summer they met every evening after dinner on the old metal bench beneath his aunts' grape arbor. Candy had to wash the dishes before she could come outside, and she always smelled like Joy detergent. They sat on the bench with the flat dark grape leaves curling about their heads and they talked.

Candy spoke of the friends she had left behind in Chillicothe and her worries that she might not be able to make the varsity cheerleading squad at Clearbrook High. Mitch talked about how he'd like to have his own car and whether or not he would be able to get a scholarship to college. He kept the darker bitterness of his life hidden away, out of fear that her affection for him would turn to disgust.

The adoration in Candy Fuller's deep blue eyes grew stronger every evening. Her reaction left Mitch breathless. No girl had ever looked at him that way. His stomach cramped as he remembered that Candy was from Chillicothe. She didn't know about the sissy boy, the diaper baby who wasn't allowed to play sports. All she saw when she gazed at him was a tall, lean fifteen-year-old, with sandy hair, light blue eyes, and a broad, handsome face.

They lived in splendid isolation through those dog days of summer, drenched in the scent of grapes and Joy and the infinite, unspoken promise of young love. The night before school started, they were quieter than normal, each sensing the changes that the next day would bring. Candy scratched a thin white line in the suntan on the top of her thigh.

"I don't hate moving here anymore, Mitch. This month, it's been special. Meeting you. But I'm scared about tomorrow. I'll bet all the girls at school are crazy about you."

He shrugged, trying to act cool, although his heart was thumping so hard it was painful.

She studied the toe of her once-white sneaker and her voice began to quiver. "I'm afraid you won't still like me after school starts."

He couldn't believe it. This soft, pretty, bubble-haired cheerleader with her sweet mouth and pointy breasts was afraid that she would lose him. The stirring of emotions that gripped his chest was the sweetest pain he had ever experienced. "I'll still like you tomorrow," he murmured. "I'll always like you."

She tilted her face up to him, and he realized that she wanted him to kiss her. Closing his eyes, he leaned forward and touched that sweet Candy-scented mouth with his own. Although dark, sexual thoughts of her had tormented him for weeks, the kiss was pure. It was a gesture of adoration, a symbol of promise, a farewell to summer.

"Will you walk me to school tomorrow?" she asked when they finally drew apart. Her eyes were large and beseeching, as if she still wasn't certain that he cared for her.

"Of course," he replied. He would have walked with her to the moon.

And then they kissed again. This time it was different. Their mouths met hungrily. Their young bodies joined with a raw, untried passion. He felt the thrusts of her young breasts against his chest and the small bumps of her spine beneath his fingertips. Dark longings raced through his body and heated his blood. A man's need surged through him, its urgency blocking out everything but the feel of Candy's body pressed next to his.

"You can touch my chest if you want," she whispered.

He couldn't believe he'd heard her right. For several seconds he did nothing, and then he gingerly slid his hand between their bodies. The well-worn fabric of her blouse was soft beneath his palm. When she didn't stop him, he let his hand creep upward, still staying outside her blouse. He felt the bump that marked the bottom edge of her bra and waited in agony for her to push him away.

But she didn't move. He slid his fingers higher until he touched the slope of her breast. Through the fabric of her blouse and the sponginess of her padded bra, his hand closed over her. He groaned and held the soft mound as if it were a fragile baseball. They kissed and he gently kneaded it. The Fuller's back porch light snapped on and they sprang apart.

Her eyes were misty with the depth of her feelings for him. "I never let a boy do that to me," she whispered. "Don't tell anybody."

He shook his head and silently pledged to keep the precious gift she had given him their secret forever.

At seven-thirty the next morning, she met him on her front porch. He could see that she was embarrassed about what had happened between them the night before, and he was overwhelmed by her fragility. She was so vulnerable, so needful of his protection. As he watched the tip of her tongue flick nervously over her lips, he determined to shield her from all the spiteful demons at Clearbrook High.

"Do I look all right?" she asked, as if her entire future depended on his response.

He took in her white blouse with its gold circle pin on the collar and her pleated green plaid skirt. "You'll be the prettiest girl in the sophomore class," he replied earnestly.

They walked to school hand in hand, her small fingers curled through his bigger ones. He felt the morning sun warming his face, and shortened his strides so she could keep up. His shoulders drew back. A slight swagger appeared in his walk. With Candy Fuller walking at his side, he was no longer Mitchell Blaine. He was Mitch. Mitch the Indestructible. Mitch the Mighty. Mitch the Manliest of the Manly.

"Do you think the other kids will like me?" she asked.

An uneasiness passed through him, a vague foreboding. But he was Mitch the Fearless, Mitch the Brave, and he shook it off. "You shouldn't pay too much attention to what the other kids think."

He could see that his response mystified her, and he remembered that she was a cheerleader—part of a group that was dedicated to conformity. His uneasiness grew.

"Don't you think they'll like me?" Anxiety had crumpled her brow.

"Of course they will."

The American flag cracked in the morning breeze as, hand in hand, they walked into the school. They were in different homerooms, and he had promised to stay with her until second bell. As they walked down the main hallway, he was lulled by the joy of entering Clearbrook High with Candy Fuller at his side, and so he wasn't prepared when he rounded the corner by the sophomore lockers and the taunts began.

"Here's Mi-*chull*," the boys clucked, imitating his aunts. "Mi-*chull*, Mi-*chull*." There were five of them leaning against the metal locker doors, five scrubbed-up would-be rebels made omnipotent by banding together.

"Who's that you got there, Mi-*chull*? Hey, baby, come on over here and meet some real men."

Candy looked first at the boys and then at Mitch. She was bewildered by their behavior. None of the boys was as good-looking at Mitch, none as tall and well-built. Why were they taunting him?

Mitch tried to appear tolerant, as if they were children and he was a world-weary adult. "Why don't you guys grow up?"

They hooted with laughter and catcalls, pounded their fists in merriment against the locker at his absurd attempt to defy them.

Candy grew more befuddled. She gazed at him, accusation and betrayal beginning to form in her eyes. She had thought he was one of the special, one of Clearbrook's chosen. Now she realized that wasn't true. She had somehow managed to ally herself with an outcast.

He felt her fingers slackening in his and panic filled him. She wanted to get away from him, to distance herself. In those few seconds, everything changed. Without knowing any of the facts, without understanding a single detail of his past, she understood that he was a social pariah and that she should not have let herself be seen with him. He was going to lose Candy Fuller, and with that knowledge came the certainty that he didn't want to live anymore. If he couldn't be Mitch the Brave with Candy Fuller at his side, he didn't want to be anyone.

The girls had gathered around the boys, and they were laughing, too. Their amusement was easy and untroubled. Mitch had been the target of their jokes for so long that their attacks upon him were inspired more by habit than venom. They even felt a distant sort of fondness for the boy who had been the source of so much amusement over the years.

Candy was pulling at his hand now, trying desperately to get away from him, to take the small steps that would transport her from the land of the untouchable to the arena of the acceptable.

"Mi-*chull*, Mi-*chull*," Charlie Shields called out in a high, good-humored falsetto. "Come here and get your diapers changed."

A blue-black vortex of rage and pain consumed him. The rage caught him in its grasp and sank its talons through his flesh. A cry built inside him as he let that small, sweet hand go, a roar of outrage at this loss of his fresh new manhood. And with that roar, years of dilligent self-control gave way inside him.

He launched himself at the boys. They were five and he was one, but he didn't care. It was a suicide attack, a kamikaze mission with no hope for personal survival, but only a distant yearning for some posthumous dignity of the spirit. They laughed as he came toward them. They catcalled at the hilarity of Mitchell Blaine attacking them. But then they saw the expression on his face and their mockery died.

He began to throw wild, vicious punches. The girls

screamed and a crowd gathered in response to the invisible radar that instantly detected a hallway fight.

Charlie Shields shrieked in pain as Mitch's fist snapped the cartilage in his nose and sent blood spurting out. Artie Tarpey gave a grunt of agony as he felt a rib crack. Mitch was indiscriminate with his violence, propelled by a rage that had been building inside him for nearly a decade. He hit anything he could touch, and barely felt the blows he suffered in return. Two of the boys were finally able to pin him long enough to slam him into a locker. He smashed the thin metal door with his body and then hurled himself back at them.

The boys had fought among themselves since they were children, and there were unwritten rules of conduct they all followed. But Mitch hadn't been part of their fights, and he didn't know their rules. Now the boys found themselves the targets of a vicious, single-minded attack that was outside their realm of experience. Mitch brought Herb McGill down with a flying tackle and pinned him to the tiled floor. Charlie, holding his broken nose and whimpering with pain, tried to rescue Herb, but Mitch shook him away.

It took three male teachers to put an end to the violence, and even then Mitch didn't give up easily. As the men dragged him away to the principal's office, he refused to meet the eyes of Candy Fuller.

The aunts were summoned. They cried when they saw him slumped forward on the office bench with his bruised elbows propped on his thighs, bloody hands dangling between his splayed knees. His white starched shirt was torn and gore-spattered, his eye swollen closed. He looked up at their frail, birdlike frames and saw their fear for him.

Aunt Theodora recovered before her sister and advanced like a brigadier general upon the principal. "Explain this outrage at once, Jordan Featherstone. How could you allow something like this to happen to our Mitchell?"

"*Your* Mitchell just sent three of his classmates to the emergency room at the hospital," Mr. Featherstone replied sharply. "He's suspended for the next two weeks."

The aunts listened in horror to the details of their nephew's hallway brawl. They gazed at Mitch, first with bewilderment and then condemnation. Amity's eyes grew fierce behind her wire-rimmed spectacles. "You will come home with us at once, Mitchell," she ordered. "We will deal with this in private."

"We are extremely disappointed in you," Theodora exclaimed. "Extremely!"

He could see them conjuring up their most terrible punishment. A stern lecture, a hundred sentences instead of fifty. His heart contracted with love for them and regret at the distress he had inflicted. "Go on home," he said gently. "I'll be there in a little while."

Flabbergasted, they repeated their commands. He shook his head sadly. When they saw that they couldn't sway him, Amity tried to tidy the torn shoulder seam of his shirt, and Theodora told Jordan Featherstone that his school was full of hooligans.

Mr. Featherstone began to lecture him, but Mitch had something else to do. He apologized politely to the three adults. "I'm sorry," he said. "I don't mean to be rude, but there's something I have to do."

He walked out of the school and made his way on foot to the emergency room at Clearbrook Memorial Hospital.

There he found Artie Tarpey, Herb McGill, and Charlie Shields, who was holding an ice pack to his nose. Mitch sat quietly with them while they waited their turn to get patched up. They talked about the Warrior's football team and whether they had a shot at division finals. They talked about the sophomore teachers and the tunes on the Top Forty. None of them mentioned the fight.

That fall Mitch broke forever his aunts' gentle domination. He landed a part-time job at a local television repair shop and fell in love with the relentlessly masculine world of electronics. When his school suspension was over, he patiently endured all of their cluckings and twitterings, then kissed them affectionately on their papery cheeks and went out to train with the football team. Although the squad had already been chosen, his dogged persistence won him the admiration of the coaches, and by the end of the season he was playing.

In the next two years Mitch Blaine re-created football at Clearbrook High. No one had ever seen a boy play the game like he did. He wasn't the fastest wide receiver in the state, but he was so strong, so ferocious in his concentration, so single-minded in his race for the goal line, that it was almost impossible to stop him. The college scouts began sending him love letters.

Off the playing fields, Mitch was still the most well-behaved boy in Clearbrook, Ohio—quiet, polite, conservatively dressed, academically brilliant. The girls who had once laughed at him left notes in his locker and fought with each other for the right to ask him to a turnabout dance. One of those who fought for his attention was Candy Fuller. He was consistently courteous to her and relentlessly unforgiving.

In a cabin on the shores of Lake Hope, he and Penny Baker lost their virginities together. The experience was better than anything he had ever imagined, and he determined to repeat it as often as possible.

"Would you raise your seat back, Mr. Blaine? We're getting ready to land."

The flight attendant who smelled like his aunts' bathpowder stood next to his seat. He still missed those dear old ladies. They had died a few years ago, Amity passing on within three days of Theodora.

The flight attendant leaned over him deferentially. "Is Boston home, or are you here on business?"

"Home," he replied, although it no longer felt that way.

She chatted with him for a few minutes and couldn't quite hide her disappointment when he didn't ask for her phone number.

Mitch had long ago accepted the fact that he had a strong effect on women, but he hadn't given the matter much thought since his undergraduate days at Ohio State. He still didn't understand that the contrasts in his nature were what fascinated them. Women were drawn to his quiet courtesy and impeccable manners, but it was the juxtaposition of those gentler qualities with an almost ferocious masculinity that had made so many of them fall in love with him over the years.

Mitch didn't worry about his masculinity any more. He didn't have to. But when he had graduated from high school, it had been very much on his mind. He remembered leaving his aunts behind for his freshman year at Ohio State, and then he remembered his sophomore year, when he finally found the father figure he had been seeking for so long—Wayne Woodrow Hayes, the Buckeyes' legendary football coach.

Mitch smiled and shut his eyes. While the plane circled Logan Airport, he thought back to those Saturday afternoons when he had carried the football to glory in the horseshoe-shaped stadium on the banks of the Olentangy River. Even now he could hear the chimes of "Carmen Ohio" ringing in his mind. But most of all, he remembered Woody.

Everybody called the Buckeye football players dumb. A lot of them *were* dumb. Woody knew that. But he didn't like everybody else knowing it. When Woody first saw the hard-hitting, clean-living boy from Clearbrook, Ohio, in action, his eyes got misty. Not only did Mitch play the kind of single-minded, no-holds-barred football that Woody had invented, but he was carrying a 3.7 grade average in Electrical Engineering to go along with it.

Not Phys Ed.

Not Communication Arts.

Electrical Engineering.

Woody was a scholar, and he loved intelligent minds. His hobby was military history, and he laced his pregame speeches with references to his favorite men—Napoleon, Patton, and General Douglas MacArthur.

Mitch Blaine knew who they were.

Every Buckeye football player who wore the scarlet and gray respected and feared Woody Hayes, but that didn't keep them from joking about his old-fashioned sentiments behind his back. Mitch saw the humor in Woody, but he still loved listening to him talk. Woody believed in God, America, and Ohio State, in that order. He believed in back-breaking hard work and a strict moral code. And, gradually, Woody Hayes helped define for Mitch what it meant to be a man.

Mitch grew close to the crusty coach. Even after he was graduated from Ohio State and had gone on to MIT for his master's degree, he still telephoned him. One evening in the summer of 1969, Mitch called with the biggest news of his life.

"Coach, I've decided to get married."

There was a long silence on the other end of the phone. "That red-haired young lady you brought over for me to meet the last time you were in Columbus?"

"Yes. Louise."

"I remember." Woody seemed to be collecting his thoughts. "She's from a rich family, you told me."

"Her people came to Boston with the Pilgrims."

Another long silence, and then Woody delivered his verdict. "She has thin blood, son. I advise you to reconsider."

Like a fool, Mitch hadn't listened.

Mitch's house smelled damp and empty when he let himself inside. He set his suitcase down and wished it could all be different, that he could walk upstairs and find David, his five-year-old son, and Liza, his three-year-old daughter, curled beneath the covers in their bedrooms. But those bedrooms were empty now, stripped of their furniture and the sweet scramble of toys he used to stumble over when he kissed them good night.

His housekeeper had cleaned up the mess from his alcoholic oblivion. As he carried his suitcase upstairs, he felt a curl of disgust in his gut from all that self-pity he had been wallowing in. During the first few weeks after Louise had left with the children, he had been able to function normally. But the house had been so empty at night that he had begun keeping company with a bottle of scotch, not the best companion for someone who had never been much of a drinker. Eventually, he had conceived an alcohol-inspired plan to stop working, buy a boat, and sail around the Caribbean for a while. He had managed to implement the first part of his plan, but the second and third parts had required too much energy. And then Sam Gamble had kidnapped him, and the small wonders he had seen in that garage in Silicon Valley had forced him to rejoin the world.

As he stripped off his clothes and turned on the shower, he

reminded himself that Sam Gamble hadn't been his only kidnapper. His mouth tightened with displeasure as he thought of Susannah Faulconer. Of all the women Sam could have taken up with, Susannah Faulconer had been the worse possible choice. Mitch knew from experience, since he had married a woman just like her. Susannah and Louise even looked a little alike. Both were tall and slender. They had discreet private-school voices and carried themselves with that special air of composure that only those born into privileged families seem to possess. And both obviously got a kick out of slumming with men who were their social inferiors.

He had even considered warning Sam about Susannah, but Mitch hadn't listened to Woody, and Sam wouldn't listen, either. Only experience would teach Sam that women like Susannah Faulconer were dilettantes. They were fascinated by men who weren't part of their upbringing, but that fascination faded in the day-to-day drudgery of living.

"I'm tired of being married to you, Mitch," Louise had said one evening a month ago, when he'd come home from work. The sight of his cool, sophisticated wife sitting on the couch toying with a set of car keys was imprinted on his mind forever.

"We don't have anything in common," she had gone on. "You like to work. I like to go to parties. I want to have fun some place other than in the bedroom for a change."

Mitch had refused to admit even to himself that he no longer loved her. Their marriage had its roots in a youthful attraction of opposites instead of commonality of interests, but it was too late to remedy the mistake. They had children, she was a good mother, and marriage was forever.

"If you're unhappy, we'll make changes," he had said immediately. "We're a family, Louise, and we made vows to each other. If we have problems, let's get some counseling to help us work them out."

"Why bother?" she had retorted. Then she had told him that she had already taken the children to her mother's and she was on her way to join them. Picking up her purse, she had left the house without another word.

And that was what he couldn't forgive. She had simply

walked out, abandoning a seven-year marriage without making any effort to solve the problems between them.

Mitch understood bored socialites like Susannah Faulconer. He knew what they could do to a man, and he pitied Sam Gamble for what lay in store for him. But at the same time, he couldn't stop thinking about the excitement taking place in that Silicon Valley garage.

15

• •

Susannah was sitting at the assembly table soldering some connections on the board she had just finished stuffing when Mitchell Blaine walked back into her life. It had been nearly a month since he had returned to Boston, and although he and Sam had talked on the phone a number of times, Mitch had shown no signs of changing his mind about joining them. Now, as he gave her a coldly courteous nod, she experienced an uneasy combination of hope and dismay.

Sam was obviously glad to see him, but he refused to give anything away. His lip curled as he surveyed Mitch's conservative navy-blue suit and maroon tie. "Somebody die? You look like a fuckin' pall bearer."

"All of us don't have your flair for fashion." Mitch gazed with distaste at Sam's ragged jeans and a faded T-shirt that was stretched nearly to transparency over Sam's chest.

Sam grinned. "So what are you doing out here?"

"I had an interview this morning. I thought I'd stop by to invite you and Yank for dinner. There's a French place in Palo Alto, or we could go into the city if you prefer."

Susannah's grip tightened on her soldering iron and she glanced sharply at Sam to see how he would react to the fact she had been neatly cut from the picture.

Once again Sam let his eyes rove over Mitch's business suit. "Let's make it Mom and Pop's."

She waited for him to say more—to mention her—but he didn't. Mitch agreed to Sam's choice of restaurant. They chatted for a while and looked over the latest work Yank had done on the prototype.

Susannah confronted Sam as soon as Mitch left, but he shrugged off her indignation. "Give him time," he said. "Once he gets to know you, he'll change his mind. You're too sensitive." He reached for her, ready to quiet her protests with kisses, but a new stubbornness took hold of her, and she resisted him. For some unfathomable reason Mitch disliked her, and he was giving no indication that he intended to change his mind. Getting up stiffly from the table, she went into the house so she could collect her thoughts. Sam didn't follow her.

That evening, she took her clothes into the bathroom and got dressed. She told herself she wouldn't let them dismiss her without a fight, but courage still didn't come easily, and she fumbled with the button at the waistband of her skirt, and then snagged her hair in the inexpensive loose-knit mauve sweater she had bought at Angela's favorite outlet store. Brushing her hair to the nape of her neck, she tied it back with a scarf. Angela came into the bathroom and fluffed the curls that had formed around her face.

"Don't let them push you around, Suzie," she said, attuned as always to what was happening around her. "Stick to your guns." She clipped a pair of beaded pink and purple triangles to Susannah's lobes. "I won fifty dollars at the slots when I was wearing these in Vegas last June. They'll bring you luck."

Susannah smiled and gave her a fierce, impulsive hug. She felt closer to Sam's mother than she had ever felt to her own.

Yank and Sam were both in the kitchen. Sam looked surprised when she walked in, as if he hadn't expected her to come with them. The sharp corners of the pink and purple triangles banged into the hollows beneath her ears.

"I don't know why you're making such a big deal of this," he said defensively. "It's just a meeting."

Instead of replying, she walked out to the car.

Mitch was already at the restaurant when they arrived. He had traded in his suit for dark brown slacks and a gold sport shirt. A Rolex gleamed in the sandy-brown hairs at his wrist. He stood as she approached, but made no attempt to hide his displeasure at her appearance. The men slid into the booth on each side of him. She took the seat on the end, keeping her back as straight as Grandmother Bennett's yardstick.

"This is supposed to be a business meeting, Sam," he said, nodding in her direction.

"That's why I'm here," she replied before Sam could answer.

The jukebox began to play a Linda Ronstadt hit. "Roberta isn't coming," Yank said abruptly.

Susannah gave him a sharp glance. Yank was hardly given to idle chatter, so he obviously wanted to make a point, but she had no idea whether he was indicating that she shouldn't be here either or whether he was making a distinction between the two women in her favor.

He began to draw an abstract figure in the moisture on the beer pitcher—another one of his diagrams. Did he design circuitry even in his sleep? she wondered. For the moment, it was easier to watch Yank's finger than deal with the tension that permeated the booth.

A circle appeared. A transistor maybe?

Two dots. A curve.

Yank had drawn a happy face.

"So . . . did you take a job with IBM yet?" Sam's voice snapped with sarcasm.

"I've been asked," Mitch replied as the waitress approached with the pizzas he had ordered. "Actually, I've had a number of interesting offers in the past few weeks. A lot of high-tech companies, naturally, but Detroit, too. And the soft drink people have been pretty persuasive." As they ate, he detailed several of his offers, including one from Cal Theroux at FBT.

Sam listened with increasing impatience, then pushed away his pizza and leaned back in the booth. "Sounds safe. Safe and predictable."

Mitch gave him a long stare. "It's a miracle that you've managed to keep SysVal alive this long. You don't know anything about selling a product. You don't have any organization, any definable market. Your company is so eccentric that it's a joke." He went on and on, detailing their shortcomings until Sam's mouth had tightened in a grim line and Susannah felt as if someone was banging her head into the wall. Yank drew three more happy faces.

Finally, Sam had had enough. He wadded up his paper napkin and tossed it down on the table. "If we're such a joke, then why did you come back, you son of a bitch?"

For the first time, Mitch seemed to relax. A smile spread slowly over his broad, good-looking face. "Because you hooked me. You hooked me good. SysVal is all I've been able to think about since I went back to Boston. I told myself I needed a vacation. I've tried to take some time off. But nothing's worked."

Sam sat slowly upright, his expression cautious, afraid to hope. "Are you telling me—"

"I'm in." Mitch shook his head. "For better or worse, I'm in all the way."

Yank smiled. Sam let out a whoop that startled one of the waitresses so badly she dropped a pie.

"That's great! God, that's really great!"

"We have to deal first," Mitch said, holding up his hand. "I have some conditions."

Sam could barely contain his excitement. "Name them."

"I want an equal partnership with you and Yank. Each of us takes one third of SysVal. In return, I'll guarantee a $100,000 line of credit at the banks. That'll keep us away from the venture capitalists for a while." He opened a leather folder he had brought with him and pulled out a gold pen. "Yank, you have to leave Atari. The SysVal I is only a toy. Our future is locked up in that prototype you're building, and you have to commit to it full-time."

"I like Atari," Yank said. "I have this new game coming out in a couple of months."

"Are you crazy?" Sam exclaimed. "This is a hell of a lot more important than a goddamn video game."

"I don't know about that, Sam," Yank replied earnestly. "It's one heck of a good game."

Sam rolled his eyes to the ceiling and turned to Mitch. "I'll take care of him. I promise."

Mitch began to discuss contingencies, eventual strategies for venture capital, a marketing plan, but Susannah didn't hear anything more. All the muscles in her torso seemed to have contracted into tight, painful bands. At the same time, her legs were rubbery and her pulse was beating much too fast. On and on they went—their exclusive male chatter cutting her out and pushing her aside like a whore who has been well-used and is no longer wanted. She drew herself up and tried to calm her heartbeat, but her voice was unsteady. "What about me?" she said.

Sam immediately grew cautious. "Let's talk about this later."

No scenes, Susannah. Be good. Be polite. The voices of the past whispered their earnest cautious messages. But she had learned brashness from Sam Gamble, and she pushed the voices away. "No. I think we need to talk about it now, since this concerns everyone here."

Mitch crossed his arms over his chest and looked irritated. "Another item on my list of conditions, Sam. Keep your woman troubles away from the company."

Susannah could feel her cheeks burning. Sam put all his weight on one hip and pulled Yank's car keys from his opposite pocket. "Look, Suzie. Take the car. I'll meet you at home in a couple of hours and we'll go over this."

"No!" She found herself on her feet, standing at the end of the booth and glaring down at the three of them. A pulse throbbed in her neck beneath skin as tight as a drumhead. She was dizzy and reckless with anger, uncaring of the scene she was creating for the people in the neighboring booths. "None of this is satisfactory to me, Mr. Blaine. None of it."

He waved his hand dismissively. "Miss Faulconer, I—"

"I've got the floor now, and it's my turn to talk. Sam seems to have forgotten to give you one important piece of information. If you intend to work with him, you need to know that he's quite brilliant in defining the big picture, but abysmal when it comes to details. He should have told you that tending to the details has been my job. Like finding the money to build those first forty boards. And paying our bills. And making certain dealers took us seriously when we went to Atlantic City. The fact is, Mr. Blaine, SysVal wouldn't exist today if it weren't for me."

She looked first at Sam and then at Yank, daring them to contradict her. Sam was scowling and Yank was studying the beer pitcher. Neither of them said anything.

"Vision isn't enough to run a company, and neither is genius. A company needs somebody to do the work, somebody to see to the everyday details, somebody to get the job done. That person has been me. And if any of you—if any *one* of you—thinks he's going to cut me out now, he's grossly mistaken."

Sam looked down at the table, refusing for the first time since she had known him to meet her eyes. Only Mitch met her gaze directly. He was tough. She could see that. And his stiff, starchy exterior hid the instincts of a street fighter.

"Aren't you being a little melodramatic, Miss Faulconer? Perhaps you'd better separate your romantic difficulties from company business." His voice was silky with condescension.

She had no one to help her. Only herself. Her intelligence and her guts. If she didn't stand up to this man right now, he would gun her down and leave her for dead. "This has nothing to do with my personal relationship with Sam. You've deliberately ignored me from the beginning, but you're not going to do it again. I told you that Sam wasn't good with details, so I'm not surprised that he seems to have forgotten to discuss one of those details with you."

"And what's that?"

"SysVal already has a binding three-way partnership agreement. And I'm one of those three partners."

Sam's head shot up. She saw consternation in his face, and realized that he had actually forgotten about the piece of paper she'd thrust under his nose that afternoon before they'd gone to Atlantic City.

"We all signed it, Mr. Blaine—even though one of us seems to have forgotten." She didn't mention that the paper hadn't been witnessed, that it probably wasn't legal at all, that the socialite was once again trying to pull a hustle.

"I see."

Her voice had begun to shake ever so slightly. "I'm not just Sam's tootsie, Mr. Blaine, as you seem determined to believe. Whether you like it or not, I'm the president of SysVal."

221

"That title doesn't mean anything!" Sam exclaimed. "We were just using the Faulconer name on those business cards. It was your idea."

"And without my name on those business cards, we wouldn't exist today."

Sam's arm shot out across the table. He grabbed her wrist and pulled her roughly down on the seat. His eyes were hard, glittering with anger. "You're going to ruin this for us, you know that? You're going to fucking ruin everything. What difference does it make how we divide things up? If you and I get married, what difference does it make?"

The pain was so sharp, she had to close her eyes for a moment. A knife, diamond-edged and lethal, sliced through her. She wanted to buckle over and curl into a tiny ball. Whenever she had wanted to talk about their feelings for each other—about their future together—he had evaded her. Now he was using marriage as a bargaining chip to manipulate her, as a carrot to dangle in front of her so she would do as he wished. Her body managed to feel both cold and hot at the same time. For the first time, she wondered if SysVal was worth it.

Yank spoke, apropos of nothing. "If I leave Atari, I won't have any health insurance."

His interruption gave her the chance to steady herself. Later. She would think about Sam's emotional betrayal when she was alone. For now she would force herself to separate the personal from the professional, just as men had been doing for centuries. Like a child playing in a sandbox, she would bury every one of her feelings to be retrieved later.

Sam's fingers had loosened on her wrist. She drew away from him, then crossed her hands on the table to keep them steady. She forced herself to forget about Sam, to concentrate only on Mitchell Blaine. "You have the reputation and the experience we lack. On the other hand, we have something you need. I've studied your career, Mr. Blaine. Sometimes you've been a bit too bold for your employers, haven't you? It must be frustrating to have some of your most innovative ideas curbed by men who are more conservative than you."

She thought she saw a flicker of surprise, and she pressed

her point home. "At SysVal, you'll find the aggressive, creative climate you've been looking for—something to relieve that boredom that's been bothering you. Because of our inexperience, we don't have preconceived notions of how things have to be done. We have a chance to build a humane, progressive company from the bottom up—a company that cares about people as well as its product. The three of us would very much like to have you as a fourth partner, Mr. Blaine; however, as president of this company, I have some conditions of my own."

Sam made a small exclamation, but she ignored him. "Your offer of a $100,000 line of credit with the banks is generous, but not quite generous enough if you want an equal partnership. I handle the books, Mr. Blaine, and we're going to need double that if we want to put the self-contained computer on the market without going to the venture capitalists right away. I'd also like to see you toss in $25,000 of your own money as soon as possible to show good faith and get us out of our immediate cash bind." She turned to Yank. "Is that agreeable with you?"

Yank nodded vaguely.

"Sam?" She forced herself to look at him.

He had clamped his teeth together so tightly that a pale rim had formed around his lips. "What the hell do you think you're doing? Mitch is holding all the cards. We're not in any position to bargain with him."

"That's not true. This is our company. As much as we may want him to be part of it, we have the final say. Isn't that correct, Mr. Blaine?"

"Up to a point, Miss Faulconer. But only to a point." His voice was soft, barely above a whisper, but it conveyed a cold authority. "Without me, you won't have a company much longer."

"Without you," she said quietly, "Sam will find someone else."

Silence fell over the table. For the first time since their confrontation had begun, Mitch had lost some of his composure. She continued to press her advantage. "Don't make the mistake of underestimating him. Sam is brash, arrogant, and lousy with details. But he has a gift. It's a gift few people have and even fewer know how to use, but he happens to be one of them. Sam has the ability to make sensible people do impossible things."

"Sensible people like you, Miss Faulconer?"

"And like you, Mr. Blaine."

For a moment he looked at her thoughtfully, and then he rose and tossed some bills down on the table. Without saying another word to any of them, he left the restaurant.

The air outside was chill. Mitch picked up his steps as he crossed the parking lot, the soles of his loafers slapping angrily on the pavement. He prided himself on his analytical mind, his ability to make decisions without being influenced by emotional overtones. But he had blown it badly in that restaurant tonight.

She wasn't anything like Louise. He couldn't imagine the woman who had gone into battle with him tonight abandoning a seven-year marriage without making any effort to confront her husband with her grievances. Despite her distant air, she was a fighter and not quite the dilettante he had imagined.

But then, maybe he was wrong. Maybe he was still so shell-shocked from his impending divorce that he couldn't judge women anymore. He slipped the key to his rental car out of his pocket and fit it in the lock. What would happen if she got her way? Would she grow bored and start looking for a new diversion?

"Mr. Blaine."

He reluctantly turned his head.

Although she was walking toward him quickly, she gave no real appearance of haste. He had noticed that about her from the beginning—the restraint in her movements, the stillness about her, the closed, cool facial expression. Those mannerisms reminded him of someone else. Louise, of course. But no, that wasn't quite right. Now that he had watched Susannah in action, he realized that she wasn't like Louise at all. She was like someone else. But who?

She stopped next to him. He drew his eyes away from her and removed the key from the door lock. "Haven't you finished raking me over the coals yet, Miss Faulconer?"

She started to speak and then stopped, no longer quite the confident woman she had been a few moments earlier. Her hesitation pleased him. He didn't enjoy finishing second place to a woman, and certainly not to one who was a neophyte.

"Just one more thing," she said. "I'd like to know why you dislike me so much. It's because of my father, isn't it?"

She was so earnest, so proper. Once again he experienced that twinge of familiarity, the nagging sense that he had met her before. "I don't like your father, but I respect him. He has nothing to do with this."

He saw that his response had thrown her off balance, and he was pleased.

"Then what? Have I done something specific? I know it can't be because of what I said tonight. You've disliked me from the beginning, haven't you?"

She was determined to press him, and he was equally determined not to put himself at any further disadvantage. He certainly wasn't going to tell her about Louise. "Do you mind if we just let this discussion go?"

She caught her bottom lip between her teeth, and he knew she hadn't finished with him. To his surprise, he heard himself saying, "Whatever my original opinions were, you've changed them this evening."

The slow smile that captured the corners of her mouth was hesitant, but so winsome that he felt his own lips begin to curve in response.

"Is that actually a compliment?" she asked.

"It's a compliment, Miss Faulconer. Definitely a compliment."

And then he realized what it was about her that seemed so familiar. The perfect manners, the quiet courtesy, the steely determination. She didn't remind him of Louise. She reminded him of himself.

The realization floored him, and then, unexpectedly, he felt his spirit lighten. In that moment, he made his decision, knowing even as he said the words that he had set his life on a new and dangerous course. "I'll accept your terms, Miss Faulconer. But don't feel too confident, because I'm going to be looking over your shoulder every minute."

"Fair enough, Mr. Blaine. Because I'll be looking right back."

He laughed. In her own way, she had as much gall as Sam Gamble, but she packaged it so much more discreetly.

Pulling the car door shut, he pressed the button to lower the window. "Tell our business partners that I might have a better name for our new computer than the SysVal II."

"Oh?"

"Maybe we should name it after you."

Her eyes widened in surprise. "After me?"

"Yeah." He leaned out the window. "Maybe we should call it the Hot Shot."

She laughed, a lovely sound, like the tinkle of antique bells. "Hot shot? Me?"

He drew in his head and slipped the car into reverse. "You, Miss Faulconer."

Susannah watched him pull his car out of the parking lot. She was still smiling as he turned out onto the highway. Imagine anyone calling her a hot shot. It was ridiculous, of course. But nice.

She heard footsteps approaching from behind, and her smile faded. Sam's hand touched her shoulder. He sounded more weary than angry.

"Just what in the hell do you think you're doing? God, you're the last person in the world I would have ever expected to have hang-ups about power."

She wanted to make some scathing retort that would hurt him as he had hurt her, but all the spirit she had summoned for her confrontation with Mitch faded. She followed Yank to the Duster, which was parked at an awkward angle in the next row.

Sam stayed on her heels. "This company isn't going to work if you pull any more power plays like that. That's not what we're about. It isn't going to frigging work!"

Yank began tapping his pants pockets in search of his keys. An eddy of cool night wind whipped Sam's hair up from his neck. Her heart ached. Why did he have to be so fierce? So driven?

"You've blown this deal, Suzie. I mean you have destroyed everything. Everything we've been working for. Everything we've tried to do. It's like you deliberately set out to sabotage us."

Yank tapped his shirt pocket and said in a distracted voice, "She didn't blow it, did you, Susannah?"

"No," she replied. "I didn't blow it."

"She didn't blow it, Sam."

Sam stared at both of them, and then at her. "What do you mean? Did he say something to you? What are you talking about?"

Without bothering to consider how Yank had known what would happen, she managed to say, "Mitch has accepted. He's joining SysVal as our fourth partner."

Sam's face shattered as if a sunlit prism had broken apart inside him. "He told you? He's accepted? That's fabulous! I mean, that is freaking fabulous!" He grabbed her and pulled her to his chest. But the moment of shared joy that should have been perfect had been ruined for her.

He released her and threw his arms into the air. "This is going to be fantastic!" With his neck arched, he began drawing word pictures of the revolution they were about to begin. He wasn't as tall as either Yank or Mitch, but as he sliced the air with sweeping gestures and spangled the night with his grandiose dreams, he seemed so much bigger than either of them.

She could feel his energy pulling at her, that indomitable force of will tugging her up toward his personal rainbow. She wanted to go with him on his climb, but this time something within her resisted. Only when he saw how rigidly she was holding herself did he grow quiet. After studying her for a few moments, he said, "Yank, Suzie and I are going to take a walk. Wait for us, okay?"

Yank began searching the ground at his feet. Sam extracted the Duster keys from his own pocket and tossed them over. "We won't be long."

He caught her arm and began drawing her back toward the row of stores. "You're still too chicken to fight with me, aren't you? You're incredibly pissed, but you're going to sulk instead of fight."

Some of her spirit began to come back. Was it his touch? Did he have a magical way of passing his energy through his skin and into hers? "I'm not afraid of fighting with you," she said. "But right now, I'm just not certain you're worth it."

Even as the words were slipping from her mouth, she couldn't believe she was uttering them. His steps faltered, and she knew that she had hurt him. It was a strange feeling to realize she had any power over him at all. She moved up onto the sidewalk. An ice cream cone lay deflated in an ugly brown puddle on the pavement. They walked past the door of Mom & Pop's. She stopped in front of the dry cleaners and stared blindly at a wedding gown entombed in a windowed cardboard box. Once again, she reached deep inside herself to find the courage to say what she must.

"Don't ever try to cut me out again, Sam," she said quietly.

"Is that what you think I was doing?"

"Yes. You excluded me and then used marriage as a bargaining chip to keep me in line."

"You're getting paranoid. I assumed we'd get married one of these days. You're not the sort of woman who's going to be happy shacking up for very long." He slipped one hand out of his jacket pocket and laid it over her shoulders. "Suzie, I'm sorry. I wasn't trying to pull any sort of power play. I just didn't understand you were so hung up about crossing all the t's and dotting the i's."

"To me, it was more than crossing t's."

"But I don't see it that way. You and I are a couple, aren't we? What one of us has, the other has."

He was so earnest, so persuasive, but this time she wouldn't let herself be swept away. "Then why didn't *you* drop out?" she asked gently. "Why didn't you say, 'I'll step aside. Let Susannah be your partner. What she's got, I've got'?"

He pulled his arm from her shoulders. "That's ridiculous! It's not even logical. This whole thing was my idea. SysVal means everything to me."

"I lost my father, Sam. SysVal means everything to me, too."

The harsh glare faded from his features as he took in the significance of what she was saying. Slowly he smiled—a rueful, apologetic smile. Some of the ice inside her began to melt. He tilted his head toward her and touched her forehead with his own. Her eyelids drifted shut. They stood like that for a moment, with their eyes closed and foreheads touching.

"I'm sorry," he whispered.

She knew that she was near tears, and she forced them

back so that she didn't sound self-pitying. "I want to be as important to you as the company."

"You and the company are all mixed up together in my mind."

They stood like that for a few moments with only their foreheads touching. Then their noses brushed, and their mouths. Although their lips were together, they didn't kiss.

"I love you, Suzie," he whispered, his voice sounding young and scared. "I know I get crazy sometimes, but you've got to promise me you'll stick with me. Please, babe. I need you so much. Oh, God, I love you. Promise me you'll always be there for me."

He gripped her hands at her sides so tightly he seemed to be trying to couple their flesh. At that moment, she realized how fiercely she loved him. Her throat had constricted and she couldn't talk—she couldn't force out the words he needed to hear. Instead, she parted her lips and gave him a dark, desperate kiss.

16

• •

Slap some paint on his shirt, Susannah," Sam said three
weeks later, as he placed a two-by-four over a pair of
sawhorses. "I'm embarrassed to be in the same room with
him."

Mitch looked down at his crisply pressed work shirt and a
pair of dark blue jeans with razor-sharp creases. "What's the
matter with the way I look? We're building a wall, for Pete's
sake, not going to a fashion show."

Sam snorted, and Susannah smiled to herself. Building
the partition to separate the assembly and storage areas in
their new office space was the first job the four of them had
done together, and despite the fact that Sam and Mitch had
been trading jibes all morning, the wall was taking shape
rapidly.

She had spent the first two weeks of October scouring the
Valley for office space, but it had been difficult finding
something that was adequate and yet met their limited
budget. With Mitch as a partner, they had easily secured a
bank loan. Each of them was now drawing a minuscule
salary, and their cash flow problems had temporarily eased.
But they all knew the loan was only a temporary stopgap,
and in order to postpone going to the venture capitalists,
they had to scrimp wherever they could.

She had finally found office space at a reasonable rent in the back of a tilt-up, one of the low rectangular buildings that filled the Valley's industrial parks. It wasn't a large area, but it was bigger than the garage and, with a few additions, would meet their needs. They had begun constructing the dividing partition the day before.

"I'll bet you go to a tailor to get your underwear made," Sam said to Mitch as he held the board for Yank to cut.

"My tailor doesn't make underwear," Mitch replied. And then, "I've heard there's a market in the Orient for human hair, Sam. It occurs to me that if you'd sell yours, we could buy this building instead of just renting it."

Susannah groaned. "Tell them both to be quiet, will you, Yank? They're giving me a headache."

"You didn't have a headache this morning." Sam leered at her, and then swung the two-by-four around so that it gently slapped her rear.

She absolutely refused to blush. If she were going to work with men all day, she at least had to pretend to be one of the guys. "That's true," she countered sweetly, "but I'll certainly have one by tonight."

Mitch smiled. Although she knew he was still watching everything she did and waiting for her to take a misstep, their relationship was at least superficially cordial.

She went over to help him support a joist he was nailing into place. "Boy, are you lucky you joined up with us. They wouldn't have let you do work like this in Boston."

He looked down at her from his perch on the ladder, with a hammer in his fist and a satisfied expression on his face. "This is great, isn't it? I haven't had so much fun since I was in college."

She grimaced as she tried to ease the cramp in her shoulders. "You were supposed to be the sane person in this partnership. Now you're as crazy as the rest of us."

On the other side of the room, Yank was driving Sam wild by insisting on measuring every board to the sixteenth of an inch. Finally Sam couldn't stand it any longer. "We're not doing brain surgery, for chrissake! It doesn't have to be exact. Just saw the son of a bitch in half."

But Yank, with his engineer's passion for precision, didn't know how to compromise. By afternoon, Sam refused to work with him any longer, and Susannah was forced to take his place.

As Susannah worked, her eyes followed Sam. She kept wondering when it would wear off, this need to touch him every moment they were together. She knew that he was arrogant and frequently self-centered, but he was also the most compelling person she had ever met. He waved challenges in her face like red flags, and pushed her into another universe with his lusty lovemaking. With Sam, she could be bold and strong. Without him— But she couldn't bear to think about life without Sam. Left on her own, she would probably crawl back into her proper hollow shell and stay there until she died.

She realized that the events the night Mitch had joined the company had changed their relationship. Both of them sensed that they had nearly lost something precious. Ironically, Sam was the one who had begun to press the idea of getting married. Being Sam, he had painted word pictures for her of what their marriage could be—the endless *possibilities* of a union both spiritually and physically sublime, the *power* of that sort of synergy, the *unlimited potential* of the joining of matched minds. As always, his rhetoric had mesmerized her. They had even gone so far as to apply for a marriage license and to get their blood tested. But then Susannah had found office space and everything else stopped.

They christened the wall with a six-pack of beer that evening and spent the next day moving in. At ten that night, dirty and exhausted, they made their way to Mom & Pop's.

Mitch had been talking for some time about the need for a formal organizational chart. Yank had said that he wouldn't accept any title except Engineer, but even Sam knew that the rest of their responsibilities had to be better defined. After the waitress had taken their order, Mitch pulled a neatly folded piece of paper from his pocket and slid it toward the middle of the table. Even before he opened it, Susannah suspected that it was the organizational chart he had been talking about.

It was illogical to hope that she could retain her position as president. Mitch had far more experience and was the better choice to head the company. But although she was reconciled to the fact that she would be demoted, she wasn't going to let Mitch give her an empty title. If it meant another fight, then so be it.

Mitch unfolded the paper and straightened it with his fingers. It was the roughly drawn chart she had expected, and her eyes first fell on Yank's name written in neat block letters slightly below center. He was listed as Head Engineer.

Sam gave a hoot of laughter and pointed to his own name. "Chairman of the Board. Yeah, I like the sound of that."

And then, to her astonishment, Susannah saw she was listed as President and Chief Operating Officer, while Mitch had appointed himself Executive Vice-President of Sales and Marketing.

Mitch took in the expression of surprise on her face. "Being president sounds impressive, Susannah, but it'll be mainly dirt work for a long time. I hope you're up to it."

"But you're far more qualified. Why——"

"Marketing technical products is what I do best, and it's why you recruited me. I don't want to be distracted with day-to-day operations. You've said that you're a detail person. Now you're going to have to prove it."

Her mouth felt dry. Even though this was what she had wanted, she was frightened. They weren't operating out of a garage anymore. What did she know about running a real company?

Mitch called for a vote, and before the pizzas arrived, she had been officially elected SysVal's first president.

On a warm and sunny afternoon just before Halloween, Susannah was in the Gamble garage packing up the last of the equipment. Mitch had been right, she thought, as she slapped a pile of tools in the carton with a little more force than necessary. Being president sounded a lot more impressive than it was. Everyone had gone off and left her to do the final cleanup. Yank was working on the prototype, and Mitch had flown to Boston to see his children. Sam was supposed to be helping her, but he had run off a couple of hours ago and not returned.

In the past two weeks she had been able to handle most of the emergencies that had popped up, and the company was still running. Although Yank continued to grumble about the way the three of them had strong-armed him into leaving Atari, the work on the prototype for the self-contained computer was now progressing much faster. They had hired a talented engineer from Homebrew to design the power supply, and spent hours debating what they would name the machine. All of them had discovered they liked images that had to do with heat and fire. After much discussion, they voted to name the machine the Blaze.

Sometimes as she studied its emerging circuitry, Susannah found herself remembering the evening at the playground with Sam. *Do you know what Yank's machine is going to give you?* he had told her. *It's going to give you courage.* In a funny way, Sam's prophecy had come true.

As if she had conjured him with her thoughts, he poked his head in through the garage door. His hair was even longer now than when they'd met. At night, when she was naked, she liked to comb it through her fingers and pull the inky strands across her breasts.

"It's about time," she said grouchily.

He grinned like a kid who'd just gotten away with something. "Sorry. Things to do."

"I'll bet. You've probably been out joy riding."

Removing the wrenches she was holding, he cupped her bottom and pulled her hips forward so that their jeans rubbed together. Then he kissed her. "You're sounding like a nagging wife. Come to think about it, that's not a bad idea. Go get your face washed. We're getting married in half an hour."

Her head shot back. "What?"

He grinned. "It's all arranged. Mom just left to pick up Yank, and they're meeting us at the tire playground. I like the idea of doing it there. The guy who's marrying us is the brother of this guy I know. He's got another ceremony at one o'clock, so we sort of have to rush."

She stared at him.

He stepped back, tilted his head to one side and gave her that cocky I-dare-you look. A police siren whined in the distance. She could see him waiting for her protests, waiting for her to give him a long list of all the sensible reasons they couldn't do something this impulsive. She thought of the hundreds of phone calls and endless rounds of appointments that had gone into the preparations for her wedding to Cal—all those intricate, elaborate, ultimately useless preparations.

Although she had known him only six months, her mind refused to consider the possibility of a future without Sam. She needed to touch his skin and breathe his air for the rest of her life. "All right," she said breathlessly. "I'll do it."

He let out a whoop of delight and drew her back into his arms. "God, I love you." He pulled her into the house, where he barely gave her five minutes to comb her hair and dab on a few cosmetics. She substituted a purple gauze blouse for her T-shirt, but before she could unfasten her jeans to exchange them for slacks, he was dragging her back outside toward the Harley.

They arrived at the playground just as Yank and Angela climbed out of Angela's red Toyota. Yank was at his worst, so distracted he didn't seem to have the vaguest idea what was happening. Angela was talking a mile a minute and dabbing her eyes with tissue. To Susannah's surprise, Sam pulled a florist's box from the bike's saddlebag. Inside was a bridal bouquet of yellow roses.

The minister, whose name was Howard, appeared in a Grateful Dead T-shirt and told Sam how cool he thought all this was. Neighborhood children playing on the tires and riding along the bike path came over to see what was going on. Susannah felt as if she had been thrown back to the sixties.

They stood in front of a dome made of tractor tires, with Yank on Sam's right and Angela, sniffing and holding a rosary, on Susannah's left.

"Listen, you guys," Howard said as he began the ceremony. "I don't know either of you, so what I have to say isn't important. Why don't you just look at each other and make the promises you think you can keep. Sam, you go first."

Sam turned to her and squeezed her hand. "I promise to give you everything it's in my power to give, Susannah. I'll be honest. I'll speak the truth for both our sakes. And I won't be afraid to walk into the future with you."

They were strange vows, but they stirred threads of emotion deep inside her because they were so typical of Sam, so exactly right.

It was her turn. She gazed into his eyes and tried to find words to express the inexpressible. "I promise to give you my best, Sam, whatever that may be." She paused and the traditional wedding vows of love and honor passed through her mind. She searched for a new way to say them, a way that would reflect the passion and joy she felt in his presence, but her silence lasted too long, and Howard spoke before she could finish.

"That's cool. That's really cool." He picked up both their hands in his and squeezed them. "The law says that you're married, but only the two of you know what that really means." He then went on to ruminate about the universal powers of light and harmony and concluded with the words, "Be groovy."

The children on the playground giggled as Sam kissed her, and then Angela kissed them both. Yank and Sam shook hands, and Howard hugged everybody, including the kids. Sam made a mad dash over to a set of playground rings suspended from a heavy chain and pulled himself across them, hand over hand. When he dropped to the ground, he threw back his head and laughed. He was exultant, as if he had claimed some priceless possession. Together, they raced to his bike.

Angela had not been able to find a box of rice in Yank's kitchen cupboards and had grabbed a box of elbow macaroni instead. She quickly distributed its contents, and the motley assortment of wedding guests pelted the bride and groom with it as they roared away.

They took a wild ride into the hills. Sam's hair had come loose and it blew into her face, stinging her cheeks. She pressed her breasts to his back and held him tightly against the chill cut of the wind. They left civilization behind and climbed higher. Eventually he steered the bike onto a narrow, rutted road that soon dwindled to an overgrown path. When even that disappeared, he slowed and drove through the dry brush to the edge of a steep bluff. Only then did he stop.

The sound of silence was sharp after the roar of the engine. The Santa Clara Valley lay below them, its highways, industrial parks, and rectangular buildings laid out so that it look like an enormous integrated circuit. "I've put the world at your feet, Suzie," he said, his voice husky. "The two of us together—we can have whatever we want. By ourselves, we're not anything. But together, the Valley's ours. Yours and mine. We'll be king and queen."

There was a strange intensity about his words that made her uneasy. She broke the tension by saying lightly, "Queens are supposed to have crowns. I don't even own a baseball cap."

He smiled and the sunlight sparked silver lights in his black hair. She drank in the sight of the wild, free lover who was now her husband. "One of these days I'll buy you your own Harley," he said. "How about that? It'll be a royal Harley." He tugged her blouse from the waistband of her jeans and pressed his lips to her temple. "You'll ride it naked right down the middle of El Camino Real, just like Lady Godiva."

As he reached behind her for her bra clasp, she instinctively closed her hands over her breasts. Although the area was deserted, she was hardly used to taking off her clothes outside, and she laughed nervously. "It sounds uncomfortable. Won't I be cold?"

He gave her a sexy, half-lidded look and pushed her hands away. "Baby, I'm going to keep you so hot that you'll never be cold again."

Her bra fell to the ground. He gazed at her breasts and used the tip of his finger to draw a line down the center of one. She had a crazy desire to lift her arms high over her head and display herself to him.

He tugged down her jeans and her panties at the same time and pulled them off along with her shoes. The air was crisp and chill on her skin, the ground cold beneath her feet, but she barely noticed.

For a moment he rested the flat of his hand over his stomach. Then he lowered the zipper. The denim fell open in a deep V. Her lips parted slightly as she saw his bare stomach and the line of dark, crisp hair and realized that he wore no briefs beneath.

"You ever done it on a bike before, Suzie?"

"A thousand times," she said breathlessly.

"Big talk." He cocked his head toward the black leather seat. "Straddle it."

Her mouth had grown dry. Once again he was daring her, testing her, pushing her beyond the safe boundaries of her experience. Without taking her eyes from his, she did as he said, keeping her back to the handlebars so she was facing him. The black leather was chill against her bare buttocks and the soft insides of her thighs.

His mouth cocked insolently. Facing her, he swung his leg over the seat and slipped his hands under her knees. Lifting and spreading them, he pushed his own legs beneath her. The inside of her bare calves rubbed against the outside of his denim-clad ones, the underside of her thighs lay over the top of his. He looked down at her. Through her excitement, she thought how vulnerable her position made her to him. She was open and assailable while he was a hard, strong, denim-encased ridge hidden beneath her.

"You're going to be a great queen." He played with her breasts until she moaned, and then he indented her nipples with his thumbs as he pressed her back against the handlebars. She tilted her neck and looked at the sky. Her hair tumbled over the tachometer and the headlight. Thin blue-white clouds skidded across the sky while he pulled at her nipples until they turned into hard, swollen buds.

Finally, he moved the flat of his hand down between her breasts and over her abdomen, skimming her body as the clouds skimmed the sky. His hand came to rest on her tight, auburn curls. "Snooty and cool on the outside . . ." He moved his fingers. "Hot on the inside."

She moaned and drew up her feet. Her toes curled over the rear pegs as he caressed her. She felt as if she were moving out of her body into the sky. The Northern California sun came from behind a cloud and struck her skin. Her hands clutched his calves. She arched her back and turned her breasts upward like some primitive human sacrifice offered for the pleasure of a god.

Beneath her hips he opened his jeans the rest of the way and released himself. His boots were still on the ground, steadying the bike as he shifted his hips, poised himself, and entered her. She clutched his calves harder, arched higher. But as he began to move inside her, she couldn't get enough of him.

She pulled herself up to straddle his lap. Her hair fell over his shoulders and down his back, the auburn strands drifting like fine silk over the tough black leather. She was the aggressor now. She impaled herself deeper on him and made him adjust his rhythm to hers. A lock of his hair brushed her lips. She took it in her mouth. Wrapping her arms around his neck, she arched her waist and took him all.

He groaned. "That's good . . . That's so good."

Tears stung her eyes as she moved upon him. "Oh, yes. Yes."

"More . . . Give me more."

"I love . . ." she cried. "I love you . . ."

"Harder . . . More . . . Yes . . . more."

Her orgasm was quick and shattering. ". . . love you so much," she sobbed as she died upon him.

He dug his fingers into her buttocks and thrust himself hard up into her. As she felt him reach his crisis, she pressed her damp cheek to the top of his head and willed him to speak the love words she craved.

His cry was hoarse and strangled deep in his throat. "More," he demanded. "Give . . . me more."

17

The SysVal offices were sparsely furnished. Three battered steel desks sat in separate corners of the open room, and two long worktables occupied the fourth. A few rock concert posters and a fold-out Harley-Davidson ad hung on the wall. As Mitch walked through the door, he couldn't help but compare the posters to the Helen Frankenthaler canvas that had hung in his last office.

Although it was only a little after seven on Monday morning, Susannah was already sitting at her desk. Her feet were tucked under her, and she had a pencil stuck behind her ear. As he walked inside, she looked up from her notepad and smiled at him.

"I know all about the early bird and the worm," she said, "but don't you think you should have gone home to get some sleep first?"

"I slept a little on the plane."

"How was Boston?"

"Fine."

She didn't press him, and he was glad. He still felt bruised from having left his kids last night. Liza's dark curls had smelled like baby shampoo when he'd kissed her good-bye. David had locked his arms around his neck and begged him

240

not to leave. Mitch blinked his eyes and headed for the coffeepot.

Susannah spoke hesitantly. "I don't want to pry, but I know having your children so far away can't be easy on you. If you need a friend . . ."

"Yes, thank you." He spoke briskly, pushing away her concern so that she would know his personal life was off limits. He took care of his own troubles, and he didn't need anyone's sympathy.

As he carried the coffee mug over to his desk, he glanced at the oversized calendar that hung on the wall. "Did anything come up this weekend?"

"Nothing much. I processed some new orders, took care of the mail, washed my hair, got married. Nothing really."

He spun around, sloshing coffee onto the floor. "You got married?"

She laughed. For the first time he noticed that she was carrying her own private glow with her. Her skin was luminous and her features seemed to have blurred at the edges, as if they were being photographed through a Vaseline-smeared lens.

"We've been talking about it for some time. You know Sam. He gave me half an hour's notice."

As she told him about the playground ceremony, his hands convulsed around his coffee mug. He was furious. He must have been crazy to have left his children on the other side of the continent for this.

When she finally paused, he set down his cup and regarded her steadily. "Quite frankly, I can't believe you've done this."

Some of her glow faded. He felt like a schoolyard bully, but he pushed away any remorse. He should have seen this coming, but he had been too caught up in the risk and excitement of their venture to dwell on the relationship between Sam and Susannah. Besides, he certainly hadn't envisioned Sam as a family man.

He watched her gather her dignity about her. "You know how Sam and I feel about each other."

"Didn't it occur to either one of you that we should have discussed this first?"

"We don't need your approval, Mitch."

"You may not need my approval, but you're damned well going to need a lawyer. Have you thought about what this marriage does to our partnership agreement?"

She was smart, he'd give her that. It didn't take her long to see that she and Sam had neatly managed to take control of half the company. "I—I'm sorry. I didn't think— We'll get it all ironed out with an attorney this week. You surely realized that neither of us was trying to pull any sort of power play."

She was probably telling the truth, he thought. That's what was so incredible. He had known from the beginning that he was getting involved with amateurs, and he had no one to blame but himself. Her expression was so stricken that he softened. "Is the lucky bridegroom in the back room?"

She cautiously accepted his peace offering. "Still in bed."

"I saw his bike outside. I thought—" He broke off at the self-satisfied expression that had begun to form on her face. "You rode the Harley over here by yourself?"

She smiled. "It was wonderful, Mitch. I beat the morning traffic, so I was only slightly terrified."

He tried to imagine his ex-wife jumping onto a motorcycle and failed abysmally. But then, he had given up the notion weeks ago that Louise and Susannah were anything alike.

Her laughter faded, and she gave him a look so earnest that his anger began to dissolve. "Be happy for us, Mitch. Sam and I need each other."

He didn't want to be on the receiving end of any intimate confessions. Taking a sip of his coffee, he nodded his head toward her hand. "No wedding ring?"

She smiled slightly. "An antiquated symbol of enslavement."

"That sounds like Sam talking, not you."

"You're right. But I'm the one who made the decision to keep my own name instead of taking his."

"Not all of the old traditions are bad ones."

"I know. But my name is my last link with my father." She hesitated. "I guess I'm not ready to give that up."

By now he had heard the story from Sam of the way Joel

Faulconer had turned his back on her. He tried to imagine doing something like that to his own daughter, but he couldn't.

"How does Sam feel about your not taking his name?"

"He harangued me for at least an hour. But I think it was more a training exercise than a sign of real conviction. He wanted to make certain marriage hadn't turned me into a yes-woman."

"Sam definitely likes a good fight."

Susannah's expression turned serious. "I'm not afraid to fight with him, Mitch. Just because we're married doesn't mean I'll rubber stamp his opinions. When it comes to SysVal, I'm my own woman."

We'll see, he thought to himself. *We'll see.*

By the end of the following week, they had taken the legal steps necessary to protect the company in the event that Sam and Susannah's marriage failed. Documents were drawn up to make certain that partnership shares couldn't change hands in a divorce settlement and upset the balance of power. If either Sam or Susannah found it depressing to sign papers that dealt—theoretically, at least—with the end of a marriage that had just begun, neither of them commented.

As fall slipped into winter, Mitch watched for signs that Sam and Susannah's marital relationship was affecting their business decisions. Finally, he was forced to admit that, more frequently than not, he and Susannah joined forces against her husband.

While the SysVal partners were growing accustomed to their new office, the little Apple Computer Company continued to operate from the Jobses' family garage in Cupertino. Its founders were also at work on a prototype of a self-contained computer, which they were calling the Apple II. One night early in December, over video games at Mom & Pop's, Mitch discovered that Yank had openly discussed his work on the Blaze with Steve Wozniak. His expression grew incredulous as he absorbed this casually offered piece of information.

"Are you out of your mind?" he exclaimed, angrily

confronting Yank, who was standing at the next video machine. "Your designs are this company's most basic asset. You don't share them with a competitor. Don't *ever* let anything like this happen again! Ever!"

Yank was completely mystified by Mitch's anger. "Woz and I like each other's work," he said in his reasonable, logical voice. "We've always helped each other out."

Sam and Susannah had been playing Super Pong together when the eruption occurred. Observing the curious stares of a couple in a nearby booth, she moved her body slightly, hoping to block some of the confrontation from public view while Sam tried to calm Mitch.

"Look, it's a different world out here," Sam said. "Yank's a hacker. Hackers can't even understand the *concept* of proprietary information."

Mitch's expression grew fierce. "Listen to me, all of you. We're not playing games with SysVal. From now on every piece of information on the Blaze design is proprietary— right down to the number of screws holding on the case. This is not debatable! No one talks publicly about anything, do you hear me? No one!"

Yank turned away from Mitch to gave Sam a long, piercing gaze, and then he said distinctly, "This is crap."

It was the first time Susannah had ever heard him use a vulgarity. Without uttering another word, he stalked away from the three of them and left the restaurant.

Mitch was as angry as she had ever seen him. Sam, in his impulsive manner, wanted to deal with the situation in the middle of Mom & Pop's, but she hustled both men outside and they drove to Sam and Susannah's apartment.

The apartment was small and dingy, with a view of the trash Dumpster, but Susannah loved having a place of her own and didn't mind its shabbiness. They had neither the time nor the money to improve it, which was probably just as well because Susannah had finally admitted to herself that domesticity had never interested her. When it came to a choice between spending her time working on the development of the Blaze prototype or picking out living room draperies, the Blaze won hands down.

Sam grabbed a beer from the refrigerator for Mitch and a

Coke for himself and then began to pace the floor. Susannah took a seat in the room's only armchair. Mitch, whose outrage over Yank's breach of security hadn't eased at all, sat on the couch and scowled. They were in the positions they usually occupied late at night when the three of them got together to refine their business plan and define exactly what they wanted their company to be.

How many nights had they spent like this, with Sam painting word pictures of a company that had glass walls, open doors, and rock music playing, while Mitch countered with his own, more pragmatic vision—one centered on swelling market share and snowballing profits instead of a Utopian working environment? Despite the friendship between the two men, they were frequently at loggerheads, and Susannah had to act as mediator. She realized that this night would be no different.

Sam planted his hands on his hips and looked over at Mitch. "You've got a Master's from MIT, but Yank and I are Valley kids. We weren't trained in colleges. Our roots are in the suburbs—in garages. For hackers, the rewards come in breaking codes and in getting into closed systems—in showing your design to someone who's smart enough to understand the dazzle of what you've done. When you tell a hardware hacker like Yank that he can't show off a brilliant piece of design to one of the few people he knows who can really appreciate it, it's like you've cut off his oxygen supply."

"Then we have a serious problem," Mitch said coldly.

Silence fell between them.

Susannah sighed in frustration. Why couldn't either of them ever see the other's viewpoint? Once again she found herself wanting to bang their heads together. Mitch grounded everything in reality, Sam in possibility. She alone seemed to understand that only with the melding of both philosophies could the true vision of SysVal emerge.

She slipped into her customary role of mediator as if it were an old, comfortable bathrobe. "Don't forget that while Yank is showing off the Blaze, he's also looking at the Apple II. Surely there'll be some benefits in that."

"That's nuts," Mitch protested. "What if—by the grace

of God—we actually manage to make a success out of this ridiculous company? We can't function indefinitely with our newest technology flying out the window all the time."

"You're right," she said, "but in this case being right doesn't make any difference, because Yank simply won't pay attention." She had already given the matter some thought, and now she shared her ideas with them. "As soon as we're able, we need to begin surrounding him with the most brilliant young engineers we can find—eccentric thinkers like he is. We have to create the Homebrew environment internally."

Sam's head snapped up, his eyes grew bright. "That's no problem. The best people in the world will be standing in line to work for us. There won't be any time clocks. No assholes in three-piece suits telling people what to do."

"But everything will be directed," Mitch said. "Everybody will be working together toward a common goal."

"The goal of giving the world the best small computer ever made," Sam said.

"The goal of turning a profit," Mitch replied.

Susannah smiled and took a sip of tea. "You're absolutely right."

December passed—sometimes a blur of activity, at other times painfully slow. Christmas was difficult for Susannah. While they exchanged presents around Angela's artificial tree, garishly decorated with plastic ornaments and ropes of pink tinsel, Susannah's thoughts wandered to the towering Douglas fir that would have been erected in the entrance hall at Falcon Hill, its branches glimmering with French silk ribbon and antique Baroque angels. Had Joel and Paige thought about her at all today? It had been foolish of her to cherish even a dim hope that the Christmas season would magically bring them all back together again. As she looked up at the plastic Santa on the top of Angela's tree, she felt unbearably sad.

She told herself she mustn't do it, but late that afternoon, while Sam and Angela were watching a football game on television, she slipped into the kitchen and dialed Falcon Hill. The phone began to ring, and she bit the inside of her lip.

"Hello."

Her father's deep, abrupt voice was so familiar, so beloved. Her own voice sounded thin in response. "Father? It's—it's Susannah."

"Susannah?" His voice lifted slightly at the end of her name, as if he might have forgotten who she was.

Her knuckles grew white as she gripped the receiver. "I—I just called to wish you a Merry Christmas."

"You did? How unnecessary."

She squeezed her eyes shut and her stomach twisted. He wasn't going to give in. How could she have let herself hope, even for a moment, that he would? "Are you well?"

"I'm fine, Susannah, but I'm afraid you've picked rather a bad time to call. Paige has planned a marvelous meal, and we're just sitting down to eat."

She was overwhelmed with memories of past Christmases —the sights and smells and textures of the season. When she was a little girl, her father used to lift her high up on his shoulders so she could put the angel on top of the tree. An angel for an angel, he had said. Now Paige would be sitting in her seat at the bottom of the table, and that special smile he had once reserved for her would be given to her sister.

She was afraid she was going to cry, and she spoke quickly. "I won't keep you, then. Please tell Paige Merry Christmas for me." The receiver hung heavily in her hand, but she couldn't sever this final connection by hanging up.

"If that's all?"

She hugged herself. "I didn't mean to interrupt. It's just—" Despite her best efforts, her voice broke. "Daddy, I got married."

There was no response. No words of acknowledgment, let alone expressions of affection.

Tears began to run down her cheeks.

He finally spoke, in a voice as thin and reedy as an old man's. "I can't imagine why you thought I'd be interested."

"Daddy, please—"

"Don't call me again, Susannah. Not unless you're ready to come home."

She was crying openly now, but she couldn't let him go. If she held on just a little longer, it would be all right. It was Christmas. If she held on just a little longer, there would be no more angry words between them. "Daddy—" Her voice broke on a sob. "Daddy, please don't hate me. I can't come home, but I love you."

Nothing happened for a moment, and then she heard a soft click. In that moment she felt as if the remaining fragile link between father and daughter had been broken forever.

In the kitchen at Falcon Hill, Paige held the receiver tightly to her ear and listened to the click as her father hung up the telephone on her sister. She replaced the receiver on the cradle and wiped her damp palms on her apron. Her mouth was dry and her heart pounding.

As she returned to the stove, she refused to give in to the memory of herself standing in a dingy hallway with a dirty telephone cord wrapped around her fingers while she tried to pry some words of tenderness from her father. She refused to feel sorry for Susannah. It was simply a matter of justice, she told herself as she turned the heat down under the vegetables and pulled the turkey from the oven. She had spent last Christmas stoned and miserable in a roach-infested apartment. This year Susannah was the outcast.

The servants had the day off, so she was responsible for Christmas dinner. It was a task she had been looking forward to. The turkey finished baking in the oven along with an assortment of casseroles. The counter held two beautiful fruit pies with an elaborate network of vines and hearts cut into the top crusts. In the past seven months she had received a surprising amount of pleasure from simple household tasks. She had planted a small herb garden near the kitchen door and livened up the corners of the house with rambling, old-fashioned floral displays, instead of the stiff, formal arrangements Susannah had always ordered from the florist.

Not that her father ever noticed any of her homey touches. He only noticed the jobs she forgot to do—the social engagement she had neglected to write down, the closets she hadn't reorganized, the plumber she had forgotten to hire—all those tasks her sister had performed with such relentless efficiency. As for the latest Ludlum thriller she had left on his bedside table, or the special meal waiting for him when he got back from a trip—those things didn't seem to matter.

"Do you need some help, Paige?"

She smiled at Cal, who had poked his head into the kitchen. She knew that Cal was an opportunist, and she doubted that he would have proven to be such a good friend if she hadn't been Joel's daughter. But he understood how difficult Joel could be, and he listened sympathetically to her problems. It was wonderful to feel as if she had someone on her side.

"Let me just set the turkey on the platter, and you can carry it in," she said.

Since there would only be the three of them for dinner, she had decided to forgo the huge, formal dining room with its long table for a cozy cherry drop-leaf set up in front of the living room fireplace, where they would be able to see the Christmas tree through the foyer archway.

When all the food was in place, she seated herself and removed the red and green yarn bow from her napkin. The center of the table held an old-fashioned centerpiece she had put together the day before with evergreen bows and small pieces of wooden dollhouse furniture she had unearthed in the attic. It had amazed her how many of her childhood toys had survived, even a few sets of tiny Barbie doll shoes. She couldn't believe those little plastic shoes hadn't been lost over the years, until she remembered how careful Susannah had always been with their toys.

While her father carved the turkey, old memories slipped over her. She saw Susannah's auburn hair falling forward in a neat, straight line as she dug out a tiny Monopoly house Paige had lost in the thick pile of her bedroom carpet. She saw Susannah in spotless yellow shorts stooping down on the brick terrace to rescue crayons her sister had left in the sun. Paige wouldn't use the crayons once the sweet, sharp points had worn off, but Susannah used them forever, patiently peeling back the paper until only a waxy nub was left. Unexpectedly, Paige felt a hollowness inside her.

Despite her careful preparations and Cal's attempt at conversation, the meal wasn't a success. Joel seemed tired and said little. Her own conversation was stiff. Paige didn't blame Cal for taking his leave not long after they had finished dessert. When she walked him to the door, he gave her a sympathetic glance and a friendly peck on the cheek. "I'll call you tomorrow."

She nodded and returned to the living room. Joel had seated himself on the couch with a book, but she had the feeling he wasn't really reading it. She felt even more lonely than when she was by herself.

"I think I'll go clean up the kitchen," she said abruptly.

Joel slapped down the book and jabbed his hand toward the remnants of their Christmas dinner. "I can't imagine what possessed you to crowd us around that ridiculous table when we have a perfectly good dining room that cost me a fortune to build."

Paige could barely keep herself from lashing out at him. She struggled with her hurt. "There were only three of us. I thought it would be cozier in here."

"Don't do it again. Susannah would never have—" He broke off abruptly.

She went cold all over. "Susannah isn't here anymore, Daddy. I am."

He seemed to be waging some kind of internal war with himself. It was the first time she could remember her father looking uncertain, and she felt a queer stab of fear prick at the edges of her hurt.

He rose from his chair and said stiffly, "I know you think I'm unreasonable, but I'm accustomed to having things done a certain way. I realize that may not be fair to you."

It was the closest she had ever heard him come to an apology. He began walking toward the door. Just as he passed her, he reached out and gave her arm a single awkward pat.

At least it was something, she told herself as she watched him disappear. She went back over to the window and looked out on the immaculate December gardens of Falcon Hill. An image formed in her mind of another sort of Christmas Day. She saw herself wearing blue jeans instead of a silk dress, and standing next to a Christmas tree decorated with construction paper chains rather than antique Baroque angels. She saw noisy, rumpled children tearing at wrapping paper, a long-suffering golden retriever, and a faceless husband in a sloppy sweatshirt pulling her into his arms.

Angry tears stung her eyes. "Fucking Norman Rockwell," she muttered in disgust.

18

• •

We can't afford it," Mitch protested, dropping a heap-
ing teaspoon of sugar into his coffee.

"We can't not afford it," Susannah countered.

Sam grinned, thoroughly enjoying having someone besides himself deal with Miss Appearances-Are-Everything
for a change.

It was March, and they had been in their new offices for
nearly five months. The three of them were sitting in a booth
at Bob's Big Boy, where they had gotten into the habit of
meeting for breakfast most mornings so they could coordi-
nate their activities for the day.

Sam took a swig of Coke. "You might as well save your
breath and give in, Mitch. Susannah's still a socialite at
heart. She's almost always right about this crap."

"It's not crap," she said, planting the heels of her hands
on the edge of the table and getting ready to dig in. "The two
of you think anything that's not immediately quantifiable is
unimportant. That's the problem with you technical types.
You're either punching calculators or walking around with
your head in the clouds."

She settled back in the booth and waited for her jibe to
pierce through their early morning grogginess. Neither man

252

was at his best until ten o'clock. She, on the other hand, jumped out of bed full of ideas.

"You've got to control her better, Sam," Mitch said earnestly. "There's a definite pattern developing here. Have you noticed how she always picks mornings to attack?"

Susannah gave Mitch a smug smile and turned to her husband. "He's joking, Sam. The way we know that Mitch is joking is that his jaw is in its unclenched position. God knows, if we waited for the man to crack a smile, we'd be here forever."

Mitch shook his head sadly over his coffee cup. "Vicious personal attacks at seven-thirty in the morning."

"Stop distracting me," she said. "You know I'm right."

Mitch grunted and took another swig of coffee.

They had decided to unveil the Blaze at the First West Coast Computer Faire to be held next month at San Francisco's Civic Auditorium. This trade show, capitalizing on its California location, promised to be larger than the one in Atlantic City, although no one was exactly certain how many disciples of small computers would attend.

Unfortunately, the Blaze wasn't ready. They were still having difficulties with the power supply, and Yank wasn't satisfied with the cassette tape version of BASIC that would be used to operate the machine. In addition, the cases for the two models they intended to have on display had been delayed. And they were nearly broke.

Susannah had done her best to push the large, unsolvable problems to the back of her mind and focus on those she could solve. Foremost in her mind was making certain that the launching of the Blaze wasn't overshadowed by all the other products that would be on display at the Faire.

She picked up half a slice of toast that Sam hadn't eaten and renewed her attack. "This is going to be a huge show. Our booth is impressive, but the Blaze could still get lost. To make sure that doesn't happen, we invite the press and the most important members of the trade to a private party the night before. They'll all be in town for the Faire. We'll give them something to drink, some food, and we'll show them the Blaze then instead of waiting for the next day."

"Sorry to side with the enemy, Mitch," Sam said. "But I

like Susannah's idea. We'll be able to jump start all the competition."

Susannah was grateful for Sam's support. She never knew which side of an issue he would come down on. But then, Sam was unpredictable about everything. Being married to him was like existing on a constant adrenaline high. Although it was frequently exhausting, she had never felt so alive in her life. Alive, but on edge, too. He wanted something more from her, something that she wasn't giving him. But she couldn't imagine what it might be.

Mitch threw up his hands. "All right. I admit it's a good idea. But you know our financial picture as well as I do, Susannah. You have to do everything on a shoestring."

"A thread," she promised, crossing her heart. "I'll do it on an absolute thread."

Susannah arrived early at the downtown restaurant where they were holding the party to launch the Blaze. Her clothing budget still limited her to shopping at Angela's outlet stores, but she wasn't displeased with her inexpensive black crepe trousers and the tunic top she had spruced up with a sequined appliqué from a fabric shop. Her hair was pulled away from her face and confined at the nape of her neck with a silver metallic scarf. She was alone. The men had been working on the software and she hadn't seen them since early afternoon.

She paused just inside the doorway of the private party room to take in the effect of the decorations. Bunches of balloons in lipstick red and lacquer black—the colors of the new Blaze logo—gave everything the festive atmosphere of floral arrangements, but without the expense. At one end of the room, a dais dramatically displayed the only two fully assembled Blaze computers in existence.

Behind the computers hung an enlarged reproduction of the spectacular new logo. The Blaze name, in curving letters that were black at the bottom and gradually turned into hot red at the top, rose in a stylistic pyramid of flames with the central A forming the apex. SysVal was neatly printed beneath.

Walking forward, she stopped in front of the machine that held the key to all of their futures. The physical design of the

Blaze had been Sam's. From the beginning he had known what he wanted—something small and sleek that would look comfortable in people's homes, a friendly machine with rounded edges instead of sharp corners and a soft ivory-colored case that didn't fight its surroundings.

As Susannah gazed down at the Blaze, she saw the embodiment of Sam's dream. The computer and the keyboard were one harmonious unit. Instead of duplicating the shape of a typewriter, the Blaze keyboard was wide and shallow with keys contoured to fit the fingers. She ran her hand over the flat top that housed Yank's genius compacted onto only sixty-six chips, an incredible engineering feat.

Someone entered the room behind her. "Hi, baby. It's beautiful, isn't it."

She turned, then sucked in her breath as the man she loved walked toward her.

"Oh, Sam . . . What have you done to me?"

His beautiful hair was gone—that wild black biker's hair she loved to crush in her hands when they made love, the long, dark strands that sometimes slipped between her lips when he drove high and hard inside her, his rebel's hair, the hair that had snapped in the breeze like a pirate's flag the day he had stolen her from her father's care.

It still hung bone-straight, brushed away from his ears, but the back didn't even reach the top of his white shirt collar. White shirt collar, dark blue necktie, sport coat. Each item was more loathsome than the last. Those were Cal's clothes, her father's clothes, not the clothes of a blue-skies thinker who dreamed of changing forever the dying days of the twentieth century.

Only the jeans were familiar, but even they weren't right. The denim was new, the seams dark and tightly stitched instead of soft and frayed. The stiff zipper lay nice-boy flat over his crotch, the prim new denim de-sexing him.

She hated it. She hated every bit of it. Her eyes returned to his hair. It swept back from his temples, revealing two ordinary ears unadorned by a swaying silver Easter Island head. They were the respectable ears of an IBM salesman, of an FBT vice-president. How could those ears belong to a small computer evangelist who sold the future instead of bibles?

Behind her the gay red and black balloons bounced forgotten, and her palm left a sweaty imprint where it had rested on the top of the Blaze.

"What have you done to me?" she whispered again.

Sam looked at her quizzically, but before he could say anything, the door swung open again and Mitch walked in with Yank. Mitch was unbearably smug as he slapped Sam on the back and patted his lapel. "Doesn't your boy look great, Susannah? He and I went on a little shopping trip. He changes his tune when you dangle a three-hundred-dollar imported Italian sport coat in front of him."

Yank was wearing his version of dress-up, a wrinkled brown corduroy suit with a narrow, mustard-colored tie hanging askew. The underside of the tie extended barely three inches below the knot.

Mitch shrugged apologetically at Susannah. "I only had so much time. Do something, will you?"

She busied herself reknotting Yank's tie. As she worked, she tried to calm her inexplicable feeling of panic. Sam was Sam, she told herself. Cutting his hair and putting on a sport coat didn't change anything for either one of them. Besides, she had said from the beginning that he needed to look more like a business man, and now she had her wish. She glanced over at him busily loading the Blaze display programs. They were married, but marriage didn't feel the way she had always imagined. She had no sense of safety or stability. Instead, every day was an adventure full of new battles to be fought. Sometimes, she was almost overwhelmed with the intensity of just being alive on the same planet with Sam Gamble.

The guests began to arrive, and she had no more time for personal ruminations. She had sent out over a hundred invitations to members of the press and other influential people in the trade, and she watched nervously as they critically circled the two machines, guzzling beer, munching on pizza and firing questions at all of them. Before long, they were watching in fascination as the large television monitors began to display the games and programs that had been designed to show the little computer's awesome power.

More than one skeptic pulled up the bright red cloth that draped the display table in search of the larger computer they were certain was hidden beneath. They shook their heads in amazement when they found only electrical cords and cardboard cartons.

"Amazing."

"Son of a bitch."

"This is freaking fantastic!"

The SysVal founders were hackers at heart, and it wasn't long before Sam slipped the case from one of the prototypes. (Neither he nor Yank had even considered designing a computer that couldn't be opened up.) Within minutes, a hundred guests were craning their necks to see the internal poetry of Yank's wondrous machine. By midnight it was evident that the launching of the brash little Blaze was an unqualified success.

The restaurant finally forced them to disband at two in the morning. The men loaded the equipment into Mitch's car, and the four partners headed for the hotel where they had booked rooms for the night. Sam and Mitch were still wired from the excitement of the evening, and neither wanted to sleep, even though they had to be at the Civic Auditorium in a few hours to set up. But Susannah was exhausted, and she declined an invitation to go to the bar with them for a drink. Yank also refused, and they crossed the lobby together.

In many ways Yank still remained a mystery to her. Angela had told her that Yank's ability to shut out the world when he worked had begun when he was a child growing up in the Valley. His mother and father had fought bitterly, but as good Catholics, they wouldn't divorce. From a young age he had learned to immerse himself in electronic projects so that he could transport himself to another world, where he wouldn't have to listen to the ugly sounds of their arguments. His parents had retired to Sun City several years ago and apparently still fought as bitterly as ever. He seldom saw them.

As they stepped into the elevator, Susannah made a stab at polite conversation. "Roberta wasn't at the party. She's not sick, is she?"

"Roberta?" Yank didn't seem quite certain who Susannah meant.

Normally Susannah would have been amused, but despite

the enthusiastic reception the Blaze had received at the party, she was on edge, and her tone was unnaturally sharp. "Roberta Pestacola, your girlfriend."

"Yes, I know."

Susannah waited. The elevator doors opened. They got off together. After a few steps Yank stopped walking, stared for a moment at a fire extinguisher, then began walking again.

She was suddenly determined to have a normal conversation with him. "Is anything wrong between you and Roberta?"

"Roberta? Oh, yes." He began patting his pockets for a room key.

They continued down the corridor. Although she was tall, he topped her by a good seven inches. Thirty more seconds of silence passed. Susannah was exhausted from the evening and still unsettled over the changes in Sam's appearance. Her already frayed nerves snapped. "The purpose of conversation is to exchange information. That's difficult to do with someone who hardly ever finishes his sentences and never seems to have the vaguest idea what anyone is talking about. It's really irritating."

He stopped walking and looked down at a point just behind her right ear. "It's probably not a good idea to take out your frustration on one person when you're really upset with someone else."

She stared at him. How did he know she was upset about Sam? He shifted his gaze and looked directly at her.

She nearly winced. His eyes were so clear and so strongly focused that she had the feeling he could see the smallest cells inside her.

"Roberta and I are no longer together, Susannah. I'm not proud of staying with her for as long as I did, since I wasn't too fond of her even at the beginning. But it's difficult for me to attract women, and I like having sex very much. This means I sometimes make compromises. Is there anything else you want to know?"

Susannah actually felt herself flush. "I—I'm sorry. It's none of my business."

"No, it isn't."

Embarrassed, she fumbled in her purse for her own room key, and managed to drop it just as they reached her door.

Yank stooped over to pick it up off the carpet. As he straightened, he once again looked at her with that penetrating gaze she found so disconcerting.

And then, more quickly than she could have believed possible, she lost him to the gods of genius. His eyes grew vague and his face emptied of all expression. Muttering something that sounded like "zany diode," he began moving off down the hallway as if she didn't exist.

Black sock.
Brown sock.
Black sock.
Brown sock.

None of them were prepared for what happened the next day. By early that morning thousands of computer enthusiasts had formed five lines that wrapped around both sides of the block-long Civic Center. No one had expected so many people, but despite the crowded conditions, everyone was good-natured and enthusiastic.

Throughout the day loudspeakers blared out announcements, computer-generated music played, and printers clattered. Lines formed to attend the event's workshops and people stood four and five deep at the booths. They could get their biorhythms charted at the IMSAI exhibit and play a game on the Sol at the Processor Technology display. Many companies—some actually larger than SysVal—were still showing their products on draped card tables with hand-lettered signs, but they were dwarfed by exhibitors like Cromemco, MITS, and even the tiny Apple Computer Company, which had apparently learned its lesson about appearances at Atlantic City. Even though they had only moved out of their garage a few months ago, they were introducing their Apple II in an impressive booth complete with a backlit plexiglass sign bearing their new brightly-colored Apple logo.

While Mitch spent his time making contacts with distributors and dealers and Yank wandered the hall to survey the competition, Sam and Susannah, along with several teenage employees they had recently hired to help manage the increasing workload, manned the SysVal booth. Sam was everywhere at once, holding four separate conversations at the same time and telling all who came within the sound of his voice about the miraculous little micro called the Blaze. Yank's splashy graphics display was a big hit with the crowd, as well as a target-shooting game people were standing in line to play.

Susannah distributed hundreds of expensively printed color brochures, smiled until her cheeks ached, and began taking orders for the Blaze almost immediately. As she discussed memory expansion, switching versus linear power supply, and eight-slot motherboards, she realized how far she had come from a woman who had once regarded her most strenuous challenge to be finding a good caterer.

At the end of the weekend, when one of the Faire's organizers announced that thirteen thousand people had been in attendance, a huge cheer went up from the crowd. Trade shows had been held in Atlantic City, Trenton, and Detroit, but the overwhelming success of the West Coast Computer Faire had put all of them to shame. On this April weekend in 1977, California had finally taken command of its own small computer kingdom.

Sam caught Susannah in his arms as the attendance was announced. "We've made history today! This is our Woodstock, baby. A digital love-in for a new generation."

That night, when they headed back to the Valley, they had orders for 287 Blazes in hand.

19

By August the hills of the Santa Clara Mountains were brown from lack of rain. Joel Faulconer squinted at the sun through the windshield of his tan rental car and wished for the winter rains. He was finding it difficult to breathe. There was too much dust in the air.

He had parked the car so that he had a clear view of the single glass door that led into the SysVal offices, but the van parked on one side of him made the car barely noticeable to anyone walking through the lot. Over the past six months, Joel had learned to choose his locations carefully. He rented inconspicuous cars, and he always brought a newspaper with him so that if Susannah should appear unexpectedly, he could block his face.

The indignity of what he was doing was something he refused to dwell on. He didn't think of it as spying on his daughter. He tried not to think of it at all. Coming here was necessary. That was all. He had to find a way to get her back.

In an hour he was due in his office for an afternoon meeting with one of the most important industrialists in Japan. It was the kind of encounter that had once sent adrenaline pumping through his veins. Now what he really wanted to do was take a nap.

He continued to have difficulty sleeping at night, and last night had been particularly bad. He should have been more honest with his doctor when he had finally gone to see him a few weeks ago, but he couldn't bring himself to confess to a medical lackey twenty years younger than himself that he was suffering from a depression so deep and so black that he didn't think he could ever climb out of it. The night before, he had spent hours locked in his library, gazing down at the Smith & Wesson revolver he kept in a mahogany case.

Sweat broke out on his body. For weeks now he had felt as if he were living on the jagged edge of something monstrous. He told himself not to think about it. He would be better soon. Any day now.

The door of the building opened and Sam Gamble walked out. Joel's stomach pitched. The bastard. Gamble moved across the parking lot toward the used Volvo he had bought a few months ago. His walk was cocky, as if he were a king instead of an arrogant upstart. Joel consoled himself with the thought that the Gamble car was merely another item that would fall to the bankruptcy court when this harum-scarum operation went belly up. He was both incredulous and frustrated that it hadn't already happened. Of course, he hadn't counted on Mitchell Blaine throwing his hat into their circus ring. Still, even Blaine couldn't work miracles.

Cal had been as bewildered as Joel when he had heard the news. "Why is Blaine doing something so bizarre?" Cal had asked.

Joel had kept his response casual. He saw no sense in letting the younger man realize how much the news had shaken him. "His wife left him. He's obviously not thinking clearly. But I don't believe we need to worry too much. Even Mitch Blaine won't be able to keep them afloat much longer."

Cal had pressed him to move more aggressively against SysVal, but once again Joel had demurred. Susannah was going to fail on her own. Only then—only when she had suffered defeat at her own hands—could he possibly take her back. He envisioned her remorse, the way she would beg him to let her return to Falcon Hill.

The sound of tires squealing distracted him from his thoughts. Gamble was just reaching for his car door when a small red Toyota shot into the parking lot and jerked to a stop near the Volvo. A woman jumped out and began rushing toward him. She wore a purple elasticized top, black jersey wrap skirt, and high heels with ankle straps. It took Joel only a moment to recognize her as Gamble's cheap little floozy of a mother.

Gamble had already spotted her. She had left the engine of her car running and the door open. He hurried forward in concern. She grabbed his arm and began to speak with enormous agitation. Joel could pick out a few isolated words but not the sense of what she was saying. Gamble looked as if he were growing angry. She clutched harder at his arms. He shook her off and went back to his car.

"Sam!" she cried.

Gamble jumped into the Volvo without sparing her another glance. Gunning the motor, he peeled out of the parking lot. She crumpled like a rag doll against the trunk of her car.

Joel watched her clutch her arms in front of her stomach and begin a slow rocking that sent her gold hoop earrings swaying. Her dark hair was mussed and her expression was full of despair. Perversely, the sight of her misery lifted his spirits as nothing had in weeks. It made him feel more in control of his own life, more like his old self. At the same time, curiosity piqued him. Anything that made Sam Gamble angry might be good news for him.

He hesitated for only a moment before he got out of the car and walked toward her. The pavement began to tilt under his feet. He wasn't feeling well, not well at all. Perhaps he should cancel his appointments this afternoon and go home. But no. Someone might discover that he wasn't feeling like himself. That wouldn't do at all.

Several moments passed before the woman seemed to recognize who he was, but even recognition didn't alter the misery on her face.

"Is there anything I can do?" he inquired. Despite his solicitous words, he felt no particular sympathy for her—she was cheap and common—and yet the strength of her misery gave him a peculiar sense of relief. No matter how difficult the past year had been for him, he hadn't once been reduced to this sort of excessive display of emotion.

"It's over," she said, a black trail of mascara running down her cheeks. "There's nothing anyone can do."

Once again he had the sense that the pavement was tilting beneath him. He concentrated on keeping his balance and on trying to decipher her words. What was over? Did she know something about SysVal? Was that why Gamble had been so angry?

"Have you ever lost someone?" she went on in a broken voice. "Someone important to you."

For a moment, he was afraid something had happened to Susannah, and fear rushed through him. Then he remembered Gamble's anger and realized it was something else. This woman had probably had a squabble with one of her aging boyfriends. All of this hullabaloo undoubtedly had its roots in a middle-aged lovers' quarrel.

"Part of me wants to die, too." She dabbed at her eyes with the back of her hand, leaving a dark smear on her first two knuckles.

"Nonsense," he replied sharply, wincing as a dull stab of pain went through his shoulder. He wanted to rub it, but he forced himself to keep his arm still. "It's ridiculous to make a fuss over trivialities. I suggest you go home and fix yourself a drink."

"I can't go home now. There's something I have to do. Someplace I have to go." She turned away from him and walked toward the front of the car.

He looked down at his watch and saw that if he didn't leave soon, he would be late for his meeting. And then the numbers began to waver in front of his eyes. He swayed and braced himself on the trunk of her car. His own car suddenly seemed to be miles away.

She bent to get into the Toyota. Pain gripped his chest. He leaned against the car trunk, using it for support. The pain didn't ease. For the first time it occurred to him that he might actually faint. The idea horrified him. What if Susannah found him helplessly crumpled in the parking lot? He had to sit down. He had to rest for a moment, but his car was so far away, and he didn't have the strength to get there. He took several awkward steps forward, moving along the side of the car to the open door.

She looked up at him curiously. His mind raced, but his

brain was dull with pain and he couldn't think what to say. He had to sit down. He couldn't stand any longer. "You— you need to go home," he stammered. "You're not—not in any condition to drive."

She reached for a pair of oversized sunglasses. "I can't go home. I have something I have to do."

He had begun to sweat profusely. In a breathless, choppy voice that didn't seem to belong to him, he said. "Not—not alone. You shouldn't go alone." His hand convulsed over the roof of the car. He couldn't faint. He couldn't let Susannah see him like this. "I'll—I'll go with you. Make certain you're safe."

"Whatever," she said dully. "It doesn't really matter."

He barely made it around the front of the car, but she was so caught up in her own misery that she didn't notice. As he slumped down into the passenger seat, he gasped for breath. The car began to move. He no longer cared about his meeting or the rental car he had abandoned in the parking lot. All he cared about was the fact that he hadn't crumpled like an aged fetus onto the asphalt where his daughter could see him.

They had begun to move out into the traffic on El Camino, and the pain was easing. He noticed that her fingernails were too long and covered with a garish purple-red polish. She pushed a tissue underneath her sunglasses to dab at her eyes. He thought about asking her what was wrong, but he didn't really care. He was too tired. His legs felt rubbery, his head hurt. He would just stay with her for a while, until he felt more like himself, and then he would call his driver to come and get him. Once again he shut his eyes. If he rested for just a few minutes, he would feel more like his old self.

When he awakened, the sun was sinking. He blinked with alarm and tried to get his bearings. They were moving fast. A road sign for Interstate 5 whipped by on his right. He saw a herd of cattle grazing and the ridges of the Sierra Nevada Mountains in the distance. They must be somewhere in the San Joaquin Valley.

The radio was playing softly, a pop tune. He looked down at his watch and was startled to see that it was nearly seven o'clock. "Where are we? Where are you going?"

She jumped as if she had forgotten he was there. Her

sunglasses were off, and the lap of her skirt held a collection of damp, wadded tissues. She tilted her head toward the radio. "I—I can't talk now. When the song is over."

The voice on the radio was familiar—a male pop singer. He dimly recognized the song, something about a child being born in a ghetto.

There were so many things he needed to do. He should tell her to get off at the next exit so he could call his driver. How would he explain this? Everyone would be alarmed because he hadn't shown up for his meeting. He had a full work schedule planned for tomorrow. He tried to arrange his thoughts in proper order, but he couldn't manage it. All he could see was the Smith & Wesson revolver lying in its mahogany case. His eyes drifted shut again, and he was consumed with a sense of his own helplessness. The song came to an end.

Her voice quivered. "They've been playing all-Elvis for hours. I—I still can't believe that he's dead. He was so young. Only forty-two."

His eyes shot open. "What are you talking about?"

"Elvis," she whispered softly. "Didn't you hear? Elvis Presley died today. August 16, 1977."

Was that what this was about? He wanted to roar his anger at her, but his brain felt foggy and his head seemed to have been wrapped in hot, wet wool. She stared straight ahead at the road. A tear dropped off her chin and made an amoeba-like stain on the front of her purple stretch top. No wonder Gamble had been angry with her in the parking lot. It was beyond Joel's comprehension that someone could be so distraught over the death of a celebrity when there were so many real problems in the world.

"I have to go to Graceland—in Memphis. I have to pay my respects." Her voice caught on a sob.

He couldn't believe he had heard her right. "You're driving to Tennessee?"

"I have to." She blew her nose, dropped the tissue into her lap, and picked up another. And then she said something that sent a chill slithering up his spine. "The King is dead. I can't believe it. I just can't believe that the King is dead."

He could feel sweat breaking out on his forehead. No! *He*

was the King! He had years ahead of him. Decades. He had so many things left to do and endless time in which to do them. The interior of the car was cool, but he couldn't seem to stop sweating, and he made a dash at his forehead with the sleeve of his suit coat.

Her mouth trembled. "I never imagined it. I thought he would live forever." She turned to look fully at Joel. Her face was stripped bare of makeup, her lipstick eaten off. "I'm only forty-three. That's not old. Only a year older than Elvis. It's just— How can I ever be young again if Elvis Presley is dead? How can any of us ever be young again?"

Joel no longer even remembered what it was like to feel young. He closed his eyes again, not to sleep, just to escape.

South of Bakersfield she exited to get gas. He went into the phone booth and called his secretary. He made up an excuse for his absence and began to tell her to get hold of his driver, but he ended up telling her to inform Paige he wouldn't be coming home tonight.

It was irrational. He was feeling better and he couldn't justify what he was doing. Even so, he couldn't seem to change his course. He decided to go just a little farther with Angela—only a few more hours. Then he would have her drop him at one of the hotels on the interstate, where he would spend the night. In the morning he would call his driver so he would be back in time for his meetings.

When he returned to the Toyota, Angela was sitting in the passenger seat holding two cans of soda pop and assorted packages of junk food. He got behind the wheel. She popped the top off one of the soda cans and handed it to him. He was thirsty, so he took a sip. It was overly sweet and awful. He couldn't remember the last time he had tasted soda pop. The second sip wasn't quite so bad.

His suit coat was mussed and damp. He took it off and turned to lay it carefully over the backseat. Then he started the engine and pulled back out onto the road. "I'm not going much farther."

"I don't even know why you're here."

The thought sprang into his head that he was there because he didn't want to die, but that made no sense. He wasn't old, only fifty-nine. And he was an important man.

He tried to distract the direction of his thoughts with a question. "Why are you doing this? Why is this so important?"

"Elvis is Sammy's father."

Joel snorted.

"You don't believe me, do you? Nobody believes me." He could see her marshaling her forces, but then she turned to stare out the window. Several long moments passed, and her shoulders slumped in defeat as if she had just given up something precious. "I wish he'd been Sammy's father. I wish I'd been able to meet him. They tell such lies about him. That he wasn't faithful to Priscilla while they were married, that he used drugs and acted strange. I never believed any of it. Elvis loved the little people. He cared about people like me. Going to Graceland to pay my respects is the least I can do for him."

She leaned back against the seat and eventually shut her eyes.

The rhythm of the interstate and the soft Presley ballads playing on the Bakersfield radio station began to lull him. It was growing dark, and he turned on the headlights. It had been years since he had driven any distance himself. Angela fell asleep next to him with her mouth slightly open. He yawned, feeling relaxed for the first time in ages. Driving was good for him. He would do more of it from now on. That was all that was wrong with him. He just needed to relax more.

The radio was fading, so that the words to "Kentucky Rain" were interlaced with static, but he didn't change the station. He noticed the St. Christopher medal affixed to the dashboard and a bottle of nail polish lying overturned on the floor. A litter bag advertising State Farm Insurance swayed from the cigarette lighter. He didn't feel sleepy, merely relaxed.

Next to him, Angela's breathing came in soft, sibilant puffs. Her skirt had ridden up above her knees. He noticed that her legs in their dark stockings were good, but nothing about her stirred him sexually. He had never liked cheap women, not even when he was young. By the time he reached Barstow, she had tucked her legs under her.

He had to stop again for gas around midnight. She woke up and took over the driving. He immediately fell asleep in the passenger seat.

They crossed Arizona during the night, shifting drivers whenever they stopped for gas. The next morning they had breakfast at a truck stop near Albuquerque. Angela went to the rest room to wash her face, and when she came out, she had reapplied her makeup. Her figure in its purple stretch top attracted the attention of some of the truckers, and they watched her over the top of their coffee cups. Joel was embarrassed to be seen with her. He took comfort from the fact that no one knew who he was.

When he went to the men's room to wash up, he saw a stranger in the mirror. His face looked bloated, his skin chalky and unhealthy, and his jaw was covered with stubble. Usually he shaved twice a day, so he wasn't reminded of the fact that his beard was mostly gray, but he didn't have a razor, so he splashed water on his face and looked down at the faucets instead of into the mirror.

He wasn't conscious of the moment when he made the decision to go all the way to Memphis with her. He simply couldn't make himself do anything else. The driving was good for him, he told himself. He needed a vacation.

As they approached the eastern border of New Mexico, Angela began to cry again. When he couldn't bear it any longer, he snapped at her. "Will you stop it, for God's sake. You didn't even know the man."

"I'll cry if I want to. I didn't invite you to come with me. You can get out any time." She reached for the radio and spun up the volume. Since morning she had been listening to news reports coming from Memphis.

". . . the twenty thousand mourners who were lined up along Elvis Presley Boulevard this morning have now swelled to fifty thousand, all of them hoping for a chance to view the body of the King of Rock and Roll as he lies in state in the drawing room at Graceland. Vernon Presley, the father of the singer, has ordered that doors to the estate be opened to allow as many of his fans as possible to file through and pay their respects. Thousands of floral tributes have arrived from all over the world since yesterday afternoon, many of them bearing the simple inscription, 'To the King.' All of the mourners share disbelief that the King is dead. . . .''

Joel snapped off the radio dial. He didn't want to hear about kings dying. He didn't want to think about . . .

Angela turned the radio back on. He gave her an icy glare—the glare that had intimidated heads of state and corporate presidents. She ignored it.

Outside of Amarillo they blew a tire. The service station was dry and dusty and the heat rose in waves from the cracked asphalt. They sat at a rickety picnic table in the sparse shade of a dying ailanthus tree while they waited for a new tire to be put on.

"Elvis gave so much to me," Angela said. "When I was upset or sad, when my husband Frank treated me like dirt, Elvis was always there. His songs made me feel at peace with myself. This might sound sacrilegious, but I don't mean it to be. Sometimes when I'd kneel in church to pray, I'd look up at the statue of Jesus. And then it would seem like it was Elvis hanging there. He sacrificed so much for us."

Joel couldn't think of a single thing Presley had sacrificed except dignity, but he didn't say so. The woman was crazy. She had to be. But then, what did that say about him?

"Did you go to high school, Joel?" she asked. It was the first time she had addressed him by name. He wasn't accustomed to women like Angela calling him by his first name. He would have preferred her to call him Mr. Faulconer.

"I went to a military academy," he replied stiffly.

"Did they have cheerleaders?"

"No. Certainly not."

"I used to be a cheerleader. I was one of the best." Softly, sadly, under her breath she began to chant, "We've got the team, we've got the steam, go fight. We've got the team, we've got the steam . . . I was so popular in high school. All the kids liked me because I was never stuck up, not like some of the other girls. I was nice to everybody. You know what I liked best about high school? Your whole life was ahead of you, and in your mind you made all the right choices. In your mind everything came out perfect. Not like real life, when you marry the wrong man and have trouble with your kid. Not like what's happened to you and me."

He jumped up from the picnic bench so suddenly that it tilted, nearly unseating her. "Don't you dare presume to speak for me. My life is perfect. I wouldn't have it any other way."

She gave him a look so sad that it cut right through him. "Then why are you going to Graceland?" she asked softly. "If your life is so perfect, why are you going with me to Graceland?"

He turned away from her. High, dusty weeds spoiled the polish on his expensive shoes. A coffee spot marred the spotless white of his custom-made dress shirt. "I've been tired, that's all. I needed to get away. I need a rest."

This time she was the one who gave a soft snort of disbelief. "Never kid a kidder, Joel. You're even lonelier than me."

He wanted to strike out at her for her presumption, but he couldn't summon up words that were cruel enough. She came up behind him. A hand settled in the center of his back and rubbed gently, like a mother comforting a child. His eyes drifted shut with the pain of her soft, soothing touch.

The service station attendant called out that their tire was ready. It was Angela's turn to drive.

"God has Elvis now," she said as she merged with the traffic in the right lane. "I keep trying to tell myself that."

"Do you really believe that?" he scoffed.

"Don't you?"

"I'm an Episcopalian. I give to the church. Sometimes I even attend, but—no—I don't believe in God."

"I'm sorry," she said sympathetically. "I think it must be harder for men like you to believe. You have so much power that you start thinking you're God, and you forget how unimportant you really are. Then, when bad times hit, you don't have anything to fall back on. With me it's different. I've never been important, and I've had faith all my life."

"God is nothing but a crutch for the ignorant."

"Then I'm glad I'm ignorant, because I don't know what I'd do without Him."

They continued their odyssey—Amarillo to Oklahoma

271

City, Oklahoma City to Little Rock, Little Rock to Memphis—two middle-aged people on their way to Graceland, one of them mourning the passing of her youth, the other on his way to see death so he could make up his mind if he still wanted to live.

They reached Memphis early Thursday morning. A crowd of several thousand had kept vigil at Graceland throughout the night, and it was already difficult to find a parking place anywhere near. Angela parked the Toyota in front of a fire hydrant some distance away. Joel badly needed a shower and clean clothes, as well as a decent meal. He thought of calling a taxi to take him to a hotel. He thought of a dozen things he could do, but he ended up walking to Graceland with her.

The day was already heavy with humidity. Helicopters circled over the mansion, and all the flags they passed hung at half mast. The sight of the flags deeply disturbed him. It seemed inappropriate to mourn a rock and roll singer so lavishly. Would the California flags be flown at half mast when he died? He shook off the thought. He didn't intend to die for a very long time. When he got back home, he would see his doctor and tell him how badly he had been feeling. He would tell him about the tightness in his chest, about the fatigue and depression. He would get some pills, watch his diet, start exercising again.

Although it was still early, souvenir hawkers plied the crowd that had gathered around Graceland's high brick walls and spilled out onto Elvis Presley Boulevard. Weeping mourners hugged Elvis T-shirts to their chests along with photographic postcards and plastic guitars made in Hong Kong. Joel found the vulgarity unspeakable.

The funeral cortege would be emerging through Graceland's famous music gate, and Angela wanted to be able to see it all. Joel moved her to the front of the crowd that had gathered in the shopping center directly across the street. It took some time, but despite his disheveled appearance, people sensed his importance and made way for them. He noted the heavy police presence and numerous first-aid stations set up to tend to those who were fainting from heat or hysteria. The city officials were obviously worried about the temper of the crowd, which seemed to change indiscriminately from a noisy outpouring of grief to almost carnival gaiety. A woman in green rubber shower thongs told Angela that at four o'clock that morning a kid in a white Ford had jumped the curb and hit three teenage girls who were keeping vigil. Now two of them were dead. Life seemed increasingly arbitrary to Joel.

Cars began entering through the music gate for the funeral service which was to be held inside the mansion. Angela thought she spotted Ann-Margret in one of them. Another bystander said he had seen George Hamilton, and there was a rumor that Burt Reynolds had slipped in through the back. It amazed Joel that these people actually cared about minor motion picture celebrities, not one of whom could possibly have been accepted for membership at his country club.

Joel could probably have gained entrance to the funeral with nothing more than a few well-placed phone calls, but the idea repelled him. He was not a participant, but an observer of this plebeian carnival of loud voices and excessive emotions.

The morning dragged on, and the heat grew so oppressive, breathing became difficult. He bought two rickety camp stools from a vendor. They sat on them in sight of the gates and waited for the funeral cortege to emerge.

"What's important to you, Joel?"

The question was presumptuous, so he remained silent.

She lifted her hair off her neck and fanned herself with a flattened red and white cardboard popcorn box. "Sammy and my friends are important to me. Your daughter. Going to Vegas. Going to church. I like doing hair and being with my girlfriends. The old ladies laugh at my jokes, and I make them feel pretty again—I like that. But most important is Sammy." She set down the popcorn box and studied one fingernail where the purple-red nail polish had started to chip. "I know I embarrass him—the way I look and the kind of person I am—like telling a few people that Elvis is his dad. But I won't change, not even for him. I tried changing for Frank, and it didn't work. A person has to be what they are. I like wearing flashy clothes and having a good time. Otherwise, before you know it, you're fifty and you haven't ever lived."

273

He was fifty-nine years old. Did she think she was talking about him? "I live on one of the most beautiful estates in California," he said coldly. "I have homes all over the world, cars, everything a man could possibly want."

"Despite all that, I feel sorry for you."

He was furious with her. Where did she get the audacity to pity him? "Save your pity for someone who needs it."

"You seem to be missing out on all the good parts of life." Once again she began to fan herself with the popcorn box. "You don't believe in God, and you won't make up with your daughter."

"You leave Susannah out of this!"

"She's a special girl. She's kind and sensitive, and Sammy's probably going to hurt her. You should be there for her."

"She doesn't deserve anything from me. She's made her own bed, and now she can damn well lie in it."

"Sometimes the best part of loving somebody is loving them even though they've hurt you. Listen to me, Joel. Any fool can love somebody who's perfect, somebody who does everything right. But that doesn't stretch your soul. Your soul only gets stretched when you can still love somebody after they've hurt you."

"Your husband for example?" he said scornfully. "You women are amazing. You let men walk all over you because you're too spineless to stand up to them, and then you hide your weakness under the cover of sacrificial love."

"Loving never makes you weak. It's being untrue to yourself that does that. It's like with Sammy. He wants to make me over into somebody like Florence Henderson. That's how he is. He buys me things like little pearl earrings and white cardigan sweaters. I always thank him, but those things aren't my style, and as much as I love him, I won't let him change me. That's how I stay true to myself. So I keep saying my prayers and hoping one day it'll be better between us. It should be like that with you and Susannah. Just because she did something you don't approve of doesn't mean you should cut her out."

His face was stony. "I refuse to have anything to do with someone who has betrayed me."

"She wasn't betraying you. She was just following her own star. It didn't have anything to do with you."

"It would be impossible for me to forgive her after what she's done."

"But, Joel—that's what makes it love. Otherwise it's just shaking hands."

He didn't want to think about what she'd said, but he couldn't help it. Was it possible that this cheap, gaudy woman knew something about life that had escaped him?

Suddenly the music gate opened. A limousine as white as Elvis's Las Vegas show costumes crept forward, followed by another. Next to him Angela gave a dry, broken sob. One by one, sixteen white limousines passed in a mournful parade through the gate. People were crying. Tough-faced men and overweight women let tears fall unashamedly down their cheeks. And then Angela clutched his arm as the white Cadillac hearse appeared—the hearse bearing the body of the King of Rock and Roll.

Angela took a deep, shattered breath and whispered, "Good-bye, E."

Joel watched the hearse turning slowly out onto the boulevard. He felt a sharp pain in his shoulder and rubbed it. He didn't want to ponder the fate of kings. He didn't want to think about his own mortality and why he had come on this strange odyssey, but suddenly the emptiness of his life pressed down on him with so much weight that he felt as if he were being pounded through the pavement into the dry, hot, Tennessee earth. He thought about what Angela had said—that the best part of loving was being able to love someone who had hurt you. He pressed his eyes shut and remembered just how badly Susannah had hurt him. But in the face of death and funerals, it no longer seemed to matter quite so much.

And then he finally admitted how badly he wanted her back. He wanted Susannah back, and he wanted to be able to love Paige the way a daughter should be loved. He envisioned his family gathered around him at Christmas dinner with rosy-cheeked grandchildren at the table and Kay at his side—silly, frivolous Kay, who used to make him laugh and helped him forget the pressures of holding power.

As he clutched his shoulder and struggled to breathe, he saw his faults stretched out in front of him like a long unbroken line on a sales graph. He saw his sins of pride and selfishness, he saw his small cruelties and his foolish belief that he could shape the world through the strength of his own will. He saw the arrogant way he had squandered the love of the people who cared for him.

The pain gripped him, traveling from his shoulder down into his chest, and he thought of the little girl he had pulled from her grandmother's closet so long ago. She had given him perfect, unconditional love—the most precious gift of his life—and he had thrown it away. Panic swept over him as he realized all he had lost. Was it too late? Could he have her back?

With astonishing suddenness, a wave of euphoria swept over him, riding right alongside his pain. It didn't have to be too late! As soon as he got back, he would tell her. He would fly home tonight and go to her. He would tell her that he forgave her, that he loved her. His life would once again have meaning. Everything would be all right again.

Angela's eyes were still on the white hearse, and her face, even in profile, looked stricken. "I know I'm not young anymore," she whispered, "but—do you think I'm still attractive, Joel?"

He clutched his chest, no longer able to draw a breath that wasn't pain-wracked. There was no more time. He felt the chill coming over him, the fading of light, and he knew he had to give something back quickly, something good and precious. With his last remaining bit of strength, he pushed out the words.

"You'll always . . . be quite . . . beautiful, Angela. . . ."

And then, in the shadow of the hearse bearing a king, another king slumped to the ground.

20

Susannah had just fallen asleep when the phone rang shortly after midnight. She groaned and rolled over, automatically reaching out for Sam before she remembered that he was still at work. She should be there, too, but she had been exhausted and had finally gone home.

She fumbled for the phone, wondering why her husband and her partners couldn't leave her alone for even one night. "Hello," she murmured thickly.

"Susannah?"

"Paige?" She was instantly alert to the strangled sound in her sister's voice. "Paige, what's wrong?"

"It's—it's Daddy."

"Daddy?" Her spine stiffened and she braced herself for something horrible.

"He's—he's dead, Susannah. He had a heart attack."

"Daddy's dead?" The words slipped from her lips, the syllables distorted as if they had been spoken underwater.

Paige was crying. It had happened in Memphis, she said. No one knew what he was doing there. Susannah gripped the sheet as her sister went on. The night closed around her like a small, tight box.

Paige hung up. Susannah continued to hold the telephone. She didn't want to replace the receiver. She didn't want to break her last fragile link with someone in her family. *Daddy*, she cried out silently. *Daddy, don't do this to me. I'm your sweetheart, remember? I'll be good. I promise. I'll never be bad again.*

A monster pressed down on her chest. Her golden prince had gone. There would be no more chances to win back his love. She began to cry—deep, wracking sobs that came from her soul. There was no more time left to receive her father's forgiveness. Her daddy was dead.

Sam heard the sounds when he walked in the door—soft, animal sounds. Fingers of fear shot through him as he ran toward the bedroom. Susannah was huddled in the far corner with her back smeared against the wall and her hands tangled in her nightgown. "Suzie . . ."

He rushed toward her, knelt down on the floor and pulled her against him. The expression on her face chilled him. Someone had broken in the apartment and raped her. He drew her closer, rage and fear shaking him. "It's all right, baby. I'm here. I'm here."

"Sam?" Her voice quivered like an old woman's. "Sam? Daddy's dead."

Relief coursed through him. She was all right. Nothing terrible had happened to her. Hearing the news of Joel's death didn't particularly trouble him, and instead of trying to offer her phony words of comfort about a man he had detested, he stroked her.

It felt strange to have her clinging to him so helplessly and to hear those broken little sobs coming from her. Their position on the floor was awkward. He lifted her and helped her over to the bed. Her body was naked underneath the thin nightgown, and as he lay down with her, he could feel himself starting to get hard. Jeezus, she would never understand that in a million years.

He hated anything that had to do with death. Once, he had heard a priest say that death was what gave life its meaning, but he didn't believe that. Death took away meaning. Death robbed life of any sense. When he was ten, the inevitability of his own death had struck him for the first time, and he had been consumed with a cold, gripping terror. For months afterward he had been afraid to go to bed at night, until, finally, he had told himself it wouldn't happen. The rules of the universe would change for him. Death was one more barrier to be smashed, one more hurdle to overcome.

He wished she would stop crying. He wished she hadn't brought death into their bedroom. He began stroking her breasts. In the midst of death, there is life. In the midst of death, there is—

"Sam." She pushed his hand away.

"No, Suzie," he whispered. "Let me. I'll make it better. I promise."

She continued to cry as he lifted her nightgown and pushed open her thighs. "I'll make it go away," he promised. "I'll make it all go away."

But he couldn't make it go away, and when he finally shuddered inside her, she felt even more alone.

For the next two days, he treated her tenderly, but when she awakened the morning of the funeral, he was gone. Frantically, she called the office, but neither Mitch nor Yank had seen him. Angela had been away for days and no one answered the phone at her house. Finally, she realized that he had deliberately disappeared and she would have to go to the funeral alone.

She picked up the keys to the old Volvo they had bought and squeezed them so tightly that the ridges bit into the palm of her hand. She needed Sam, and he wasn't here for her.

A dark maroon Cadillac Seville was pulling into the parking lot as she walked unsteadily from the apartment building. Mitch got out and came toward her. "Get inside," he said quietly. "I'm coming with you."

She nearly slumped against him with relief. He took her elbow and helped her into the car. As they drove toward Atherton, she stared blindly through the windshield. "Sam's afraid of death," she said numbly. "If he weren't afraid, he would have come with me."

Mitch made no response.

Solid, strong, and immovable, he stayed by her side throughout the ceremony. Sometimes it seemed as if only his presence was keeping her from flying apart. Spasms kept wracking her body, but he held tightly to her hand. She refused to cry. Once she started, she would never be able to stop.

Whenever she looked at the sleek black coffin, her teeth chattered. She tried to talk silently to her father. *It's not finished between us, Daddy. Nothing's finished. I love you. I still love you.* But no comforting messages came to her from the other side of the grave.

Cal sat with Paige, and when the ceremony ended, a crowd gathered around the two of them, offering their condolences. But hardly anyone spoke to her, not even people she had known for years. It was as if—in running away from her wedding and breaking the rules—she had betrayed them all.

As they left the church for the cemetery, she overheard a guest mutter, "Not his real daughter, of course. Adopted." The word was delivered as if it had been sucked from a particularly juicy lemon. Mitch heard it, too, and squeezed her hand.

The gravesite ceremony was mercifully short. As Mitch was leading her away, Cal approached. "Susannah?"

It had been a year since they had spoken. The eyes that had once gazed at her with pride were now full of venom. This was the man she had planned to spend her life with. Now his hatred struck her like a blow.

"I hope you're satisfied," he sneered. "You killed him, you know. He was never the same after you left."

Susannah felt as if she had been punched in the stomach. Mitch stiffened and took a menacing step toward Cal. "Get away from her, Theroux," he said harshly.

A soft touch penetrated Susannah's pain, the brush of a hand on her arm. It settled there only for a moment and then lifted away like a butterfly in flight. She turned numbly toward her sister.

Paige of the tight jeans and saucy walk was conservatively dressed in Kay's old pearls and a subdued black dress. Her rock and roll sister who used to whip her hair to the beat of the Stones looked as proper as an old dowager. Susannah waited for Paige to condemn her, too, but her sister wouldn't even meet her eyes.

"Come along, Paige," Cal said, his lips thin and tight. "There's no need for you to be subjected to her presence."

Mitch drove her home and offered to come inside with her, but she knew she couldn't hold herself together much longer and she refused. Before she got out of the car, she leaned over and pressed her cheek to his jaw. "Thank you," she whispered. "Thank you so much."

The radio was playing softly in the kitchen as she entered the apartment. She expected to see Sam there, but instead she found Angela washing dishes in the kitchen. She set down the dish she had been drying and opened her arms. "Poor baby."

Susannah felt something break apart inside her. She went toward her like a three-year-old running to her mother with a mortal wound. She cried in Angela's arms while Angela stroked her back and said, "I know. I know, baby."

Her nose began to run and tears dripped off her chin onto the shoulder of Angela's blouse. Her body no longer seemed to belong to her. What had happened to the woman who never cried?

"My father's dead," she said. "I won't ever see him again."

"I know, honey."

"I never—I never got to say good-bye. Now I'll never get the chance to put it right."

"You tried, honey. I know you did."

"I didn't think he would die. Not ever. He always seemed like God."

Angela led her to the living room sofa. She rubbed her arms and held her hands, but Susannah couldn't be comforted. "I loved him. I always loved him. He just didn't love me back."

Angela stroked her hair. "That's not true, honey. He loved you. He told me so."

Several seconds passed as her words penetrated Susannah's deepest misery. She looked up and saw Angela's face wavery through her tears. "He told you?"

Angela brushed Susannah's hair back from her wet cheeks, freeing the strands that were stuck there with the lightest scrape of her fingernail. "We were together at the end. Your father went with me to Graceland for Elvis's funeral."

"Graceland? My father?" Susannah stared at her without comprehension.

"I don't think he meant to come with me. But it just sort of happened."

Gradually, Angela unfolded the story of the trip. Susannah listened, stunned by what she was hearing.

"The day he died, he talked about you," Angela said.

Susannah went cold all over. "What did he say?"

"He didn't hate you, Susannah. I think he hated himself."

The horrid words Cal had assaulted her with kept punching at Susannah's brain. "I think I killed him," she whispered. "I did a terrible thing to him. If I hadn't run away, he would be alive today."

"Don't say that! Don't say that, honey. You weren't responsible." Angela spoke in quick, breathless tones. "Those last few hours, we were sitting on these camp stools across from the music gate, waiting for the hearse to come out. We started talking about both of you—about you and about Sammy. Just before the hearse came out, he looked me straight in the eye and he said, 'Angela, I've been wrong to cut Susannah out like I've done. She had to get away. I understand that now. I love her, and as soon as I get back to California, I'm going to tell her so.'"

Susannah held herself rigidly. "He told you that? He told you he loved me?"

"As God is my witness. He told me he was going to call you that very day."

Susannah pressed her eyes shut and tears slithered from beneath her lids. "Oh, Angela."

Angela took her in her arms once again. She was much smaller than Susannah, but she sheltered her. "I—I couldn't bear the idea that he went to his grave hating me."

"He loved you, honey. He went on and on about how much you meant to him."

Susannah pulled away, her forehead crumpling. "You're not making this up so I'll feel better, are you, Angela? Please. I have to know the truth."

Angela squeezed her hands tightly. "It's true. I'm Catholic, Susannah. If I didn't tell the truth about somebody's last moments on earth, it would be a mortal sin. He loved you so much. He told me again and again."

Angela's eyes were wide and earnest, and Susannah wanted desperately to believe her. But although grief had dulled some of her senses, it had sharpened others. As she gazed at her mother-in-law, she knew with absolute certainty that Angela was lying from the bottom of her loving, generous heart.

Sam came home that evening with an expensive handwoven shawl she had admired in a boutique a few weeks earlier. He made no mention of his disappearance, and she was too drained to ask him about it. As she tucked the shawl away in a bottom dresser drawer, she told herself that no one was perfect and she had to learn to accept Sam's faults. But a fissure had been ripped in the fabric of their marriage.

Several weeks passed before she learned that she had been cut from her father's will and that he had left everything to Paige. Millions of dollars were involved as well as a huge block of FBT stock. But it wasn't the financial loss that devastated her. It was the additional evidence of her father's lack of forgiveness.

Sam argued with her for weeks because she refused to challenge the will. Even in death he hated for Joel to get the best of her. But she didn't want money. She wanted her father alive. She wanted another chance.

Sometimes Susannah thought it was only the overwhelming work load that kept her going through the next few months. She had little time to wallow in either grief or guilt, no time at all to try to decide how she would live the rest of her life, knowing that she could never be reconciled with her father. All of the hours that would have been devoted to introspection were occupied with keeping their small company alive; ironically, success was proving to be even more dangerous to SysVal than failure.

"Will you relax, for chrissake," Sam said, glaring at her as he paced the carpeted reception area of Hoffman Enterprises, one of San Francisco's most prestigious venture capital firms. "If they see how nervous you are, you're going to blow this whole deal. I mean it, Susannah, you could personally screw us up—"

Mitch slapped down the magazine he had been pretending to read. "Leave her alone! Susannah, why do you put up with his nonsense? If I were you, Sam, I'd worry about what I was going to say instead of giving her a hard time."

"Why don't you go fuck yourself?"

"Why don't you—"

Susannah whirled around. "Stop it, both of you! We're all nervous. Let's not take it out on each other." Mitch and Sam had always argued, but in the four months since her father's death, it had grown worse. While their relationship had deteriorated, her own relationship with Mitch had grown closer. She would never forget the way he had stood beside her when she had most needed it.

These past months had been unusually difficult. Not only had she been faced with a searing personal crisis, but SysVal was in deep trouble. Despite the fact that stacks of new orders were coming in every week for the Blaze, the company had run out of money.

Sam glared at her and resumed his pacing. Mitch continued to brood. She wandered over to the windows, where she stared at the view of the ocean, the Golden Gate, and the distant hazy outline of Marin beyond. The chill December rain that splashed against the skyscraper's windows matched her mood.

It bothered her that Sam always seemed to be at his worst when she most needed his support. Today, for example. This meeting meant everything to them. If they couldn't get the financing they needed, they simply wouldn't be able to survive. As orders poured in for the Blaze, they had been feverishly adding new staff, expanding their facilities, and searching out additional subcontractors to assemble the machines—all within the space of a few months. Now they simply couldn't pay their bills. The money was there on paper in future orders, but it wasn't in hand where they needed it.

They had known from the beginning that they were dangerously undercapitalized, but now she and Mitch estimated that their precarious financial balancing act was within thirty days of collapsing. They could no longer put off going after venture capital.

Mitch studied the straight line of Susannah's back as she

stood at the windows. He had grown to care very much for her in the past year, and he was worried. The strain of her father's death had taken an enormous toll, and the business of running SysVal grew more complicated by the day. God knew, Sam wasn't any help. The more Mitch watched them together, the more he saw that Sam was a user. He took everything Susannah had, but he gave very little back.

All of them knew how important this meeting was. Granted, there were firms other than Hoffman Enterprises they could have gone to for financing, but Mitch had both his heart and his head set on making this deal. Leland T. Hoffman was a wily old fox who had written the textbook on venture capital and financed some of the biggest success stories in American business. If Hoffman put his money behind SysVal, it would legitimize them in a way that nothing else could.

The general public was gradually becoming aware of the microcomputer. Commodore had introduced the PET. The TRS-80 was on display at Radio Shack stores all across the country, and both SysVal and the little Apple Computer Company had begun to find a small, but loyal following. But was that enough to convince a man of Hoffman's reputation to make a substantial investment in SysVal?

A secretary appeared to usher them into a conference room, which was furnished in lush art deco. Hoffman, white-haired and plump with prosperity, sat at the center of a burled walnut table and leafed through the folder of material they had prepared for him. None of the half dozen other men who were seated rose to greet them or acknowledged their presence in any way, an obvious intimidation tactic that Mitch hoped wouldn't rattle his partners.

Sam curled his lip at the opulent surroundings, then sprawled down in a chair. He tilted it back and stretched his legs out under the table like a sulky James Dean. Susannah smiled pleasantly, but fumbled with her papers as she sat. She smoothed the skirt of the conservative pale gray business suit that Mitch had asked her to purchase for the occasion. Mitch knew that Susannah was irritated with him for being so specific about her wardrobe, while he totally ignored the jeans that Sam was wearing with his sport coat.

But Mitch had a clear idea of the impression he wanted to give today, and his partners' manner of dress was all part of it.

Hoffman finally raised his head and studied Mitch over the top of his half glasses. Then he shifted his gaze to Susannah.

"Hello, Uncle Leland," she said.

Mitch nearly fell out of his chair. *Uncle* Leland?

Sam seemed to be as surprised as Mitch to discover that his wife knew Hoffman. Mitch wanted to strangle her for springing something like this on them.

"Susannah. It's good to see you again." Hoffman's tone was brisk and formal. "Now what can we do for you and your friends?"

Mitch's stomach sank. Hoffman wasn't taking them seriously at all. He hadn't agreed to meet with them because he was interested in backing SysVal, but merely as a courtesy to Susannah.

Mitch wanted to bang his head against the table in frustration. He forgot that only a few minutes before he had been worried about the strain Susannah was under. Now he wanted to kill her.

Susannah was to make the first presentation. She picked up her leather folder and proceeded to the front of the room. She looked so cool and composed that even Mitch, who knew better, was nearly fooled.

"Gentlemen." She gave all of them a polite smile. "I have to begin with an apology to my business partners for not telling them that we're meeting today before an old family friend. Although Leland and I aren't blood relatives, he was a longtime acquaintance of my father and has known me for nearly as long as I can remember. I didn't tell my partners about this acquaintance because I didn't want them to believe—even for a moment—that an old family connection would make Hoffman Enterprises magically open up its checkbook to SysVal."

Looking thoughtful, she took a step forward. "If I were a man—my father's son instead of his daughter—this old family relationship would almost certainly work to my advantage. But as a woman—my father's daughter—I find myself at a distinct disadvantage."

She smiled at Hoffman. "When I was growing up, Leland, you didn't watch me climbing trees and getting roughed up in football games. Instead, you saw me cutting out paper dolls and having tea parties. Although a grown woman stands before you now, in your mind you're undoubtedly scoffing at the idea of putting your money behind someone who once—and it pains me to admit this—came running to you for protection from an exceedingly ugly earthworm."

The men around the table chuckled, and Mitch felt himself beginning to relax. It was impossible to read Hoffman's expression, but Mitch had to believe that he was impressed by Susannah's good-humored introduction. His admiration for his business partner grew. She was really good at this. As he watched her, he realized that she had actually begun to enjoy herself.

"Women in the business of electronics are a rare species," she went on. "Ironic, isn't it, since women are destined to become major users of small computers? I regard being a female in this industry as an advantage, since I look at everything from a fresh viewpoint. But if my being a woman bothers any of you, I do offer some consolation." She nodded her head toward Sam and Mitch at the foot of the table, and grinned wickedly, "My partners have more than enough testosterone to put all of your minds at ease."

Even Hoffman smiled at that.

Now that she had them relaxed, she launched into her presentation. In her efficient, no-nonsense manner, she offered the business plan they had all labored over for so long, outlining market projections and five-year goals that were aggressive, but credible. As she spoke, her private-school voice and calm assurance gave their renegade company an air of old world stability, despite the fact that Sam had propped his motorcycle boots on the polished tabletop.

She finished her presentation and returned to her seat. Mitch noticed that the men were looking at the papers in front of them with a bit more interest.

Sam dropped his feet to the floor and rose slowly from his chair. "There are winners and losers," he muttered. "Fast buck artists, con men, bullshitters." He glared at all of them. "And then there are champions. And do you know what separates them?" He punched the air with his fist. *"Mission. Mission* is what separates them."

Brother Love's traveling salvation show was off and running. For the next twenty minutes he paced the room, tugging his necktie loose with one hand, shedding his sport coat with the other, jabbing a hand into the pocket of his jeans only to pull it out and shove it through his hair. With a spectacular display of verbal pyrotechnics and oral gymnastics, he painted a picture of a shining future with a Blaze microcomputer beating solidly as its heart.

Hallelujah, brother. And amen!

When it was all over, Mitch was exhilarated. His intuition had been right and he hadn't needed to speak at all. Together, Susannah and Sam had formed exactly the company image he wanted to present—rock-solid respectability countered with outrageous razzle-dazzle. Only a fool could resist them, and Leland Hoffman was no fool.

Although it would be several days before Hoffman got back to them, at least they knew they had given him their best. They went to Mom & Pop's that night to celebrate. Sam immediately claimed Victors, a new high-tech target game that all of them, with the exception of Yank, had decided was the best video game ever made.

Sam called her over. "Come on, Suzie. Cheer me on." Her earlier resentment had dissolved, and she went to join him. He kissed the corner of her mouth without taking his eyes off the screen. "I've got a good game going here. Give me a couple of minutes and then I'll let you play."

She slid behind him so that her breasts were pushed up against his back, and propped her chin on the top of his shoulder while she watched him maneuver the joystick. Her high-tech, whiz-bang husband. Her body began to feel hot, the way it did before they made love. She slipped her hands down onto his upper arms, conscious of the movement of his muscles on the controls through the sleeves of his T-shirt. Sometimes he made her feel as if she was tottering on the edge of a deep precipice. What if she fell off? Would he be the one who would catch her or the one who had pushed her? It was a disconcerting thought, and she shook it off.

Mitch was playing Space Invaders at the next machine.

Releasing Sam, she stepped over to watch him. He glanced longingly toward the Victors game. "Is Sam about done?"

"Forget it. I'm next."

"Are you open to negotiating for position?"

"Unless you're talking diamonds, forget it."

Mitch smiled. "At least I don't have to beat off Yank, too. I can't understand why he won't play Victors. He loves good video games."

"Who can understand what goes through Yank's head?"

Just as she spoke his name, the restaurant door opened and he walked in. She looked more closely and then let out a soft, incredulous exclamation. Distracted, Sam glanced up. "Jesus . . ." he murmured.

Mitch had fallen into a disbelieving silence.

Although Yank was walking toward them, he wasn't the one who had caught their attention. Instead, it was the woman sashaying at his side who had temporarily stunned them into speechlessness. She was a traffic-stopping redhead with crimson lips, elaborate makeup, and leopardskin pants that looked as if they had been tattooed on her hips. Overshadowing all that jutted a pair of breasts so spectacular that only a miraculous feat of engineering seemed to be holding them within the confines of her gold tank top.

"Maybe she's his wet nurse," Susannah whispered, unable to take her eyes off the monumental mammaries.

"Are you kidding?" Mitch whispered back. "He'd suffocate to death."

Yank walked up to them and nodded. He refused to have anything to do with the day-to-day business operations of the company; typically, he didn't ask about their meeting with Hoffman Enterprises, but about a problem they'd been having with their keyboards. "What'd the manufacturer say, Sam? Did you talk to them?"

"Uh . . . static." The woman's presence seemed to have robbed Sam of his capacity for coherent speech.

Yank looked irritated. "Of course it's static. We've known that for weeks. What do they intend to do about it?"

"Do?"

Susannah stepped in and extended her hand to Yank's companion. "Hi, I'm Susannah Faulconer."

"Kismet," the woman replied in a breathy, affected voice.

"I beg your pardon?"

"Kismet Jade. My numerologist picked it out. You're a Sagittarius, aren't you?"

"Actually, no." Susannah quickly introduced her partners, but Kismet barely spared them a glance. She was too busy cantilevering her left breast over Yank's upper arm.

"I'm hungry, Stud Man," she purred. "You gonna buy me something to eat, or do I have to work for my dinner?" She gave him a wicked, moist-lipped smile that clearly indicated exactly what sort of work she had in mind.

Yank calmly adjusted his glasses on his nose. "I'll be happy to get you something to eat. The pizza is excellent, but the burgers are quite good, too."

"Stud Man?" Mitch muttered at Susannah's side.

"I ordered some pizzas," Susannah said quickly.

Kismet walked two vermilion fingernails up the length of Yank's arm. "Play Victors with me while we wait."

"I'm sorry, Kismet, but I don't play Victors."

Kismet began to pout. "Why not? It's the best arcade game that's come out this year."

Yank looked genuinely distressed. "I'm awfully sorry, Kismet. I really don't like to play Victors. Sam is our champion. He's the best Victors player you've ever seen." He gave Sam a pleading glance. "Would you mind playing a game with Kismet?"

"Uh—sure. No problem."

Mitch abandoned Space Invaders and walked with Susannah to the table. "She certainly is a far cry from Roberta," he said. "Sam's going to have a hard time keeping his eyes on the screen."

"So would you," she pointed out as they slid into the booth.

Kismet released a giggling obscenity as Sam annihilated her before she even reached the second screen. She took the quarter Yank handed her.

Susannah studied them. "Have you spent any time at all thinking about what it will mean if this deal goes through?"

"That's about all I've done lately."

"I don't mean the company. I'm talking about how it will change us personally. On paper, anyway, each one of us will be worth a lot of money."

"I have money now. You've had it before. We know what it's like."

She studied Yank and Sam. "They don't."

"Nothing ever stays the same, Susannah."

"Uhm. I guess you're right." She picked up her beer and took a sip.

On the opposite side of the room, Kismet arched her arms around Yank's thin neck, pressed her lips to his, and thrust her long experienced tongue deep within his mouth.

Susannah experienced a moment both bittersweet and poignant. Mitch was right. Nothing was ever going to be the same again.

BOOK
TWO

• • • • • • • • • • • • • • • • • • • •

THE
MISSION

We have set out together on an adventure to give the world the best computer humankind can produce. We will support and stand by our products, placing quality and integrity above all else. We relish the adventure because it gives us the opportunity to put ourselves to the test of excellence.

Statement of Mission
SysVal Computer Corporation

21

The money came rolling in. Slick, green, fast money. Hot money. New money. Money aching to be spent.

The seventies whirled into the eighties, and the greatest industrial joy ride of the twentieth century picked up speed. Silicon Valley was awash in electronic gold as capitalism struck its finest hour.

Home video games had already captured the imagination of the American family, and by 1982, the idea of having a computer in the house no longer seemed strange at all. Firms sprang up overnight. Some of them collapsed just as quickly, but others left their founders with almost unimaginable riches.

In the posh communities of Los Gatos, Woodside, and Los Altos Hills, the electrical engineers stepped out of their hot tubs, stuffed their plastic pocket protectors into Armani shirts, hopped into their BMW's, and laughed like hell.

By the fall of 1982, the nerds owned the Valley. The bespeckled, pimply-faced, overweight, underweight, dateless, womanless, goofiest of the goofy, were the undisputed, unchallenged kings of the entire freaking Valley!

Man, it was sweet.

Yank pulled his Porsche 911 crookedly into a parking space at SysVal's main building and then headed up the walk toward the main entrance. He nodded absentmindedly at the two female account executives who had stopped in mid-conversation as he approached and gazed wistfully at the retreating back of his leather bomber jacket. Once inside the lobby, he determinedly ignored the security guard stationed behind the elliptical-shaped desk.

Everyone else who worked at SysVal had to show a plastic security badge to be admitted. Even Sam wore a badge. But Yank pretended the badges didn't exist, and Susannah had left orders that the guards were to admit him on sight.

Logically, he understood that those golden days of Homebrew were gone forever—the days of free and open information, of one for all and all for one. It was September of 1982. John Lennon was dead, Ronald Reagan was in the White House, and Uncle Sam had just busted up AT&T. The world was changing, and the Valley was filled with industrial spies intent on stealing the latest American technology and selling it to the Japanese, the Russians, or even a new start-up in the next industrial park. SysVal's astounding success had made it a prime target for those roaches of humanity. Yank understood all that. But he still wouldn't wear a security badge.

As he headed down the hallway toward the multimillion-dollar lab that had been built especially for him, he had the nagging sensation that he had forgotten something very important. But he dismissed his worry. What could be more important than solving the problem with the trace lines of solder on their new circuit board? They were too close. He had an idea . . .

Ten miles away, in the gilt and brocade bedroom of his Portola Valley home, lingerie model Tiffani Wade's carefully arranged seductive pose was ruined by the frown marring her forehead. "Yank? Yank, you can come back in now. I'm ready."

She called out three more times before she realized that no one was going to answer, then she sagged back into the pillows. "You son of a bitch," she muttered. "You've done it to me again."

* * *

Susannah shut off the Blaze III that rested on the credenza behind her desk and stretched. Somewhere in the building one of the employees fired off an air horn. She barely noticed. At SysVal, people were always firing off air horns or calling out Bingo numbers over the loudspeaker system, just so no one ever made the mistake of confusing them with IBM or FBT.

As if someone had overheard her thoughts, the loudspeaker began to squawk. "Mayday, Mayday. The Japanese have just attacked the parking lot. All employees driving domestic cars should immediately take cover. This is not a drill. I repeat. This is not a drill."

Susannah rolled her eyes. God forbid they should ever have a real emergency. No one would believe it.

SysVal's employees were primarily men in their twenties, and they prided themselves on being bad. In the six years since the company was founded, Sam Gamble's personality had become their model. Even the whiz kids at Apple Computer weren't as raunchy, as brazen, as wild as the rowdy bunch at SysVal. At Apple they held Friday afternoon beer blasts, but at SysVal they showed stag movies, too. The boys of SysVal strutted their stuff—their youth, their audaciousness, their sense of destiny. They were the ones who had made the magical little Blaze available to the world and helped humanity learn the beauty of personal computing. Like their brash, charismatic founder, they were young, invincible, immortal.

Taking off her glasses, Susannah rubbed the bridge of her nose, then looked across her office at a much-abused dart board with the Apple logo painted on it. She thought about the five of them—Jobs and Woz, Sam, Yank, herself. All of them college dropouts. Freaks, nerds, rebels, and one overly polite socialite. In the five years that had passed since the West Coast Computer Faire, everything they touched had turned to gold. It was as if the gods had blessed them with youth, brains, and unlimited good luck. On paper, anyway, she and her partners were worth over a hundred million dollars each, while at Apple, Steve Jobs was worth more than three hundred million. Sometimes the enormity of their success scared Susannah to death.

The battered Apple dart board gave visual evidence of the

early rivalry between the two young companies, but in the past few years that had changed. With the dawning of the 1980s, the Big Boys had finally lifted their heads and realized that they had been left behind. Late in 1981, IBM had introduced the IBM-PC. Apple Computer, in a display of bravado that Susannah still wished SysVal had thought of first, had taken out a full-page ad in the nation's newspapers. The ad said, WELCOME IBM. SERIOUSLY. A paragraph of copy had followed in which the brash young upstarts at Apple had assumed the role of the wise old men of the industry and spelled out for Mighty IBM all of the glories of personal computing—as if IBM were too inexperienced, too stupid, too wet-behind-the-ears, to figure it out for themselves. The sheer audacity of it had kept the business community laughing for months.

A custom-designed radio-controlled car zoomed into her office, did a three sixty in the middle of her carpet and zoomed out again with no sign of a human operator. SysVal's engineers were entertaining themselves again.

Rubbing her eyes, she pushed a stray lock of hair away from her face. Her hair was shorter now, cut in a breezy style that feathered around her cheeks and softened the sharp, aristocratic features of her face. Since no important meetings were on her docket for that day, she had dressed informally in a coral cowl-neck sweater and tight, straight-legged jeans. Two slim gold bangles glittered at one wrist and a wide gold cuff hugged the other. The third finger of her right hand sported a two-karat marquis-cut diamond that she had bought for herself. More, she had definitely concluded, was better than less.

On impulse, she reached for her telephone and dialed the number that connected her directly with Mitch's private office. But before the phone could ring, he walked through her door.

"Mental telepathy," she said, some of her tension slipping away merely at the sight of his solid, comforting presence. "I was just calling you."

He slumped wearily into the chair opposite her desk. "Somebody left a bra in the hallway."

"As long as the person who lost it isn't running around bare-chested, don't complain."

298

Of them all, Mitch had changed the least. The blunt planes of his face had hardened a bit, and a few strands of gray had begun to weave through the sandy hair at his temples. But his body hadn't lost any of its tone. At thirty-seven, SysVal's Executive Vice-President of Sales and Marketing was still as solid as the Buckeye wide receiver who had won a place in Woody Hayes's heart.

Mitch was the most respectable corporate officer SysVal had, a wonderful piece of white bread who thought nothing of flying across the country to watch one of his kids play soccer, and was recently honored as the Bay Area Jaycees' Man of the Year for his civic contributions. Over the years, he and Susannah had developed a deep friendship.

She saw at once that he was exhausted. He had been driving himself for months, trying to win a multimillion-dollar contract with the state of California to install the Blaze III in hundreds of its state offices. The contract would provide the capitalization SysVal needed to finish up the work on the Wildfire and launch their new business computer ahead of the competition. Unfortunately, SysVal's competition for the contract was FBT, and Cal Theroux had been lobbying hard for the Falcon 101, FBT's new personal computer. Although the entry of giant corporations like IBM and FBT had legitimized the personal computer, it had also made things a lot tougher.

"Be honest with me," he said, as he stretched out his legs. "Do you think I'm stuffy?"

"You? Perish the thought."

"I'm not joking. I want to know."

"You're serious?"

He nodded.

"Yes. You're definitely stuffy."

"Well, thank you. Thank you so very much." He glared at her, a picture of offended dignity.

She smiled. "Does this sudden soul searching have anything to do with your relationship with the beautiful, talented, and terminally obnoxious Jacqueline Dane?"

"Jacqueline is not obnoxious. She is one of the finest actresses in this country."

"As she is quick to point out. Did you see that television interview she gave last week where she went on and on about

299

the importance of making *serious* films and doing *serious* work? She kept pushing her fingers through her hair like she had mange or something. I have never yet seen that woman give an interview where she hadn't managed to work in the fact that she has a degree from Yale. She bites her finger-nails, too."

He gave her his best stony-eyed gaze. "I suppose you would prefer it if I started dating bimbos like Yank does."

"You and Yank could do each other big favors by trading women for a few months. Yank needs to date someone with an IQ that's higher than the speed limit, and you need to find a woman who can lighten up a little. Honestly, Mitch, I can't believe Jacqueline had the nerve to call you stuffy. I think her face would crack if she ever tried to smile."

"You just said I was stuffy," he pointed out.

"I'm allowed to say that because I'm one of the best friends you have, and I adore you. She, on the other hand, only cares about dead philosophers with names no sensible person can spell."

"I had my fill of party girls when I was married to Louise. I like serious women."

Susannah shook her head in disgust. There was simply no reasoning with him. In the past six years, Mitch had had long-term relationships with three women, all brilliant, beautiful, and sober-minded. Susannah still couldn't make up her mind which one of them she detested the most. At heart he was a family man, and Susannah was afraid he might actually marry Jacqueline Dane. And if her suspicions were right, the actress would jump at the offer. Mitch had a funny effect on women. For someone who was basically a stuffed shirt, he certainly didn't have any trouble finding bedroom companions.

She knew she was beating a dead horse, but she plunged in anyway. "Why won't you let me pick out some women for you? Really, Mitch, I know just the sort of person you need. Someone who's intelligent, but warm. Someone who won't try to mother you, since I know you hate that. A woman with a sense of humor to make up for the fact that you have absolutely none." It wasn't true. Mitch had a wonderful sense of humor, but it was so dry that most people didn't appreciate it. "A woman without much libido, since you're getting older and you probably don't have the sex drive you used to."

"That's it." He stood and glared at her. "My libido isn't any of your business, Miss Hot Shot."

"Touchy, touchy." She tried to imagine herself joking with a man about his sex drive six years ago and failed. SysVal had changed them all.

He finally smiled. "Now that you're filthy rich, you've turned into a real brat, do you know that?"

"We're all filthy rich. And I'm not a brat."

She noticed the strain that had been evident when he had come into her office had dissipated. The company was a pressure cooker of activity with a new crisis popping up every hour, and she and Mitch had long ago discovered that baiting each other worked as well as anything else to relax them both.

An angry male voice blared through the loudspeaker. "Whichever son of a bitch took DP27E's new HP calculator had better get the fucker back to the office right now!"

Mitch's expression grew pained, and he lifted a disapproving eyebrow toward the speaker. "Susannah?"

She sighed. "I'll put out another obscenity memo." They had learned years ago that it was useless to lock up the loudspeaker controls. There was nothing the SysVal engineers loved better than breaking through anything that bore even a passing resemblance to a closed system.

She asked him about his visit to Boston. Over the years, Mitch's children had visited him frequently, and she had grown fond of them. She kept a framed picture nine-year-old Liza had drawn for her on her desk next to a paperweight David had made in his sixth-grade art class.

Mitch walked over to her window. "I finally met Louise's new husband. He and I had a couple of beers and talked about the kids. He said they were getting along well, and he wanted me to know that he wasn't going to try to take my place with them. He saw himself as a big brother, not a father, that sort of thing. Heck of a nice guy."

"You hate his guts, don't you?"

"I wanted to slam my fist right through his face."

301

She gave him a sympathetic smile. Not for the first time, it occurred to her that Mitch was a much better friend to her than Sam had ever been.

They chatted for a few more minutes, and then Mitch left. Her stomach rumbled and she realized she was hungry. Maybe she could talk Sam into leaving early tonight. It would be wonderful to have dinner at home for a change and spend an evening alone together—something they hadn't done in longer than she could remember.

She got up from her desk, deliberately pushing away the painful knowledge that Sam wouldn't want to spend an evening alone with her. She had made it a habit not to dwell on the problems in her marriage when she was at work, but it was difficult. As she walked out of the office, she forced herself to think about the company instead.

SysVal had become one of the most glamorous privately owned companies in the world. Thanks to Mitch's brilliant financial strategies, the original four partners had each held onto a whopping fifteen per cent of the company. Susannah didn't like to think about how much money they had. The amount was almost obscene.

As she turned the corner into the next hallway, she ran into two of the engineers who were playing with the radio-controlled car. She chatted with them for a few minutes and admired their toy. When she finally moved on, she wasn't aware of the fact that they still watched her.

Even though Susannah wasn't beautiful, there was something about her that drove the young engineers at SysVal slightly crazy. Maybe it was those tight jeans—those long slim legs. Maybe it was the way she moved—tall and proud. But physical appearance was only part of their attraction to her. There was the aphrodisia of her wealth and the ever-increasing influence she held in a male-dominated industry. All in all, at the age of thirty-one, Susannah was a potent combination of style, sex, brains, money, and power, qualities that were irresistible to the brilliant young men who came from all over the world to work for SysVal.

They joked about what it would be like to sleep with her, but behind their sexual bantering lay a genuine respect. Susannah was tough and demanding, but she was seldom unreasonable. Not like some people.

Sam wasn't in his office.

Susannah moved on. SysVal headquarters occupied three large buildings, grouped together in an informal campus arrangement. Her office was in the main building, the center section of which was open, with glass block walls and partitions that didn't quite reach the ceiling. A Joan Jett song blared from one of the labs, and she passed a group of video games that occupied a cranny in the brightly painted hallway. At SysVal, the boundaries between work and play were deliberately obscured.

Lights were coming from the left, and she took a sharp turn in that direction. Although it was after six o'clock, the New Product Team was still meeting to talk about the problems they were having with the Blaze Wildfire, the revolutionary new business computer they hoped to launch within a year.

For all the future promise of Sam's Wildfire project, the Blaze III was SysVal's workhorse, the bread and butter of the company. The Blaze III was the computer that America was buying for its kids, the computer that small offices were growing to depend on, and the computer that—along with its ancestors the I and II—had made them all rich.

Sam's voice punched the air and spilled out into the hallway from one of the conference rooms. She paused inside the doorway to watch him. Once just the sight of him had sent thrills of excitement through her body. Now she felt a sense of despair. Somehow she had to make things right again between them. But how could she do that when she wasn't even certain what was wrong?

He was straddling a chair backward, straining the fine woolen material of his charcoal slacks. His white shirt-sleeves were rolled to the elbows, his collar was unfastened, and the heels of his Italian loafers were propped up on the chair rungs. A dozen young faces sat cross-legged on the floor around him, gazing up at him as he spoke, their expressions rapt while they listened to Brother Love's new-age Sermon on the Mount. Blessed is the microchip, she thought, for its users shall inherit the earth.

The employees both loved and hated Sam. With his evangelist's zeal, he inspired them to do the impossible, but he had no patience for incompetence and was brutal in his criticism. Still, very few of them left, even after suffering one of his humiliating public tongue-lashings. He gave them the sense that they had a mission in life. They were soldiers in the final crusade of the twentieth century, and even those who had grown to detest him continued to scramble all over themselves to please him.

She frowned as she watched those young, eager faces soaking up everything he said. An aura of hero worship had developed around Sam that bothered her. It might be good for the company, but it wasn't good for Sam.

Her presence in the doorway caught his attention. He turned his head and frowned at the interruption. She remembered how his face had once softened when he caught sight of her. When had it begun to change? Sometimes she thought that it went as far back as her father's funeral.

She gestured toward the kitchen at the back, signaling him that she would meet him there. He returned his attention to the group without making any acknowledgment. She straightened her shoulders and walked on with quiet dignity. Just before she reached the kitchen, she passed a woman with two very young children on their way to the large cafeteria. All of them wore visitor's badges, and the mother was carrying a picnic basket.

Her depression burrowed in deeper. It wasn't the first time she had seen something like this. SysVal's employees worked such long hours that spouses—usually wives—sometimes showed up with their children so they could provide some facsimile of a family dinner. SysVal didn't hire anyone who wasn't a workaholic, and the long hours were taking a toll on family life—something Sam hadn't taken into account when he constructed his Utopian vision of their company. But then, families weren't important to Sam. She touched her fingers to her waist, feeling the hollowness inside. How much longer was he going to ignore this pressing need she had for a child? Just because she was SysVal's president didn't mean she wasn't a woman, too.

She made her way to the refrigerator in the back of the kitchen and pulled out a carton of yogurt. But as she began to peel off the lid, her fingers faltered and her eyelids squeezed shut. What was she going to do about her marriage? Far too many times, Sam felt like the enemy, like another person for her to please, another person with an invisible checklist of qualities she had to live up to.

He shot through the door, wearily shoving his right hand through his short black hair. "Susannah, you're going to have to get on Marketing again. I'm sick of their bullshit. They either have to buy into the Wildfire—and I mean total commitment—or they can take their asses over to Apple. They're like a bunch of goddamn old ladies . . ."

She let him rant and rave for a while. Tomorrow he would undoubtedly storm the Marketing Department and throw one of his famous temper tantrums. Then she would have to clean up after him. Sam was thirty now, but in many ways he was still a child.

He collapsed into one of the chairs. "Get me a Coke."

She went over to the refrigerator and pulled out a can from his private stock. The top hissed as she popped it. She set it in front of him, then bent forward and brushed his mouth with a soft kiss. His lips were cool and dry. After he had been speaking to a group, she was always surprised that they weren't red hot.

She began to knead the tight muscles of his shoulders with her thumbs. "Why don't we take off early Friday night and drive down to Monterey? There's an inn I've been hearing about. Private cottages, ocean view."

"I don't know. Maybe."

"I think it would do us both good to get away for a while."

"Yeah. You're probably right." Despite his words, Susannah knew that Sam didn't really want to get away. He fed off the furious pace of the company. Even when he was at home he was thinking, working, lambasting people over one of their seven telephones. Sometimes she thought that Sam was trying to outrun life.

Her hands grew still on his shoulders. "It's a good time of the month. Full moon, baying wolf, ripe egg."

He pulled abruptly away from her. "Christ. Don't start the baby shit again, all right? Just don't start. You can't even find time to help me look for that new Oriental rug for the dining room. How do you expect to take care of a kid?"

"I don't like picking out rugs. I do like children. I'm

thirty-one, Sam. The clock's ticking. SysVal is going to have on-site child care by the end of the year. That'll make a big difference to me and the rest of our female employees."

As soon as she had spoken, she wished she hadn't brought up the child-care issue. She had given him an excuse to divert their conversation from the personal back to the company, and she knew he would take advantage of it.

"I don't know why you act like this child care thing is all signed, sealed, and delivered. I'm not backing you, and I don't think Mitch will, either. It's not a corporation's responsibility to take care of its employee's kids, for chrissake."

"It is if the corporation wants to hang onto its female work force. I'm going to fight you on this one, Sam. I'll take it right to the Board of Directors if I have to."

"It wouldn't be the first time." He rose abruptly from his chair. "I don't understand you anymore, Susannah. You seem to fight me on everything."

It wasn't true. She still believed that of all of them, Sam had the truest vision of what SysVal could be. Because of him, the company had never been loaded down with hierarchies. The organization was fluid, lean, and profitable.

"I don't know, Susannah. You've changed. And I'm not sure it's all for the better." His eyes skimmed down over her clothing. He didn't like it when she wore jeans. He hated her shorter hair. If he overheard her swearing, he staged a major confrontation. She had finally realized that a big part of Sam wanted her back the way she had been when they had first met.

"Sam, we need to spend some time together without telephones ringing and people showing up at the front door. We have some problems we have to work out, and we need time alone to do it."

"You're turning into a broken record, you know that? I don't want to hear about it anymore. I've got enough on my mind without a load of crap from you."

"Excuse me. Uh—Sam?"

Mindy Bradshaw walked into the kitchen in such a gingerly fashion that the floor might have been covered with rattlesnakes. She was a thin, anemic-looking blonde, with baby-fine hair that fell like a veil over the sides of her face.

Mindy was one of the most recent additions to the New Product Team. Although she was bright, she lacked self-confidence and was frequently at the receiving end of one of Sam's more humiliating public tongue-lashings. Several times in the past few weeks, Susannah had seen her running from a meeting in tears, not exactly the behavior Susannah wanted to see from the company's minority female work force—a group of which she was fiercely protective. Despite Sam's abuse, however, Mindy continued to hang on to his every word and gaze at him as if—at any moment—he just might levitate.

Sam was obviously relieved at the interruption. "Yeah, Mindy, what is it?"

"Pete and I wondered— That is—"

"Christ, Mindy. Start all over, will you? Walk into the room like you own it for a change. Stand up straight, look me in the eye, and tell me to go to hell if you feel like it."

"Oh, no," she said breathlessly. "It's just—Pete and I have been crunching some numbers. We have some ideas about pricing on the BDI that we want to go over with you."

"Yeah, sure." He pitched his empty Coke can into the recycling bin and left the room without a backward glance.

Susannah walked listlessly back toward her office. These past few years had turned her into a fighter, but she didn't know how to fight this. On impulse, she took a detour that led to the east wing of the building. Maybe Yank was still working in his lab. Sometimes when she was rattled, she liked to drop in there and spend a few minutes with him. They seldom talked, but being with Yank was soothing. She enjoyed the quiet patience of his movements, the steadiness of his eyes when they actually focused on her. His presence settled her.

And then she hesitated. She wasn't going to get into the habit of using other people as a crutch simply because she couldn't solve her own problems. She returned to her office and flicked on her Blaze III. The light began to glow on the screen. For a moment, she regarded the machine with a mixture of love and bitterness. And then she lost herself in her work.

* * *

Long after midnight that same evening, Sam eased naked into the hot tub. The house that rose behind him was a stark ultramodern structure with a roof line that jutted at sharp angles like bats' wings against the night sky and held eighteen solar panels to provide energy. He and a team of architects had worked on the design for nearly a year, and it had taken another two years to build. Everything was the best. The interior held free-form couches upholstered in white suede and jagged-edged tables chiseled from rock-crystal selenite. The deck was made of marble and sculptured black granite. Rigidly geometric furniture constructed of cold-rolled steel glimmered faintly near the perimeter of the hot tub. The hot tub itself, made of black marble, was the size of a small swimming pool.

He had settled into a ledge contoured to fit his body. Although he was tired, he couldn't sleep. As the inky water swirled around him, he gazed down at the lights in the valley below and pretended that they were stars and that he was hanging upside down in the universe. He let himself float, concentrating only on the surge of the waters and the feeling of rushing through unexplored space.

He had more money than he had ever dreamed existed. He could buy anything he wanted, go anywhere, do anything. But something was missing. The water sucked at him and he raced deeper into space. *Find it,* a voice whispered. *Look around you and find what's missing.*

He was only thirty years old, and he didn't want life to be safe and settled. Where were the challenges? The thrills? SysVal wasn't enough anymore. And neither was Susannah.

A sound intruded on his thoughts. One of the doors that led out from the house to the deck had opened behind him. Susannah came into his line of vision. He watched with resentment as she pulled her silk robe tight and hugged herself against the night chill.

"You couldn't sleep?" she asked.

He settled deeper into the bubbling waters and wished she would go away.

"Would you like me to get in with you?" she said softly.

He shrugged. "Whatever."

She unfastened her robe and let it slide from her shoulders. She was naked beneath. There was a momentary shift in the rhythm of the water as she settled onto the ledge next to him.

"The water's hot."

"One hundred and two degrees, like always." He arched his neck and laid his head back in the water, closing his eyes to shut her out.

He felt her fingers on his arm. "Sam, I'm worried about you."

"Don't be."

"I wish you'd tell me what's wrong."

His eyes snapped open. "You're what's wrong! Why don't you leave me alone?"

For a moment she did nothing, and then she rose silently from the tub. Water glistened on her body. His eyes roved down over her small breasts, her waist, the soft auburn tuft. She didn't have any idea how hot she still made him. He grabbed her hand before she could move away and pulled her down. She lost her balance and landed awkwardly beside him.

He pushed her back onto the ledge. "Open your legs."

"I don't want to." She tried to twist away.

"Open them, damn it," he insisted.

"Sam, this isn't right. We need to talk. Sex isn't enough this time."

She started to get up. He clenched his teeth and moved on top of her. He didn't want to listen to her. He wanted to get the fire back, the challenge, the thrill of conquest. Wedging open her thighs, he thrust hard and buried himself inside her.

She wasn't ready for him and she winced, but he tilted up her hips and drove deeper.

She dug the heels of her hands into his chest, trying to push him away. "Dammit, Sam. Don't do this!"

He refused to let her up. The night-black water swirled around him like a witch's caldron. Steam rose from his shoulders as he arched his back and thrust again and again, cursing her in his mind. In the old days, she had made him happy . . . In the old days, life had been exciting . . . Everything had been new—the company—Susannah . . . In the old days, life had thrilled him.

He cried out when he came, shuddering violently and

falling heavily on her. With a hard shove, she pushed him off her body and rose from the tub.

"Susannah . . ."

She spun around, steam coming from her body. Her light gray eyes blazed with fury. "Don't you ever do that to me again."

Naked and fierce, she stood over him. She was silhouetted against the sky, her head in front of the moon, so that a halo of silver light had formed around her wet hair and spilled down over her shoulders. Water sluiced like quicksilver over her skin. As he stared at her, her entire body glowed with an eerie moon-induced incandescence. She looked both holy and profane.

He hated the strength he saw there. The strength and power and courage that hadn't been there when they had first met. When had she gotten ahead of him? How had she learned secrets he didn't know?

A dam of emotion burst from inside him, and he shouted at her. "Why should I worry about how you feel? You don't care about me!"

She stared down at him, the moonlight forming an unearthly aurora behind her. "You don't even know what you want."

He wanted that *click* he used to feel, that sense that she would fill in his missing parts, that she would give him some of her serenity, polish off his rough edges, soothe his impatience. He wanted her to take away his fear of death. He wanted her to relieve his boredom, offer him a fresh challenge. Make life exciting again. And she wasn't doing it.

He rose from the hot tub and angrily slicked the water from his body with the flat of his hand. "If you haven't figured out what's wrong by now, I'm not going to explain it to you."

"You'll have to make peace with yourself," she said flatly. "I can't do it for you."

His anger swelled. "I should have known you would try to make it my fault. What's happened to us is *your* problem, Susannah. Yours, not mine."

He turned to stalk away from her, but he hadn't finished punishing her for not being able to help him. Spinning back around, he made a final cruel attack. "I'm warning you right now. You'd better not be playing any games with those birth control pills."

Her hand spasmed at her side. "You bastard."

Water was glistening on her cheeks, but he didn't know if it was from the hot tub or because she was crying. "If you get pregnant, I'll leave you," he said viciously. "I mean it."

She spun away from him and stalked toward the house, her robe lying forgotten on the deck.

"Things had better start changing around here," he shouted after her.

But she had disappeared inside, and he was left alone with himself.

22

F BT had been caught with its pants down. All of its sophisticated forecasting tools, its graphs and charts and leather-bound strategy statements, its legions of MBA's and Ph.D.'s and decades of experience, hadn't been able to predict the public's growing fascination with the personal computer.

Personal computer. Just the name made the FBT executives cringe. What kind of name was that? It sounded like a douche, for godsake.

As the seventies had come to an end, the executives had kept themselves busy smiling and harumphing and doubletalking the press, referring to stable product line and the fickleness of the consumer products market. They had talked about FBT tradition, waxed poetic over the majesty of their giant mainframes and those eye-popping profits listed in crisp black ink in their annual reports. And the more they had talked, the more they had qualified and quantified away, the more the world's business community had laughed behind their backs at them for having been so woefully left behind by a bunch of wild-eyed kids.

For Cal Theroux it had been unbearable.

He was the one who had given FBT back its self respect with the launching of the Falcon 101 in January of 1982. It had been his baby from the beginning, and its success had given him the final leverage he needed to consolidate his power within FBT. Now Cal was riding the small computer's success all the way to personal glory.

On the other side of the office, his secretary was unpacking the last of his personal effects and arranging them in the bookshelves. She had been at the task for some time, and he was growing impatient. The ceremony that marked his appointment as the new chairman of FBT would begin in less than an hour, and he wanted a few moments to himself.

"That's enough for now, Patricia. When my wife arrives, send her in."

His secretary nodded and left.

Finally alone, Cal allowed himself the liberty of sliding back in his chair and contemplating his imposing surroundings. Some men were obsessed with sex, others with wealth. But for Cal, power had always been the ultimate prize.

He stroked the polished malachite top of the chairman's desk and touched the panel of switches that controlled the FBT fountains. Since the grounds were crawling with members of the press, he suppressed the urge to manipulate the switches as he had seen Joel do so many times. Even Paul Clemens had not been able to resist toying with those seven fountains during his reign as FBT chairman following Joel's death. They were the final symbol of command, and now they belonged to Cal.

The door opened and his wife Nicole entered. "Hello, darling." As she walked across the carpet toward him, her shoulders tensed almost imperceptibly. He knew she was awaiting his verdict on her appearance.

She looked reed-thin and stylish in a black suit with tan piping. Her dark hair fell in a smooth page boy that formed identical sickles over her ears and revealed the small diamond studs he had given her last week for their third wedding anniversary. Although she was only thirty-four, faint lines had begun to appear near her eyes. It would not be long before he would have to arrange plastic surgery for her.

"Take off the bracelet," he said, eyeing the silver bangle at her wrist with distaste.

She obeyed him instantly. Nicole's dedication to pleasing

him was one of the qualities he liked most about her. He had chosen well. Not only was she the daughter of one of the more prominent members of the FBT Board of Directors, but she had been in love with him for years, even when he was engaged to Susannah. At the time, however, Joel Faulconer's daughter had been the bigger prize. His jaw tightened. How he would love to see that bitch's face when he took office today as FBT's chairman.

"It's a zoo in the lobby," Nicole said. "Half the world has shown up to watch you take office." She gazed around her at the well-appointed office. "I can't believe this has finally happened. I'm so proud of you, darling."

As she chattered on, he watched the adoration glimmering in her eyes, and he could almost pretend that he loved her. But he wasn't a sentimental man, and he no longer believed that he was capable of that sort of emotion. The closest Cal had ever come to love had been with Susannah, and that had led to the greatest humiliation of his life.

Even after six years, his stomach still churned when he remembered standing at the altar and watching her run away on that motorcycle. Instead of easing his desire for revenge, the passing years had fueled it. He had been patient for so long. While Joel was alive, the old man had prevented him from doing what needed to be done. In the years after his death, during Paul Clemens's reign, Cal's position had been precarious and he hadn't been able to allow himself the luxury of taking even the mildest risks. But with the success of the Falcon 101, all of that had finally changed.

His intercom clicked on, interrupting the monologue Nicole had been delivering on the suitability of the dress she had chosen for the reception that evening.

"Miss Faulconer is here."

"Send her in."

He could feel Nicole's resentment, and he smiled inwardly. His wife made no secret of the fact that she detested Joel Faulconer's daughter. But that was all right. His long-term friendship with Paige kept Nicole on her toes.

The door burst open and Paige breezed in, carefree and beautiful, her skin golden from the sun. She greeted Nicole with a cool cheek-press and headed toward Cal. "I can't believe you made me come back for this hideous ceremony,

Calvin. One of the photographers goosed me on my way in through the lobby. He had a great ass, but even I draw the line at body odor." She slid into his arms. "No tongue, sweetie. Your wife is watching."

He brushed a suitably chaste kiss across her lips. Being with Paige was exhausting, but necessary. It was ironic that she, rather than Susannah, had provided the weapon that had allowed him to rise to his current position. From the beginning, Paige had hated the responsibilities that went along with the huge block of FBT stock she had inherited, and Cal had made certain he was always there to advise and comfort her. Within a year of Joel's death, Paige had given him her proxy so he could vote her shares in any way he wished. In return, he had promised not to burden her with the FBT responsibilities she detested. Heads, he won. Tails, he won.

"You know I wouldn't have asked you back today if it hadn't been absolutely necessary," he said.

She stuck out her lip in a playful pout. "But there are going to be speeches. I hate speeches."

"Really, Paige," Nicole said stiffly. "Life can't always be one of your parties."

"Who says?" Paige settled on the edge of Cal's desk and crossed her long legs. They were bare of stockings, he noted with disapproval. At least her raw silk suit was appropriate, although he doubted that she had bothered to put on a bra beneath it. He remembered with some nostalgia the time before Joel's death, when Paige had dressed conservatively and behaved with at least a modicum of dignity. That had changed within a year of her father's funeral—about the time he and Paige had made their agreement.

"I haven't bothered you for months," he said. "You know I wouldn't have asked you to fly in if it hadn't been absolutely necessary."

She regarded him evenly. "You couldn't miss having your picture taken with me today of all days, could you, Calvin? A photograph for all the world to see of Paige Faulconer symbolically passing on the mantle of her father's power."

Sometime Paige was smarter than he gave her credit for. He always tried to remember that.

Nicole fluttered near the doorway, obviously reluctant to

leave the two of them alone. "I'm supposed to meet Marge Clemens. I'm afraid I have to go."

"I'll be down in a few minutes," he told her.

She had no choice but to leave. As the door shut, Paige regarded him with cynical amusement. "Poor Nicole. Doesn't she realize that if we had wanted each other, we would have done something about it long ago?"

She slid down off the corner of the desk. In a manner that was too offhand, even for her, she said, "I'm cutting out of the FBT dinner early tonight."

"Any reason?"

"Susannah sent me an invitation for some sort of party SysVal is holding." She tucked a wayward strand of blond hair behind her ear and wouldn't quite meet his eyes. "I decided to stop by."

Cal kept his voice carefully neutral. "You've received lots of invitations from Susannah over the years. I don't remember that you've ever been inclined to accept one. Why now?"

"I'm in town."

"The only person who detests Susannah as much as I do is you. Why now?" he repeated.

She hesitated for a moment and then, withdrawing a folded white card from her purse, passed it over for him to read. It was an invitation to a party SysVal was holding to celebrate having reached half a billion dollars in sales for their fiscal year. Handwritten at the bottom of the invitation in Susannah's neat script was the message, "How long are you going to keep running away from me, Paige? What are you afraid of?"

Paige snatched the card from him and shoved it back in her purse. "Can you believe it? That prissy bitch actually thinks I'm afraid of her."

"She's very successful," he said calmly, even though the word tasted like poison in his mouth. "Probably the most prominent female executive in the country today."

"And I ended up with FBT and all of Daddy's millions. Well, tonight I'm going to rub every one of them in her face."

The enlarged Blaze logo that took up much of the back wall was the first thing that caught Paige's eye as she entered

SysVal's soaring lobby. As she stared at the logo, she thought of how much her sister had accomplished in six years, and she was so filled with envy that she felt dizzy. Her eyes darted through the crowd. When she saw no sign of Susannah, she forced herself to relax. If only she hadn't shown Cal the invitation, she could have backed out, but now it was too late.

A bar was set up off to the left. As she made her way toward it, she noted that SysVal's party guests favored denim and old running shoes. The beaded white satin gown that had looked so stunning at the FBT dinner she had just left was distinctly out of place here, but she didn't care. She had never been the sort of woman who needed to dress like everyone else to be comfortable.

Most of the guests were drinking beer, and the bartender had trouble finding the champagne she requested. While she waited, she thought about checking into a hotel instead of returning to Falcon Hill. The furniture was under dust covers and the house still bore the faint, sweet smell of death. Falcon Hill carried too many memories of that year when she had tried so desperately to make a home— running around baking pies and planting herb gardens like a demented Betty Crocker. She had even worn her sister's clothes. In the end it had been meaningless. She still hadn't been able to make her father love her.

She blinked her eyes hard and wished she hadn't come. After all of these years, why had she given in to the impulse to see her sister tonight? Maybe if she hadn't felt so rootless and alone after that horrible scene at her Malibu beach house three days ago, she would have tossed Susannah's invitation into the trash where it belonged.

She had actually thought she'd found Mr. Right. He was a documentary filmmaker, and they'd been seeing each other for six months. She should have realized that he was more interested in having her finance his new film than in everlasting love, but she had steadfastly ignored all of the warning signs. God, she was stupid. She had even been planning a wedding in her head.

The bartender finally handed her a glass of champagne. She decided to cancel her plans and leave tomorrow for her new villa in Sardinia. She could spend some time with Luigi or Fabio or one of the other minor Italian princes who drank Bellinis with her at the Hotel Cervo's piano bar in the evening and accompanied her back to her villa to spend the night. She had bought five houses in the past three years, each time throwing all of her energy into renovations and decorating, certain that this was the house that would finally make her happy. But happiness was proving to be one commodity that the millions her father had left her couldn't buy.

The lobby was crowded, but she found a spot along the side wall of windows where she could study the other guests. The men had already begun to notice her, which was predictable. It never took long. She looked through the windows toward the parking lot. In the reflection of the glass, she saw one of the party's male guests break away from his friends and come toward her. He had wild-looking hair, wire-rimmed glasses, and a knobby Adam's apple bobbing up and down in his throat. Terrific, she thought wearily. Just what she needed.

He planted the flat of his hand on the window next to her head, a cool operator leaving a big sweaty palm print on the glass. "I never forget a pair of beautiful eyes, and yours are gorgeous. My name's Kurt. Haven't we met somewhere before?"

"I doubt it, Kurt. I make it a practice never to talk to weenies."

He tried to smile as if she'd made a joke, but when her expression remained cool, his lips began to droop at the corners. "I, um, do you want me to get you a drink?"

She lifted her full champagne glass, making him feel even more awkward and stupid.

"Uh, how about some food? There's, uhm, some real good meat balls."

"No, thank you. But there is something you can do for me."

The muscles of his face lifted into an eager, puppy dog grin. "Sure."

"You can fuck off, Kurt. Would that be all right?"

He flushed and mumbled something before slinking away with his tail between his legs.

She bit down on the inside of her lip, making a little raw

place. He had been harmless, and she could have let him down easily. When had she become so unforgivably cruel?

"Quite a performance." A crisp, male voice spoke from behind her.

She never forgot a handsome face, and it didn't take her long to place Mitchell Blaine. The day of her father's funeral had been a blur, but she could still remember him standing at Susannah's side. He was blunt-featured, good-looking. And proper. God, was he proper. She bet he had a drawer full of perfect attendance Sunday school pins stuck away at home.

"Glad you liked it," she replied.

"I didn't like it at all. He's a nice kid."

Screw him. Screw everybody. Not a bad idea, as a matter of fact. She drained her glass. "You want to get out of here and go to bed with me?"

"Not particularly. I like women in my bed. Not children." His eyes were light blue, cold and unsmiling.

Anger rushed through her. "You bastard. Nobody talks to me like that. Do you know who I am?" Her words echoed in her ears—petulant and obnoxious. She wanted to erase them so she could say different words, words that would turn her into someone else, someone sweet and warm.

"I imagine you're Paige Faulconer. I was told that you'd been invited."

She maintained her lofty bitchy pose. "And doesn't that mean anything to you?"

"Just that the gossip I've heard is true."

"What gossip?"

"That you're a spoiled, rude little girl who should have been turned over somebody's knee a long time ago."

"Kinky. Want to give it a try?" She gave him a phony, moist-lipped smile.

"I think I'll pass. I already have two children, and I don't need another."

She didn't let him see by so much as a flicker of an eyelash how humiliated she felt. Instead, she let her words drip with condescension. "You're married. How unfortunate."

"Why? I can't imagine what possible difference that could make to you."

She swept her eyes down over his body, then lingered for

319

one long moment on his proper, gray-flannel-clad crotch. "I don't *do* married men."

To her astonishment, he laughed, a short bark of sound. "But I'll bet you *do* everybody else, don't you?"

His amusement infuriated her. Nobody laughed at her. Nobody. But before she could come up with a sufficiently cutting reply, he touched her chin with his index finger and said softly, "Ease up, honey. Life's good."

"Mitch?"

The expression that softened his blunt features as he turned his head toward the woman who had come up behind him was so warm and affectionate that Paige felt sick. She turned, too, and all the old emotions surged through her, making her bitterly regret giving into the loneliness that had led her here tonight.

She and Susannah had only seen each other a few times since their father's death, not enough for her to grow accustomed to the changes in her sister. Susannah's hair was shorter—barely reaching her jaw line—and her carriage was more relaxed. She looked free and funky, not at all like old uptight Miss Goody-Two-Shoes. Tonight she was wearing chunky gold hoops with a persimmon-colored blouse and beige slacks cinched at the waist with a fish-scale belt. But the expression on her face as she caught sight of Paige was the same as ever—tense, wary, overly conciliatory.

"Paige! No one told me you'd arrived. I'm so glad you came. Have you met my partner, Mitchell Blaine?"

"We've met," Mitch said.

Paige's lips curled in a sleek cat's smile. "I offered to go to bed with him, Susannah, but he turned me down. Is he gay?"

Susannah got that old tight look on her face, the one she use to wear every time Paige and Joel were trapped together in the same room. "Paige—"

"I'm not gay," Mitch replied. "I'm just discriminating." He brushed his lips against Susannah's cheek, squeezed her shoulder, and walked away.

"I wish you hadn't done that," Susannah said softly. "Mitch is a good friend—probably the best friend I have."

"If you don't want me to insult your friends, you shouldn't send me nasty little invitations."

"It got you here, didn't it?"

Paige lifted a glass of wine from the hand of one of the male guests who was passing and gave him a sexy smile as a reward. She tilted her head back toward her sister. "I don't think I've ever seen so many nerds gathered together in one place in my life."

"Talented nerds. Some of the most brilliant people in the Valley are in this room tonight."

"And you seem to fit right in. But then, you were always pretty much of a nerd yourself, weren't you, Susannah?"

Susannah smiled—patient, saintly Susannah. "You haven't changed, have you, Paige? You're still as tough as nails."

"You bet I am, sis."

"I wanted you to meet Sam, but he seems to have left."

Paige had avoided meeting Sam Gamble for six years, and she had no interest in doing so now. Besides, she had spotted him when she had first come into the lobby. He had been on his way out, and he had been surrounded by fawning people, just as Cal had been surrounded at the FBT reception. Although Gamble had acted as if he weren't aware of all the attention he was receiving, she hadn't believed it for one minute. Men like her sister's husband always knew exactly what they were doing. That's why they bored her.

"I recognized him when I first came in."

"He's very special," Susannah said. "Difficult, but special."

There was a burst of laughter, and someone began playing the Brady Bunch theme song over the loudspeaker. Quickly, Paige drained her wineglass. She couldn't handle this any longer.

"Sorry I can't stay, Susannah, but I've got to get back to Falcon Hill and count all the money Daddy left me."

Susannah flinched, but she didn't give up. "Let me show you around first."

"Don't take this the wrong way," Paige sneered, "but a company tour isn't exactly my idea of a good time."

Her sister stubbornly stayed by her side as Paige headed for the door. "Then let's get out of here," Susannah said, following her outside. "Come on. We'll go for a drive."

"Forget it."

"Afraid I'll eat you up?"

Paige came to a halt in the middle of the sidewalk. "I'm not afraid of you."

"Prove it." Susannah caught her arm and began steering her toward a late model BMW parked close to the building. "We'll take a drive, and I'll show you my house."

Paige jerked her arm away. "I don't want to see your house. I don't want to have anything to do with you."

Susannah stopped at the side of the car. The lights in the parking lot reflected off the hoops swinging at her ears and sent golden lights shimmering through her deep auburn hair. Susannah's new prettiness felt like another wound to Paige.

"You *are* afraid of me, aren't you, Paige?"

Paige gave a hollow laugh. "What is this? A grown-up version of I-dare-you? That was always my game, not yours."

Susannah opened the door on the driver's side and nodded toward the interior. "It's a good game. If you're not chicken, get in."

Paige knew that she didn't have to give in to Susannah's childish taunts, but she hated the smug look on her sister's face. The night stretched ahead like a hundred years, and she told herself that anything was better than going home alone to Falcon Hill. Shrugging indifferently, she got in. "Why not? I guess I don't have anything better to do at the moment."

Susannah carefully concealed her satisfaction as she pulled out of the parking lot. The more trouble she had with Sam, the more important it became to her to establish some sort of connection with her sister. Paige was her only blood relative, and surely they were both old enough by now to find new ground for a relationship. As she pulled out of the industrial complex onto the highway, she kept the conversation light. Paige answered in monosyllables or not at all. Some of Susannah's satisfaction began to fade. Paige's hostility seemed to be growing stronger instead of easing.

They left the highway and drove up into the hills. After several miles, Susannah turned into the drive that led to her house. A thick wall of shrubbery offered privacy from the road. Ahead of her the roof line rose in forbidding angles against the sky, and once again she realized how much she detested the harsh chill of this house. It was a cold temple dedicated to the worship of high technology, designed by a man who had always been obsessed with having the best.

"Cozy," Paige said sarcastically.

"Sam designed it."

"Didn't your big bad husband let you have any opinions?"

Susannah tried not to jump at the bait. "Houses aren't important to me."

Paige's evening gown rustled as she got out of the car. Instead of walking toward the pair of bronze doors that marked the entryway, she took the lighted path that led to the back of the house. Susannah followed, feeling increasingly uneasy. The beads on Paige's gown glittered like ice chips. Everything about her radiated hostility, from the stiff line of her neck to the harsh rhythm of her stride.

They cleared the side of the house and were met with the breathtaking view of the Valley. Paige stalked up the granite steps onto the bottom level of the deck and stared out at the lights. "I'll bet you're really proud of yourself, aren't you, Susannah?"

There was an ugly sneer in Paige's voice that made Susannah want to turn away. This had been a terrible idea. Why had she ever thought she could change the path of their relationship? "I've worked hard," she replied, trying to keep her tone neutral.

"I'll just bet you have," Paige spat out. "How much of that work did you do on your back?"

Susannah was stunned into silence by her sister's maliciousness.

"Now you can spend your days and nights counting your new money and laughing at Daddy in his grave."

All of Susannah's determination to renew their relationship disappeared, replaced by her own rage. "Don't say that. You know it's not true."

"It's true, all right," Paige retorted. "You showed him, didn't you? Too bad he's not still alive so you can throw your success in his face."

"I didn't do this because of him. I did it for myself."

"You're so goddamned sanctimonious. So smug and

self-righteous." Paige spoke with deadly quiet, but her words struck Susannah like small bursts of venom.

She gripped the keys she still held in her hand. "Stop right there, Paige. You're acting like a child, and I've heard enough from you."

But Paige didn't want to stop. The poison stored inside her bubbled to the surface and burst forth in short, caustic spurts. "You've always been perfect. Always right. So much better than everyone else."

"That's enough! I've tried for years to establish some sort of adult relationship with you, but I'm not going to try any longer. You're spoiled and selfish, and you don't care about anyone but yourself."

"How would you know?" Paige shouted. "You don't know anything about me. You were too busy stealing my father to ever try to understand me."

"Get out of here!" Susannah threw the keys at Paige. "Take my car and get out of my sight." Turning her back on her sister, she walked rapidly toward the door on the far side of the deck.

But Paige wasn't finished. Propelled by years of self-loathing, she came after her, running almost, ready to pummel Susannah with more hatred. Susannah couldn't bear anymore. She shoved the door open.

"Do you have any idea how much I've always hated you?" Paige shouted, rushing into the house behind her. "I'm his real daughter! Not you. But I couldn't compete with your perfection act. Do you understand that a day doesn't go by when I don't wish that you'd never been born."

Susannah stalked through the back hallway and down the steps. Paige was still at her side when she dashed into the living room.

"Why did you have to come live with us?" Paige cried. "Why did you have to be so much *better* than me?"

Susannah gasped and then the gasp turned into a soft, kittenlike mew.

On a white suede couch in the center of the room, Mindy Bradshaw was jerking her skirt down over her naked thighs, while Sam fumbled awkwardly with his trousers.

Susannah mewed again. She could feel her hands opening and closing at her sides. The world reduced itself to the scene before her and the awful mew of pain that kept rising from her throat. And then her lips began to move, to form words. They came out tinny, like the computerized voice of a robot.

"Excuse me," she said.

The apology was idiotic, obscene. Susannah staggered blindly out of the room. She knew her legs were working because the walls were moving past her. She walked up one ramp and down another, past the massive mantelpiece of stainless steel. After every four or five steps, that awful sound kept sliding out. She tried to stop it, tried to clamp her lips together, but it wouldn't be contained.

Someone touched her elbow. For a moment she thought it was Sam and tried to shake him off. Her arm was clasped more firmly, and she realized that Paige was at her side.

It was easier to concentrate on her sister than on the obscenity she had just witnessed. The lesser pain of Paige's hatred seemed almost a safe harbor in comparison to the starkness of Sam's betrayal.

Susannah felt her lips quivering again. Sam and Mindy. Sam was having sex with Mindy. Her husband. The man she had loved so blindly for so very long.

She realized she was in the kitchen. An awful pain traveled from her throat down through her stomach, a pain that crushed her heart and filled her breasts like bitter milk.

Paige spoke hesitantly. "Let's get out of here."

"Go away." Susannah shoved the words through a narrow passageway before her throat closed on a sob.

Paige's fingers grasped her arm. They were icy cold, distracting Susannah from her desperate need to draw another breath.

"Let me take you somewhere."

Susannah couldn't tolerate pity, especially coming from someone who hated her so much. "Just leave me alone," she said almost desperately. "I don't ever want to see you again."

Paige released her arm as if she had been burned and closed the keys Susannah had thrown at her in her fist. "Suit yourself. I'll send your car back in the morning."

Susannah stood at the kitchen windows and stared out into the darkness. Seconds ticked by. Paige's icy white dress whipped past. Before long, footsteps clicked on the floor behind her.

She kept her eyes on the blackness beyond the window. It was as dark as the inside of her grandmother's closet, as malevolent as a shed on the edge of the desert.

"The old silent treatment, Suzie? It's so goddamned typical of you, I don't know why I'm even surprised."

Her breath caught on a sob. He had gone on the attack. Why hadn't she realized that was what he would do? The pain was so fierce, she didn't think she could bear it. She gathered herself together as best she could and turned slowly to face him.

His black, straight hair fell over his forehead and stuck out near his ear just the way it did when she ran her fingers through it as they made love. Except this time it had been Mindy's fingers that had rumpled that beloved hair.

"I sent Mindy away," he said, as if that would make everything all right.

Tears were sliding over her lips. She tasted their salt and thought of how hard she had been fighting for her marriage, of the baby she had wanted so badly. "Was Mindy the first?" The question slipped out unwanted, but the moment she heard the words, she knew she had to have an answer.

He combed one hand through his hair. She could almost see him gathering his forces for the struggle—relishing the fact that there would be a struggle. This was what he did best—charging blindly at an insurmountable obstacle and pounding away until it gave. Her chest shuddered as she tried to hold back another sob.

"It doesn't make any difference. How many doesn't matter. Infidelity. Fidelity. Those are just words. That's not what you and I are about."

He was angry, defensive, electric with restless energy. He began to pace the kitchen, his body vibrating with tension as he dodged the black granite islands. "We've never tried to push our marriage into someone else's mold. That's why it's worked for us. We're smarter than that. We know what we want. . . ."

He talked and talked and talked.

". . . the two of us are bigger than convention. We can do

anything together. That's what's made us strong. What happened tonight is little shit, Suzie. Maybe I shouldn't have done it, but it's not important. Don't you see? It's little shit. It's not goddamned important!"

Her hands closed over a ceramic bowl on the counter in front of her. With a slash of her forearm, she sent the bowl crashing to the floor at his feet and expelled the questions that were killing her. "I want to know if she was the first! Were there others? How many others?"

Some of his belligerence began to fade in the face of her agony. For the first time he looked frightened.

"How many?" she screamed.

He was an idealist, a man dedicated to speaking the truth, and he kept to his code. "A couple of times on the road," he mumbled. "A girl I used to go with. What difference does it make? Don't you understand? This doesn't have anything to do with us."

"Yes, it does!" she screamed as she snatched up another bowl and threw it across the kitchen. "We're married. When people are married, they don't fuck other people!" She punished him with the tough, nasty obscenity that she knew he would hate.

"Stop it!" He lurched toward her, his expression vicious. "Stop doing this!"

She hissed with pain as he caught her shoulders and then, without warning, backhanded her across the cheek.

She slammed up against one of the counters. With a gasp of pain, she lifted her fingers to her face. Her nose was running. She dabbed at it with the back of her hand. As she drew it away, she saw a smear of blood.

He saw it, too. His eyes widened, stricken at what he had done. He took a step forward. "Suzie, I—"

The sight of her blood chilled her. She moved backward.

His face crumpled like a child's. "I didn't mean to hurt you. I—God, how could you do this to me? How could you make me do something like that?"

She walked past him with uneven steps, crossing the kitchen and making her way to the foyer. The closet was tucked behind a slab of polished granite that looked like a tombstone. She pulled out the small traveling bag she kept packed with basic necessities. Her cheek throbbed and her hands trembled as she snagged the strap, but a deadly calm had settled over her.

"Don't do this." Panic rang in his voice as he came up behind her. "Don't you leave me! I mean it, Suzie. If you leave, don't plan on coming back. I mean it, do you hear me?"

Tears were running down her cheeks. She turned toward him, and when she spoke, her voice was as rusty as an old saw. "You've made a mistake, Sam. Don't you see? I've turned into your vision of me. And the woman you've created won't put up with you any longer."

• • • • • • • • • • • • • • • • • • • •

23

Susannah rushed from the house. Dimly, she remembered that she had no keys and that Paige had taken her car, but she didn't care. She would walk. Nothing could make her go back in that house.

She fled past a row of shrubbery and saw her car still parked in the drive. Paige sat behind the wheel, waiting like a vulture to pick the bones from her carcass. Susannah bit back a sob. She couldn't bear any more. Why hadn't Paige gone away? Didn't her sister have a speck of compassion left?

The front door banged open behind her. "Suzie!"

She heard his voice calling out to her just as he had the day he had stolen her away from her father. She stumbled, righted herself, and rushed awkwardly forward. He called out for her again. She saw Paige reach over from behind the steering wheel and push open the passenger door.

"Suzie!" he cried.

Paige's gloating seemed the lesser evil. Thrusting her traveling case into the car, she jumped in after it. Sam reached her just as Paige threw the car into reverse. She glimpsed his contorted face at the window, and then they hurled backward down the drive.

She knew Sam's ruthless determination, and she waited

with dread for him to run for his car and give chase. But he stood in the glare of the headlights without moving. She felt an absurd surge of gratitude that at least he was giving her this. Then she remembered Mindy and realized that Sam wasn't letting her go out of compassion, but because he had given Mindy his car.

The tires squealed as Paige spun onto the road and raced down the mountainside toward the highway. As times, she barely seemed to have the car under control. Maybe they would die. The prospect didn't seem so terrible.

As they moved out onto the freeway, a broken sound slipped from Susannah's lips. Her cheek still stung from his blow. Her throat was burning and her eyes were filled with hot tears. Small spasms began to wrack her body.

She had no idea how much time passed before they stopped. Numbly, she lifted her head and saw that they were at the airport. Paige walked around the front of the car and opened the door to pull her out.

"I can't— Please, Paige."

Paige gripped her arm firmly. "You'll do what I say."

Susannah tried to push her away, but her limbs had no strength. Although it was late, people were still milling around. She realized with paralyzing certainty that Paige was going to parade her in front of everyone in the airport and that she couldn't do anything to stop her.

She was wrong. Her sister led her into a private lounge and immediately brought her a cup of coffee. Her stomach rebelled at the smell and she pushed it away. Paige searched through her case and pulled out the passport that Susannah always kept there. She slipped it into her own purse, then went over to a phone bank and began making calls. A little later she returned.

"There's a British Airways flight leaving for Heathrow in an hour. I've booked us seats. We'll pick up a plane to Athens from there."

"Athens?" she repeated dully. "I can't go to Greece. I have a job."

"Your job will hold for a few weeks. I've got this house on Naxos." For the first time, Paige hesitated. "It's nice there. The sun's hot and everything's white and pure." And then

330

her mouth grew sullen, as if she didn't really care whether Susannah accepted or not.

Susannah covered her cheek with her hand. "I can't possibly go away. I have responsibilities." Even as she forced out the words, she couldn't imagine going to work on Monday and facing Sam again.

Paige stared out into the middle of the lounge and plucked at one of the bead-spangled flowers on the skirt of her evening gown. "I have these cats. They're silly, really. Not pedigreed or anything. But I want to show them to you."

A strange combination of belligerence and yearning mingled in Paige's voice. She continued to pick at the beads on her skirt. Susannah stared across the lounge and tried to take in what had happened to her, but the pain kept her mind from working. Suddenly, it seemed perfectly reasonable that she should fly halfway around the world to see Paige's cats. At least she wouldn't have to go to work on Monday.

The rocky islands of the Cyclades lie spattered over the turquoise waters of the Aegean like so many pebbles flung by a giant fist. Birthplace of ancient myths and legends, the islands are a mecca for lovers of Greek antiquity. The spirit of Narcissus is said to have been reincarnated on Mykonos, Thira is suspected to be the lost continent of Atlantis, and Naxos was the refuge of Ariadne after she saved Theseus from the labyrinth of her father, King Minos.

Susannah had been to the Greek islands several times before, although never to the island of Naxos. As the battered jeep made its way inland from the dusty airstrip, a white-hot sun hovered in the bleached sky overhead. They had left the tourist town of Chora with its discotheques and Coca-Cola signs far behind and were crossing the heart of the island. Susannah was barely aware of the breathtaking contrasts around her—the stark moonscape of rocky hills silhouetted against the brilliant blue green of the sea. Squat windmills perched near slopes terraced with vineyards, fruit, and olive trees. The gears of the old jeep ground ominously as they made their way through the steep twisting streets of the villages, some so narrow that the driver had to stop and wait for a donkey to pass because there was not enough room for both animal and vehicle to travel side by side.

Susannah's eyes scratched like sandpaper against splintered wood and her body ached with exhaustion. They had been traveling forever. She was no longer even certain what day it was, and she couldn't remember why she had ever agreed to come on this trip.

Paige sat silently next to her. The fierce glare of the late afternoon sun turned her tumbled hair into tarnished silver. In her rumpled, soiled evening gown, she looked beautiful and dissolute, like a ruined playgirl left over from a Fitzgerald novel. She had handled passports and tickets, the delay at Heathrow, the complex arrangements to get to Naxos, all the business of traveling that Susannah normally managed so expertly. In all that time Susannah hadn't spoken a word to her.

It was evening when they reached the cottage on the eastern side of the island. Susannah stumbled numbly into the room Paige indicated. She was aware of the sound of the sea and clean lavender-scented sheets. Then she slept.

When she awoke late the next morning, sunlight was trickling through the closed shutters and throwing hyphens of light on the white stucco walls of the room. Her body felt heavy and sore as she made her way into the tiny bathroom. She showered, then slipped into a pair of seersucker shorts and a light blue halter top she found lying across the foot of the bed.

She winced as she stepped out into the rustic interior of the cottage's main room and a blaze of sunlight hit her full in the face. A sharp pain pierced her temple. She made her way over to the open screenless windows and saw that the white stucco cottage clung precariously to a barren hillside overlooking the sea. Even though she had vacationed on the Aegean several times before, she had forgotten the depth of the water's jewellike tones. It spread before her like a bottomless pool of azure tears.

She turned back to the room and tried to find some sense of peace in the simplicity of her surroundings. An earthenware bowl of peaches sat on the scrubbed wooden table, while a basket of geraniums caught the sunlight in one of the windows. The windowframes, shutters, and door were all painted the same bright cerulean blue as the Aegean, and the thick stucco walls of the cottage were so crisp and clean, they looked as if they had just been whitewashed. She felt as if she had been plunged into a world where only three colors existed—the dull gray-brown tones of the bare hillside, the blazing white of stucco and sky, and the rich, cerulean blue of sea, shutters, and doorway.

A fat tabby walked across the flagstone floor and rubbed against her ankles. "That's Rudy," Paige said, coming into the room from outside. "Misha's taking a nap on the patio."

Paige wore a faded bandanna top and a pair of cutoffs so threadbare that her skin beneath was visible in several places. Her feet were bare, her face free of makeup, and she had snared her hair into an untidy ponytail. Even so, she looked beautiful.

Susannah couldn't believe that she had put herself in the position of being dependent on Paige. She had to get out of here. As soon as possible, she had to leave.

"You look like shit," Paige said, picking up the blue and white striped dish towel that hung next to the stone sink in the kitchen and using it to pull a fragrant loaf of brown bread from the oven. "Go keep Misha company on the patio. The table's all set and breakfast is almost ready."

"You shouldn't have bothered," Susannah said coldly. "I've made a mistake. I have to get back."

Paige set a sweating pitcher of fruit juice on top of a tray that held two blue glass goblets. "Carry this out. I'll be there in a few minutes."

For the moment it was easier to do as she was told than to argue. Susannah stepped through the door onto a patio paved with smooth brown pebbles. She squinted while her eyes adjusted to the light and the breathtaking view of sky and sea below. An old olive-wood gateleg table holding handwoven place mats, ceramic plates, and cutlery was sheltered from the sun by a lacy network of jasmine trees growing up from the other side of the stucco wall. Wooden chairs sat at each end, their rush seats covered with plump blue pillows. Flowers spilled over the tops of fat pottery crocks, and the old stone head of a lion provided a spot of shade for a sleeping cat.

The animal looked up as Susannah set the tray on the table. Then he stretched, yawned, and went back to sleep. Paige began bringing out food: mugs of coffee, a bowl of eggs soft-boiled in their speckled brown shells, a majolica plate arranged with a sunburst of melon slivers. She cut the bread she had just baked into thick slices and then spread one with butter. It melted into little amber puddles as she held it out to Susannah.

Susannah shook her head. "I'm sorry. I don't feel like eating."

"Give it a try."

Susannah couldn't remember the last time she had eaten —not on the plane, certainly. She hadn't eaten at the party. Her stomach rumbled as the warm, yeasty scent pricked her nostrils. She took the bread, and as she bit into it, she discovered that the simple act of chewing provided a momentary distraction from the pain that wouldn't go away. She sipped at a glass of freshly squeezed orange juice and ate part of a melon slice. When her stomach began to rebel, she cuddled a mug of coffee and gazed out at the sea.

With the meal over, the awkwardness between them increased. In the past she would have broken it with inconsequential chatter, but she no longer cared enough about her relationship with Paige to make the effort. The fantasy of sisterly love had died along with everything else. Paige began to tell Susannah about the cottage and how she had restored it. Then she fetched a San Francisco Giants baseball cap for herself and a straw hat for Susannah and announced that they were going to walk down to the beach.

Susannah followed, simply because she couldn't summons the energy to do anything else. Paige led the way around to the side of the house where there was a gentler drop to the beach than the sheer cliff face that fell from below the patio. Even so, the descent exhausted Susannah. Paige walked over the rocks and hot sand to the water's edge, then dipped her toes in the sea.

"You didn't say anything about breakfast. How did you like my homemade bread?"

"It was delicious," Susannah replied politely. What had

she done wrong? her brain screamed. Why had Sam gone to other women?

Paige kicked at a wave. "I love to cook."

There was a long pause. Susannah realized that she needed to say something. "Really? I hate it."

Paige looked at her strangely. "You always took over the kitchen on the cook's days off."

"Who else was going to do it?"

Paige leaned over and picked up a small smooth stone. "I might have."

"Maybe," Susannah said bitterly. "Or maybe you would have just told me to go to hell."

It was the first time she could remember inflicting the initial blow, but Paige didn't respond. Instead, she pulled off her baseball cap and tossed it down on the beach.

Susannah gazed up the hillside. The cottage seemed miles away. "I think I'm going to climb back up and take a nap. Then I need to make arrangements to get back."

"Not yet." Paige unsnapped her cutoffs. "We're going to swim first."

"I'm too tired to swim."

"It'll do you good." Paige pulled off her cutoffs to reveal lacy white underpants. She slipped them down with her thumbs and then unfastened her top. "This is my very own nude beach. Nobody ever comes here."

As Paige discarded her clothes, Susannah looked at her sister's body. Paige's breasts were larger than her own. Her waist was trim and her stomach flat. She was golden all over. Sam would have liked Paige's body. He liked big breasts.

"Come on," Paige taunted, dancing backward into the waves. "Or are you chicken?" She slapped the water, sending a splatter of drops in Susannah's direction.

Susannah was pierced with a desperate longing. She wanted to forget what had happened, to be young and carefree and splash in the waves like her sister. She wanted to touch the childhood that had been denied her, to go to a place where betrayal didn't exist. Instead, she shook her head and climbed the hill back to the cottage.

That afternoon, Paige went off to the village on a battered moped while Susannah lay in the shade of the jasmine trees and punished herself. She should have cooked more meals for Sam. She should have shared his passion for that awful house.

A chill settled over her that even the Greek sun couldn't dispel. Hadn't these last six years taught her anything? Why was she so quick to assume blame for the problems in their marriage? Sam had been betraying her for a long time—and not just with other women. He had been passing judgment on everything she did and criticizing her when she didn't live up to his invisible spec sheet. He had scoffed at her need for a child, ignored her attempts to repair their marriage. And like a little boy, he had looked to her to fix all the problems he had within himself. She had endured Sam's bad temper, his arrogance, and his small cruelties. But if she endured his infidelity, he would have swallowed her whole.

They ate an early dinner and went to bed not long after dark. In the morning she told herself to make arrangements to return to San Francisco, but she dozed on the patio instead. One day slipped into the next. Paige fed her and made her walk down to the beach every morning, but otherwise she left her alone. Toward the end of the week, she produced a second moped and decreed that Susannah was riding into the village with her to help shop for dinner. Susannah protested, but Paige was insistent, so she did as she was told.

On the way, Paige pulled into a lovely old olive grove that had been part of the island for centuries. As they wandered silently through the trees, Susannah breathed in the fresh scent of earth and growing things. She rubbed her palm over her slim waist and pressed that barren flatness. The tears she had been repressing pricked her eyes. Now there would be no baby to grow inside her.

She stopped under a twisted old tree and stared off into the distance. Paige plopped down in the shade. The afternoon was so still, Susannah felt as if she had found the end of the world. If only she could locate exactly the right place, she might be able to drop off the edge.

After days of barely speaking at all, words began to tumble from her lips. "I didn't know he was sleeping with other women. I knew we had problems, but I thought our sex life was all right. I really did."

"It probably was."

Susannah turned on her. "It couldn't have been or he would have stayed faithful."

"Grow up, Susannah. Some people don't feel alive unless they're having sex with half the world." Paige's face took on a closed, hard expression.

"But he loves me," she said fiercely. "Despite everything he says and everything he's done, he loves me."

"What about you?"

"Of course I love him!" she cried, furious with Paige for asking the question. "I gave up everything for him. I have to love him!" She sucked in her breath as her words hit her. What was she saying? Did she truly love Sam or was she still caught up in an old, worn-out obsession?

"I'm definitely not an expert on love," Paige said slowly. "But I think there are lots of different kinds. Some are good and some are bad."

"How do you tell the difference?"

"The good love makes you better, I guess. Bad love doesn't."

"Then what Sam and I had was definitely good love, because he made me better."

"Did he? Or did you do it yourself?"

"You don't understand. Daddy wanted me to be his perfect daughter, Sam told me I should be strong and free. I listened to Sam, Paige. I listened to him and I believed him."

"And what happened?"

"A miracle happened. I discovered that Sam's vision was right for me. It was a perfect fit."

"That should have made him happy." Cynicism edged Paige's words.

Susannah blinked against the sting of tears. "But it didn't. A big part of Sam liked the old Susannah Faulconer. Deep inside, I don't think he wanted me to change at all."

"I like the new Susannah."

The unusual softness in Paige's voice pierced through Susannah's misery, and she looked at her sister as if she were seeing her for the first time. Against the sunlight, Paige's profile was as soft and blurred as an angel's. "Did I treat you so terribly when we were growing up?"

Paige plucked at a blade of grass. "You treated me

wonderfully. I hated you for it. I wanted you to be awful to me so I could justify how awful I was to you."

Something warm opened inside Susannah like a loaf of her sister's bread. The awful chill that wouldn't go away thawed a little.

"I thought if you were out of the way, Daddy would love me," Paige said. "But he never did. Not really. You were everything to him. Even after you left, he let me know I couldn't compete. The irony of it was that I did so many things better than you—the meals were more imaginative, the house prettier. But he never saw that. He only saw the things I didn't do well."

Paige's unhappiness touched a chord inside Susannah. "After the way you've taken care of me, I can't imagine you not doing anything well."

Paige shrugged off the compliment. "Look at my checking account some time. And I'm completely disorganized. I hate everything connected with FBT business. Daddy should never have left the company to me. I don't know what I would have done without Cal."

Susannah looked away.

"He's been a good friend to me, Susannah," Paige said earnestly. "You really humiliated him."

"I know that. And the selfish part of me doesn't care. Isn't that awful? I'm so glad to have escaped marrying him that I'm willing to feel guilty about what I did to him for the rest of my life."

"Even though escaping Cal meant that you married Sam?"

Susannah stared at the dappled shadows on the ground. Nothing had changed, but some of the turmoil inside her seemed to have eased. "I could never regret having had Sam in my life. In a funny way, he created me, just like he created the Blaze. In the end I guess his vision of me wasn't right for him. But it was right for me."

"Are you going back to him?"

The pain that was never far away spread through her again. She was a fighter, and she didn't take her marriage vows lightly. In the deep quiet of the olive grove, the vow she had made on her wedding day came back to her as clearly as if she had just spoken it. *I promise to give you my best, Sam, whatever that may be.* As the words echoed in her mind, she knew that she had done exactly that, and she finally understood the time had come to begin fighting for herself.

"No," she murmured. "No, I'm not going back."

"That's good," Paige said softly.

For dinner that night, Paige fixed a cheese pie with fresh marjoram and tossed a handful of pine nuts into a dish of green beans. As Susannah ate her sister's wonderful food, she began to feel at peace with herself. Something important had happened in the olive grove. Maybe she had finally completed the task she had begun when she'd run away from home. Maybe she had found herself.

The next morning after breakfast, Paige once again dragged her down to the beach. As she stripped off her clothes, she said, "This time you're going in the water. No more excuses."

Susannah began to protest, but she stopped herself. How much longer was she going to wallow in self-pity? Reaching for the tie at the back of her neck, she unfastened her halter top, then pulled off her clothes until she was as naked as her sister.

"I've got bigger boobs than you," Paige called out in a deliberately taunting voice as Susannah waded into the surf.

"I've got longer legs," Susannah retaliated.

"Giraffe legs."

"Better than duck legs."

The water was sun-warmed and wonderful, the surf gentle. Susannah bent her knees and settled down so that the water covered her shoulders. The sea was gentle and soothing. For a while, anyway, it made her feel well again.

"You can't stay out too long," Paige said, flipping over onto her back. "You're a real paleface. Not to mention other parts of you." A wave passed in a swirl of foam beneath her. "What should we have for dinner tonight?"

Susannah turned on her back to float. "We just finished breakfast."

"I like to plan ahead. Lamb, I think. And a tomato and

339

cucumber salad with feta crumbled on the top. Stuffed eggplant— You're starting to drift out. Come back in."

Susannah obediently did as she was told.

That evening they worked together in the kitchen. Paige opened a bottle of Skeponi, a local wine, and poured two glasses for them to sip while they worked. "Slice that cucumber thinner, Susannah. Those things look like hockey pucks."

"I'm not enjoying this," Susannah grumbled after she produced another slice that was too thick to meet her sister's approval. "Why don't you cook while I straighten out your checkbook?"

"You're on," Paige said, laughing.

Five minutes later, both sisters were happily occupied— Paige with a hollowed-out eggplant and a mixture of pine nuts, herbs, and currants; Susannah with her pocket calculator and what she quickly labeled "the checkbook from hell."

Just as they were getting ready to eat, Susannah heard the sound of a moped approaching the cottage. Paige stiffened. The moped stopped, and several seconds later someone knocked. As Paige opened the door, Susannah glimpsed a handsome young Greek with thick curly hair. Paige immediately stepped outside, but Susannah could hear bits of conversation through the open window.

". . . in village today. Why you not come to me?"

"I have company, Aristo. You shouldn't have come here."

The conversation went on for several minutes. When Paige reentered the cottage, the old hard look had settled over her face. "One of my legion of lovers," she said tightly, picking up the last of the serving dishes and carrying them to the old kitchen table.

Susannah brought over the wine bottle and poured them each a second glass. "You want to talk about it?" she asked cautiously.

Paige's tone immediately grew caustic. "What's there to say? Unlike you, I've never been Miss Pure and Innocent."

It was Paige's first attack. Susannah set down her wineglass. "What are the new ground rules between us, Paige?"

340

"I don't know what you mean."

"If it weren't for you, I'd probably be curled up in a ball someplace. You've taken care of me in a way no one else ever has. But does that mean we can only get along if I need you? Not if you need me?"

Paige toyed with one of the wrinkled oily olives in her salad. "I like taking care of people. I just never get the chance."

"You're getting the chance now, and I'm not ready to give it up." Her voice broke a little. "I feel battered, Paige. You've given me sanctuary. I'm not used to needing people, and it scares me to think about how much I need you right now."

Paige's eyes filled in response. "I always wanted to be just like you."

Susannah tried to smile, but couldn't quite manage it. "And I wanted to be like you—a rebel giving the world the finger."

"Some rebel," Paige scoffed. "I don't want my life to be this way. I'm tired of running all over the world and having sex with men I can't stand."

"Then why do you do it?"

"I don't know. Sex lets me connect, you know. Except I don't connect at all, and that makes me hate myself."

And then she told Susannah about the boy who had raped her when she was sixteen. She spoke of Aristo and Luigi and Fabio and the string of lovers who existed like spoiled meat everywhere she went. She talked about the filmmaker she had imagined she was in love with and the abortion she couldn't quite forget.

Afterward, they were silent. Susannah thought of the roles they had been assigned from the time they were small children. Paige played the rebel daughter while she took the part of the obedient conventional one. But all along it should have been the other way around. They were like two sisters who had gotten their parts mixed up at some cosmic version of Central Casting.

Paige abruptly shattered the silence. "I'm starved."

Their dinner had long grown cold, but they fell on it

anyway, both of them suddenly lighthearted from the connection they had made with each other.

"You know what I really want?" Paige said, stuffing a gooey chunk of eggplant into her mouth with her fingers. "I want to mother the whole world. Sort of like a slutty version of Mother Teresa."

Susannah, who hadn't imagined she would even be able to smile again, burst out in laughter. They drank more wine and Paige told terrible jokes and they cleaned up the dishes together. Afterward, Paige moved a small lamp into the center of the kitchen table. She gave Susannah her old mulish look. "I bought something for us in the village. If you start laughing again, I won't speak to you for the rest of my life."

"All right. I won't laugh."

"Promise?"

"I promise."

Paige reached into one of the cupboards and pulled out a cheap coloring book along with a brand new package of Crayola crayons.

Susannah hooted with laughter. "You want us to color?"

Paige gave her a snotty look. "Do you have a problem with that?"

"Oh, no. I think it's a wonderful idea." Without thinking about what she was doing, she swept her sister into her arms and hugged her so tightly that Paige let out a yelp.

They settled down at the table, chairs butted up next to each other as the two Faulconer sisters bent their heads over the coloring book. Susannah worked on the left page, her sister on the right. Paige fancifully shaded her cartoon cow in pinks and roses, then added a comically oversized hat. Her artistic eye held no regard for the thick black outlines of the drawing, even as her homey soul craved strong, respectable borders.

Susannah neatly outlined all the separate parts of her lady pig before she dutifully filled in the blocks of color. Constriction was fine in coloring books, she discovered, but it wouldn't do at all in real life.

"Not fair, Susannah. You wore the point down on the blue crayon. I can't stand it when the points aren't sharp."

And because Susannah cared more about pushing life to its limits than she did about crayons, she gave Paige the sharp ones and used the dull, blunt nubs herself.

It was an arrangement that made them both blissfully happy.

24

• •

Mitch stood at the edge of the patio and gazed down at
the secluded beach from behind a pair of silver-rimmed
aviator's sunglasses. A sweat stain had dared to form a patch
on the back of his pale blue knit shirt, and his gray slacks
were rumpled from the long plane trip. But fresh clothes
were the furthest thing from his mind as he watched the two
women playing in the surf below.

Paige's body, with its full centerfold breasts, was the more
voluptuous, but it was Susannah's lean, thoroughbred form
that held his attention. Water glittered like crystals on her
shoulders, her breasts, and the flat plane of her belly. It
slithered down the small of her back and glossed her small,
sweet ass as she waded at the edge of the waves.

He knew he shouldn't watch, but the sight of her held him
in a grip that was so powerfully erotic, he couldn't turn his
head away. Thou shalt not covet thy partner's wife, a voice
whispered. But he had been coveting his partner's wife for a
very long time.

He didn't know exactly when in the past few years
friendship had turned to love or affection had become
desire. There was no specific moment he could point to and
say—now! Right now I know that Susannah Faulconer is
the woman I've been looking for my entire life. He certainly

hadn't wanted to fall in love with her. It was messy. Inconvenient. It absolutely violated his moral code. But just the sight of her filled him with a piercing sweetness that transcended anything he had ever felt for a woman.

Except now that her farce of a marriage was finally over, that sweetness had been distorted by anger. For years he had kept his emotions firmly leashed when he was around her. He had never slipped, not once. But when he had heard what had happened, something inside him snapped. He wanted to shake her for her stupidity, for all those wasted years she had held on. He wanted to shake her until he rattled loose whatever it was inside her that had made her an emotional slave to Sam Gamble.

And now he would have to comfort her. He would have to be good old Mitch, patting her back and pretending to be sad right along with her. He would have to be her compassionate and understanding friend when he didn't want to be a friend at all, when he wanted to kick up his heels and shout, "Good riddance."

That's what he wanted her to do, too. He wanted her to look up into his eyes and say, "Thank God that's over. Now you and I have a chance."

But Susannah wasn't frivolous with her emotions, and he knew that wouldn't happen—not for a very long time, if ever.

The recent turn of events at SysVal made everything more complicated. As he remembered the crisis that had arisen so abruptly, he wondered what he would do if she weren't ready to go back with him.

Paige looked up at the cottage, interrupting his thoughts. He could tell by the way her body grew still that she had spotted him, but he didn't back away. Susannah continued to play in the waves, so he knew that her sister hadn't shared the news that they had an observer. If Paige wasn't going to tell, neither would he. He continued to watch.

Susannah was astonished to see the back of a man's head and shoulders rising above one of the patio chairs as she came up from the beach. He turned and smiled at her, the sun glinting off the metal rims of his aviator glasses as he stood.

"Well, if it isn't SysVal's lost lady."

"Mitch! What are you doing here?"

"I was in the neighborhood."

She rushed toward him and then remembered that she was naked beneath her beach towel. Clutching it more tightly in her fist, she leaned forward and kissed a jaw that bore an uncharacteristically rakish stubble.

His hand pressed flat against the small of her back for a moment and then he released her. "I've been worried about you. It's been three weeks."

Had it been so long? September had slid into October and she had barely noticed. "You came this far just because you were worried?"

To her surprise, the corners of his mouth tightened in the subtle sign that indicated he was upset. "You could have telephoned, Susannah. You must have known—" He broke off as something just behind her caught his attention.

Susannah turned her head to investigate, and to her dismay saw Paige standing on the edge of the patio, the beach towel wrapped low on her hips, her breasts as brown and bare as one of Gauguin's Tahitian women.

"Well, well, well," Paige said. "If it isn't Mister—Black, is it?"

"Blaine," he said. He gazed at her for a moment, and then dropped his head so that it was obvious he was deliberately staring at her breasts through his sunglasses. "You're looking well, Paige."

Susannah was embarrassed. And then she wondered why she should be uncomfortable. These two were both pros. Mitch certainly knew what he was doing, and Paige had to work out her devils in her own way.

Paige looked over at Susannah, obviously expecting her to intercede in some way. Susannah lifted an eyebrow. *You got yourself into this, sister mine. Now you can get yourself out.*

She could see Paige begin to grow flustered. Mitch stubbornly refused to redirect his gaze. Paige made an elaborate show of yawning as if all this were too, too boring for words. "I'm thirsty," she said. "I guess I'll go get us something to drink."

Susannah had to suppress the urge to applaud her sister's

feistiness. Paige knew she had lost the battle, but she was going down fighting.

Paige, however, had one final salvo to deliver. "You really should have come swimming with us, Mr. Blaine, instead of standing up here spying. It would have been so much cooler." With a smug glance at her sister, she disappeared inside the cottage.

Susannah rounded on Mitch. "You were spying on us?"

He slowly pulled off his sunglasses and folded in the stems. "Not spying exactly."

"Then what, exactly?"

"Just sort of watching."

"I don't believe this! Mitch, how could you do something so slimy?"

"Aw, come on, Susannah. Ease up, will you?" He stuffed his glasses in his shirt pocket. "What would you have done if you were a healthy heterosexual male who just happened to stumble on the sight of two beautiful naked women cavorting in the water?"

She saw his point, but she didn't have too much fondness for any member of the male sex at the moment, and she refused to give in. "I'm not beautiful, and I'm not a woman. I'm your business partner."

"Ri-i-ght. And for a business partner, you've got a terrific—"

He broke off as he found himself on the receiving end of one of the more chilling of her glares—the glare that, five years ago, she had reserved for anyone who had the audacity to ask SysVal to pay its bills on time.

He studied her for a few moments and the teasing light faded from his eyes. Once again, she observed an almost imperceptible tightening at the corner of his mouth. "Are you okay?" he asked.

She shrugged, then sat down on one of the rush-seated chairs, keeping her towel tucked securely beneath her arms. With the tip of her finger, she traced a bright terry-cloth stripe that ran across the tops of her thighs. "Did you know, Mitch?"

He wandered over to the stucco wall and looked down at the sea. "Know what?"

"About Sam and Mindy? About the others?"

347

The breeze lifted his hair as he turned back to her. He nodded.

She felt as if she had been hit with a new betrayal. "Sam's infidelity was common knowledge, wasn't it? Everyone knew but me."

"I wouldn't say it was common knowledge, but . . ."

Slowly she rose from the chair and gazed at him. "We're friends. Why didn't you tell me?"

He studied her and said quietly, "I thought you knew."

She felt sick at her stomach. Was this the opinion Mitch had of her? Did everyone see her as some spineless creature who turned a blind eye to Sam's wanderings? "Don't you know me better than that?"

"Where Sam is concerned, I don't know you at all."

He seemed to be condemning her, and she resented it. "You're blaming me, aren't you?"

"Sam is one of the greatest visionaries in our business, but when it comes to personal relationships, everyone knows he's pretty much a loser. I guess what I don't understand is why you're the only one who was really surprised. Why is that, Susannah?"

Hurt welled inside her. She couldn't believe that Mitch was attacking her. "I didn't ask you to come here, and I don't want you prying into my life."

He glared at her, the corners of his mouth growing tighter by the second. And then something seemed to give way inside him. "Aw shit." He closed the distance between them in two long strides and wrapped her in his big, bear arms.

She needed his comfort, and she was more than willing to forgive him. Wrapping her own arms around his waist, she laid her cheek against the solid wall of his chest where she could hear his heart pumping beneath her ear. "I loved him, Mitch," she whispered. "I loved him and I didn't want to know."

He drew her closer, rubbing his hands up and down her back through the towel. "I know, honey," he murmured, his voice sounding slightly hoarse. "It'll be all right."

As he spoke, the motion of his chin scraped her temple. His fingers rose above the top edge of the beach towel and touched her skin. She closed her eyes, drawing comfort from his presence in a way she had never been comforted by Sam.

And then something changed. His body began to grow tense. The muscles in his arms hardened until she felt as if she were being imprisoned instead of sheltered. A warning bell went off inside her. His leg pressed against the center line of her thighs as if he were trying to push them apart. She had never been so aware of his greater strength, never before felt threatened by it. This was Mitch, she told herself. It was only Mitch. And then he crushed the beach towel in his fists.

"Mitch!" She rescued the towel and pushed herself away at the same time.

He let her go so abruptly that she stumbled. She trapped the towel before it could fall and righted herself. "Mitch, what—" But as she raised her eyes to his face, she couldn't remember what she had been about to say.

"Yes, Susannah?" he asked calmly.

He looked as solid and unflappable as ever. She began to feel stupid. What was wrong with her? Mitch didn't present any threat. Was this going to be another legacy that Sam had left her—the sense that all men were dangerous?

"Hors d'oeuvres, anyone?" Paige appeared with a tray of cheese, black olives, and crackers.

Her head had begun to ache, and she was grateful for her sister's interruption. Excusing herself, she went into the cottage to shower.

Paige—out of pure mischievousness, Susannah was certain—insisted Mitch stay with them in the cottage. That evening she outdid herself with a meal of plump prawns sautéed in butter and herbs, rice pilaf, Greek salad, and a chewy loaf of fresh, warm bread. Mitch was effusive with his compliments, and Paige's cheeks took on a rosy flush. Neither of them paid much attention to Susannah.

Over bowls of apple cobbler drizzled with cream, Mitch entertained them with a story about Yank losing his new Porsche at a shopping mall. He was so amusing that before long Susannah relaxed and joined in. The tension between Susannah and Mitch dissipated, and they were soon trying to top each other, telling Paige stories about Yank.

When they began describing Yank's habit of misplacing

his girlfriends, Paige accused them of exaggerating. "Nobody's that much of a nerd."

Susannah and Mitch looked at each other and laughed.

But Susannah's lighter mood vanished after dinner when Mitch broached the subject of her return to California. She knew she couldn't stay here forever—she had already been away much too long—but the thought of returning made her insides twist. "I'm not ready. I can't go back yet."

His brow furrowed and he looked as if he were about to say something more, but he merely took a sip of coffee and asked Paige about the island. The strain between them was back.

For the next two days, Mitch and Paige baited each other until Susannah wanted to slap them both. Mitch continued to bring up the subject of Susannah's return, but she refused to discuss it. He began to make vague allusions to a new problem at SysVal. She ignored him. For the past six years she had dedicated herself to the company. Someone else could take over for a while.

By the third day, Mitch could no longer postpone his departure. "We need you in California, Susannah," he said once again, as he handed over his suitcase to the driver of the jeep that was taking him to the airstrip in Chora. "Come with me. We can get a later plane." Once again, she had the sense that he was holding something back.

"Soon," she replied quickly. "I won't stay much longer."

"When? Damn it, Susannah—"

Paige quickly intervened, jumping into the fray like a mother bear defending her cub. Using tactics that were distinctly her own, she brushed her small body against Mitch's big one and gave him her poutiest smile. "So long, Mitch. Look me up whenever you decide you're man enough to go skinny dipping with me."

Instead of ignoring Paige's baiting, he smiled. For a moment his eyes flicked to Susannah, and then he cupped Paige by the back of her neck and gave her a long, deliberate kiss.

When Susannah saw his tongue slip into her sister's mouth, she looked away. She was well aware that Mitch had a strongly sexual nature tucked away beneath his endless supply of navy-blue suits, but it made her uncomfortable to witness it.

Mitch pulled back and slapped Paige's rear. "Keep it warm for me, lamb chop. One of these days, I just might run out of interesting things to do and take you up on your offer."

He brushed Susannah's cheek with a friendly kiss and climbed into the jeep. Paige shaded her eyes with her hands and watched the vehicle disappear. "Mitch Blaine is definitely one hell of a man."

It was the first time Susannah had ever heard her sister speak about any male without cynicism. She suppressed a stab of jealousy because Paige was forming a relationship with Mitch while her own friendship seemed to be showing mysterious signs of strain.

"I should have gone back with him," she said stiffly. "I don't know what's wrong with me. I can't stay here forever."

Paige draped a comforting arm over her sister's shoulders. "Give yourself a little more time."

Time didn't help. Another week passed, but whenever Susannah thought of returning to California, her heart began to race. One afternoon, she stood at the stone sink washing up their luncheon dishes while Paige went into the village, and as she dried a serving bowl, she told herself she had to do something soon. It wasn't fair to impose upon Paige much longer. For the first time, she let herself think about leaving SysVal and going to another company. Her misery was so encompassing that she didn't hear the jeep pulling up outside the cottage.

Yank hated to travel. He could never find his tickets and his boarding passes disappeared. He picked up the wrong luggage and always seemed to end up next to crying babies. Occasionally he became so absorbed in his thoughts that he missed his boarding call altogether and the plane took off without him. As a result, SysVal had an unwritten policy that he was never to be sent on a business trip alone. But Mitch hadn't been able to retrieve Susannah, and they certainly couldn't send Sam. That meant Yank had to do the job.

His coworkers would have been surprised to know how efficiently he had managed the complicated trip to the island of Naxos. They still didn't understand that he was able to function quite well when he chose to. It was just that most of the time he didn't choose to.

As he got out of the jeep in front of the cottage, he made a precise currency conversion in his head and then tipped the driver exactly fifteen percent of the fare, counting out the drachmas and organizing them into precise piles in the palm of his hand. When he was done, he carefully slipped his wallet back into his pocket so he wouldn't lose it and picked up his suitcase. It was leather and monogrammed with matching Y's. A former girlfriend had given it to him as a present for his thirtieth birthday. Later, his accountant told him that she had charged it on one of Yank's own credit cards.

While he walked up the path to the cottage, he organized his thoughts and mentally prepared himself for the task of retrieving Susannah. This was a job he couldn't afford to bungle. It was too important to all of them.

She answered the door after his first knock. She appeared so tired and sad that Yank wanted to hug her, but of course he didn't. All the feeling he had held for her since the evening Sam had brought her to the Homebrew meeting rushed through him like a bombardment of electrons.

"Yank!" Susannah's mouth grew slack with astonishment. She glanced past his shoulder to see who had brought him. He could almost feel her dread that it might be Sam.

"Hello, Susannah." He watched as she tilted her head to the side to look behind him again. "I'm alone."

"Alone?"

He nodded.

Her forehead wrinkled. "Did someone come part of the way with you?"

"I came all the way alone."

"All the way to Greece?"

"Could I come in, Susannah? And if it isn't too much trouble, I'd very much like something to drink."

"Of course." She stepped aside to admit him, but she couldn't resist one last peek outside before she shut the door.

"I think we have some Greek beer," she said. "But— Why are you here, Yank?"

"I've come to get you," he said simply. "I've come to take you home."

The sun was in Paige's eyes, so for a moment she thought the man standing with his back to her on the patio was Mitch. A flash of pleasure washed through her at the idea of engaging in another round of sexual dueling with the delectably stuffy Mr. Blaine. But then she realized that the man looking out toward the sea was much leaner than Mitch and even taller—maybe four or five inches over six feet.

As he turned toward her, she caught her breath. What an incredibly arresting man! His brown hair was side-parted and well-cut. His features were unusually sharp: bladed cheekbones, a thin straight nose, finely chiseled lips—all of it topped by a pair of light brown eyes that were widely spaced and compelling. He was casually dressed in a charcoal shirt with a pair of chinos and a webbed belt. A nearly empty bottle of Greek beer was clasped in his hand, and a gold watch with a leather strap encircled his wrist. All in all, he was an extremely tempting piece of male flesh.

She took a step toward him and stopped as a prickle of unease traveled up her spine. He was looking at her so strangely, almost as if he were taking her apart and examining the separate pieces—the iris of an eye, the curl that brushed her cheek, her chin, a breast. He shifted his gaze to her other breast, regarded it with great concentration, and then moved his eyes down over her torso to her hips. Instead of being insulted, she felt curiously flattered.

"Should I turn around so you can see the rest?"

"Not unless you'd like to." His voice was so deep and soft that it almost seemed to have blown in off the sea.

The door of the cottage opened and Susannah came out with a glass of ice water. She looked tense and frazzled. "Paige, you're back. I didn't hear the moped."

"Just got here." Paige set down the string bag of produce from the market and once again glanced curiously toward their visitor.

"Paige, this is Yank Yankowski. Yank, my sister Paige." Paige nearly choked. This was Yank? This was the dopey genius that Susannah and Mitch had told her all those stories about? Had Susannah gone blind or had she simply lost her mind?

Paige let her gaze drift appreciatively over Yank. "No wonder big business fascinates you, Susannah. Do you have any more male partners tucked away?"

Susannah looked at her blankly.

Paige returned her attention to Yank and saw that his eyes had grown unfocused. He began patting his pockets, muttering something indecipherable, and then—without a word to either of them—walked past them into the cottage.

Paige watched him with amazement. "What on earth—"

"He's working on something. He does that all the time." Susannah took a sip of her ice water and set it down. Her hand shook ever so slightly. "Paige, don't let him take me back."

"What are you talking about?"

"Yank's come here to take me back. I—I'm not ready yet."

Paige regarded her curiously. "Then don't go. I've told you that you can stay as long as you like."

"You don't know the way he is. When he has his mind set on something, it's impossible to distract him. He's like Sam, except different. He's so gentle. Kind. It's difficult to explain."

"That's ridiculous, Susannah. He can't take you back unless you decide to go with him."

Susannah didn't look convinced. "I never expected him to show up here. Yank doesn't travel by himself. He can't manage things."

"He seems to have managed things just fine." Paige shook her head in amusement. "I can't believe that's the same man you and Mitch were telling me all those dopey stories about. Susannah, he's incredibly sexy."

Susannah seemed vaguely startled. "Well, he's changed a lot since we started the company. He's certainly a lot better looking than he was when I met him. All the women he's had in his life these past few years have put him together. I guess it happened so gradually that those of us who are with him all the time barely noticed."

"What do you mean, 'put him together'?"

"They've done his clothes shopping for him and thrown out the awful stuff he used to wear. He had this terrible crew cut right out of the 1950s, and these ugly black glasses with Coke-bottle lenses. His girlfriends cleaned him up, organized his wardrobe, and made him get contacts—that sort of thing. But it's all surface cosmetics. Yank is still Yank. And—" She shivered slightly. "Sometimes he can be scary."

It was the first thing Susannah had said about Yank Yankowski that made any sense to Paige.

As she had done with Mitch, Paige invited Yank to stay the night and fed him a delicious dinner. To Yank's credit, he managed to keep up his end of the conversation throughout most of the meal and only faded out on them a time or two. After the dishes were cleared, he asked Susannah to show him the beach.

She made a great play out of pushing the cork back into a bottle of wine they hadn't quite finished. "Let's do it tomorrow. I'm a bit tired tonight."

"I'd very much like to see the beach now," he said quietly.

"It's late, Yank. And it's a steep climb."

"There's a full moon. We can see quite well."

Susannah shot Paige a pleading glance, and her sister's maternal instincts took over. She set down her dishrag and touched Yank's arm lightly. "Beach tours are my specialty. If you treat me right, I might even let you cop a feel behind the rocks."

Susannah's hands stilled on the cork as Yank's mouth curved in a slow sleepy smile that was almost mesmerizing. Paige was right. Yank had turned into an incredibly attractive man, and she had barely been aware of it.

Paige wove her fingers through his and pulled him toward the doorway. "Don't wait up for us," she called over her shoulder. "I'm not letting him back until I've had my way with him."

For all her bravado, Paige felt awkward the moment the cottage was behind them and they were alone. There was something spooky about him—as if he knew all sorts of things other people didn't. She didn't like being put at a disadvantage with Yank, but she wasn't quite certain how to take control.

The moon lit their way, shining silver on the harsh rocks

as they headed down the path to the beach. The night was warm and still, and the waves lapped softly at the shore. She walked to the edge, pretending to be mesmerized by the water, while she tried to ignore the fact that Yank was studying her quite openly.

His scrutiny made her increasingly uncomfortable. She fell back on her old tricks. "Did anyone ever tell you that you're incredibly sexy?"

"Yes."

"Susannah thinks you're a nerd."

"I know."

"Doesn't that bother you?"

"Do you think it should?"

"How would I know? If you want to go through life having everyone think you're weird, I guess that's your problem."

He laughed softly.

His amusement irritated her. It suggested that he understood something she could not even begin to perceive. In retaliation, she reached for the tail of her T-shirt and began to pull it up over her bare breasts. "Let's go in for a swim."

He caught her hands, stilling her movement in a surprisingly firm grip. "No, I don't want you to take off your clothes in front of me."

"God, not another one. First Mitch and now you. What are you? A couple of Buddhists or something?"

"Maybe Mitch understands, too. Seducing either one of us isn't the right thing for you to do. Not now."

"Who made you God? How do you know what's right and wrong for me?"

"I just know, that's all. It occurred to me at dinner exactly how all this might turn out. If we're very, very lucky, of course."

"How what will turn out? What are you talking about?"

He brushed the side of her cheek with his hand in the gentlest gesture she could ever remember receiving from a man, and she looked into eyes that were as wise and compassionate as the eyes of a dime-store Jesus. "You mustn't give yourself to anyone for a while, Paige. Not sexually. It's quite important."

She slapped away his gentle touch with the flat of her hand. "I'll 'give myself' to anybody I like! God, you really are a nerd! From now on, you mind your own goddamn business, do you hear me? Fuck you, mister. Just . . . fuck you."

He gave her a sweet sad smile and turned away to watch the waves.

Susannah made certain she was in bed before Yank and Paige returned from the beach. She couldn't bear the thought of another discussion about leaving. As she plumped her pillow, she remembered Paige's astonishing reaction to Yank's appearance. Her sister's sexual sparring with Mitch hadn't been at all surprising—Mitch was an incredibly attractive man—but Paige had seemed just as captivated with Yank.

She shut her eyes and tried to relax so she could sleep, but her eyelids kept jumping open. To distract herself, she began to imagine what it would be like to make love with Yank. Try as she might, all she could picture was Yank getting distracted at the crucial moment.

And then, to her utter shame, she felt a flash of desire. For the first time it occurred to her that sexual frustration was something she would have to learn to live with. She was a sensual woman, and that part of her wouldn't go away just because she no longer had a husband to satisfy her. At the same time, she was so bruised that she couldn't imagine ever again making the deep emotional commitment that she needed before she could go to bed with someone.

A picture of Sam hovering over her as they made love took shape in her mind. The pain that accompanied it was so sharp she bit down on her lip. *Don't think about it,* she told herself. *Think about someone else.*

She pondered the bleak sexless years ahead. Once again she tried to envision herself with Yank, but the picture wouldn't take hold. Another picture took its place, one of herself and Mitch. Fantasy was a harmless pursuit, so she gave herself permission to strip off the black trunks that he had worn on the beach. She imagined his shape and size, and her limbs began to feel pleasantly lax. She let him pick her up and lay her down on a blue silk sheet. She conjured up the scent that he carried with him of starched shirt and clean skin. Her body felt heavy and languid.

She groaned and buried her face into the pillow. As her eyelids squeezed shut, Sam's mouth took shape in her mind. Sam's mouth—hard and determined—whispering a life-long litany of traitorous love words.

She got up very early the next morning, still groggy from her awful night. Holding her sandals in her hand so she wouldn't make any noise, she slipped across the front room toward the door so she could get away before Yank awakened. Later she would be ready to face him, but not yet.

"Susannah?"

She moaned with frustration as Yank slipped out of his bedroom. His hair was tousled and he had pulled on the wrinkled chinos he had been wearing the night before. The rest of him was uncovered. She didn't realize until that moment that she had never seen Yank without a shirt. His chest was lean almost to the point of boniness, but there was a tautness about his flesh that made his thinness appealing.

"I'm going into town," she said, anxious to get away before he stopped her. "I thought I'd get some pastries for breakfast."

"We don't actually need any pastries." He walked over to the kitchen table, where he picked up a ripe peach from a bowl of fruit and bit into it. He chewed slowly, then looked down at the peach as if he had never seen one before. "It would be easiest on you, Susannah, if you simply resigned yourself to going back with me this afternoon."

"This afternoon? That's impossible."

"Would you prefer to wait until tomorrow morning?"

"No, I—"

"This afternoon, then." He made the statement with ominous finality.

"Yank, I don't want to go back. Not yet. Don't press me on this."

"Someone has to press you. I was very disappointed with Mitch. He should have brought you back last week."

"I'm not a piece of cargo! Listen to me, Yank. The thought of facing Sam— I just can't do it yet."

"Of course you can. You're quite strong, Susannah. You need to remind yourself of that."

She didn't feel at all strong. She felt like a little girl with a string of broken balloons woven through her fingers. "Being forced to face Sam a dozen times a day is a little more than I can handle right now."

"The company depends on you."

She threw down her sandals. They skidded across the floor and banged into the leg of a chair. "Forget about the company! I'm sick of hearing about it. If we believe the Gospel according to Gamble, SysVal is just as important as Christianity. I don't buy that anymore. We're making a computer, for God's sake. A machine. That's all." She waved her hand toward the ceiling. "See! The sky didn't fall. I spoke blasphemy and nothing happened."

Yank looked strained, as if being near such an outpouring of emotion had exhausted him. He dropped the peach pit into the waste basket. "SysVal isn't three kids in a garage anymore. It's a company filled with people who have to pay their mortgages and support their families."

"I'm not responsible for that. All those people aren't my responsibility."

"Yes, they are. You're essential to SysVal."

"I'm the most replaceable of the partners, and you know it."

"You're the least replaceable. I'm surprised you don't realize that. From the very beginning, you're the only one of us who has always been able to see the whole picture. The rest of us only see parts."

"That's ridiculous. Mitch sees it all."

"Better than I do. Better than Sam, maybe. But Mitch's business background has given him biases you don't have. And Mitch and Sam give each other energy, but they don't really understand each other. Without you interpreting for them, they can't even talk."

It was a long speech for him. He began to stare off into space, and she assumed that he had worn himself out. But he was merely taking a few moments to arrange the rest of his thoughts properly. "You're not a visionary like Sam or a marketing strategist like Mitch. You can't design like I do. But you understand people, and you're the one who keeps us on track. If it weren't for you, SysVal would have been lost in chaos long ago. You have this way of keeping order."

The part of her that wasn't miserable was gratified that Yank thought so highly of what she did. Somehow, his praise meant more to her than any compliments she had ever received from either Sam or Mitch.

"Mitch wants you to come back when you're ready, Susannah. He told me quite explicitly that I was not to force you to return."

"I'm a free human being," she said with what she hoped passed for conviction. "You can't force me."

"That may be, but freedom is relative. I have information that Mitch has ordered me not to divulge. If you knew this information, you would immediately return."

Although she had known Mitch was keeping something back from her, for the first time she grew alarmed. "What information? What are you talking about?"

"It's quite disturbing, Susannah."

"Don't you dare do this to me! If you know something I should know, tell me. I don't care what Mitch says."

"Oh, I intend to tell you. I was quite surprised that Mitch thought he could bully me like that."

"What's happened, Yank? What's this all about?"

Yank wandered over to the window and looked out at the view for a few moments. Then he turned back to her. "A few days after you left, Sam began to lobby our Board of Directors."

"That's not unusual. Sam is always lobbying the board for something."

"This time his goal was quite different."

Susannah felt a chill of apprehension deep in the pit of her stomach. "What do you mean? What's he done?"

"Susannah, I'm sorry to have to tell you this, but Sam is trying to convince the board to sell SysVal."

25

When Paige awakened, Susannah told her what had happened and tried to convince her sister to return to San Francisco with them. But Paige shrugged her off, insisting she had already made plans to go to Sardinia. She immediately began the business of closing up her cottage and arranged for a jeep to come and get all three of them. Their relationship was still so fragile that Susannah was reluctant to press her. At the same time, she felt so emotionally intertwined with her sister that she didn't want a lengthy separation. What if they fell back into their old antagonistic pattern?

Their parting at the airport wasn't as difficult as it might have been because Yank disappeared at the last moment and both of them had to set off after him. Paige found him with a group of passengers ready to board a flight to Marrakech. She took him back to the proper gate just as Susannah had given up all hope of locating him.

He absentmindedly passed his ticket and boarding pass over to Susannah, then turned back to Paige. "Please remember that request I made when we were on the beach. It's very important."

Susannah looked at them curiously, trying to figure out what Yank was talking about.

Paige ran her fingers along her purse strap. "What's it worth to you?"

"Worth?"

"Yeah. Are you willing to put your money where your mouth is?" Her eyes swept over him insolently. "And I'll just bet your mouth has been in some very interesting places."

Yank flushed. "You're suggesting I make the same agreement?"

"Why not? Misery loves company."

"I hadn't thought that far ahead."

"Maybe you'd better."

"You have a point. Although—"

"Do you agree?"

He considered her question for a few moments and then nodded.

Susannah was mystified by the conversation, but her speculation was stopped short as the loudspeaker announced the final boarding call. Neither she nor Paige seemed to know quite what to say. Susannah smiled shakily. "Thanks. Thanks so much for everything."

Paige shrugged off Susannah's gratitude. "I owed you one."

Yank had begun to wander away. Susannah grabbed him and steered him toward the gate. Just before they passed through, she gave Paige a final wave.

Paige stood in the middle of a bustling crowd of tourists and watched her sister and Yank Yankowski disappear. As they slipped out of sight, a deep ache passed through her like a dark wave on her private beach. Something important was slipping out of her life, and she didn't have the faintest idea how to get it back.

On the trip from Athens to Heathrow, Yank told Susannah what he knew about Sam's sudden determination to sell the company. He offered the details in his customary systematic fashion, laying out the facts as he knew them and refusing to speculate on anything he wasn't certain of.

Sam wanted to sell SysVal to Databeck Industries, an international conglomerate. Databeck had offered to buy SysVal a year ago, and at the time Sam had scoffed at them, even though several of the board members had urged that the offer be considered. No matter how hard she searched, she could find only one explanation for Sam's change of heart. He wanted to get back at her for leaving him. The idea that he would sacrifice the company that meant everything to him just to punish her sent a chill to the very marrow of her bones. How could she have thought she knew someone so well and not have known him at all?

They had to lay over for several hours at Heathrow before their plane left for San Francisco. When they finally boarded, Yank fell asleep quickly, but Susannah couldn't rest. Instead of concentrating on the crisis at SysVal, she kept imagining herself walking into the lobby. Everyone would be watching her. She envisioned the pity in their faces, imagined the whispers behind her back. The images were unbearable, and she forced herself to concentrate on the implications of Sam's turnabout.

They all had been so certain that nothing like this could ever happen. The four partners each held fifteen percent of the company, giving them a controlling sixty percent. The other board members held the remaining forty. They had always felt so safe with this arrangement. But if Sam could unite the board, and if he then threw his fifteen percent in with them, nothing that she, Yank, or Mitch could do would keep the company from being sold.

They arrived in California at six in the morning. Even though it was early, Susannah asked Yank to drop her at Mitch's house. He lived in a charming California-style ranch that sprawled over several acres in Los Altos Hills. As he opened the door, she saw that he was clad only in a pair of running shorts. Sweat gleamed on his arms and darkened the pelt of sandy hair on his chest. He looked surprised to see her, but he was so hard to read that she wasn't certain whether he was pleased or not. The strange, erotic fantasy she'd had about him when she was in Greece slipped back into her mind, and for a moment she couldn't quite meet his eyes.

"Welcome home," he said, stepping aside to admit her. "I just got back from my run." He took her traveling case and led her into the living room. Normally it was one of her favorite places in the house, a happy hodgepodge of American Southwest and French Riviera. Chairs and couches were upholstered in nubby, neutral-colored fabrics brightened up with throw pillows printed with colorful geometrics. The stucco walls held large canvases splashed with tropical flowers, and tables with curly wrought-iron legs were placed at convenient intervals. But the pleasure she usually felt at being in such cheerful surroundings eluded her.

He set down her case next to one of the couches. "Give me a minute to take a shower and then we'll talk. There's a pot of fresh coffee in the kitchen."

She stopped him before he could leave the room. "You should have told me what Sam was doing when you came to Naxos." She hadn't intended to sound so condemning, but there still seemed to be some mysterious strain between them and she couldn't help it.

"You had plenty of chances to ask questions," he replied. "I don't remember hearing any."

"Don't you play games with me, Mitch. I expect better of you."

He picked up a wadded T-shirt from one of the end tables and began to rub his damp chest with it. "Is that an official reprimand, Madame President?"

A month ago she could't have imagined being intimidated by him, but now there was something so forbidding about the way he was looking at her that she had to force herself to hold her ground. "You can take it any way you want."

He yanked his T-shirt on, then pulled it down over his chest. "I tried every way I knew to talk you into coming back, Susannah, but I wasn't going to force you if you weren't ready. We've got a big fight ahead of us, and your personal problems are going to make it more complicated. If Yank and I couldn't have one hundred percent from you, I wanted you out of our way."

He was acting like she was an encumbrance. "That wasn't your decision to make," she snapped. "What's wrong with you, Mitch? When did you turn into the enemy?"

Some of his stiffness faded. "I'm not your enemy, Susannah. I don't mean to be abrupt. Sam's called an informal meeting of the board tomorrow at three o'clock. My guess is that he intends to tighten the screws."

"Forget it," she said fiercely. "He can call any meeting he

wants, but his partners aren't going to be there to see the show. I'm not going to meet with anybody on the board— formally or otherwise—until I've had a few days to ask some questions. Without us, they can't have much of a meeting."

"We have to confront the board sooner or later."

"I know that. But I'm taking the ball into my court for a while. Make sure that you're unreachable tomorrow after- noon at meeting time. I'll take care of Yank."

Mitch seemed to be thinking over what she'd said. "I'll give you a couple of weeks, Susannah, but no more. I don't want anyone to think we're running. That'll hurt us nearly as badly as what Sam is doing."

She didn't like the fact that he was questioning her judgment, but at least some of his stiffness had dissipated. What was happening to the two of them? She'd grown to take Mitch's friendship for granted, and she couldn't imag- ine losing it, especially now when she felt so fragile. The burst of adrenaline that had kept her going had begun to fade, and she sat down on the couch.

He saw that she was exhausted, and went to get her a cup of coffee. As she sipped it, he told her he had reserved the town house SysVal owned for its traveling executives so she had a place to stay until she got resettled. He had also reclaimed her car from the airport and stored it in his garage. His thoughtfulness made her feel better.

Forty-five minutes later, she climbed the stairs to the town house's second floor, slipped into the freshly made bed and fell into a troubled, dream-ridden sleep. She awoke around noon and telephoned home to make certain Sam wasn't there. When she received no answer, she dressed and drove over.

She half expected to find the locks had been changed, but her key worked without any difficulty. The house looked the same—cold and uninviting. She went into the bedroom with its steel-framed furniture and gray suede walls. Every- thing was exactly as she had left it. Everything except—

Her eyes widened as she saw a small oil painting hanging on the wall between their matching bureaus. It was a seascape in soft feminine pastels that were at odds with the room's cold gray interior. She had found the painting a year ago in a gallery in Mill Valley and immediately fallen in love with it. But Sam had hated it and refused to let her hang it. This was the first time she had seen it since she had come home from a business trip and discovered that he had sent it back.

She sagged down on the side of the bed and stared at the painting. Tears welled in her eyes. How could he be taking the company away from her on one hand and, at the same time, giving her this painting? The pastels blurred through her tears, swimming together so that the painting seemed to be in motion. The waves of the seascape heaved toward the shore in watery blue and green swells.

She thought of Sam's wave—the wave of the future he had told her about all those years ago. That wave had swept over them just as he had promised, and just as he had promised, they had been changed forever. She stared at the painting, and the great vat of grief that had been sealed shut inside her opened up, sending dark eddies through every part of her. She hugged herself and stared at the painting and rocked back and forth on the edge of the bed while she truly mourned the death of her marriage.

And with the death of her marriage, she mourned the death of the child she had hoped to bear, that dark-haired, olive-skinned child of feisty spirit and soaring imagination who would never be born. She hugged that child to her breast and loved it with all her might, pouring years of maternal care into a few brief moments. She cried it a bleak lullaby, that unconceived child of her imagination, and let her heart tear apart as she laid it in its grave.

When she left the house, she felt as old and empty as a hollowed-out stone.

26

• •

Walking into SysVal that same afternoon was one of the hardest things Susannah had ever done. She wore an unadorned black knit, garbing herself in its severe lines as if it were a suit of armor. As she flashed her pass at the front desk, the security guard wouldn't quite meet her eyes. A group of jeans-clad workers conversing in the lobby stopped talking as she came toward them. They looked down at the floor; they looked at the walls. The company grapevine was powerful, and Mindy Bradshaw obviously hadn't kept her mouth shut. By now every SysVal employee must know that Susannah had walked in on Sam and Mindy making love.

As she moved through the halls, several of the men called out cautious greetings, as if she were a terminal cancer patient and they didn't know what to say. She nodded graciously and kept walking—spine straight as a ramrod, posture so perfect she would die before she bent. She had been San Francisco's Deb of the Year in 1965. She had been trained in the old ways to retain her dignity regardless of provocation and to hide her emotions behind a mask of serenity.

As she neared her office, her palms began to perspire, but she didn't lower her head by so much as a fraction of an inch. Ahead of her a technician ducked into an office so he could avoid the embarrassment of having to greet her. The corners of her mouth began to quiver, and she realized then that she couldn't carry it off. She was no longer San Francisco's perfect socialite or SysVal's efficient president. She was a woman who had learned to feel and bleed and care. Her steps faltered. She couldn't do it. She simply couldn't go through with this.

Her muscles were so tightly wound that she jumped when a voice sounded over the loudspeaker. It was a voice that had never before been heard over the SysVal system because it belonged to the man who had been trying for several years to have that same system disconnected. It was Mitch, clearing his throat and speaking in the dry, businesslike fashion of someone whose idea of fun was spending an evening reading sales forecasts.

"Ladies and gentlemen, the security desk has informed me that our president and chief operating officer, Susannah Faulconer, has just arrived back in the building. I feel compelled to address all of you today and set the record straight. The rumors that Ms. Faulconer has been hiding out in Las Vegas and dancing in a nude review are absolutely untrue, and anyone repeating such rumors will be dismissed at once. We have it on good authority that Miss Faulconer was not nude. She was respectably clad in a leopardskin G-string." And then the music of "The Stripper" blared out.

Heads popped out of offices. A hoot of laughter went up around the building. Susannah wanted to kill Mitch, to kiss him. He had known how hard it would be for her to come back, and this was his strange—and typically SysVal way—of making it easier. After the strain of their encounter that morning, this gesture of friendship meant everything to her.

Mitch's announcement pushed away the awkwardness and gave people something to say to her. For the next few hours, everyone teased her unmercifully. But there was still an edge of caution to their laughing remarks. Normally when she was away from the office for even a day, Sam's name would have come up a dozen times within an hour of her return. Now no one mentioned him.

More than anything, she wanted to put off seeing him. But she knew she couldn't hide away forever, and the longer she postponed meeting with him, the more difficult it would become. When Helen, her secretary, brought in the most urgent of her mail, Susannah forced herself to look up from her notepad and ask as coolly as she could manage, "Is Sam in today?"

"Gee, I— Yes, I think so."

"Good," she said briskly. "Call his office. I'd like to see him as soon as he can get free."

She forced herself to concentrate on her work. So much urgent business had piled up while she was gone that it was difficult even to prioritize it. And there were small irritations. When she turned in her chair to flick on the Blaze III she kept on her credenza, she was annoyed to discover that it had been replaced with a newer III. The machines were identical, but she had a sentimental attachment to her old Blaze. It was one of the thirteen original test models that Sam had insisted be put into use for a few months before the Blaze III was released to the general public, so that all the bugs could be worked out ahead of time.

When she asked Helen what had happened to her old computer, she was told that a technician had come for it. "He transferred all of your files to the new machine, so it shouldn't be a problem."

"Get hold of him and tell him I want my old Blaze back," she said. She didn't care if she was being illogical. She'd had enough changes forced upon her in the past month, and this was one she could control.

Helen nodded and then told her she had a call from Mitch. Susannah picked up her phone. "A nude review? Couldn't you have done better than that?"

"I'm an engineer, not a poet. I thought I told you not to come in to work until tomorrow."

"Too much to catch up on."

He hesitated. "Susannah, I'm afraid I've got more bad news. I don't like hitting you with everything on your first day back, but I just got a call from Sacramento."

She rested her forehead on the tips of her fingers, bracing herself for the next disaster.

He said, "The people we're dealing with in the state government got wind of the rumors that SysVal is up for sale, and that tipped the scales in favor of FBT and the Falcon 101."

She rubbed her temple with her thumb. A multimillion-dollar contract was lost; Sam wanted to sell the company. A month ago they had been sitting on top of the world. Now everything was coming apart.

She spent the next two hours on the phone to Sacramento, talking to everyone she could reach and trying to convince them that the rumors were untrue. The officials were polite but unbending. They had made the decision to go with FBT's Falcon 101 instead of the Blaze III, and that decision was irreversible. She turned to her computer and began crunching numbers, trying to determine how this financial setback would affect the new Blaze Wildfire project.

Sam came to her office around five. She sensed his presence in the doorway before she looked up.

"Hi, Suzie."

For so many years every part of her had jumped alive whenever she caught sight of him, but now she felt numb. She swiveled slowly in her chair and for a few brief moments saw him as others did, those who hadn't fallen under his spell. He looked tired and nervous. He needed a haircut, and his slacks and shirt were wrinkled, as if he'd fallen asleep in them.

"Did you go over to the house?" he asked as he walked into her office.

"I stopped in to pick up my things."

"You can't run away if we're going to get this worked out."

Now that she had left him, he finally wanted to work out their problems. She could almost have predicted this would happen, so why was it so hurtful? "We're not going to get our problems worked out. It's over, Sam. I've had enough."

He drove his hand through his hair, plunged his fist into the pocket of his slacks. "Look, Susannah. I'm sorry. I fucked up real bad. I know that. But it doesn't have to be the end of everything. If I'd known it was going to be such a big deal to you—"

"I don't want to talk about it!" She fought for composure. Years of bitter experience had taught her how easy it was to get caught up in Sam's twisted logic, and her emotional control was too fragile for her to argue with him now. "These are business hours, Sam, and we're going to talk business."

Rising from behind her desk, she forced herself to come around to the front. "Mitch just told me that we lost the contract with the state of California because they heard a rumor that we're going to sell SysVal. Tell me why you sandbagged us like this."

He flopped down in a chair, stretching his legs out and hunching his shoulders like a sullen schoolboy. "It's obvious, isn't it? It's time for us to sell. The economy is heading for a recession, and companies are going belly-up all over the Valley. We've been lucky, but I don't think we should push it. That contract with the state was fool's gold, anyway."

"And so, without consulting any of your partners, you took it upon yourself to approach the rest of the board about selling SysVal."

"What was I supposed to do?" he replied belligerently. "You'd run away, remember? How was I going to consult you?"

She wouldn't let him draw her into a fight. "What about Mitch and Yank? They didn't run away."

"Mitch and Yank don't understand things, not like you do. Listen, Susannah, this may seem like it's come out of nowhere, but everything's going to be okay. We can take all that we've learned and start a new company—something a lot better than SysVal. We've gotten too big too fast. This time, we'll keep ourselves even leaner and trimmer. Think how much we know about manufacturing. We can automate everything. Robotics is exploding. We'll save millions in labor costs. With our track record, we'll have every investor in the country standing in line to back us."

He was saying the right words, but the energy wasn't there. His eyes weren't shining with any mystic vision of the future. She sensed that he was throwing up some sort of elaborate smoke screen. Stalling for time, she walked over to the window and gazed out on a small, grassy courtyard. It was pretty, but uninspired compared to the elaborately landscaped grounds at FBT's Castle.

"What's this really about, Sam?" she asked quietly. "Are you trying to get back at me? Is that what you're doing?"

"No! God, don't you know me any better than that? What kind of a shit do you think I am?"

She didn't say anything.

He got up from the chair, looked down at the carpet and jabbed the leg of her desk with the toe of one of his custom-made Italian loafers. "Suzie, don't do this. Don't throw everything away because of what happened. I got rid of Mindy. I didn't think you'd want her around, so I fired her. And I went back to the shop and got that painting you wanted."

He was laying small gifts in front of her like a child who had misbehaved and wanted to make up with his mother. The betrayed wife in her felt a vindictive satisfaction that Mindy had been fired. The female corporate president noted the injustice and knew she would have to correct it right away.

She wasn't going to discuss their marriage, and she certainly wasn't going to discuss Mindy. "Why do you want to sell SysVal?"

"I told you. We've made a fortune, and we need to get out now. You have to listen to me, Suzie. It's all going to crash down. I can feel it. We need to get out while we can."

The old passion was back in his eyes, and it stirred a sense of apprehension within her. "You know something that you're not telling me."

"When did you get so goddamn suspicious? There aren't any hidden secrets here, Susannah. Just look at the fucking economy."

"We're not selling SysVal."

"The hell we're not. The rest of the board will go along with me. They're bean counters, Susannah. They don't like it when I get nervous. In the end, you won't have any choice. You'd better trust me on this, because if you don't, you're going to end up looking like a fool."

"I don't think so. I think you're the one who'll look like a fool."

"We went into this together, and I'm going to see to it that we go out together." He strode past her toward the door. "Don't fight me on this one, Susannah. I'm warning you. If you fight me, it'll be the last big mistake you make with this company."

*　*　*

At three o'clock the next afternoon, when SysVal's Board of Directors convened, Mitch, Susannah, and Yank were conspicuously absent. Sam paced the floor of the board-room while one of his assistants scurried to locate them. The assistant returned with the news that Mitch had made an emergency trip to Boston and that Susannah and Yank were nowhere to be found. The board overruled Sam's objection and voted to postpone their meeting.

Sam stalked out into the corridor. He couldn't believe she was defying him like this, that she was being so goddamn stubborn about everything. He should have known she would freak if she ever found out he slept with other women. She didn't understand that sort of shit didn't mean any-thing. She didn't understand that she was the only woman he wanted to spend his life with.

When he reached his office, he pushed through the line of people waiting in the reception area to see him and told his assistants they had fifteen minutes to find out where she was. Then he shut himself in his private office. She wanted a baby. Okay, he'd tell her a baby was okay. Maybe having a kid was what he needed. Maybe it would settle him down.

He realized he was sweating. Jesus, he was scared. Every-thing was happening so fast. Somehow he had to convince his partners to sell SysVal. And he had to get Susannah back. Not because of the company, either. Because of him.

Now that he was seeing things a little more clearly, he realized that it wasn't all her fault he wasn't happy. Maybe most of it was his fault. But she knew how crazy he got sometimes. She should have understood that he was just going through a hard time. She knew he loved her. He needed her. And if she left him, she was going to take all his missing parts with her.

"I don't mind coming with you, of course," Yank said to Susannah as they explored the empty bedroom of a newly built, multimillion-dollar luxury condominium that came complete with indoor pool, solarium, and a spectacular view. "But I don't need a babysitter. I wish you had trusted me to make myself unavailable this afternoon."

Susannah glanced at her watch. It was four o'clock. The

meeting should have broken up by now. She gave Yank an apologetic smile. "I couldn't afford to take a chance that you'd get distracted today and forget the time."

He didn't return her smile. He merely gazed at her, his expression inscrutable.

Feeling uncomfortable, she looked away. There was something so mysterious about Yank. She never knew what he was thinking. She doubted anyone did.

The realtor had left them alone so Susannah could go through the house a second time. This afternoon had seemed as good an opportunity as any to find a permanent place to live. She gazed unenthusiastically through the arched windows to the mountains beyond. "I guess this is all right."

"It seems adequate. Furnishings will add a lot, of course."

Susannah thought of the gaudy gilt and brocade interior of Yank's house, a decorating scheme favored by one of his early girlfriends.

A noise sounded below—the bang of the door being pushed open and then slammed shut. She caught her breath as she heard a pounding on the stair treads. Yank frowned.

Sam burst into the room. "I can't believe this. It's like I don't know who to trust anymore."

Susannah's control snapped. "Don't you talk to me about trust."

"You have a house, Susannah!" he exclaimed. "My house. Our house. You don't need another one."

"I don't want to talk about this now, Sam. I want you to leave."

He stalked toward her. Yank stepped forward, moving without any appearance of haste, but effectively blocking Sam before he could reach her. "You'd better leave, Sam," he said quietly. "Susannah doesn't want you here."

"Get out of my way!" Sam punched at Yank's chest, trying to push him aside. But Yank was wiry, and although he swayed to the side, he didn't budge. A vein in the side of Sam's neck began to pulse as he shouted, "I thought you were my friend. You should have been at the board meeting today. Instead, you were helping my wife leave me."

"Yank came with me because I asked him to," Susannah said. Sam's rage was embarrassing. Once again she had a sense of detachment as she studied him, a feeling that she was seeing him with newer, wiser eyes.

"I'll just bet he jumped all over himself trying to help you out," Sam retorted nastily.

Yank pressed his eyes shut and his mouth twisted with pain. "I think I'm going to have to give up on you, Sam. Susannah and I—we're both going to have to give up on you."

Sam winced and for a moment his face seemed to crumple.

"I saw a lawyer this morning," she said quietly. "Nothing you do now will make any difference." Clearing a wide berth around him, she walked out into the hallway.

"Don't do this, Susannah," he called from the doorway. "Come home with me right now."

But she wasn't going into battle with him, and she walked away.

Instead of returning to SysVal, Sam found himself driving to his mother's house. She was sunning herself in the backyard, wearing a bikini in some shiny bronze fabric that didn't look as if it had ever seen water. The headset of a Walkman was strapped over her ears, and her eyes were closed beneath a pair of sunglasses with the gold script letters A.G. glued to the bottom of one lens.

Even though he had offered to buy Angela a new house anywhere she wanted, she had refused to move out of the old neighborhood. She said she liked living here because she knew all the neighbors and her old ladies depended on her. He'd told her that she didn't have to work anymore—he had more money than he knew what to do with—but she said she liked her independence. He'd even offered to buy her a first-class salon that she could run any way she wanted, but she'd said she didn't want to work that hard.

As he reached down and shut off the Walkman, her eyes snapped open. "Hi, baby." She pushed her sunglasses on top of her head and sat up a bit. Her stomach wrinkled a little as she moved, but she still had a great body for someone who was forty-nine.

"Don't you look snazzy," she said, as she always did. "If anybody had told me when you were eighteen that you'd be running around someday in eighty-dollar neckties, I'd have told them they were crazy."

He took the webbed chair next to her, noticing as he sat that rust had formed around the screws on the arms. "Clothes aren't important."

"Try giving them up."

He stretched out his legs, looked up at the sky and closed his eyes. "Did you talk to Suzie?"

"She called me yesterday."

"She's got this stupid-ass idea that she's moving out."

"Uh-huh."

"Well?"

"You want some spaghetti?"

"So what did you tell her?"

"I didn't tell her anything. Suzie's a grown woman."

"So what did she say to you?"

"She said she's leaving you, Sammy."

He pushed himself out of the chair. "Yeah, well that's what she thinks. See, she wants a kid."

"I know. She wants a husband, too. You're getting what you deserve, kiddo. I've been trying to tell you that for a long time."

"You know, you really piss me off. You're my mother, not hers. You're always taking her side. Right from the beginning."

"I'm my own woman, Sammy. I call it like I see it."

He splayed his hand on his hip and glared at her. "Yeah? Well, you see it all wrong. She's important to me, you know. I need her."

Angela sighed and reached out to touch him. "Oh, baby. You're so hard to love."

"Databeck tendered an excellent offer, Susannah," Leland Hayward said over lunch at a pretty café in Ghirardelli Square. The venture capitalist was still one of SysVal's most influential board members. In addition to Hayward and the four founding partners, SysVal's board consisted of bankers and investors who had been brought in as they needed expansion capital. They were, by nature, conservative men, and as Susannah had visited privately with each one over the past four days, she had been dismayed to discover how nervous they were. Even Hayward, who was accustomed to taking risks, was worried.

He sprinkled Sweet'N Low into his coffee and shook his head. "You have to understand that when someone who's as much of a wildcatter as Sam starts getting cold feet and says we should sell, I have to listen."

"The company is solid," she insisted. "There's no reason to sell."

"You're behind schedule on the development of the Wildfire. You've just lost the contract with the state of California. That doesn't seem so solid to me."

"We only lost the contract because of the rumors about the sale."

"Maybe. Maybe not."

Susannah understood only too well. If she or Mitch had expressed worry over the financial state of the company, the board members would have been concerned, but not frightened. But when a swashbuckler like Sam said he wanted out, the board was thrown into a panic.

They finished their coffee and prepared to leave. As Leland rose from his chair, he frowned. "By the way, Susannah, I'm not too happy with your service people right now. They picked up my computer a few weeks ago when I was on vacation, and they haven't returned it or brought me a replacement."

Susannah pulled out the small notebook she kept in her purse and jotted a reminder to herself. SysVal policy dictated that any employee who received a complaint was responsible for following through on it. No one at SysVal—from the Chairman of the Board to the newest member of the typing pool—was exempt.

"I liked that machine," Leland went on. And then he chuckled. "Having one of those Blaze III test models made me feel like a pioneer."

Susannah looked at him curiously. "You had one of the test models?"

"Sam gave it to me. He found out I hadn't been using a computer and said I was a disgrace to the company. It took me a while to get used to it, but now I can't get along without it."

Susannah thought of her own missing computer and

wondered if someone in Engineering had pulled in all thirteen of the original test models to troubleshoot them. She reassured Leland that she would have a replacement machine sent over that afternoon, and once again asked him to reconsider his position.

"I've learned to trust my instincts," he said. "And right now my instincts are telling me that SysVal is in trouble."

She returned to her office frustrated and depressed. Her secretary handed her a pile of phone messages and she flicked through them, hoping to find something from Paige. For days, she had been leaving messages with the maid at Paige's villa in Sardinia, but so far she had heard nothing.

She was still thinking about her sister the next morning when Lydia Dubeck, an eager young MBA from Harvard who was one of the company's newest directors, poked her head into her office. "It's the darndest thing, Susannah. No one in Engineering seems to know anything about a recall of those thirteen test models. There aren't any work orders, and no one has heard about any problems. I guess that's good news."

Susannah was still troubled. "Sam's assistants should have a list of all the people who have one of those computers. Have someone get hold of it and find out the status of every machine."

But when Lydia caught up with her late that afternoon, she looked tired and irritated. "I don't know what the big deal is. Sam's apparently the only one who has a list. You'd think it was some sort of state secret. None of his assistants will give it to me, and he was in one of his moods when I finally ran him down."

Susannah didn't have to ask what that meant. Lydia had obviously received one of Sam's famous tongue-lashings. She thought for a moment, and decided that it was unwise to go into battle with Sam over something that was probably trivial, especially when a much bigger fight loomed ahead. "Thanks for trying, Lydia. Forget it for now."

She spent the rest of the afternoon in meetings. When the last one broke up at six, she decided to see if Mitch was still around so she could run some new ideas about financing the Wildfire past him.

His office was more formal than any of his partners'

offices. The windows were draped in a cream and maroon stripe, the chairs deep-seated and comfortable. Various civic awards hung on the walls, along with framed photos of his children.

He was deeply engrossed in a meaty-looking report lying open on his desk, and she paused for a moment to study him. Gold cuff links glimmered discreetly at his wrists. His collar button was securely fastened, his necktie neatly knotted. As he looked up at her, the lenses of his horn-rimmed glasses flashed in the light of his desk lamp. For a moment she tried to reconcile this bastion of corporate respectability with the man who had soul-kissed her sister.

"You want to go get some dinner?" she asked.

"Sorry. I'm meeting Jacqueline." He quirked an eyebrow as she made a face at him. "You're welcome to come with us, Susannah. Jacqueline enjoys your company."

"Thanks, but I think I'll pass. I'm not in the mood to discuss dead philosophers tonight." She settled down in the chair across from his desk and kicked off her heels. "Are you going to marry her?"

He immediately turned stuffy. "Really, Susannah."

"Well, are you?"

The loudspeaker crackled in the hallway outside. "Attention everyone. We have a lost pig in the building. Anyone spotting a two-hundred-pound porker answering to the name of Yoda should notify security at once."

Mitch sighed and Susannah cast her eyes to the ceiling. "Oh, Lord, I hope they're kidding," she said.

"Around here you never know."

Susannah's smile died on her lips as she thought how much this company meant to her, especially now that her marriage was over. "God, I love this place. I don't want to lose it, Mitch."

He took off his glasses and slowly folded in the stems. "I don't want to lose it, either, but it's not the worst thing that could happen. If we sold SysVal, we'd all end up with more money than we could spend in six lifetimes."

Susannah had refused to think about defeat herself, and she hated the idea that Mitch had even considered it. "This isn't just about money. We've built a wonderful company, and nobody is going to take it away from us."

"Sam has a lot of support, Susannah. Don't try to kid yourself about that."

"We have support, too. You know as well as I do that most of the board members don't even like Sam."

"Maybe not. But when he starts screaming 'fire,' they certainly start thinking about running for the nearest exit."

She poked her feet back into her shoes. Not for one moment had she considered the possibility that Mitch might change sides, but now she was no longer so certain. "I'm getting the feeling that you have some sort of contingency plan in mind, and I don't like it. We're not going to lose this company."

"That's emotion speaking, not logic. We have to be ready for anything. As much as we may want to deny it, we need to face the fact that we might not win."

She jumped up from her chair. "You face the fact. You and that computer brain of yours. I'm going to be too busy trying to keep us together."

"Susannah, you're overreacting."

The fact that he was right didn't make her any more conciliatory. She had imagined Mitch fighting at her side forever. Now she realized that might not happen. If at some point Mitch decided that the battle wasn't winnable, he would regroup. And that might very well put him on the other side.

Her fingers closed tightly around the papers she was carrying. "You're either with me or you're against me, Mitch. There's no middle ground. If you're with me, don't waste my time waving yellow flags. And if you're against me—then you'd better stay the hell out of my way, because this is one fight I'm not going to lose."

He slapped down the report he had been reading and stood. "SysVal isn't life and death, Susannah. It's only a company."

"No! It's an adventure." She threw SysVal's Mission Statement in his face, speaking Sam's words from the depth of her heart. "'We have set out together on an adventure to give the world the best computer humankind can produce. We will support and stand by our products, placing quality and integrity above all else. We relish the adventure because

380

it gives us the opportunity to put ourselves to the test of excellence.' I believe it, Mitch. I believe every word."

"Don't confuse rhetoric with real life."

"It's not rhetoric. We have to have standards. Not just as a corporation, but as human beings. Otherwise, we've wasted our lives."

She stalked out the door and down the hallway. The tight bonds of their partnership seemed to be unwinding in front of her. She found herself heading for Yank's lab. It was late, but he would probably still be there. She would only stay a few minutes so she could watch him work. Just a few minutes in Yank's presence would steady her.

27

The SysVal town house where Susannah was staying was located at the end of a narrow road and tucked away on a hillside thick with redwood and oak. She had just carried her first cup of Saturday morning coffee out onto the small private patio to enjoy the solitude when she heard her door bell ring. Setting down the cup, she went inside to answer it. As she crossed the small kitchen on her way to the foyer, she found herself hoping it was Mitch. Sometimes he stopped by on Saturday mornings, and she needed a chance to mend her fences with him, especially after their argument last week. But when she opened the door, she found her sister standing on the other side.

"Paige!"

"Don't slobber. It's only been a couple of weeks."

Susannah pulled her sister into the small foyer and gave her a hug. "Long weeks. I missed you."

Paige hung in her arms a moment longer than necessary, then pushed herself away. "Sardinia was a bore. I flew in last night." She tossed the strap of her purse over the banister, then glanced around at the foyer and into the living room. "This place is a dump."

The town house wasn't palatial, but it was hardly a dump.

Even so, Susannah didn't argue. "Temporary housing. I can't find anything I want to buy. How did you find me?"

"I called Mitch. What's wrong with him, anyway? He sounded funny on the phone."

"He was probably in bed with Jacqueline Dane." Susannah was surprised at how sharp she sounded. "Come on into the kitchen. You can fix us some breakfast."

"Me! I'm company."

"I know, but you're a better cook than I am."

Paige grumbled the entire time she was preparing their breakfast, but Susannah noted that she still made the effort to hunt through the shelves for cinnamon to add to the French toast, and that she refused to put the bread slices on the griddle until they had soaked in the egg batter a full ten minutes.

Susannah sank her teeth into the first bite. "Ambrosia. It's almost worth putting up with your nasty temper just to taste your cooking."

Paige ate a few bites, then set down her fork. Her hair tumbled forward, spilling like rumpled silk over the shoulders of her expensive designer blouse. She looked deeply unhappy.

"What's wrong?" Susannah said, putting down her own fork.

"Nothing, really. Nothing and everything. I don't know. What happened between you and that bastard you married was awful, but those weeks in Greece . . . They were nice, that's all."

Paige wasn't demonstrative, and Susannah knew this was the closest she could get to a statement of affection. "You're right," she said. "They were nice." She toyed with the handle of her fork while she chose her words carefully. "Paige, all that time we were together in Greece, you played the big sister and I got to be the little sister. I loved it. But right now I need to be the big sister again for a few minutes."

"Terrific," Paige said scornfully. "This is just what I need after traveling halfway around the world."

Susannah reached out and cupped her sister's arm. "You have a gift that's in short supply these days, kid. You're a natural-born nurturer. But you keep turning your back on that gift, acting like it's not important. And I think that's why you're so unhappy. Why don't you give yourself a chance?"

"A chance to do what?" she said fiercely. "I don't have a husband or kids. Men are jerks. The ones who aren't gay are sex maniacs."

"Paige, it's 1982. Marriage isn't the only way you can fulfill yourself. Why don't you stop whining about how awful your life is and start looking around you? There are hospitals full of sick children who could use a little of your attention. There are schools that need teacher aides, community centers looking for volunteers."

"I'm one of the richest women in California, Susannah. I can't just call up the Girl Scouts and tell them I want to help sell cookies."

"I don't know why not. Money should give you freedom instead of hemming you in. Figure out for yourself what you want to do and then do it."

Before she could go on, the telephone rang. She went over to the counter to answer it.

"Hi, baby doll. It's me."

At the sound of Angela's voice, Susannah smiled. She was grateful that her estrangement from Sam hadn't marred her relationship with his mother. Angela had changed very little in the past six years. She continued to fight off her birthdays as if each one were a lethal dose of poison, and she was having a high-voltage relationship with a man nine years younger than herself who adored her.

"Sorry to bother you, honey, but I had a broken water pipe in the garage sometime last night—one of the pipes that goes to a shampoo sink. Anyway, a neighbor got the water turned off, but everything's a mess."

Susannah was puzzled. It wasn't like Angela to worry her with household emergencies. She listened as Angela detailed her problems getting a plumber.

"Is there something I can do to help?" she asked.

"I tried to get hold of Sam, but he didn't answer."

If Sam wasn't home this early on a Saturday morning, he obviously hadn't spent the night in his own bed. This time the ache was less noticeable.

Angela went on. "I just thought someone should know

about it because of all those computers that are stored on the other side of the wall. I'm afraid the water might have gotten to some of them."

"What computers?"

"The ones Sam sent over a few weeks ago. Part of a new project or something. He was worried about security."

Susannah had no idea what Angela was talking about. Why would Sam be storing SysVal equipment in a garage? She reassured Angela that she would take care of it. They chatted for a few more minutes. Susannah hung up, then began punching in the number of SysVal's switchboard.

Her finger stalled before she completed the call. Something wasn't right.

"Paige, I have to run out for a while. It can't be any fun for you staying alone at Falcon Hill, and there's a perfectly good extra bedroom here. Why don't you pack a suitcase and move in with me for a few weeks?"

"You just want a free housekeeper," Paige grumbled. But Susannah could see that she was pleased with the invitation. By the time she left for Angela's, Paige had started making out a grocery list.

Angela let Susannah into the garage and left to meet a friend in the city. The garage smelled damp from the broken water pipe, but still familiar. A rush of nostalgia came over her as she remembered the hope and excitement of those early days. This part of the garage was now used only for storage. Boxes of beauty supplies took up the shelves that had once held those first SysVal computer boards. The abandoned burn-in box housed crimped rolls of old hairstyle posters. Her eyes swept from the burn-in box to the dusty workbench and then to the wall that divided the beauty shop from the rest of the garage.

Two rows of cartons marked with the Blaze logo had been stacked there. She carefully counted them. There were thirteen.

Flipping on all the lights so that she could see better, she stepped through a shallow puddle of water and made her way over to the boxes. The flaps weren't sealed. Pulling them back, she saw a silver-gray computer inside. It wasn't packed in molded Styrofoam like a new machine, but had been stored unprotected. With some effort she wrested it from the carton and set it on the floor. Although she could see that it had been used, she didn't have a list of serial numbers, and she had no way of knowing for certain if it was one of the thirteen test models or not.

Pushing up the sleeves of her sweater, she opened the next carton and continued to unpack the machines. Perspiration formed between her breasts and tendrils of hair stuck to her damp cheeks. She was breathing heavily by the time she maneuvered the eleventh computer from its box.

Her eyes swept over the case and then stopped as she found what she had been looking for—a brightly colored sticker mounted crookedly on the side of the metal housing. In hot pink letters it announced BOSS LADY. One of her assistants had put the sticker on the machine as a joke. This was her missing computer.

She called Yank from the telephone in the beauty salon. He was awake but vague. She repeated her instructions twice, hoping he would follow them. Then she sat down in the quiet garage along with the ghosts of her past and waited.

He arrived more quickly than she had expected. Without asking any questions, he set four of the computers on the workbench, including Susannah's old machine, and turned them on. Two of the machines were completely dead, and their screens remained dark. Two of them, including her computer, responded normally.

He tilted one of the nonfunctioning machines onto its side and unscrewed the case. "Somebody's been here first," he said. "The board is missing."

Susannah peered inside and saw that the printed circuit board that held many of the computer's components had been removed.

Yank moved the two machines that were still working over to the old burn-in box and left them running. Then he turned his attention to the computers on the floor. "Let's see what we've got here. One by one."

By the time they were finished, they discovered six dead machines and seven that still worked. Two of the dead machines still contained their circuit boards. Yank removed them and began testing them.

She pulled up one of the old metal stools and watched

him, taking care not to disturb his concentration, even though she itched to question him. Eventually her back began to ache. Slipping off the stool, she went into the Pretty Please Salon, where she made a pot of coffee.

She was walking back into the garage with two steaming mugs in her hand when a banging noise erupted from one of the working computers that had been plugged into the burn-in box. Startled, she moved closer, only to realize that the awful noise was coming from her old machine. It sounded as if the disk drive head was slamming back and forth. Coffee splashed over the side of the mug and spilled on the back of her hand as the noise grew worse. Instead of behaving like a sweetly engineered piece of high-tech equipment, her beautiful little Blaze was banging away like an old Model T.

Abruptly, the machine grew quiet and the screen went dark. A tiny wisp of smoke curled from the case.

"Interesting," Yank murmured, with typical understatement.

"Interesting? My God, Yank, what happened?"

"It died," he said.

She wanted to scream at him to be more specific, but she knew it wouldn't do any good.

He pulled her old machine from the burn-in box and carried it to the workbench. As he tilted it onto its side, he said, "Why don't you go on? This is going to take a while."

She hesitated, then decided she would go crazy just standing around watching Yank and waiting for him to say something. When Yank knew what was wrong, he would tell her. Until then, not even the threat of torture could pull an opinion from him.

She picked up her purse. "Work on this by yourself, Yank. When you find out what's happening, report to me directly. Don't talk to Sam. And don't talk to Mitch, either." She felt guilty for cutting Mitch out, but she wanted a little time to absorb the facts first before she told him what was happening.

He studied her closely, but didn't comment.

She had an appointment with her attorney that afternoon to discuss the divorce. Paige went with her, and afterward they did some shopping together. Although Susannah enjoyed her time with her sister, her mind was back in the Gamble garage trying to sift through what she had seen.

Only one moment of tension marred their afternoon together. As they were driving back to the town house, Susannah, in an attempt to encourage her sister to look for organizations where she could be useful, mentioned some of the local charities SysVal had involved itself with over the past few years. Perhaps it was because she was so worried about what she had discovered in the garage that she didn't guard her tongue carefully enough.

"I don't know whether or not you're aware of it, Paige, but ever since Father died, FBT has been doing a lousy job of getting money into the community. It's gotten even worse lately. Cal's great on high-profile grants—museums, symphonies—but he won't involve the company with drug programs, alcoholism, the homeless—anything that's down and dirty."

Paige's expression grew distant. "I won't talk about anything that has to do with Cal. He's the one subject that's off limits between us. There aren't very many people on this planet I owe any loyalty to, but Cal stood by me when I didn't have anyone else, and he's one of them."

Susannah didn't say anything more.

When they got back to the town house, Susannah found a message from Yank asking her to come to the garage at seven that evening. Paige had already made plans for dinner with a friend. Susannah did some chores around the town house and then drove to Angela's.

The lights were on in the garage when she got there. As she let herself in, she saw that Yank was still hunched over the workbench, his shirt pulled tight across his back. For a fraction of a moment the years flew away and she was a runaway bride again, watching a skinny egghead genius at work. But then Yank turned toward her and the illusion slipped away. The face of the man before her was strong and arresting, full of character and an almost unearthly sweetness. This man was self-confident in the deepest, most private way.

"The others will be here soon," he said quietly.

She stopped in her tracks. "Others?"

"We're partners, Susannah. We have to solve this together."

She experienced a disturbing combination of anger and guilt. "I gave you a direct order, and you chose to disregard it."

"Yes."

"I told you not to talk to anyone until you'd talked to me."

"It was an improper order, Susannah. Mitch should be here soon. I didn't call Sam, however, until just a few minutes ago. It will take him a while to get here, so the three of us will have a little time to talk first."

Headlights flashed through the side window as another car pulled in. Moments later Mitch stalked through the door. "What's this about?" he asked abruptly.

"We have a problem, I'm afraid," Yank replied.

Mitch's eyes roamed the garage, taking in the computers, the workbench, and coming to rest on her. She hoped he didn't guess that he was here at Yank's invitation, not her own.

Yank cleared his throat and began to speak. "We produced thirteen test models of the Blaze III because Sam wanted the computer in use for at least four months before it went on the market."

She could almost see Mitch mentally counting the machines scattered around the garage. "I remember. They've performed like champions. A few of the employees had them. Some of our customers. A couple went to elementary schools."

"Susannah had one in her office," Yank continued, "but it disappeared while she was in Greece. When she tried to find it, she discovered that hers wasn't the only one missing."

"Why didn't you tell me about this?" Mitch asked.

"In light of our other problems, I didn't think it was that important."

"Our test models disappear, and you don't think it's important?"

"It wasn't like that." She didn't like the way he was putting her on the defensive, so she recited the sequence of events coldly.

After she told of her phone call from Angela, Yank took

over and described what he had found. He mentioned the missing circuit boards on some of the machines and recounted the failure he and Susannah had witnessed in her computer. "It was an amazing piece of luck for me to actually be able to watch Susannah's machine fail. If that hadn't happened, it would have taken me much longer to understand the problem. All of the trouble has its source in one of the ROM chips."

ROM—standing for "read only memory"—was a custom microchip containing instructions that allowed the computer to perform automatically a specific set of tasks. Susannah listened carefully as Yank detailed how he had pinpointed the source of the trouble.

While Mitch questioned him more closely, Susannah mentally reconstructed the process of making a ROM chip. First the SysVal engineers decided what specific jobs the chip was required to perform. Then they wrote a list of instructions for those tasks in machine language. When the instructions were complete, the listing was sent to a ROM chip manufacturing firm where the chip was produced. For years, SysVal had used an Oakland-based firm named Dayle-Wells. The firm was efficient, reliable, and stood by its work.

"We've had chip failures before," Mitch said, when he was finally satisfied with Yank's explanation. "It's not something we take lightly, but it certainly doesn't justify all this secrecy."

Susannah had been thinking the same thing. Each tiny Sen-Sen-sized microchip was housed in a rectangular casing about an inch long. The casing had always reminded her of a caterpillar because it had a series of pointed legs at the bottom that fit into miniscule slots on the computer board. It was a relatively simple matter to unplug a faulty chip and plug in a good one.

Once again Mitch turned his attention to Susannah. "I assume Sam is behind this. Do you think this is related to his rush to sell the company?"

"I can't imagine what the link is, but it's difficult for me to believe this is coincidental."

Mitch gestured toward the computers. "But why all the

subterfuge? Just because one batch of chips fails doesn't mean that they're all bad. It's a problem, but it's not unsolvable."

"Remember that we're dealing with a ROM chip that contains software," Yank said, "and the possibility that I find alarming—"

But whatever Yank was about to say was cut short as Sam slammed into the garage. He looked wild, like a man on the brink of losing control. "Is it coincidence that I'm the last person here, or did my invitation have a different time printed on it from everyone else's?"

Mitch's features hardened. "You're lucky you got an invitation at all."

Sam turned on Susannah. For a moment, she almost thought he would strike her. Mitch must have thought so, too, because he took a step forward.

"This is your fault," Sam shouted. "You pick away and pick away without the slightest goddamn idea of what you're doing—always second-guessing me, thinking you know better."

"That's enough," Mitch interrupted. "Why don't you just cut through all the crap and tell us what's going on here."

Sam looked around at the empty cartons and the machines scattered everywhere. The tendons of his neck were stretched taut, his eyebrows drawn so close together they looked like a single line. "You should have done it my way. All of you should have trusted me. I was willing to take the responsibility. You should have let me do it. Why didn't you let me do it?"

"Because it's not your company," Susannah retorted.

His arm slashed the air. "It's not going to be yours, either, for very long because it's going up in smoke."

"A chip failure is hardly the end of the world," she countered.

"Oh, no? How many Blaze III's have we shipped since we introduced the machine?"

"Nearly two hundred thousand. But just because we have a bad part in the test models doesn't mean the ROM chip in every III we've manufactured is bad."

"Wrong again," Sam sneered.

391

"How can you know that?" she asked. "You can't possibly—"

"They're all bad. Every III we've shipped is going to fail after one thousand hours of use. Statistically, that'll average out to about a year—less time under office use, more time under home use."

"One year!" She caught her breath while Mitch swore softly. She wanted to reject Sam's conclusion, but she couldn't. He would never have predicted something this dire if he weren't absolutely certain.

She tried to sort through the facts logically. They'd faced recalls before, but never one this massive. She began thinking aloud, hoping to reassure herself as she reassured them. "It'll be a huge headache, but we can deal with it. Dayle-Wells is a reliable firm. If they've made a bad chip, they'll take financial responsibility for it." In her mind, she was already envisioning the logistics of this kind of recall. Once the outer case was opened, the actual replacement of the ROM chip was a relatively minor procedure. The old one was simply unplugged from its slots and a new one inserted. But the sheer number of machines involved made the recall complex, and it had to be done before the faulty chip physically destroyed the computer by smashing the disk drive head.

"Little Miss Pollyanna," Sam scoffed. "Always looking for the bright side. Well, babe, this time there isn't one. Dayle-Wells isn't responsible for the bad chip. We are."

Mitch's head shot up. Susannah felt as if a cold fist had clutched her spine.

Sam began to pace. "The ROM listing Dayle-Wells received from us was buggy."

Mitch spun around. "That's impossible. We have a dozen safeguards built in to keep that sort of thing from happening."

"Well, it happened this time. Five lines—just five lousy lines of bum code out of a hundred—but those five lines programmed a time bomb into the machines. Every Blaze III we've shipped will work for exactly one thousand hours, and then it will fail. The disk drive slams its head back and forth. It destroys itself and burns out the power supply.

After that—nothing." His voice had a harsh, raspy edge. "One thousand hours from the date the computer is first turned on, every one of those III's is going down."

Yank spoke thoughtfully. "The first of those failures will be showing up any day now, if they haven't already. Others are going to take years."

Dates and numbers spun like a roulette wheel in Susannah's head. They had charts that were amazingly accurate at predicting computer-use time. At best, they had only a few months to prepare. Once again, she began to think aloud. "We can handle the recall. It'll be expensive— it'll definitely hurt—but it won't kill the company."

"Susannah's right," Mitch said. "We can set up some sort of centralized system. Move a few hundred of our people into temporary service positions and send them out into the field. Thank God it's just one chip. We take out the old one, plug in the new one. We can do it."

Sam hunched his shoulders and turned his back to them.

Yank's voice was strained. "No. No, I'm afraid we can't. Come here and take a look."

With a sinking sensation in the pit of her stomach, Susannah got up from the arm of the couch and walked to the workbench. Mitch fell into step beside her. Sam stayed where he was with his back turned away from them. Whatever Yank was about to show them, Sam had already seen.

Susannah gazed down into the orderly, internal world of the Blaze III. Its microchips were laid out like rows of miniature houses on the neat little village streets of the green printed circuit board. With the tip of a pair of long-nosed pliers, Yank singled out one microchip. Susannah leaned forward to take a look.

"This is the bad chip," Yank said. "Look. It's soldered. The chip is permanently soldered to the board." He paused a moment, giving his words time to sink in. "We can't do a simple little chip swap. This particular part was designed to be permanent. That means we have to replace the whole circuit board on every Blaze III we've ever made."

Susannah's bones seemed to have lost the ability to support her. She felt as if she had just been punched in the belly. They couldn't afford to replace the circuit board on every machine they had manufactured. The cost would be prohibitive.

They didn't look at each other. Susannah stared down at the circuit board, Mitch at the litter of tools on the workbench. Silence ticked away like a doomsday clock. All of them knew that Yank had just pronounced their death sentence.

And I didn't let any of them know this involved anything"

28

T he four of them sat silently around Angela's kitchen
table. Mitch held his reading glasses between his fingers and
folded one stem in and out. Sam rolled an empty can of
Coke between his open palms. Susannah rubbed her right
temple with the pad of her thumb. She had just done the
unthinkable. She had made the phone call that shut down
the Blaze III assembly line.

Yank stared off into space. He had taken himself to a place
so far away he might not have been with them at all.

Mitch finally spoke. "I can't even conceive of how many
hundreds of millions this is going to cost."

No one said anything. Even a giant company like IBM or
FBT would have difficulty recovering from this sort of
financial catastrophe, and a young company like SysVal
simply didn't stand a chance.

Susannah's hand curled into a fist. If only *some* of the III's
had been bad, they could have handled it, but the fact that
the machines they had shipped last week, yesterday, the
ones that had come off the line that very morning—the fact
that *all* of them were bad—made the situation so hopeless
her mind could barely absorb it.

Yank slowly re-entered their world. "Who wrote the bad
code?"

The Coke can slapped between Sam's palms. "I don't know for sure. My guess is that it was one of the engineers who was working on the instructions for the chip. A guy named Ed Fiella. He only worked for us about six months, then he quit."

"Did you try to find him?"

"Yeah, but he disappeared, so I let it go. I couldn't ask too many questions or people would have been able to figure out that something was wrong."

"No one else knows about this?" Mitch asked sharply.

Sam shook his head. "Until today, I was the only one who had all the pieces."

Susannah rubbed the pulse in her temple. "How could you keep something like this secret?"

"I used a couple of independent engineers in Boston to run a few tests, some guys in Atlanta—people who weren't likely to bump into each other while they were out jogging. And I didn't let any of them know this involved anything more than a couple of prototypes."

Yank looked searchingly at Sam. "You realize that these failures aren't accidental. Everything happens too specifically. The machine works for a thousand hours and then it stops. And when it fails, it does it spectacularly. All that noise—the disk drive banging. That's too bizarre to be accidental."

"You're saying someone—this Fiella, probably—deliberately planted a bug in the ROM chip?" Susannah asked.

Sam nodded. "Just five lines of code, but that's all it took."

"We have so many checks and balances built into our procedures," she said. "A test team, code reviews among the engineers. How could this happen?"

"Maybe Fiella somehow managed to switch the listings at the last minute." Sam walked to the refrigerator and pulled out another Coke. "You know, I'm almost glad you found out. I was getting tired of having all of you look at me like I was Benedict Arnold or somebody."

Mitch slipped his glasses back on. "This is why you started pressuring the board to sell the company."

"If Databeck buys SysVal," Sam said, "the board swap is

their problem. We're out clean and we have the money in our pockets to start a new company. Databeck is a big conglomerate. The loss will hurt them, but they can stand it."

"There are laws against that kind of thing," Susannah said wearily. "Once those machines start to die, they'll sue us for fraud."

Sam slammed his unopened Coke can down on the counter. "No they won't. That's the beauty. It'll be months before we see anything more than a few isolated failures, and I haven't left any loose ends. They couldn't even come close to proving that we had any previous knowledge of the defect."

Susannah dropped her eyes to the tabletop. "So we dump the company on them, take the money, and run."

"Something like that," Sam replied with a shrug.

She looked up from the table and stared him straight in the eye. "That's shit, Sam. That's really shit."

He gave her the black scowl he always used whenever she uttered a vulgarity. She looked away in disgust.

Mitch's tone was cool and impersonal. "We at least need to discuss the possibility of selling out to Databeck."

Susannah felt a prickling along the back of her neck, and she turned toward him angrily. "The only way Databeck will buy SysVal is if we don't tell them about the bug."

"They have a lot more resources than we do," he said calmly. "There's a slim possibility that they could save SysVal. We already know that we can't."

Her skin felt cold. Mitch was going to betray her, too. Her friend had become a stranger. She thought she knew him so well, but she hadn't known him at all. Feeling as if she had just lost something precious, she turned toward Yank. When she spoke, her voice trembled. "Yank, what do you think?"

He returned to her from a very distant place. His eyes met hers and his expression was deeply troubled. For a moment he did nothing, and then he gently, almost accidentally, brushed the tips of her fingers with his own. They tingled slightly, as if she had been touched by a greater power. "I'm sorry, Susannah," he said softly. "I'm still processing the information. I'm sorry, but I'm not ready to offer an opinion yet."

"I see."

"I'm not offering an opinion, either," Mitch said firmly. "I'm merely pointing out that we need to discuss all the options."

She didn't believe him. Mitch was a black-ink man, a homebred, bottom-line capitalist. They could discuss all the options in the world, but in her heart of hearts, she was certain he would eventually side with Sam.

Sam began to pummel them with facts and figures. Mitch grabbed one of Angela's scratch pads and took copious notes, filling up one page and then quickly flipping to the next.

Susannah listened and said nothing.

Eventually her silence grew oppressive to Sam. He planted the flat of his hand on the table and leaned down. "We've already seen what happens when we splinter, Susannah. For chrissake, we have to work together on this as partners. We have to speak with one single voice."

"And I'll bet you think that voice should be yours," she snapped.

"That's crap, Susannah. Why don't you stop taking potshots for a while and start acting like a team player?"

"All right." She stood up and walked over to the kitchen counter. "All right, I'll be a team player. I'll reduce all this discussion to one simple question—the only question. Are we going to tell Databeck about the bug or not?"

Mitch looked down at his notepad and drew the outlines of a box. He traced the border over and over again with his pen.

As always, Sam declared a spade a spade. "Databeck would snatch that offer back in a second if they knew about these machines. Unless we keep quiet, there isn't any offer."

"Then that makes our decision simple, doesn't it? Are we liars or aren't we?"

Mitch slammed down his pen. "Susannah, I have to tell you that I resent your condescending tone. You don't have any special pipeline to heaven."

"We had a mission," she said, her voice catching on the last word. "We set out on an adventure together, and we've always been true to it. We didn't lie. We didn't cheat or steal or take shortcuts. And we made money beyond our wildest dreams. But making money was never what the adventure was about. It was only part of it. The adventure was about pushing ourselves and finding our own excellence."

Mitch stood up. "Those are wonderful words, but we're trying to decide the future of thousands of people here."

"They're not just words!" she exclaimed, her heart pumping in her chest, as she tried desperately to make them understand. "We've been put to the test."

Mitch made a dismissive sound and scowled.

"People are put to the test everyday," she declared. "Just not as dramatically as it's happened to us. A clerk puts too much change in your hands. Do you give it back? A friend tells a racist joke. Do you laugh? Are you going to cheat on your taxes? Water down the liquor? When does a person take a stand? When do we say, 'Stop! That's enough! This is what I believe in, and I'll stand by it until I die.'"

The corners of Sam's mouth twisted sardonically. "Don't you love this? Listen to the rich girl talk. Only someone who has never been poor could be so morally pure."

The muscles in the back of her neck ached with tension and her palms were damp as she pleaded with them to understand. "Don't you see? We've slammed right up against the morality of our own lives."

"This is business," Mitch said. "We're merely discussing a business deal."

"No," she retorted. "It's a lot more than that."

He gazed at her with a combination of pain and wonder. "You want us to hang on even if those beliefs are going to take us on a death ride?"

"Yes. Yes, I do." She walked closer to him, until only the corner of the table separated them. "Ever since I was born, people have been telling me what the rules of life are. My grandmother, my father." She gazed over at the man who was still her husband. "And you, Sam. You, most of all. But none of those definitions ever seemed quite right to me. Now—today—right at this moment—I know exactly who I am. I know what I believe in. And I believe in our mission. I've always believed in it. Our mission statement isn't just what SysVal is about. It's what life is about. Quality, excellence, honesty, taking pride in what we do no matter what that might be, and standing by it. That's what makes life good."

Sam's face had grown rigid and Mitch looked shaken. She turned toward Yank so she could judge his reaction, and saw that his expression was as blank as a sheet of white paper. While she had been spilling out her soul, he had been in a world of his own, not paying the slightest bit of attention.

Sick at heart, she moved away. The edge of the counter dug into the top of her hip as she sagged against it. They were going to end the adventure. She could sense it. Their brave and daring adventure was going to be transformed into something loathsome and unclean. She wanted to hurt them for what they were doing, and the only way she could hurt them was to make them speak the truth aloud about themselves.

"I'm calling for a vote." Her voice was hollow. "Are we going to tell Databeck the truth or not?"

"A vote between the four of us means nothing," Mitch said. "It's obvious that we're going to be splintered."

"No! I want a vote. I'm putting all of us to the test. Right now. Right this moment. We've slammed against the wall, and each one of us has to take a stand. We have to declare what we believe in."

Mitch reached out toward her. The gesture was awkward, almost as if he thought he could stop her flow of words with his hand. She moved past his reach, determined to see this through to the end.

"Yank, how do you vote? Do we tell Databeck the truth about the machines or not?"

Yank blinked and looked faintly befuddled. "Well, of course we tell them. It would be dishonest not to."

She stared at him and absorbed his absolute certainty. At that moment, comprehension swept over her, an awareness so new and yet so old she couldn't believe that she hadn't understood it long go. The vision of excellence and integrity that Sam carried like an evangelist into the world had come from Yank. Sam had merely found the words to define everything that Yank believed in.

She gave Yank a shaky smile and looked at her husband.

As she stared into his eyes, one part of her still yearned to reach out to him, but she understood with absolute certainty that was no longer possible. "Sam? Please, Sam."

"Sometimes the end justifies the means," he muttered.

"What about our mission? Please," she begged him. "Think about our mission. Think about what it means."

"Too many people depend on us," he said flatly. "Too much money is involved. I vote no."

Some precious spark of optimism, a naive belief in the invincibility of the human spirit, died within her. Her throat felt tight and swollen as she turned to Mitch and uttered his name.

His face was pale, his words clipped. "This is ridiculous, Susannah. Completely meaningless. There are complexities here, subtleties that need to be examined and discussed."

All the confused emotions she felt for him were choking her. "I'm putting you to the test, Mitch," she whispered. "Do we tell them or not?"

He dropped his head. Stared down at the floor. As she saw the stoop to those broad shoulders she had so often leaned upon, she was overcome with a sense of her own arrogance. Who was she to hold Mitch up to judgment? He was a good man. She had no right to do this to him.

He spoke, his voice low-pitched and sad. "Yes. Yes, we tell them the truth."

A rush went through her—hot and cold at the same time, the birth of something new and strange.

Sam slumped against the wall. His shoulders hunched forward, his head sagged. Everything about him spoke defeat. She walked over to him, her sneakers making soft little squeaks on the floor, and this time she touched him, the lightest brush of her fingers against his hand. "We have a few months," she whispered. "Help us make a miracle."

"No," he said belligerently. "No, there aren't going to be any miracles."

She laced her fingers through his and squeezed them, trying to pass her strength to him as he had once passed it to her. "You can find one if you want to. You can do anything. I believe it, Sam. I've always believed it."

"You're a fool. A stupid, self-destructive fool." He

dropped her hand and gazed at her with bleak angry eyes. "You'll have my letter of resignation on your desk Monday morning."

A murmur of protest slipped through her lips.

"I'm quitting," he said. "The terms of our partnership agreement give the three of you sixty days to buy me out. I'm going to hold you to it."

She wanted to be angry with him, but instead she experienced a splintering sensation of separation. Lifting her hand, she cupped the cheek of the man she had once loved so well and so unwisely. "Don't do it, Sam. Don't walk away from us. The adventure isn't over. Stay and fight with us."

But no sparks flashed in those deep dark eyes. Something essential had left him. He stood before her—a visionary with no vision, a missionary who had lost his faith. Gently, he removed her hand from his cheek. Then he turned on his heel and left them alone.

● ●

29

Susannah was cold with fear. She couldn't imagine SysVal without Sam. He *was* SysVal. He was the energy that propelled them, the force that guided them. Yank was gathering up his tools, and Mitch absentmindedly fingered his car key. She couldn't stand to have them leave her. "Come back to my house. I filled the freezer yesterday. We can find something to eat."

Apparently they were no more anxious than she to be alone, because they immediately agreed to her suggestion.

They drove separately. Mitch and Yank parked in front, while Susannah drove into the single-car garage. As she came in through the kitchen, she heard Paige's throaty laughter in the foyer.

"Well, well, well. If this isn't my lucky day. Tell me. Have you boys ever considered a sexual threesome?"

Susannah quickly made her way toward the foyer. She heard Mitch give a chuckle that sounded thin at the edges. "Sorry, cupcake, I only work solo."

"It figures. I'll bet you leave your socks on, too."

Susannah arrived in time to see Paige sauntering over to Yank. "Feeling left out, slugger?" She began to move closer, only to have him shoot out his hand and grasp hers, giving it a solid shake that effectively kept her at arm's length.

"It's good to see you again, Paige."

Paige's presence proved a welcome distraction. She picked up their somber mood, but she didn't ask any questions. Herding them into the kitchen, she began putting together a platter of cold cuts and making sandwiches.

Paige's position as a major FBT stockholder prevented them from discussing the crisis that was uppermost in their minds, but all of them seemed to welcome the respite. The next day would be soon enough for them to pick over the bones and see what they could salvage.

Yank was quiet and distracted throughout the meal. In contrast, Mitch teased and bantered with Paige as if he hadn't a care in the world. Once again Susannah wondered what it was about her sister that produced such a transformation in her stodgy partner.

Over scoops of vanilla ice cream smothered with home-made butterscotch syrup, Paige shifted her attention to Yank. She gave him a mischievous smile. "Do you know why female pygmies don't like to wear tampons?"

"Oh, Lord," Susannah groaned, losing interest in her ice cream.

Paige waved her to be quiet while Yank appeared to think over the answer. When nothing was forthcoming, she leaned toward him. "They trip on the strings."

Mitch chuckled. Yank's forehead wrinkled as if he were trying to sort out the physics of the whole thing.

"Paige, that's gross," Susannah protested.

The three of them gave her varying looks of disapproval, until she felt like an old maid schoolteacher with a prim mouth and chin whiskers. Slapping down her napkin, she got up from the table. "You people can party all night if you want to, but I'm going to bed. There's a cleaning lady coming in the morning, so leave the dishes."

Mitch stood up. "It's getting late. I think I'd better be getting to bed, too."

Paige lifted one eyebrow mischievously. "Why not climb in with Susannah? Now there's a combination of live-wire personalities guaranteed to set the sheets on fire. I'll bet the two of you could bring up the temperature of a bedroom—oh, maybe one and a half degrees."

"Paige, shut up, why don't you?" She scowled at her sister

and escorted Mitch to the door. Even though she knew it was silly, Paige's taunt had made her self-conscious. "In my office at eight on Monday, okay?"

He nodded and deposited a chaste kiss on her forehead. "You take care, hear? We'll work things out."

She shut the door behind him and walked upstairs to her bedroom. If only it were that easy.

In the kitchen below, Paige made a great show out of clearing the table. With far more force than was necessary, she snatched the dessert bowl out from under Yank.

He gently clasped her wrist. "You were rude to your sister."

"I'm always rude to Susannah. She wouldn't recognize me if I turned nice."

He maintained his grasp on her wrist. To punish him, she deliberately dropped down into his lap, where she wedged herself between the edge of the table and his thin, wiry body. "How's the celibacy trip going, lover boy? Ready to break your fast yet?" She wiggled the tip of her fingernail in between two of the buttons on his shirt and lightly scratched his bare skin.

He removed her hand.

She sighed dramatically and extracted herself from his lap. "Whenever I'm around you, I feel like Mary Magdalene trying to tempt Jesus."

"It's not the right time, Paige."

"And you're not the right man." She had intended to say the words lightly, but they came out with a sharp, vicious edge. She tried to cover up with a laugh, but it rang hollow.

He came up behind her as she walked over to the sink. "Please don't worry."

"Who me? Not a chance."

"Everything's quite difficult now. We have a crisis."

"Not my problem, slick. And by the way, our deal is off as of right now."

"That's not a good idea."

"Stick it, okay? I'm serving notice. Before the month is over, I'm going to tumble your good-looking buddy into a big double bed and screw his brains off."

He stood absolutely still. "You want to go to bed with Mitch?"

"Wouldn't any woman in her right mind?"

She waited for some reaction, prayed that he would yell at her or shake her or tell her he'd lock her in a room before he'd see her go back on the promise she'd made. Instead, he regarded her with great seriousness. And then to her astonishment, he leaned back in his chair and smiled in the deeply satisfied manner of a man who has the world under his absolute control.

"As long as it's Mitch, it's all right."

She wanted to slap his geeky, nearsighted face. He might just as well have stabbed a fingernail file right through the center of her heart. At that moment, she hated him, and so she gave him her bitchiest cat's smile. "Wanna watch?"

For a moment he looked so thoughtful that she wondered if he was actually considering the idea, but then he patted her arm and, as he got up to leave, told her she needed a good rest.

That night as she climbed into the guest-room bed, she heard the echo of the devil's laughter.

I can't get no . . .

I can't get no . . .

Sam's resignation lay on Susannah's desk when she arrived at work Monday morning. She stared down at it, unwilling to touch it with her fingers. The neat black and white letters swam in front of her eyes. She pushed the paper away and covered it with a folder. For now, at least, she would pretend that it didn't exist.

She managed to postpone the board meeting for another week while she brought in her key security people to begin tracing Edward Fiella, the engineer Sam suspected of being responsible for the bad code. Stressing the need for secrecy until they made a public announcement about the failures, she also had checks run on every employee at both SysVal and Dayle-Wells who had had any contact with the faulty ROM chip.

She spent the weekend preparing for the board meeting she had called for the following Monday. In hopes that bad news might be received better if it came in a brightly colored package, she dressed that morning in a hot pink suit draped at the neck with a boldly patterned Matisse scarf she had bought in the gift shop at San Francisco's Museum of Modern Art.

Mitch met her as she was walking toward the boardroom and fell into step beside her. "I just talked to Yank. Sam gave him his proxy."

Susannah didn't know what to say. Although she was glad that one of them had the proxy, she wished Sam had chosen Mitch. She would have trusted Yank with her life, but he was definitely a wild card when it came to a roll call. The men took their seats, and Susannah broke the news to them as calmly as possible. She might as well have detonated an atomic bomb in the middle of the conference table.

Leland Hayward's complexion turned gray, and he jumped up from his chair. "This is outrageous! How could something like this happen?"

"My investors are going to be wiped out," cried another board member as he fumbled in his suit pocket for a container of nitroglycerin pills. "What am I supposed to say to them?"

Mitch tried to calm the outbursts that had erupted around the table. "We have several months. Susannah and I remain hopeful that we can find at least a partial solution to our difficulty."

"Difficulty! This isn't a difficulty! It's a goddamn disaster."

They raged on, and Susannah made no effort to quiet them. For many of these board members, their jobs rode on the wisdom of their investment decisions, and the dramatic failure of SysVal would mark the end of their careers. They subtly let it be known that the partners should have kept the news of the computer failures to themselves and let the sale to Databeck go through.

"That's not what this company stands for," Susannah said. "You knew that about us from the beginning."

"Sam was going to let the sale go through," Hayward said in an accusatory voice. "Why didn't you let him do it? The board couldn't have been held responsible because he hadn't informed us. And where is Sam? Why isn't he here?"

She had dodged their previous questions about Sam's absence, but she could do it no longer, and she informed them of his resignation.

The absolute silence that fell over the table was worse than the men's anger. The news seemed to extinguish any dim hope they might have cherished of finding a way out of their disaster. The men didn't like Sam, but they believed in him.

The same emotion of despair had gripped her when she had seen Sam's letter of resignation lying on her desk, but something about their hangdog expressions sparked her anger. Sam wasn't superhuman. He didn't possess any special powers to save the company. There were other bright, inventive minds at SysVal, and one of those minds was her own.

Without clearly thinking through what she had to say, she rose from her chair and faced the board members squarely. "From the beginning, all of you knew that the SysVal adventure was one of high risk. But you were eager to go on that adventure as long as you could delude yourself into believing that the four founding partners were keeping the path safe for you. You were making so much money that it served you well to delude yourself. And so you told yourselves lies about us."

"What are you talking about?" Leland snapped. "What lies?"

"The lies that kept you comfortable so you could enjoy the fortunes you were making," she said angrily. "The lies about who we were. For all the faith you have in Sam's mystical abilities to solve any crisis, he's always frightened you. You didn't like that fear, and so in your minds you tried to overcome it by mentally transforming Mitch and Yank and myself into safe, conservative business partners who could balance out Sam's unpredictability. You didn't look at the three of us individually, only as we related to Sam. His arrogance disturbed you, so you found solace in my respectability. His inexperience terrified you, so you concentrated on Mitch's experience. When his flair for theatrics embarrassed you, you took comfort in Yank's solid silences. Always, it was Sam you turned to, Sam you believed in, and Sam you feared. You ignored the stories that I had run away from my wedding on the back of a motorcycle. You passed over any doubts you might have had about the stability of a man with Mitch's background throwing it all away to take up with three kids working out of a garage. You ignored Yank's radical genius and convinced yourself he was merely eccentric. Sam was the wildcatter. Sam was the swashbuckler. From the very beginning, you never understood that all four of us were the same. You never admitted to yourself that all four of us were renegades."

The board members were stunned by the passion of her words. Mitch leaned back in his chair and began to applaud, a lone set of hands clapping in the quiet room. Yank looked down at the notepad in front of him, a vague, satisfied smile tugging at the corners of his mouth.

"The adventure is not over, gentlemen," she said quietly. "We don't promise you that we can save this company. But we do promise you that no one—not Sam Gamble, not God Himself—has a better chance of saving SysVal than the three of us."

The meeting adjourned in a somber mood. As the members filed out of the room, Mitch came over to her and squeezed her shoulder. "Nice going, Hot Shot. What do we do now?"

"Now we get to work," she said.

SysVal teemed with the upheaval. Sam Gamble had disappeared, the Blaze III assembly line was shut down while a new ROM chip was being produced, and—incredibly—all work on the Wildfire project had been suspended. Everyone knew that something calamitous had happened, but no one was certain exactly what. The loudspeaker system was ominously silent.

Susannah and Mitch immediately went on the attack. To keep the public's confidence high in the Blaze III so that customers would continue to buy new machines, they had to move boldly. They drafted a series of newspaper ads in which they openly admitted that they had a problem with the old machines and assured their customers that a recall would be handled in a timely fashion. Before they could run the ads, however, they had to be honest with their employees.

Two days after the board meeting, Susannah appeared on SysVal's closed-circuit television system and told their employees exactly what had happened. Looking directly into the camera lens, she affirmed SysVal's intention to stand behind its product. Then came the most difficult part—announcing salary and hiring freezes and acknowledging that layoffs were inevitable. Speaking from the depths of her heart, she reminded them of SysVal's heritage and the absolute necessity of standing behind their product.

"This is a company that has always thrived on turmoil," she concluded, addressing the single camera in the small, high-tech studio. "Turmoil brings pain, but it also brings growth. Instead of complaining about our fate, let us welcome this crisis as an opportunity to dazzle the world. If we face this test valiantly, we will have taken another giant step along the continuing path of the SysVal adventure."

As soon as she had finished, the studio telephone rang. Her assistant announced that Mitch was on the line.

"Good speech," he said when she took the receiver. "Life's strange, isn't it? You sound more like Sam all the time."

She tightened her grip on the telephone receiver. "Sam is part of all of us. I just hope we got the best part of him."

The expression on Sam's face when she had last seen him continued to haunt her. She had tried to call him several times, but there was never an answer and no one knew where he was. Angela had gone over to the house, but it was empty and she was clearly worried. That night, as Susannah was getting ready to pull out onto El Camino, she decided to investigate for herself. Her marriage was over, but she couldn't turn off six years of caring.

The house smelled stale as she let herself inside. The bronze lamps shaped like Egyptian torches that sat in the foyer were dark, the living room cold and vaguely malevolent, with its sharply angled ceiling. Once again she realized how much she hated the harsh planes and unyielding materials of this building.

The telephone let out a shrill ring and she jumped. It rang again and again, scraping at her nerves. She stood motionless until it stopped and the house was once again quiet, then she moved through the empty rooms.

The heat pump clicked on. As she entered the vaulted hallway that led to the back of the house, she saw a wedge of weak gray light lying across the black granite floor. She walked closer and pushed on the partially opened door.

Sam lay on top of the rumpled bedcovers. He was unshaven, his chest was bare, and his jeans were open in a vee at the waist. One elbow was crooked behind his head. His other arm lay listlessly at his side while he stared up at the ceiling with hollow eyes.

On the side of the bed, a young woman sat in bra and panties filing a fingernail with an emery board. She was dark-haired and beautiful, with full breasts and long thin legs. She saw Susannah before Sam did. As she jumped up from the edge of the bed, her emery board hung in midair like a conductor's baton. Sam's gaze traveled from the ceiling to Susannah. He didn't show a flicker of expression.

She breathed in the thick, stale scent of marijuana and sex. Her stomach curled. A layer of dust covered the black lacquered furniture. The blinds were shut tight against the outside world. On the floor around the bed abandoned food cartons were mixed with dirty dishes. The painting Sam had bought her leaned with its face against the wall, a hole the size of a fist punched through the canvas.

"Get out of here," she said harshly to the woman.

The woman opened her mouth to protest, but apparently decided Susannah was too formidable to oppose. She glanced hesitantly toward Sam. He paid no attention to her; his gaze remained fixed on Susannah.

Susannah was dimly aware of the woman scrambling to get into her clothes and stumbling past her. Only when she heard the sound of the front door closing did she step farther into the room. "What are you doing to yourself?"

He turned his head to the ceiling.

She kicked away a damp bath towel. "Hiding is a coward's game. It won't solve anything."

"Unless you want to fuck, get out of here."

She didn't flinch from his vulgarity, even though the thought of going to bed with him repelled her. It wasn't just that he was sleeping with other women; she simply could no longer bear the idea of his touch. "Your mother is worried about you. We're all worried."

"Sure you are."

He sounded like a surly little boy. Whatever lingering elements of respect she had held for him crumbled away. His childishness, his infidelity, his self-pity had all diminished him.

"Are you going to spend the rest of your life sulking because you didn't get your way?"

For a moment he didn't move, but then he began to lever himself slowly out of bed. The dim light coming through the windows cast a blue-black shadow over his unshaven jaw. His hair was tousled, his arms hung at his sides. He began moving toward her, and she could feel his rage. She told herself not to underestimate him.

"You're not anything without me," he sneered.

"Do you have any idea how tired I am of dealing with your hostility?"

His nostrils flared and his hard dark eyes glittered with anger. "You're *nothing*, you hear me? You were an uptight socialite when I met you, and that's still what you are. Except now you're an uptight socialite playing at being a working girl."

The words hurt. She told herself they weren't true—she didn't believe them—but she was insecure enough that they still pricked.

"Madam President," he scoffed. "You think you've made so many contributions to SysVal. What a fucking joke. SysVal was always mine! You were so goddamn laughable the other night, I could hardly believe it. Talking about 'mission' and 'adventure' like you invented the words. Jesus, I wanted to puke."

She opened her mouth to defend herself, only to discover that she had no urge to do so. He was as pathetic as an overindulged child.

"I came to see if you were all right," she said. "Now that I know it's just self-pity bothering you, I'm leaving."

She turned to go, but he snatched her arm. "You got one more chance. I'm giving you one more chance to come with me."

"On a new adventure?" she shot back scornfully.

"Yeah. A new one. A better one. As soon as the word got out that I was leaving SysVal, every investor in this country wanted a piece of me. They're standing in line begging me to take their money. I'm the golden boy, babe. The goddamn dream child of capitalism."

His words sounded like braggadocio, but she knew they were true. An investor had even tried calling her that morning in hopes of locating him. She shook off his grasp. "You don't have the vaguest idea what the real adventure is. It's not just starting something—that's for kids. The real adventure is seeing it through. You bailed out at the toughest part, Sam. In your marriage and in your job."

For a moment she thought he was going to hit her, but she didn't flinch. Sam was a bully, and bullies had to be faced down.

"Get out of here," he said contemptuously. "Get out of here and learn what life's all about. Maybe then I *might* take you back."

She stared at him for one long moment. "I'm not coming back. Not ever."

Turning away from him, she left the house. As she stepped out into the cool, eucalyptus-scented air, she felt a sense of release. Whatever bonds of love and need had been tying her to Sam were finally destroyed. She was done forever with loving little boys.

30

Hal Lundeen, SysVal's head of security, was one of the company's few employees over the age of forty. A former Oakland city cop, he was a confirmed pessimist who believed that no matter how bad a situation was, it could only get worse. The hunt for SysVal's saboteur was proving his adage.

It was December now, and he had been driving himself hard since October, when Susannah Faulconer had first called him into her office and told him about the sabotaged ROM chip. Every piece of evidence Lundeen had been able to gather pointed to Edward Fiella. He even thought he knew how the switch had been made. Fiella had apparently spilled a cup of coffee just as the messenger had arrived to pick up the ROM chip instructions that were to be delivered to Dayle-Wells. That's when the substitution had taken place. Unfortunately, finding Fiella had proved a lot more difficult than any of them had ever imagined.

Lundeen looked uncomfortable as he took a seat and gazed at the woman behind the desk. She wasn't going to be at all happy with what he had to tell her. "I'm afraid I've got some bad news about Fiella."

"Terrific," she muttered. "Did you lose him again?"

"Not exactly. We finally traced him to Philadelphia. Unfortunately, we were about ten days too late."

"He took off again?"

"No. Uh . . . he's dead."

"Dead!"

"Yeah. He was killed in an auto accident ten days ago."

"Oh, no." She rubbed her forehead with the tips of her fingers. "What happened?"

"A couple of drunk teenagers ran a stop sign. He was dead when the cops pulled him out of his car. Just one of those things."

"We can't seem to buy a piece of luck, can we? Did you find out anything else about him?"

"Yeah. The car the cops pulled him out of was a Mercedes 380 SL convertible. He bought it new a few weeks after he left SysVal."

"That's an expensive car. I didn't see any mention of it on his credit report."

"Funny thing about that. He paid cash."

She slid the pen between her fingers as she took in the implications of what he had said. "That pretty much eliminates the possibility that he was just a hacker sabotaging the chip for kicks, doesn't it?"

"I'd say so, Miss Faulconer. I'd say it blows that theory right out of the water."

Since only a founding partner could purchase another founding partner's shares, she, Mitch, and Yank had been forced to buy Sam out. The Blaze III recall had severely depressed the price of Sam's fifteen percent, but the buyout was still costing each of them millions.

Susannah had been hit the hardest because she couldn't tap into any of the assets she and Sam owned jointly until her divorce was final. As a result, she was forced to deplete all of her financial reserves. She replaced her BMW with a Ford compact, and was staying in SysVal's town-house condominium on a semipermanent basis because she couldn't afford to buy anything else for a while. It was the way of the Valley, she joked ruefully to Mitch. A millionaire one day, a pauper the next.

But it was no joke. Before all this had happened, her net worth—on paper, anyway—had been close to a hundred million dollars. But as the new year arrived and she continued to pour every dollar she could lay her hands on into their dying company, she was practically broke.

The dreary, rainy months of winter slid into early spring. What had begun as a trickle of computer failures turned into a deluge. The company was hemorrhaging money. They sold off all nonessential assets—a conference center near Carmel, warehouses, land they had bought for expansion—but it was like trying to stop the flow of blood from a bullet wound with a wad of toilet tissue. By the end of June, Susannah felt as if each day they survived bankruptcy was a miracle.

As she drove home late one June evening, she wondered if Mitch and Yank would be at the town house when she arrived. Her partners had gotten into the habit of dropping by several evenings a week. Ostensibly, they met there so they could talk without the interruptions that plagued them during the day. But Susannah knew the real reason they showed up so frequently on her doorstep was simply because they knew there was a good chance Paige would be there, and Paige helped all of them forget their troubles.

She was their beautiful, blond-haired den mother. She pampered them and clucked over them, feeding their spirits as well as their bodies. When they felt too battered to go on, she restored them with her lively chatter. She was the major stockholder of their fiercest competitor, but they had stopped worrying about divulging company secrets in front of her. Paige had no interest in the business discussions that raged around her, merely in what everyone wanted to drink and eat.

Susannah's hands tightened on the car's steering wheel. She was torn between her love for Paige and the jealousy that had begun to grow inside her these past few months. If Mitch was there when she got home, he would be trading sexual innuendoes with her sister and grinning like an idiot. Frankly, she was getting sick of it. The two of them were just too revoltingly touchy-feely. Even a blind fool could see that they were ideal for each other. Yin and yang. The perfect mating of opposites. So why didn't they just get it on and put an end to her misery?

But she didn't want them to get it on. Even though she loved them both and saw how good they were for each other, the thought of them together made her insides feel raw. She hated her selfishness, but she couldn't seem to help it. She wanted her friendship with Mitch back the way it used to be, and his growing closeness with Paige was shutting her out.

She had been so upset about the situation that she had actually tried to talk to Yank about it a few weeks ago. He had given her his inscrutable smile and told her that everything had its proper time and she should be patient. She had wanted to slap him silly.

When she arrived home, she heard three voices coming from the dining room. Paige was feeding her partners just as she had expected. Susannah stood well back in the hallway and watched unobserved for a few minutes as Paige fussed over the men. She hopped up to go to the sideboard and choose special tidbits for their plates, fishing out mushrooms because Yank didn't like them, adding black olives because Mitch did. She was June Cleaver packaged in the body of the Playmate of the Month. As much as Susannah loved her, Paige's soft womanliness had begun to make her feel sexless. Paige was every man's fantasy woman—mother and sex goddess combined. How could she compete with that? Susannah wondered.

Not that she wanted to compete. It wasn't as if she were in love with Mitch or anything. She had already experienced the great love of her life, and look where that had ended up. It was just that she'd started to look at Mitch a little differently. Which was certainly understandable. She was a sensuous woman. Her body wasn't accustomed to celibacy, and Mitch was an incredibly attractive man. The past eight months had added more gray to his temples and deepened the brackets around his mouth, but, if anything, the changes had made him more appealing, certainly too appealing to be running loose around a woman who hadn't been intimate with a man for nearly a year.

He leaned back in his chair and stretched like a well-fed cat. She felt a peculiar giddiness creep over her as she watched his dress shirt stretch over his chest.

"Too bad we can't package you and put you up for sale, Paige," he said. "We'd make millions."

Paige crossed her arms on the table and leaned forward so that her breasts were propped up on them. "Exactly what part of me would you want to package? My cooking or my . . . other skills."

Mitch grinned, something he hardly ever did with anyone except her sister. "We're buccaneer capitalists. Whichever will bring us the best profit."

"Probably Paige's cooking," Yank said quietly.

Mitch shook his head in comic bewilderment. "I think you'd better start going out with women again, Yank. Ever since you quit dating, you've been losing your perspective."

"Holy men don't date." Paige's voice was silky. "Isn't that right, Yank? Holy men don't need women. They're above all that slipping and slopping around."

Yank gave her the sad, patient look he wore so frequently when they were together, and then mentally withdrew to his accustomed position on the sidelines. The bantering Paige directed toward Yank wasn't nearly as good-humored as her comments to Mitch, Susannah had noticed. Maybe that wasn't so strange. Yank and Paige were definitely from separate planets.

"Would it be possible for me to have another cup of coffee?" Yank asked.

Paige hopped up, her blond hair flying. Both men followed her round blue-jean-clad bottom as she rushed over to the coffeepot on the sideboard. As Susannah shrugged off her coat, she couldn't suppress another petty stab of envy. Even though she knew it was demeaning, she wished one of them would look at *her* bottom that way.

If only she could forget about the crisis at SysVal for a while and just be a woman. While she hung her coat away, she played a little fantasy in her mind in which she had her sister's breasts and they were barely covered by a black lace negligee. She saw herself sashaying up to Mitch and saying something sultry like, "Hey, big guy, remember me? How's about you and me go make ourselves some whoopie?"

But this particular fantasy wouldn't work. She kept seeing Mitch's face going pale with embarrassment. She heard his self-conscious throat clearing. "Susannah, I wouldn't hurt you for the world. You know how much I value your friendship. But Paige and I . . ."

"Could I have a little more coffee, too?" Mitch held out his cup for Paige to refill. He had glimpsed Susannah skulking about in the hallway, but he was pretending he didn't know she was there. Paige leaned over him and poured. He smiled at her. She was so damned good for his bruised ego. He loved having that sweet small body racing around catering to him. He enjoyed trading jibes with her smutty little mouth. There wasn't one morsel of honest sexual chemistry between himself and Paige, but apparently Susannah didn't realize it, and for the time being that was fine with him.

Susannah's feelings toward him seemed to be changing now that he had stopped playing Mitch the Buddy. He hoped so. It was about time he started getting under Miss Hot Shot's skin. Although she might not know it, he had declared war and was banking on her love of a challenge. He prayed he wasn't miscalculating. How much longer would it be before she began to understand what he had known for so long—that they were kindred spirits, like personalities who viewed the world in the same way and fit together exactly the way a man and woman should fit?

Her divorce wouldn't be final until the end of the summer, and he intended to use every moment of that time to pry her eyes open. Maybe it wasn't fair for him to play games with her when they were in the middle of such a devastating crisis, but he didn't care about fairness anymore. It was obvious by now that SysVal couldn't survive the summer. He was going to lose his company and his money, but he wanted to make damned sure that he didn't lose Susannah, too.

The only thing that worried him was Yank. Susannah kept disappearing into his lab to watch him work. It was a habit she had developed whenever she was upset about something. Mitch thought her feelings for Yank were brotherly rather than romantic, but he wasn't absolutely certain. And Yank was impossible to read. What if he was in love with Susannah? Being forced to compete with Yank wasn't something he could take lightly. The rest of the world might underestimate his partner, but Mitch had never made that mistake.

"Suze! I didn't hear you come in." Paige had spotted her sister in the hallway. "Sit down. I'll fix a plate for you."

Susannah greeted all of them and took a seat at the table. Within seconds, she was served a glass of chilled white wine and a fragrant helping of chicken provençal. Paige did everything but plump a cushion behind her back. Susannah's spirits sank lower. She felt like the world's lowest life form for being jealous of someone who took such good care of her.

"My kids are flying in the second weekend in July," Mitch announced. "I thought I'd have a barbecue for them that Saturday. You're all invited."

"Sorry, lover," Paige said. "Big bad duty calls. That's the night I have to hostess FBT's annual party at Falcon Hill. Not that I wouldn't rather spend it with you. God, I hate those things."

"Then why do it?" he asked.

"Cal does so much for me that when he asks something in return, I try to accommodate him."

Mitch and Susannah exchanged a glance. Neither of them approved of the amount of power Paige had transferred to Cal Theroux. Since he was a forbidden subject between the sisters, Susannah had asked Mitch to urge Paige to take more interest in FBT affairs and reclaim her voting rights. Paige had told him to mind his own business.

That evening after the men had left, Paige propped herself on the living room couch with a magazine, and Susannah carried her briefcase over to the armchair. When she opened it, she discovered a fat manila folder she had thrown in just as she was leaving. For a moment she couldn't remember what it was, and then she realized it was the file on Edward Fiella that the security department had finally returned to her office that day. She had tossed it in her case so she could give it one last perusal before it was put away.

She settled back in the armchair and then noticed that Paige was staring off into space, her expression troubled.

"What's wrong?"

Paige snapped back to reality. "Nothing."

420

"I thought we weren't going to shut each other out anymore. Are you having problems at the shelter?" For months now Paige had been volunteering her services at a shelter for battered women. She loved her work there, but sometimes being in the presence of so much suffering got to her.

Paige shook her head, then set down her magazine. "Nothing that noble. I was just wondering . . . How come you haven't started dating anybody? It's been nearly a year since you left Sam. Your divorce will be final before long."

"There hasn't been much time. Besides, I'm not exactly the world's best company these days. It's hard to be cheerful when you've just laid off another seven hundred people."

"But don't you miss being with a man?"

"I'm with men all day long," she replied, deliberately sidestepping the issue.

"That's not what I mean."

Susannah knew exactly what her sister meant, but she certainly wasn't going to tell her that she had been having embarrassing sexual fantasies about Mitch. Instead, she told her part of the truth. "It takes all of my energy just getting from one day to the next. I don't have anything left at the moment for an emotional involvement."

"What about sex? Don't you miss it?"

"I miss it a lot."

Paige looked deeply unhappy. "I know it's stupid, but in Greece Yank made me promise not to sleep with anybody for a while. I don't know why I agreed, except you know how he is. Right after I got back, I got mad and told him I was going to sleep with anybody I wanted. But I didn't. And last month when I flew over to Paris for a few days, I was definitely planning on having a good time. I have a friend there. He's a playboy, but he's nice. Anyway, I never called him. God, Suze, it's been forever."

"Celibacy must be catching. Even Mitch seems to have given up all those dreary women he used to date." The moment the words were out, Susannah wished she hadn't brought up his name. Of course Mitch had stopped dating. He was moving in on her sister. She recovered quickly. "Maybe you just needed some time off from men for a while."

"I guess. But I'm starting to think about sex a lot. Which is really ironic, because I didn't use to like it very much."

And then Paige got up from the couch, almost as if she wished she hadn't said so much. "I—I think I'd better sleep at home tonight. I have to meet with Cal early tomorrow about the FBT party. If I stay at Falcon Hill, I won't have to fight rush-hour traffic."

Susannah nodded. She knew she wasn't the best company right now and she didn't blame Paige for taking off. They walked to the door together. Paige grabbed her purse and jacket, kissed Susannah's cheek, and left the town house.

It was a beautiful night. The moon was full, the air sweet. As Paige drove home, she tried to concentrate on how pretty the sky was so that she wouldn't start to cry. But she had barely reached the highway before the tears were dripping down her cheeks. She hated to cry. It was weak and stupid and completely infantile. But from the time Yank Yankowski had walked into her life, it seemed as if she had been doing a lot of it in her private time. God. She had been like a crazy woman for months. Every time she opened Susannah's door and she saw him standing there, she felt as if someone had shot heroin straight into her veins.

All she had to do was shut her eyes and she could see him. She tried to read messages into every change of his expression, and to transform those short cryptic statements he uttered into complex sonnets of passion, but it never worked. She was too much a realist. Of all the jokes God had played on her, this was the biggest. She, a woman who could chose among the most fascinating men in the world, had fallen in love with the nerdy, absentminded geek who was so obviously in love with her stupid, blind sister.

Susannah carried the file on Edward Fiella upstairs. She decided that she might as well do some work, because she certainly wasn't going to fall asleep easily, not with all those dirty dreams waiting for her. After she had gotten ready for bed, she propped herself into the pillows and flipped open the file. She had been through this material months before, and she didn't really expect to find anything new, but she still wanted to take one last look.

There was a coffee ring on the first page, which held a copy of his employment application. She skimmed through the rest. They had hired Fiella right out of college. He had been with them six months and then left. She knew that he had a degree from San Jose State, and she glanced through his college history. No fraternities. No professional associations. The summer before he had graduated, he had taken a job programming the computer billing system at the Mendhan Hills Yacht Club.

Her eyes stopped moving at the reference to the yacht club. Why had she never noticed that before? She had visited the Mendhan Hills Yacht Club many times. Although it was a small club, it was one of the Bay Area's most prestigious.

And Cal Theroux had been a member for as long as she had known him.

Her pulse was racing. Moments before, the bedroom had seemed cool, but now she was burning up. Don't leap to conclusions, she told herself as she threw off the covers. Cal wasn't the only high-ranking FBT official who was a member of the club, and she couldn't make assumptions just because a former SysVal employee had been in the same room with a competitor. She reminded herself that FBT and SysVal hadn't been rivals until the Falcon 101 had gone on the market. Even then, winning the contract with the state of California had been far more important to SysVal than to FBT.

But all of the logical arguments in the world weren't enough to convince her. Snatching up her telephone, she called Hal Lundeen and told him what she had discovered.

It took two days for Lundeen to report back with the information she needed. He flipped open his notepad. "You definitely stumbled on to something, Miss Faulconer. Cal Theroux headed the committee at Mendhan Hills Yacht Club that put in the computerized billing system Fiella worked on. The two of them definitely knew each other."

Susannah's hand tightened around the pen she had been holding. Now she felt free to acknowledge her instincts. The moment she had seen the reference to the yacht club in Fiella's file, she had known in her guts that Cal was responsible for sabotaging the Blaze. She thought of all that hatred festering inside him for so many years. Had she really imagined he had forgotten what she had done to him? That he wouldn't, at some point, strike back at her?

"We need something that will stand up in court," she said. "It'll have to be more substantial than this."

"Give me a few more days, and let's see what I can dig up. The more I find out about your Mr. Theroux, the more I think he's a pretty slippery operator. He's left a lot of dead bodies at FBT on his way to the top."

As soon as Lundeen left her office, she called a meeting with Mitch and Yank and told them exactly what she had discovered. But both men had been trained in the scientific method, and neither was impressed with her conclusions.

"These are serious accusations," Mitch said, "and everything you have is circumstantial. If you're not careful, we'll be facing a lawsuit for slander on top of everything else. Unless Lundeen comes up with something more definite, I don't see how this will help."

"He'll come up with something," she said. "He has to."

But a week later Hal hadn't unearthed anything more than unpleasant anecdotes from former colleagues about Cal's ruthless but effective climb to the top of FBT.

Susannah stopped sleeping. She couldn't eat. The first week of July slipped into the second, and the weekend arrived. She spent all of Saturday at her desk. Mitch's children were in town, and he had taken them to a Giants game. Because Paige was committed to hostessing the annual FBT party that evening, Mitch had postponed the barbecue he had planned until the next afternoon. Susannah looked forward to seeing the children, but she dreaded watching Paige and Mitch together.

By seven that evening she was exhausted, but she didn't want to go home. She got up from her desk and wandered through the empty hallways. Many of the corridor lights were permanently dimmed, the offices unoccupied. She remembered when Saturday nights had been full of activity. Now her footsteps echoed hollowly on the tile floors. She peered into laboratories that only a year ago had been bursting with brash young engineers eager to strut their stuff. Now they were idle. No one announced loose pigs in the hallways or warned of Japanese invasions over the loudspeaker system. It was as if the whole brilliant, brazen world of SysVal had been an illusion.

She rested her cheek against the cool green wall. The adventure had come to an end. A sense of defeat settled over her so all-encompassing, she wanted to sink down along the wall and curl up against it. Cal Theroux had beaten her. Right now the party would be beginning at Falcon Hill. While he extolled FBT's accomplishments, he would be secretly celebrating SysVal's destruction.

She thought of the bright young kids who had arrived from all over the country to work at SysVal, of the thousands of lives his vengeance had upset. And in her mind, she kept seeing Cal dancing in the gardens of Falcon Hill.

She squeezed her eyes shut. From the beginning Mitch had called her Hot Shot, but she had never felt less deserving of that nickname. A real hot shot wouldn't stand by and let all the people she was responsible for be destroyed by a bastard like Cal Theroux. A real hot shot would do something, have some sort of a plan. A real hot shot would—

Her eyes sprang open. For a moment she stood without moving, barely breathing. Then she looked at her watch and began to run.

31

● ●

The library at Falcon Hill was unchanged. Her father's heavy mahogany desk still dominated the room. Susannah stood next to it clutching the telephone receiver in her hand while she waited for someone to answer the phone ringing in the pool house near the gardens. She was dressed in a slim scarlet chiffon evening gown with a rhinestone-banded bodice. As she waited, she remembered the night she had walked into this same room and found Sam seated behind the desk staring up at the embossed copper ceiling. A party had been going on then, too.

"Yes?" The voice that answered the pool-house telephone was male with a foreign accent. Probably a waiter.

"One of the guests is needed in the library immediately," she said. "Mr. Cal Theroux. It's an emergency." She repeated Cal's name for the waiter, reiterated the fact that the matter was urgent, and hung up the telephone.

She took several deep breaths and fidgeted nervously with the rhinestone border on the long scarlet scarf that accessorized the gown. The library faced the side of the house, so she couldn't see the party going on in the gardens at the back, but she could hear the lush sounds of an orchestra playing. She glanced toward the antique humidor on the

426

corner of the desk to reassure herself that the small tape recorder hidden within couldn't be seen.

Less than two hours had passed since she had left SysVal. In that time, she had tested the powerful little machine to make certain it was working properly, dressed in her evening clothes, and driven to Falcon Hill. Using one of the side entrances, she had made it to the library without running into her sister, or anyone else for that matter, since the staff was working out of the pool-house kitchen and the main house was deserted. Now all she had to do was wait.

She wandered restlessly over to the bookcases, reviewing what she planned to say to Cal. He wouldn't be expecting to see her, and she needed to use the element of surprise to her advantage. Once again, the socialite had to pull a hustle. She wished she had been able to reach Mitch so she could tell him what she planned, but he had been out with his children and hadn't answered the phone.

The door behind her opened. Slowly she turned. "Hello, Cal."

Surprised flickered over his features when he saw who was waiting for him, and his eyes narrowed. "What are you doing here?"

"Enjoying your party?" she asked, deliberately sidestepping his question. He was tanned and elegant in his tux, but his appearance repelled her. How could she ever have considered spending her life with this unscrupulous man? She wondered if his antiseptic lovemaking made his wife feel as unwomanly as she had once felt.

"What do you want, Susannah?"

She stepped forward, making no effort to conceal her hostility. "I want to see you sweat, you bastard."

He hadn't expected a direct attack. The woman he remembered had been obedient and aristocratic. She would never have dreamed of challenging him like this. "What are you talking about?"

"I didn't realize you were responsible until a few weeks ago," she said bitterly. "Isn't that ironic? It never occurred to me that you were capable of doing something so horrible."

He had regained control of himself. "I have no idea what you're talking about."

"I'm talking about my computers, you bastard.

"What—"

"I'm talking about the Blaze III and a sabotaged ROM chip."

"You're ridiculous."

"I'm talking about thousands of lives that have been disrupted. About innocent people who have lost everything. I'm talking about a man so twisted that he didn't care who was hurt as long as he could get even with the woman who ran away from him."

She saw it then. A flicker of satisfaction crossed his features before he could hide it. "SysVal's problems are well-known," he said. "I suppose it's even understandable for you to look for a scapegoat. After all, it's easier to blame some mysterious saboteur for your troubles than to blame your own inept management."

Her stomach curled. "You're enjoying dancing on our grave, aren't you, Cal? How can you sleep at night knowing what you've done?"

"I sleep very well. Probably just as well as you slept after you decided to humiliate me in front of all my friends and business associates."

"I didn't run away from our wedding out of malice. What you've done is obscene."

He walked over to a chest that held an assortment of crystal decanters and poured himself a small brandy. There was a smugness in his every gesture, a sense of absolute confidence. He took a sip, then smiled, showing perfect white teeth. "I heard you left your husband. Sorry it didn't work out."

"Oh, it worked out. Not forever, I admit. But I wouldn't trade those years with Sam for anything."

He didn't like her response, and his jaw set. "There's a certain vulgarity about you, Susannah, that I didn't notice when we were together. I suppose I should be grateful that our wedding ceremony was never completed. I can't imagine having been forced to live with you."

"No," she said. "I can't imagine it, either. And now after all these years have passed, you finally have what you've been waiting for. I'm sure you know that SysVal is on the verge of bankruptcy."

He smiled, a sly fox's smile that made the hair prickle on the back of her neck. "Unfortunate."

"Unfortunate for both of us."

He swirled the liquor in his glass. "I doubt that it's going to affect me very much. Except in profits on the 101, of course."

"You're wrong. It's going to affect you quite a lot." She paused for a moment and then said softly, "I don't have anything more to lose, Cal. So I'm going to take you down with me."

The room grew quiet. Only the distant sounds of the orchestra penetrated the silence. He set down his glass. "You're bluffing. You can't hurt me."

Hustle, a voice inside her screamed. *Hustle, hustle, hustle.* "Oh, I can hurt you very badly. All of those people out there in the garden. All of the FBT executives and board members. The United States senators and newspaper publishers. All those important people." Her voice dropped to a whisper as she began her lie. "I'm going to go out there in just a few minutes and entertain them with a little story about treachery."

His face took on a grayish hue beneath his tan. "Susannah, I'm warning you—"

"I'm going to move from one group to the next. I'm going to tell them about the Mendhan Hills Yacht Club and your connection with a man named Edward Fiella. I'm going to tell them about that brand new Mercedes Fiella bought after he did his dirty little job for you. I'm going to lay out every piece of evidence we've gathered."

His features hardened. "You can't prove anything."

"It's a party, not a courtroom. I don't have to prove anything."

"That's slander. I'll ruin you."

"You already have."

Silence fell thick and heavy between them. She knew that she needed something more definite on the tape. He pulled an immaculate white handkerchief from his pocket and pressed it to his forehead before slipping it back into his pocket. She could almost see the wheels turning in his head as he tried to find a way out. He couldn't know her threat to expose him to the people in the garden was a bluff. She intended to bring him to justice legally, not through gossip. But he needed to incriminate himself for her tape recorder before that would be possible.

"They'll think you're crazy." A small muscle had begun to tic near his eye. "No one will believe you."

"Some of them won't. But you've made enemies, Cal. A lot of them are out there right now. Your enemies will believe me."

His mouth twisted with suspicion. "Why are you warning me? Why not just do it?"

"I told you at the beginning. I want to watch you sweat. I want you to know what's going to happen to you. Just like I've known what would happen all these months while I've watched my company die."

"You little bitch." He gritted out the words.

"That's right, Cal. I'm the most vicious bitch you've ever met."

"I won't let you do this."

"You won't be able to stop me."

His forehead was damp with perspiration, and once again he pulled his handkerchief from his pocket.

"Did it feel good to ruin me?" she asked.

"I'm warning you—"

"Did it make your heart pump faster?"

"Shut up, Susannah!"

"Is that how you make yourself feel like a man?"

"God damn you!"

"We both know you don't get your kicks from women. Is that how you turn yourself on?"

"You goddamn bitch!" His face was full of venom as he lashed out at her. "It felt better than anything I've ever done in my life. I'm almost glad you found out. I wanted you to know. I wanted you to know exactly who was responsible for what was happening to you."

He had driven the crucial nail into his coffin, but she couldn't let him see her jubilation. She wouldn't make the mistake of celebrating until she held the tape in her hand.

"Enjoy your revenge while you can, Cal," she said quietly. "You don't have much time left." She began heading toward the door.

He followed her, just as she had anticipated. "Don't you walk away from me," he ordered.

"I don't have anything more to say to you." She wanted him to accompany her back out to the garden. He would stay at her side while she mingled with the guests, and when she didn't say anything incriminating, he would think she had lost her nerve. As soon as she was certain it was safe, she was going to return to the library and fetch the tape. Tonight she would make copies to mail to every member of FBT's Board of Directors.

She was reaching for the doorknob when she heard the sound of his breathing behind her. It was labored, as if he had run a great distance. A chill chased along her spine as his hand clasped her shoulder.

"Susannah . . ."

She shook him off and tried to take a quick step backward, but he caught her by the wrist. "You can't do this, Susannah."

Spinning around, she saw the panic in his eyes. It frightened her, and she tried to pull away. "Don't touch me."

He tightened his grip. "You're not going to do this!"

She had never known Cal to lose control, and the desperation in his face sent a cold shock through her. "Let go of me!" Balling her fist, she lashed out at him.

He caught her arm before she could connect, grabbing her so roughly that her neck snapped. She opened her mouth to scream, but the sound died as he pinned her against his body and grabbed her by the throat.

"Stop it!" he commanded.

She clawed at his arm and let out a terrible, garbled cry. The fact that she couldn't draw a deep breath intensified her panic. She kicked at him and jabbed him with her elbows, fighting for survival with an animal instinct.

"I'm not going to let you ruin me!" he exclaimed, sounding increasingly frantic.

Twisting her neck, she sank her teeth into his upper arm.

With a muffled cry, he struck her on the side of her head. The blow dazed her. She whimpered and sagged back against him, barely staying conscious as he dragged her out into the hallway.

"You can't . . . do this." His words came to her in a choppy, disjointed fashion, like the late night signal from a faraway radio station. She had the vague sense that he was talking to himself as much as to her, making up his plan at the same time he dragged her down the hall. "No . . . you can't . . . I won't . . . I know . . . I know what you'll do. . . . You're going . . . to commit . . . suicide."

She gasped out a mutated version of his name, but she needed all of her energy to draw air into her lungs, and the sound didn't carry. He was strong, so incredibly strong. She remembered how proud he had always been of his body, how hard he had worked to keep himself in shape.

"What better place . . . to kill yourself . . . than the house where you were raised?" His breathing was heavy as he pulled her down the hallway. "Your company . . . is going bankrupt, your marriage is over." She kicked weakly at him, trying to break his powerful grip, but she was too dazed to do any damage.

"Paige told me she's been . . . worried about you. Everyone will understand."

She pushed another cry through the narrow passageway in her throat. He increased the pressure on her windpipe, but she continued to make as much noise as she could, even though the sounds were too feeble to carry out into the garden. She had never been so aware of the vastness of the house, and she prayed for someone to come inside.

The back door that led into the garage tilted in front of her. Keeping one arm around her throat, he tore several sets of car keys from the pegboard. She clawed at his arm, gasping for breath and trying to stay conscious. He dragged her down the steps into the garage and pulled the door shut behind them.

They were in the far wing of the house, well away from the gardens. Her old bedroom was above them, several guest rooms, parts of the house that hadn't been occupied in years. Even if she could scream, no one would hear her. Please God, she prayed, digging her fingernails into his arm. Let someone come to the garage. Please God.

Two cars were parked inside—Paige's Mercedes and a Chevy that the housekeeper used. The Chevy was the closest, and he pulled her toward it, snatching up a pair of work gloves on the way. Her muscles turned liquid with fear. Why did he need gloves?

The pressure on her throat eased. She coughed. "Cal . . . Don't . . ."

He began to drag her toward the Chevy. A fresh rush of terror gave her new strength. She lashed out at him, summoning every bit of energy she had left. She fought with vicious determination, using fists and teeth and feet. He cursed and wrenched her around. Before she could protect herself, his arm shot back and he struck her again.

An angry black whirlpool sucked at her, drawing her inexorably toward its viscous center. Someone was pulling at her, moving her body about. No! She wouldn't be shut in the closet. The fox head was there. The balloon man. She tried to fight, but something was happening to her arms. She couldn't lift them, couldn't move them. There were furs all around, suffocating her. Garish balloons swam in front of her eyes in a slow drifting dance. She wanted to watch them, but someone was breathing harshly in her ear. Her arms. Why couldn't she move her arms?

Scarlet and the glitter of rhinestones swam before her eyes. Her head sagged forward and then back. Gradually she realized that she was behind the wheel of a car. The housekeeper's old Chevy. The scarlet and rhinestone pattern swimming in front of her came into focus. It was the long scarf from her evening gown. Cal was wearing the work gloves and tying her wrists to the steering wheel with the scarf from her dress.

"No . . ." she gasped. She tried to move, but her limbs wouldn't work and something was wrong with her legs. Her ankles were tied.

Cal's breath rasped in her ears. He was leaning in through the open car door to secure her wrists. She saw the gray lightning bolt that shot through his hair, and struggled to stay conscious. Her wrists were throbbing and the rhinestones on the scarf were cutting into her skin. He had tied the scarf much too tight. Why was he tying her wrists? He had said she was going to commit suicide.

"Don't do this . . ." she murmured, her words slurred.

He stepped back to survey his work. And then, in a gesture that seemed almost tender, he pushed her hair back into place and straightened her dress. When he was satisfied, he rolled down the car window and shut the door.

Her throat was dry, her tongue felt swollen. She was still dazed from the blow and she had difficulty speaking. "Cal . . . don't do this."

"It didn't have to happen," he whispered. She heard remorse in his voice, but the wildness was still in his eyes. "I never intended to let it go this far. But I can't have you ruin me."

"I won't . . . tell. I promise."

"I'm sorry. Truly." He checked the scarf. Her hands had begun to cramp painfully, and they twitched when he touched them. "I'll come back and untie you," he murmured gently. "Afterward."

Afterward. After she was dead. Before anyone discovered her body. They would think she had killed herself. "No," she moaned.

He turned on the ignition and the Chevy's engine sprang to life. Helplessly she watched as he went over to Paige's Mercedes and turned it on, too. The powerful German engine roared. He stood by the car and straightened his tuxedo. For a moment the scene looked to her like a slick magazine ad. Expensive car. Expensive clothes. Expensive, evil man.

She screamed and began to struggle against the knots, trying to slide her wrists along the steering wheel so she could reach the gear shift. But the knots were too tight and her struggles were pushing the sharp prongs of the rhinestones deeper into her flesh. He walked toward the door that led into the house, returned the gloves to the shelf, and then removed his handkerchief from his pocket. Using it to turn the doorknob, he disappeared.

She refused to go silently to her death, and she cried out until her throat was raw. How long did it take to die of carbon monoxide poisoning? Maybe someone would come into this wing of the house. Maybe someone would hear her.

Her wrists wouldn't move. Sobbing, she began to throw herself against the steering wheel, trying to sound the horn. But it was recessed and she couldn't reach it with her body.

Her struggles were forcing her to consume the tainted oxygen at an alarming rate. She cried out as she saw blood beginning to seep through the scarf, and she realized that the rhinestones had cut into her flesh in a dozen places. She tried to hit the gear shift with her legs, but the rope around her ankles made it impossible for her to maneuver.

While she struggled, the automobile engines roared away in a death chorus. As she watched her blood seep in rusty patterns through the scarf, her life had never seemed more precious. She didn't want to die. When the police saw the blood on her wrists, they would know she hadn't committed suicide. And sooner or later someone would find the tape recorder. But bringing Cal to justice no longer seemed to matter.

Mitch's face swam in front of her eyes. As she faced death, she knew that she loved him. She had loved him for years, but since she was married, she had made herself believe it was merely friendship. He was good and kind and strong, everything a man should be. And the fact that he loved her sister didn't diminish her feelings for him at all.

The monster engines continued to spew out their poison. The blood trickled from the wounds in her wrists. How much time had passed? Was she starting to get sleepy? Please God, no. Don't let me get sleepy.

She wanted a baby. She wanted to tell her sister that she loved her. She wanted to bask in the light of Yank's gentle eyes. She wanted to see Mitch again. Even if she couldn't have him, she wanted to watch that wonderful face soften in a smile. Please, God, don't let me die.

And, gradually, a sense of peacefulness came over her. Her head wobbled and her forehead dropped against the top of the steering wheel. She needed to rest. Just for a little while. Just until she felt stronger.

And then she heard her father's voice.

Wake up, sweetheart. Wake up right now.

She saw Joel standing before her, holding out his arms. His face was as young and as golden as a prince's. He was real. He wasn't dead. He didn't hate her.

Her eyelids fluttered. *Daddy? Daddy, where are you?*

His smile faded and he looked angry with her. Just like the

day she had run away with Sam Gamble. So fierce and angry.

Your arms, he shouted. *Move your arms!*

No. She didn't want to move them. She was too tired. But he kept calling out to her over and over again.

Your arms! Move your arms!

The scarves were too tight. Her wrists were bleeding and she was sleepy. But he looked so angry—she didn't want to make him angry—he looked so angry that she tried once more. Gathering the small amount of strength she had left, she struggled against her bonds. For the last time, she pulled at the knots.

And her wrists began to move in their slippery path of blood. Pain clawed at her as she tried to slide them down along the steering wheel. Everything was spinning. She had to rest. She had to make the pain stop. Just for a moment.

Her fingers bumped against the gear shift, but she could no longer remember why it had been so important to reach it.

Wake up! Joel shouted. *Wake up now.*

She tried to focus, tried to remember what she had to do. With a rasping breath she tugged on the gear shift and awkwardly maneuvered the car into reverse.

But she had expended the last of her energy, and there was nothing left.

Your feet, he cried. *Lift your feet.*

He expected too much of her. He had always expected too much. Her feet were heavy. Much too heavy to lift.

Now! Now!

She pushed her clumsy feet against the accelerator.

The oxygen-eating engine roared. Her neck snapped as the car shot backward. It crashed through the garage door and catapulted out onto the driveway.

The slap of fresh, pure oxygen acted like a shot of adrenaline. She sucked the life-giving air into her lungs. Several minutes passed. Strength began to flow back into her body, and with the strength came agonizing shards of pain in her wrists.

She began to sob. Blood was smeared all over the steering

wheel, and she couldn't loosen the knots that held her wrists. How much longer before Cal discovered her and finished what he had begun? The faint sounds of the orchestra drifted in through the window. The music sounded more beautiful than anything she had ever heard. Biting her lip against the pain, she worked the car into drive. Then she once again slammed her feet on the accelerator.

The car shot down a small bank and onto the side lawn. With her wrists tied, it was almost impossible to steer, but she wrenched the wheel to the right and rounded the back of the house. On the opposite side of the grounds, she could see a striped party canopy and white paper lanterns swinging from the trees. The car rocked violently as the right wheels rode up on the terraced slope of the hillside. For a moment she thought she was going to flip, and then she gasped as the wheels steadied on even ground.

A low wall of shrubbery loomed ahead. The car careened wildly as she plowed through it. She could see the people more clearly. They were turning toward her. A heavy urn planted with topiary scraped the side of the car. The vehicle shuddered but didn't stop. One of the garden's marble statues appeared on her right. She wrested her arms to the left, just missing it. Men in tuxedos and women in glimmering gowns watched in horror as she raced closer.

She lifted her legs to hit the brake, but her foot caught beneath the peddle. The fountain materialized ahead along with well-dressed party guests who were scattering in alarm. She sobbed as she freed her foot and slammed on the brake.

Stones flew up from the tires. The car fishtailed on the gravel path and skidded into the side of the fountain. Her body jolted as the engine shuddered to a stop.

She heard a woman screaming, the sound of people running, a man's voice, loud and incredulous. "It's Susannah Faulconer!"

Someone was struggling with the door on the passenger side and then crawling over the seat to help her. Hands touched her wrists and tugged at the knots on the scarf. She whimpered with the pain.

More voices.

"She's tied. Why is she tied?"

"I'll call an ambulance."

"She's bleeding."

"Don't move her. You shouldn't move her."

But her arms and legs were free, and she was being taken from the car. Held in someone's arms.

Mitch. Mitch had come to help her.

Her eyelids fluttered. She wanted to thank him. Tell him she loved him. She forced her eyes open and saw a lightning bolt of gray hair.

"Don't try to talk," Cal murmured as he held her against his chest. "Don't try to talk." And then in a louder voice. "I'm going to take her inside. She's in shock."

Susannah tried to cry out, but she was dazed. He was moving more quickly. The paper lanterns flashed by in the trees overhead. A scream rose inside her, but the only sound that passed through her lips was a weak whimper. "Paige . . ."

A flash of pink appeared at her side, a cloud of blond hair. "I'm here, Suze. I'm here. Don't try to talk. Oh, sweetie, don't try to talk."

"Stop him . . ." Susannah tried to force out the syllables. Cal's fingers dug more deeply into her ribs. "Don't let him . . . take me . . . inside," she gasped.

Paige stroked her head. "Stop who, sweetie? It's all right."

"She's in shock." Cal picked up his pace. He was at the back of the house, stepping onto the patio. "See to the guests. Make certain no one was hurt."

"Stop . . . him. He tried . . . to kill . . ."

"What's she saying, Cal?" Her sister brushed her arm. "Suzie, I can't understand you."

"She's hysterical, Paige."

"What's wrong, honey?" Paige murmured. "We'll take care of you."

Susannah pushed the words out. "He . . . tried to kill me."

"Don't listen—"

Paige's voice was flat. "Stop for a minute, Cal."

Cal kept moving. "She's been hurt. I have to get her inside. Go see to the guests."

438

"I said to stop!" Paige threw herself at him, the mother lioness protecting her cub.

Men appeared at her side. Cal let Susannah go, and Paige pulled her down onto a patio chaise. The world gradually steadied.

A crowd was forming around her. Through a breach she saw the buffet tables covered in rose-colored linen. Ice falcons with their wings spread in flight dripped into silver trays. Nicole Theroux, frightened and bewildered, was standing at Cal's side. Cal looked frantic, and people were staring at him. He tried to disperse the crowd, but no one moved. Susannah recognized several of the FBT board members and their wives, many of the same people who had witnessed her disastrous wedding.

Paige held her bleeding wrists and told her to lie down, but there was no time. Susannah turned to Paul Clemens, her father's friend. "Paul . . ." Her voice was as weak as an old woman's. "In the library. There's a tape recorder . . ." She told him where she had hidden it. The effort exhausted her.

Cal started toward the back door.

"You stay right here," Paul said sternly.

The men at the gathering were accustomed to taking command, and without a word being spoken, they began to step forward in a silent cadre. Cal looked at them, his face haggard as he tried to comprehend the fact that his world was being ripped apart. Before they could get close to him, he broke away and dashed toward the side of the house.

Several of the men gave chase, but Cal was running with a strength born of desperation, and he eluded them.

Paul had fetched the recorder, and he rewound the small tape. No one in the crowd spoke. Susannah held her sister's hand as the tape began to play.

Later there was a doctor and the police. Paige tucked Susannah into Joel's old bed, murmuring over the white bandages that encircled her wrists. The doctor had given her a sedative, but Susannah struggled to tell Paige something before she fell asleep.

"I saw him."

Paige gently stroked the damp, clean hair back off Susannah's forehead. "Who did you see?"

"Daddy." Susannah's eyes clouded with tears. "He came to me when I was dying. Oh, Paige, Daddy came to me."

Paige patted Susannah's hand. "Go to sleep, Suze. You go to sleep now."

32

I'm going to kill her!"

Pain had taken over every part of Susannah's body. She squeezed her eyes tight and wished that whoever was making so much noise in the hallway would be quiet. The sedative was powerful, and it took her a while to realize it was Mitch talking. Only a faint gray light seeped through the window. Why had he come to visit so early?

"How could she have done something so stupid?" His voice sounded like a jackhammer at dawn. "I mean it, Paige. As soon as she wakes up, I'm going to kill her."

"Shhh," Paige hissed. "You're acting like a wild man. Yank, make him be quiet."

After Mitch's angry bellow, Yank's murmurings were like a soft breeze. Susannah drifted back to sleep.

When she awakened several hours later, bright sunlight was streaming through her window. Intermingled with the stiffness in her muscles was a piercing sense of joy. She was alive for a new day.

The mattress sagged. She turned her head and saw Yank lowering himself to sit next to her. His clothes were wrinkled, his hair rumpled, his face lined with worry. At the sight of that dear sweet face, everything inside her broke apart. "Oh, Yank . . ."

Mitch had his hand on the doorknob when he heard Susannah's moan. His eyes were bloodshot, his hair standing in spikes on his head. He had been by her bedside all night and had just stepped out for a moment to help Paige deal with an overly aggressive reporter. Now he yanked open the door, overwhelmed with the irrational notion that her soft moan was a death rattle. He shouldn't have left, not even for a moment. He hadn't watched her carefully enough, and now she was going to die.

As he rushed into the bedroom, the scene in front of him gradually came into focus. She was curled up against Yank's chest as if he were the only man on earth. Mitch felt as if someone had given him a sucker punch right in the gut.

Yank lifted his head and saw him. He smiled his gentle smile. "Susannah's awake."

"Yes," Mitch said, his voice cracking with emotion. "Yes, I see."

Susannah stiffened against Yank. He laid her back on the bed. She turned toward Mitch.

"Hi, Hot Shot," he said, trying to make it easy for her by keeping his voice light.

She held out her hand. "Mitch."

He walked over to her, sat down on the side of the bed and curled her fingers through his. At the sight of the bandages on her wrists, he wanted to weep.

"I didn't think I'd ever see you again," she murmured.

He squeezed her hand tighter, pressed his eyes shut. "No more detective work, honey. Promise me."

Paige came into the bedroom leading a housekeeper and maid, all of them carrying trays ladened with food. "The police picked Cal up at a private airfield an hour ago, and the house is surrounded with three more television crews. No one is talking to anybody until everybody's had breakfast."

They didn't feel like eating, but none of them had the nerve to argue with Paige when the feeding urge was upon her.

In the aftermath of the scandal, FBT had a public relations nightmare on its hands, while Susannah became the Valley's Joan of Arc. Before a month had passed, her face had appeared on the cover of three national magazines. She sparred with Ted Koppel on *Nightline* and appeared on all three network morning news shows.

Would you buy a new computer from this woman?

You bet.

The publicity brought in an avalanche of orders for the Blaze III, and SysVal scrambled to get back to full staff to process them.

In the meantime, FBT struggled to extract itself from a public relations nightmare. Having its former CEO in jail waiting to go on trial for industrial sabotage and attempted murder definitely wasn't good for a company's image, and the corporation's stock tumbled to the price of a haircut. The state of California canceled its contract for the Falcon 101 and ordered the III. Investment money poured in to SysVal, as well as the initial payment on a huge financial settlement from FBT.

Although it was early evening, the SysVal parking lot was still half full as Sam pulled in. He turned off the ignition and sat in the car for a few minutes without moving. Six weeks had passed since Theroux had tried to kill Susannah. Sam had stayed away from SysVal while the worst of the media circus had gone on, but time was running out, and he had to make his move.

Since early spring he had devoted every minute to launching his new company. The concept was so beautiful, he couldn't believe he hadn't thought of it years ago. One night he had been handing over his credit card at a restaurant when it had hit him. He had stared down at that slim piece of plastic and felt as if the top of his head had blown off. What would happen if credit cards were embedded with microchips?

Aw, man . . . He had almost started to cry as he envisioned the beauty of it. The way the world did business would change forever. Ideas had flashed through his mind like lasers at a rock concert. An electronic credit card could handle bank transactions, dial a telephone, take care of parking meters and vending machines. A person's entire credit history could be stored on the card, their medical history, their fucking *life* history. The card could function as a door key, an ignition key, a security pass. His head had reeled. Jeezus . . .

He had more investors waiting in line to bankroll him than he needed. Money was no problem, but people were. He had gone on a raid, picking up some of the bright youngsters that SysVal had laid off, stealing a few programmers from Bill Gates at MicroSoft, a top executive from Intel. He had seduced a marketing whiz away from Apple. The Valley was churning with bright, young talent, and he had gone after the best. By mid-summer, he had money and he had a staff.

Now he needed Yank.

As he pocketed his keys and began to walk across the lot toward the building, he thought how sweet life had turned for his former partners. Hardly a week passed without another story in the newspapers about them. He tried not to resent the fact that the press had cast him as a villain because he'd bailed out of SysVal when it was in trouble. Since he'd sold his partnership at a deflated price, the bail-out had cost him millions, but he'd still made a fortune and he didn't care. Money wasn't the game. The game was vision. SysVal had gotten old and respectable. He wanted a challenge, a new adventure. He liked to be in on the beginning of the game, not the end. Some people weren't capable of business as usual, and he was one of them.

God, he was glad to get out of there. He could feel his blood pumping again.

But he needed Yank working with him. He couldn't imagine going any further without Yank's engineering genius behind him. He knew he had to stay patient while SysVal rode the crest of its publicity wave, but before long the company would stabilize, and he could have everything he wanted. Yank would freak when he found out what Sam was working on, and as long as Yank was certain that SysVal was safe, Sam would have no difficulty convincing him to come to work for his new company.

But Yank wasn't all Sam wanted. As he approached the entrance, he shoved his hand impatiently through his hair. His divorce was going to be final soon, and he had to move quickly.

His heart began to beat faster. God, he loved a challenge, and this was going to be the biggest challenge of his life. He could get Susannah back. What was it she had once said about him? That he had the ability to make sensible people do impossible things. Now he had to convince her that he'd settled down. Life was exciting again. He no longer had anything to prove by screwing around with other women, and he was finally ready to cope with a kid. Those were his bargaining chips.

Maybe it was good that they'd had this time apart, because now he understood how much she meant to him. Before she'd left him, he had been bored, restless, and he'd blamed it on her. He'd lost sight of how smart she was, how sweet. He hadn't felt complete since the night she had walked out on him. She seemed to have taken part of himself with her.

The last few times he had tried to talk to her on the phone, she had brushed him off, so he had decided to use Yank to get to her. Drop in on him at work. Make it seem casual. He had to get more aggressive with Yank anyway. This way he could kill two birds with one stone.

He didn't have any trouble getting past the SysVal security desk. Even at seven in the evening, the halls were bustling with activity, and he shot the bull with some of his former engineers before he left to find Yank. Somebody said he was eating dinner.

As he made his way toward the small kitchen in the back of the building, the loudspeaker blared. "Whoever ordered thirty-six pizzas and a box of Milk Duds, pick your order up in the main lobby now."

He shoved his hand in his pocket. It felt good to be back. And then he scoffed at himself. That was the sort of nostalgic bullshit that kept people from moving forward.

As he approached the kitchen, he saw Yank and Susannah sitting across from each other at one of the blond wooden tables. A picnic basket was propped between them. Too fucking cozy for words.

Ever since he and Susannah had split up, he'd been worried about Yank's feelings for her. He knew that years ago Yank had had a crush on her, but he'd never taken it very seriously. He'd even gotten a kick out of the way Yank used to look at her. Now he wondered if he'd been too casual about the whole thing.

Susannah laughed and Yank smiled back at her. He looked like he wanted to eat her right along with the piece of chicken on his plate. Since when had Yank ever taken time out from the lab to eat dinner?

Susannah saw Sam first and her smile faded. Her lack of welcome hurt. Jesus, he still wanted her. She was part of him, for chrissake.

"Sam." Yank put down his fork, stood, and held out his hand. As Sam shook it, he sensed a wariness in Yank, and that hurt almost as much as Susannah's lack of welcome.

He heard someone moving behind him and realized they weren't alone. Susannah's sister Paige stepped forward opening a wine bottle with a cork screw. He had only seen her once before, the night she and Susannah had walked in on him with Mindy. He could tell right away that she was a real bitch.

"My, my. Don't you look spiffy with your pants on." She ran her eyes up and down his body.

He wanted to slap her right through the wall.

Susannah didn't reprimand her sister for the wisecrack, and that really pissed him off. It scared him, too. What if he couldn't make her care again?

"Have a seat, Sam," Susannah said. "I think we can come up with an extra piece of Paige's chicken."

He sat, but refused the food. As Susannah reached for her napkin, he saw the faint scars on her wrist and remembered what she had gone through the night Theroux had tried to kill her. He felt rage, and something else he didn't want to identify. Maybe some kind of guilt bullshit.

Yank asked Sam what he had been doing, and Sam began telling him about his new company. Before long, he had thrown off his sport coat and was pacing the room, his fingers splayed, his arms making arcs in the air as he talked and talked and talked.

Hallelujah and amen! Brother Love's traveling salvation show was back on the road.

Susannah watched him without much expression, but Yank hung on to his every word. When Sam finally stopped talking, he noticed that Yank's eyes had grown unfocused, and he could sense his old partner's excitement as he pondered the miracles of engineering necessary to transform a wafer-thin credit card into a tool that could interface with the world.

Even Paige had lost her superior look. She had set down her wineglass and was staring at him as if he had just dropped in from another planet.

Susannah had noticed Yank's reaction, too, and she immediately rounded on Sam. "What do you want? Why are you here?"

He had forgotten those hair-trigger reflexes of hers, and he realized too late that he had miscalculated by talking to Yank when she was present. God, she was feisty. He had only wanted to pique Yank's interest, not steal him away in front of her.

But he could feel his adrenaline pumping at the idea of going into a battle with her again. Jesus, he loved a good fight. He had too many yes-men around him now. Not enough scrappers like Suzie. She liked everything up front, so why not give it to her? Why not have his fight and let her know what he wanted? That way she couldn't ever accuse him of having gone behind her back.

"What do you think I want?" he asked, spinning around the only empty chair at the table and straddling it.

"Suppose you tell me."

"I want the best, babe. Just like always."

"You can't have him."

"Yank's a big boy. He should be able to make up his own mind."

"He has. He's staying here."

"SysVal's getting old and respectable. Yank likes new challenges."

Paige's eyes were going back and forth between the two of them as if she were watching a tennis match. Yank was regarding them thoughtfully.

Susannah threw down her napkin. "I heard you were making some personnel raids. I thought you'd have enough decency to know that Yank is off limits."

Sam turned to confront Yank. "Still letting other people do your talking for you?"

Yank gazed at him with those gentle, infuriating eyes. "I'm not the only person you want. Am I, Sam?"

For the first time, Sam hedged. "What are you talking about?"

"Susannah's been through enough," Yank replied. "When are you going to leave her alone?"

Sam propped his arm over the back of the chair, still keeping it casual. "I'm not trying to recruit her. I know Susannah won't leave SysVal."

"But that's not what you want from her, is it? You don't want her to work for your company. You want her back as your wife, your good luck charm."

Susannah pushed her plate away and stood up. "I want you to leave, Sam. We don't have anything more to say to each other."

But Sam barely heard her. All of his attention was focused on Yank. Yank, the nerd—the goofy genius. Yank, who forgot his socks and lost his women. How could Yank think—how could be even imagine that he had a chance— at a woman like Susannah?

Sam's lip curled. He wanted to be cruel, to slice them both to the quick. "If you think I'm going to play dead and leave the field clear for you, buddy, you'd better think again. All I need is one night in bed with her. One night in bed, and I'll have her back. Isn't that right, Suzie?"

Susannah tightened her hands around the back of the chair. "Get out of here right now."

"I'm afraid this can't go on any longer," Yank said abruptly. "Susannah, we have to put an end to Sam's delusions about you right now. He's obsessed with you, and it has to stop."

"The divorce will be final in a few weeks," she snapped. "That'll put a stop to it."

"A piece of paper doesn't mean shit." Sam knocked over the chair as he leaped to his feet. "Get a divorce! Get a million of them! I don't care. Marriage doesn't mean anything, and neither does divorce. I want you back with me. We belong together. That's the only thing that matters."

Susannah slapped her palms on the table. "That's enough! Get out."

"He isn't listening to you, Susannah," Yank said. "He

refuses to listen. Sam doesn't understand about divorce papers. But he understands how to make a deal. Don't you, Sam?" Yank leaned slightly back in his chair.

Paige's eyes were huge in her face as she took in the scene these lunatics were playing out in front of her.

For a moment, Yank stared at a spot in the air directly in front of him, and then he said, "What about a contest? A contest and a deal."

Sam was poised, all his senses alert. "What kind of contest?"

"A contest between you and me. The winner gets Susannah. The loser steps aside forever."

"Are you out of your mind?" Susannah exclaimed. "Are both of you crazy!"

Sam laughed. "Wait a minute. Let me get this straight. You want the two of us to have a contest? If you lose, you'll stay away from her forever?"

Yank nodded slowly. "And if you lose, Sam, you leave her alone for the rest of your life."

Susannah made a choking noise, but neither of them paid any attention.

Sam immediately began to pace, hammering out the fine points. "You can't stay away from her if you're working with her every day. That means you'll have to get another job."

"Yes. All right. I won't sell out my partnership, but I'll get another job."

Susannah gasped.

Sam pressed his advantage. "With me."

"That's not part of the deal. The deal's about winning Susannah."

"I'm not a piece of property!" she exclaimed.

Sam ignored her. "And tell me exactly what you mean. The winner *gets* Susannah. What does *gets* mean?"

"You said you could have her back if you spent a night in bed with her," Yank replied. "Susannah will make love with whichever of us wins. Is that agreeable to you?"

"I will not!" Susannah cried. "Yank, I can't believe you're doing this!"

Yank gave her a stony look. "That's the agreement, Susannah. Do you understand it?"

She was starting to feel desperate. Yank was so serious, so determined. He was spooky when he was like this. She loved him, but she didn't desire him, and she wasn't going to go to bed with him. "No! No, I don't understand at all."

Yank turned toward Sam, who had stopped his pacing by the door. "Susannah will make love with whichever of us wins. The other one of us will leave her alone forever."

Sam's grin spread all over his face. Another challenge to face. Another barrier to smash. "Yeah. Yeah, I like this. Okay. I agree. What kind of contest?"

Yank looked at Sam as if he were the most thick-headed person left on earth. "Why, a video-game contest, of course. How else would we compete?"

"What?" Susannah shrieked.

"Oh, Jeezus." Sam began to laugh, collapsing against the doorjamb. "We're going to play a video game for her? Oh, Jeezus, I love this. The last buccaneers of the twentieth century fight a video game duel over their lady fair. What game? What game are we going to play?"

For the first time, Yank hesitated. "Why don't you chose?"

As soon as the words were out of his mouth, Susannah knew what was going to happen. She told herself it didn't matter. It didn't matter because she wasn't going along with them anyway. But still, she took a quick step toward Yank. "No! No, Yank! He'll choose—"

"Victors," Sam said. "I choose Victors."

"Oh, God . . ." She sank back down into her chair. They were crazy. Both of them were crazy, and she was even crazier to sit here listening to them. Why should she care what game Sam chose? There was no reason for her stomach to have plummeted like that. Sam could beat Yank at Victors from now until doomsday, and she wouldn't get in bed with him. The game didn't matter. Sam's choice didn't matter. But what was Yank doing? Hadn't she gone through enough? Why was he putting her through this?

Next to her at the table, Paige sat stunned.

Both men headed for the door, Sam charged with energy, Yank moving at his customary deliberate pace. An old

Victors game had been put away in one of the small storage rooms. It was a dinosaur now. Its graphics were stone age, its sound primitive. But it was still a classic—right up there with Space Invaders and Pac Man. Victors was a classic. And Yank Yankowski had never played a single game in his life.

33

● ● ● ● ● ● ● ● ● ● ● ● ● ● ● ● ● ● ●

The men wrestled the Victors game into an office near the storage room, then plugged it in and checked the controls to make certain it still worked. As Paige walked into the office, she saw that Susannah was already there. She had positioned herself as far away from the men as she could get and still be in the room with them. She looked shaken, as if these men really were deciding her future.

They said nobody could die of a broken heart, but as Paige looked from her sister to Yank, she didn't believe it. She was dying. And because she loved them both, she had to find the strength not to let either of them see it. The outcome of the video game might be meaningless as far as Susannah was concerned, but the fact that it was taking place at all had sent the dream world Paige had been building around herself crashing down.

For these past six weeks, ever since the night Susannah had almost died, Paige had been praying that she would fall out of love with Yank, but her heart continued to soar with joy whenever she looked at him. She was happy merely being in the same room with him, breathing his air and drinking in the sight of his gentle, dear face. She wanted to live every second of the rest of her life with him. Have his babies, wash his clothes, take care of him when he got sick. She wanted to sit next to him in a rocking chair when they were both old and hold his hand. She wanted to die with him and be buried next to him and believe in eternal life so she could be certain their spirits would live together forever. He was the only person who made her feel at peace in the deepest, most secret part of her soul.

Now, regardless of the outcome of this stupid video game, she had to accept the fact that she could never have him. Yank wanted her sister, and Paige had to get out of their way. The terror of knowing Susannah had almost been murdered was something Paige would never forget, and the guilt she felt for having placed so much trust in Cal had become a crushing burden. Since that night, Susannah had become even more precious to her. More precious to them all, Paige realized. Yank hovered at her side like a guard dog. Mitch had a haunted look in his eyes whenever Susannah was around. Poor Mitch. The tragedy had made him more serious than ever. He seldom smiled. He hadn't stopped by the house for weeks. All he did was work.

As Paige approached, Susannah gave her a wan smile. "I thought you'd gone home."

"No. No, I'm still here," Paige replied.

"This is crazy, isn't it? They're both crazy."

"Then why are you watching?"

"It's Yank. I can't—I can't understand why he's doing this."

"Because he loves you." The words stuck like great chunks of bread in Paige's throat.

Susannah shook her head. "That's not true. And he knows Sam will win. Why is he trying to push me back to Sam? I won't go, Paige. I don't care what Yank says or what he does. This time he won't get his way. I'm not going back to Sam."

Paige nodded numbly, unable to imagine any woman preferring a macho stud like Sam Gamble to a wonderful man like Yank.

The Victors game began to emit cheerful little beeps. Sam had unbuttoned his cuffs and was rolling up his white shirt-sleeves. "You'd better play a practice game, partner. I don't want you to say I didn't give you a chance."

Yank gazed at the game controls with distaste. "I don't think so. I don't like playing this game, Sam."

Sam slapped him on the back. "Tough shit, hombre. This was your idea."

Victors was the most complex of the early target games. It provided a miniature history of the development of weaponry, from the stone age to the atomic age. On the first screen, primitively shaped men threw stones at small four-legged creatures and dodged lightning bolts from the sky. On the second and third screens, they shot arrows at running men and then fired guns at a platoon of soldiers while they avoided return fire. The final screen featured a moving city skyline. The players controlled an airplane that dropped bombs down onto small targets as skyborne missiles moving in erratic patterns tried to blow up the plane. If the player survived all the screens, a mushroom cloud appeared with the final score and a message:

CONGRATULATIONS.
YOU HAVE SUCCESSFULLY WIPED OUT
CIVILIZATION.
NOW WHAT ARE YOU GOING TO DO?

That message had knocked everybody out.

Sam had none of Yank's reluctance about playing a practice game. As he stood in front of the machine in a white shirt and trousers, with his necktie pulled loosely down from his open collar, Susannah remembered all those nights at Mom & Pop's. Mom & Pop's was now a vegetarian restaurant called Happy Sprouts. They hadn't been there in years.

"Okay, I'm ready," Sam said. "High score wins. Let's toss to see who goes first."

"Go ahead," Yank said gloomily. "You're ready. You might as well play."

Sam limbered his fingers and gave Susannah a cocky grin. Then he turned back to the machine. "Come on, baby. Don't let me down."

Paige couldn't help it. She stepped forward to watch. Susannah seemed certain that Sam was going to win. Maybe when that happened, it would trigger something inside of Yank. Maybe he would fall out of love with Susannah and in love with her. Maybe they would get married and live at Falcon Hill. . . .

And maybe cows would fly over their wedding.

Sam Gamble was a superb video-game player, she'd give him that. He concentrated so intently on the screen and the controls moving beneath his hands that she doubted if anything could distract him. A lock of straight black hair tumbled down over his forehead as he moved through the first three screens with a ruthless efficiency. The machine beeped. The beeps got faster and faster. He hit the final screen. The muscles in his forearms spasmed as he maneuvered the controls. Missiles flew, bombs dropped. His face blazed with excitement.

Sam gave a victorious roar.

The mushroom cloud appeared and the screen flashed its message. He had scored 45,300 points out of 50,000.

He turned to Yank and grinned. "In my heyday, I made 48,000, but I guess I can't complain."

And then Paige watched while he ran his eyes over Susannah's body. The way he did it wasn't exactly creepy— Paige could see that, in his own way, he really did care about her sister. But still, the possessiveness in his appraisal made her skin crawl. Only someone who was entirely self-absorbed could be so arrogant. What a terrible man to have fallen in love with.

Yank, looking completely miserable, walked over to the machine. He sighed and stared at the screen. For a moment he did nothing, and then he turned back toward them as if he were about to say something. Apparently he reconsidered. Clamping his jaw tight, he returned his attention to the machine and pushed the button.

Sweet.

It was so sweet watching him work.

He kept his hands loose, his attention focused. Every motion was precise. He did nothing at random. One by one the screens surrendered to him. Every projectile found its target. Arrows flew, bullets whizzed. He dropped his bombs with deadly accuracy and dodged missiles before they even came close. It was as if he had envisioned every event before it could happen. Nothing was random. He was all-powerful, all-knowing. No man could be so perfect. Only God. Only the Mighty Creator Himself could play so perfectly.

Fifty thousand.

Fifty thousand perfect points.

"You son of a bitch," Sam said. Over and over. "You son of a bitch . . ."

"She's mine, Sam," Yank replied, looking even more miserable than before the game. "We have a deal, and you have to live up to it."

Sam stared down at the floor. Long seconds ticked by. He gazed at Susannah. "Do you really want him?"

"A deal is a deal," she whispered.

Paige could feel this great, awful sob rising up from the very bottom of her soul. She couldn't breathe for fear it would burst from within her. She had to hold it back and hide her grief in a deep secret place where it could never be discovered. Somehow, she had to find the generosity of spirit to give these two people she loved her blessing. And then she would disappear from their lives because she simply could not bear to watch them together.

"I love you, Suzie," Sam said hoarsely, with an expression of desperation on his face.

Slowly, sadly, Susannah shook her head.

Sam felt it then. Deep in his guts. He finally understood that he had truly lost her. That no sparkling oratory, no offensive he could launch, regardless of how brazenly conceived, how aggressively implemented, would ever bring her back. For the first time in his life, he had been defeated by a will greater than his own. And then he had a glimpse of something dark and unpleasant hovering on the edge of his unconscious. A glimpse of something Susannah had once tried to tell him—that vision wasn't enough. That it wouldn't stave off loneliness or keep old age at bay. That there was a kind of love in the world of which he was incapable. Susannah understood that love, but he didn't. And because he couldn't give it to her, he had lost her.

He blinked his eyes. Picked up his suit coat. Screw her. He didn't need Susannah. He didn't need anybody. The world of ideas stretched before him, and that was enough.

He ran the collar of his suit coat through his fingers. Then he lifted his eyes to Yank's. "Victors is your game, isn't it?"

Yank nodded slowly. "It was the last game I invented. Right before you made me leave Atari."

"Why didn't you ever tell us?"

"You all kept going on about it. I was embarrassed. I meant to tell you, but then I waited too long, and it got awkward."

Sam could have cried foul, but Yank was the greatest engineer he'd ever met, and he deserved respect. "It's a good game, Yank," he said huskily. "A real good game."

He turned to walk out the door.

And collided with Mitchell Blaine.

Mitch exploded into the office. His face was flushed, his blue dress shirt stuck to his chest with sweat. His light blue eyes held a savage, awful gleam none of them had ever seen before. "What in the goddamn everlasting *hell* is going on here?" he roared.

Paige's feet seemed to move of their own volition as she raced toward him and threw her small body into his arms. Safe, solid Mitch. He was as good as a daddy. The only force of stability in a world filled with familiar people gone crazy. She had telephoned him right away, as soon as she had realized they were actually going to play this crazy game. But he hadn't gotten here in time.

"You're too late," she said. "It's over."

Mitch circled Paige's shoulders and hugged her against him. His arm was strong and protective, like her father's should have been when she was a child. She wanted to cuddle up against him and let him keep the wolves away.

"Somebody'd better start talking fast," he hissed, hugging her close. "Right now. Susannah, tell me what happened."

She shrugged with all the nonchalance of SysVal's unshakable corporate president—the valiant female warrior who had taken on everything and everybody who had threatened her company. But as she watched her sister cuddled into Mitch's big arms, her bottom lip began to quiver. "Yank won me."

Mitch's eyes shot to Yank. He pierced him with an icy gaze as deadly as any of Victors' missiles. "What does that mean?"

"It's very simple, Mitch," Yank said. "Sam refused to accept the fact that Susannah no longer wanted him in her life, so he and I had a contest. Whoever won got to take her to bed. I won."

Somewhere in Mitch's solid thirty-eight-year-old body, the reflexes of an Ohio State wide receiver still existed. With a muffled roar, he released Paige, shot over the corner of the desk, and charged straight for Yank Yankowski.

Yank went down immediately.

Paige screamed, Susannah yelled, both women raced across the small office and threw themselves on Mitch, one of them pulling at his legs, the other at his arms.

"Get off!" Paige screamed, straddling his hips. "Get off, you'll kill him!"

Susannah grabbed a handful of blue Oxford-cloth dress shirt (light starch only) and pulled. "Stop, Mitch. No! Don't do this!"

Sam stood by the doorway and watched the four of them grappling on the floor. God, he was going to miss this place.

Susannah lost one of her high heels. Paige knocked a Rolodex to the floor and the cards went skidding everywhere. The glowing screen of the Victors game flickered above them.

Mitch shook off the women, pulled Yank to his feet, and slammed him against a dividing partition. The partition promptly collapsed, sending the men crashing into the next office.

Sam watched it all, took in the expressions on their faces, and finally understood how these people fit together. This was the vision that had escaped him, the one he had been too preoccupied to see. He shook his head at his own stupidity.

"Let him go, Mitch!" Susannah cried. She had a death grip on one of Mitch's arms. But something distracted her, a small movement in the periphery of her vision. She twisted her head and caught sight of Sam just as he was turning to leave the office.

He gazed back at her. She sucked in her breath as she saw the resignation in his eyes, and realized that he had finally let her go. "So long, babe," he said. "See you around."

For the briefest of moments, their eyes locked, and then she nodded her head in a final gesture of farewell toward her first true love. *Good-bye, Sam Gamble. Godspeed.*

His mouth curled in that old cocky grin, the grin of the motorcycle pirate who had stolen her away from her wedding and reshaped her destiny. Then he turned his back on all of them and set out to conquer another brave new world.

The loudspeaker began to play "Twist and Shout."

"Fight, dammit!" Mitch ordered. He sounded mean, but he was having difficulty summoning the will to smash in the face of an opponent who was proving to be so pathetically inept. "Fight me, you son of a bitch!"

But Yank was mystified when it came to physical violence. Although he found he rather liked the *idea* of finally being in a fight after all these years, he didn't really like *fighting*. There was no time to think anything through. No time to ponder or plan.

In actuality, Mitch was having more trouble with the women than he was having with Yank. The Faulconer sisters hung onto him like burrs. No sooner had he shaken off one than the other came back again. Paige had him by the neck, Susannah was pulling on his middle. His knee was starting to hurt, and he had banged up his elbow when the partition collapsed. What in the hell was he doing? He was thirty-eight years old, father of two, a member of the United Way Board of Directors. What in the sweet hell did he think he was doing?

He let go of Yank and loosened Paige's grip from around his neck. When Susannah realized he had stopped the fight, she relaxed the arm that had been clamped around his waist.

Yank was blinking his eyes. Mitch glared at him. "You're not taking Susannah to bed."

"No." Yank blinked. "No, I don't think that would be a good idea at all."

There was a long silence. Mitch stared at Yank. Then at Susannah. All the tension left his body like air from an overinflated balloon.

Yank continued to blink. "I'm sorry, but I seem to have lost my contact lens."

Then they were all down on the floor, relieved to have an

excuse to pull themselves back together while they crawled around to find Yank's lens. Paige located it, still intact, under one of the Rolodex cards. Mitch straightened his necktie and rubbed his sore elbow. Susannah looked for her shoe.

"It's difficult . . ." Yank said, after he had inserted his lens and inspected a scraped knuckle. "It's difficult to see exactly how we might extract ourselves from this. Sam and I had a deal. I'm not proud of the fact that I didn't behave in an entirely honorable fashion. I should have told him I'd invented Victors, of course. But in any case, two wrongs don't make a right. Sam and I had a deal, and I have a certain obligation."

Now Susannah was the one who wanted to smack him. She stalked toward Yank, wobbling because she still hadn't found her shoe. "Yank, will you let it rest? It's over. The contest was meaningless."

To her astonishment, Mitch began to yell at her. "Shut up, Susannah! You may be dynamite when it comes to running a corporation, but you're hopeless when it comes to organizing your love life. I've let all this go on far too long. For six weeks I've been walking around with my tail tucked between my legs waiting for you to stop looking like you're going to break in half. Well, I've had enough!"

"Don't you dare talk to me like that!"

"I'll talk to you any way I like. Right now, I'm in charge." He spun toward Yank. "Let's make a side deal."

"A side deal? Yes. Yes, I think that's a good idea."

Paige's heart began an arhythmic thumping against her ribs.

"How do you want to go about it?" Mitch asked, all business now that he was once again in control. "Your deal, your call."

Yank was thoughtful. "Perhaps you could make me a monetary offer for her. That should make it official."

Mitch had cut his teeth on making deals, and he knew how to go for a quick kill. "I'll give you five dollars."

"Five dollars!" Susannah lurched toward them. "Did you say *five* dollars?"

"That would be fine," Yank replied. "If you don't mind, I'd prefer cash. I lose checks."

Mitch reached for his wallet and flipped it open. "I only have a couple of twenties. Do you have change?"

Yank pulled out his own wallet and inspected its contents. "I'm sorry. I only seem to have a twenty myself. Paige?"

Paige nearly lost her balance as she scrambled for her purse. But her hands were trembling so much she couldn't find anything. In desperation, she emptied the contents out on the desk, sending lipsticks rolling and chewing gum flying. Frantically, she snatched up her wallet and pulled open the dollar-bill compartment, breathing so fast she was dizzy. "No, no, I don't," she sobbed. "Oh, God. I've only got a fifty. What good in the world is a fifty?" And then she turned to Mitch and screamed, "*For God's sake, give him the twenty!*"

Susannah had to make some attempt to reassert her dignity. In a voice as chill as the polar ice cap, she said, "If this is an auction, I'll put in twenty and buy myself back."

"It's not an auction," Yank said firmly. "That would be demeaning."

Paige started to choke. Yank tapped her gently on the back.

Mitch passed over the twenty. "I want my change back."

Yank nodded and drew Paige toward him. For a moment he closed his eyes as his bruised jaw came to rest on the top of her head.

Paige settled against his chest. And then she stiffened as she remembered everything he had put her through.

Yank had been fighting over Susannah. Three men had been fighting over her sister. Not one, but three! Didn't anyone remember that she was the pretty one? Didn't anyone remember that she was the one men went crazy over?

Yank remembered. He stared down at her, this beautiful blond creature he had fallen so desperately in love with. She was every girl who had passed him by, every girl who had laughed at his awkwardness and then ignored his existence. All his life he had stood on the sidelines and watched women like Paige Faulconer walk right past without even seeing him. But now that was over.

Who could ever have imagined that someone like Paige could have fallen in love with someone like him? And he knew she loved him. He had felt the way their souls matched up right from the beginning, that night on the beach in Naxos. But he had wanted the two of them to last forever, and so he had given her time and all the room she needed to adjust, even though from that very first evening he had wanted to bind her to him so tightly she could never get away.

And tonight he had frightened her to death. What he had done for Susannah had hurt her badly. She was in a huff. He could see that, all right. Now he had to make it up.

"Susannah, I won't be in to work for several days," he said. "Paige and I need some time alone together."

Paige curled her lip and flashed her eyes just like a prom queen who had been forced to dance with the ugliest boy in the class. "I wouldn't go anywhere with you if you were the last man on earth. You're a nerd! A complete and total nerd!"

Yank took his time to consider his options. He had a scientist's passion for the truth. Tricking Sam had made him miserable, even though he had done it for the best of reasons. He had offended his own moral sensibilities once tonight. He certainly couldn't offend them twice.

Could he?

"Very well, Paige," he said. "Susannah, would it be possible for you to drive me to the doctor's office? My arm is a bit sore. I'm certain it's not broken, however—"

Oh, Lord, he could hardly breathe as Paige cradled his arm and cooed over him and made him feel as if he were a bronzed California surfer god with sculptured muscles, a white zinc nose, and a brain too small to ever cause the slightest bit of trouble.

Susannah watched the two of them leave. They were wrapped together as if they'd been born that way. Silence hung thick and heavy in the office. Mitch stood by the doorway, one hand resting loosely on the hip of his navy-blue trousers, the other at his side.

Susannah was so nervous she could hardly think. For months she had been on a wild roller-coaster ride as she realized that she loved Mitch and tried to lock her feelings away because she thought he loved her sister. Now she wanted him to take her in his arms and speak all those tender phrases she yearned to hear. But he wasn't saying a word.

She filled up the silence with chatter. "There's not one thing wrong with Yank's arm. He's manipulating her. I swear, Yank's getting stranger all the time. And my sister . . ." Her voice faded. Didn't Mitch care for her? She told herself that he had to care, or he wouldn't have gone so crazy with Yank.

She studied a point on the wall just past his shoulder. "I thought you and Paige . . ."

Mitch didn't say anything. He just stood there and looked at her.

His look was definitely possessive. She remembered the five dollars, and she could feel her cheeks growing hot. Did he really think he'd bought her from Yank?

She lowered herself to the floor and made a great business out of looking for her shoe. Anything to avoid looking at Mitch. She peered under the desk, under the credenza, over by the doorway. Mitch's shoes were there. Unlike hers, they were on his feet. Polished black wing tips peeking out from between neatly creased navy-blue slacks.

The silence was growing more oppressive. Her cheeks still felt hot. She jumped as her shoe dropped in front of her.

Just as she picked it up, two strong hands pulled her to her feet. Mitch looked quite stern, perhaps a bit dangerous. "Your divorce isn't final yet. As soon as it is, you and I have an appointment in the bedroom."

At first she thought he said boardroom. You and I have an appointment in the boardroom. She was so shaken that she heard him wrong. And by the time she realized what he had actually said, he was on his way out of the office.

She gritted her teeth. Oh, no. It wasn't going to be all business. No way. If Mr. Stuffed Shirt thought it was going to be all business, he'd better think again. She flung her shoe at the door.

His reflexes were quick, and she hadn't been trying to hit him anyway, so the shoe missed him by a yard. That didn't seem to appease him, however.

He turned back to her, crossed his arms over his chest and said with a deadly quiet, "You've got thirty seconds, Susannah."

463

"For what?"

"To stop acting like a feather-headed female and decide what you want."

"I—I don't know what you mean."

"Twenty-five seconds."

"Stop bullying me."

"Eighteen."

"You're a real jerk, do you know that?"

"Fifteen."

"Why does it have to be me?"

"Twelve."

"Why can't *you* say it?"

"Ten."

"All right. I'll say it!"

"Five."

"I love you, you jerk!"

"Damn right, you do. And don't you forget it."

He still looked as mad as hell, but something warm and wonderful was opening inside of Susannah. She wanted to slide into his arms and stay there forever. What was it about Mitchell Blaine's arms that made a woman want to lose herself in them? Moving forward, she placed her open palms on his chest. She could feel his heart racing just as hard as hers. She shut her eyes and lifted her mouth toward his.

He groaned, caught her wrists and set her firmly away from him. "Not yet," he said hoarsely. "I bought you, and I'm in charge."

Her eyes snapped open. "You're kidding."

He gave her that narrow-eyed look he turned on competitors when he was bargaining for position. "Legally, you're still a married woman. And I'm not going to touch you until your divorce is final, because once I get started with you, I don't intend to stop."

She repressed a delicious shiver of anticipation, and then frowned. "It's going to be another month, Mitch. That's a long time."

"Use it well."

"Me?"

He gave her his best steely-eyed glare, but she saw these funny little lights dancing in those light blue irises. "You might as well know right now, Susannah, that I expect value for my money."

The sound that slipped through her lips was a garbled combination of laughter and outrage. She decided two could play his game. Recovering quickly, she sauntered back over to him and slipped her fingers underneath his necktie knot. "I know exactly what *I've* got to offer. You're the unproven commodity."

"Now *that* is exactly the sort of disrespect we're going to have to work hard to correct." His voice was as solemn as a judge's, but she wasn't fooled for a minute. "I want to see a change of attitude, Susannah. At least a semblance of subservience."

"Subservience?"

"I'm the man. You're the woman. As far as I'm concerned, that says it all. It had better be that way after we're married, too."

"Did you say married?"

"I'm considering it."

"You're considering it? Of all the arrogant—"

"First you pass the bedroom interview, Hot Shot. Then we'll talk about a contract."

As she sputtered for breath, his sober face shattered into the biggest grin she had ever seen. Before she could say another word, he walked away.

But she wasn't done with him. She rushed over to the doorway only to discover that he was already half way down the hall. "Stop right there, Mitchell Blaine," she called out. "Do you love me?"

"Of course," he replied, without losing a step. "I'm surprised you even need to ask."

Then, as she watched, he took three long strides forward, leaped off the ground, and faked a perfect jump shot at the ceiling.

His shirttail didn't even come untucked.

34

Yank and Paige left for Reno without bothering to change their clothes or pack a suitcase. Somehow, Paige had never imagined herself getting married in a silk blouse and pair of gray slacks, but no force on earth could have persuaded either of them to wait a day longer. The ceremony took place not long after midnight in a tacky little chapel with one of Elvis's guitars on display in a glass case. Yank had stared at the guitar for a long time and then said it reminded him of a woman he loved.

Paige didn't understand why one of Elvis's guitars would remind Yank of herself, but the service was ready to begin, and she didn't have time to ask any questions.

The wedding suites in the better hotels were already booked, and they had to settle for a smaller hotel. The bellhop showed them into a room that looked like a nightmare version of the inside of a Valentine candy box. The walls were covered in fuzzy zebra-striped wallpaper, and white fake fur rugs as thick as dust mops stretched from wall to wall. Festoons of shiny red and white satin draped the heart-shaped bed and were reflected in the gold-flecked mirror that served as a headboard.

"This is nice," Yank said in admiration.

Normally Paige would have laughed, but she was too

nervous. What if Yank was disappointed in her? She had faked lovemaking with some of the best, but Yank was a lot more perceptive than most men. Still, she didn't envision lovemaking as being the most important part of their life together. Anybody who was as cerebral as Yank probably wasn't going to be the world's most competent lover, which was fine with her. She'd already gone to bed with the greatest, and it hadn't been all that wonderful.

Cuddling with him appealed to her the most—so warm and cozy. The cuddling and the cooking. She wanted to fill his thin body with her rich, wonderful food. Nurse his babies from her bountiful breasts. Unaccountably, her eyes filled with tears.

She had her back to him, but somehow he seemed to know she was crying. He gathered her in his arms and held her. "It's going to be all right," he said. "You mustn't worry."

She stood on her tiptoes and buried her face in his neck. "I love you so much. I don't deserve you. I'm not a nice person. I lose my temper. I swear too much. You're so much better than I am."

He tilted up her chin and stroked her blond hair back from her face with his fingers. His eyes were filled with wonder. "You're the most wonderful woman in the world. I still can't believe you're mine."

As he gazed at her, all the goodness in his soul infused her. And then he dropped his head and kissed her. Oh, so slowly. She had never been kissed like that. His lips touched hers so lightly that at first she could barely feel them. She was the one who deepened the pressure. She was the one who opened her mouth.

The kiss went on and on. He was a man of infinite patience, and he believed in doing a job well. He kissed her cheeks and her eyelids, laid her back on the bed and tilted her chin to the side so he could kiss her throat. He found the pulse that fluttered there and counted the beats with the touch of his lips.

She felt so languid, so warm. His lips trailed down the open vee of her blouse and lingered there. Her breasts began to throb, anticipating his touch. She wanted more of him. Her fingers worked beneath his shirt. He pulled her hands away and clasped them gently between his own.

"Would you like some champagne?"

She shook her head. She didn't want any champagne. She didn't want him to stop.

But he got up anyway. He went to the ice bucket and fiddled with the bottle. It took him forever to get it open. First he had to dry it with a towel, then he made a big deal out of removing the foil neatly. He unscrewed the wire cage as if he were working with a delicate piece of machinery. She wanted to scream at him to just open it, for Pete's sake, and get back to her.

While he poured a glass for himself, she propped herself up against the pillows. He asked her again if she wanted some.

"All right," she replied grouchily. "As long as you've got it open."

He brought the glasses over and stood by the bed looking down at her. The narrow gold wedding band looked beautiful on his long thin fingers. Her body once again began to grow warm and her irritation faded. The mattress sagged as he settled on the side of the bed and put the glasses on the nightstand.

"Don't drink yet," he said. "I want to think of a toast." And he sat there.

She couldn't believe it. She wanted him to kiss her again and touch her breasts, but he was sitting there thinking up a dumb toast. And while he was thinking, he began doing this thing with the palm of her hand. Just lightly stroking it with his thumb. She had never had her palm stroked in that particular way. It was so unbelievably exciting. Before long, she began to squirm.

"Did you think of it yet?" she finally gasped.

"A couple more minutes," he said, transferring his touch from her hand to the sensitive skin of her inner arm.

She closed her eyes. Her lips parted. What was he doing to her? The stroking on her arm continued forever, and then his mouth brushed over hers again in another of his delicious kisses. This was good, she thought. Now they were getting back to business.

She moaned as he kissed the base of her throat. His fingers played with the top button of her blouse. After another few years had passed, he opened it. He kissed the spot of skin revealed there and then unfastened the next button. A button and then a kiss. A button and then a kiss.

Her breasts where they rose above the scalloped lace of her bra were covered in a rosy flush. When would he get to her bra? To her slacks?

He stopped. "I think I have the toast now."

She gritted her teeth. If he didn't get his mind back on what he was doing, she was going to toast him.

He handed her back her champagne glass. "To my wife, the most beautiful woman in the world. I love you."

It was sweet—really sweet—but hardly original enough to be worth the wait. She clinked her glass with his, downed her champagne, dropped her glass to the carpet and threw herself back in his arms.

He gently disengaged himself and slipped off her blouse.

She wanted to give a whoop of triumph. Yes! He finally had the idea. He'd finally remembered what he was supposed to be doing. Now the bra. Don't forget the bra.

He didn't forget. His agile fingers unfastened the clasp so smoothly it seemed as if it had dissolved in his hands. He slipped the lacy garment off her and laid her down on the bed.

And then he just looked at her. She lay back and he inspected her with his eyes. Her nipples grew hard and beaded under his scrutiny. He bent forward. She closed her eyes, waiting for the heat of his mouth on her breasts, and felt his lips settle . . .

. . . over the curve of her shoulder.

She gave a little sob of frustration. Her hands knotted into fists at her side while he played with her shoulder for another ten years. My breasts! she wanted to cry. Taste my breasts, my bubbies, my pretty pretty boobies.

But the booby she had married had discovered a patch of incredibly sensitive skin at the inside of her elbow and he was sucking on it.

"Your slacks are getting mussed," he said finally.

"Yes," she agreed. "Oh, yes." She began to unfasten them, but again he pushed her away. He slipped them down over her legs and started to fold them.

"It doesn't matter," she said. "Just throw them across a chair."

"They'll get wrinkled," he replied, as if a pair of wrinkled slacks were some sort of monumental crime against nature. Standing, he held them by the cuffs, snapped the creases, and began matching up the inseams with a geometric precision that would have made Euclid weep with joy.

Paige wanted to weep, but not with joy. Why couldn't he understand how difficult it was for her to get aroused? Her excitement could vanish any second. It always did. He needed to take advantage of her arousal before it slipped away. Didn't he understand that?

Apparently he didn't. He had to carry the slacks over to the closet and hang them up. And not just any hanger would do. It had to be a trouser hanger.

She whipped off her underpants while his back was turned and lifted one knee just a bit so that the sole of her right foot was pressed against the curve of her left calf.

When he turned around and saw that, his eyes opened wider. Determined to gain the upper hand, she let one arm fall languidly to the side of the bed and began rubbing the sole of her right foot up and down her calf. Yank walked back toward the bed. She caught her bottom lip between her teeth. He abruptly took a detour.

She shot up on her elbow. "Where are you going?"

He walked over to one of the tables and flipped on another lamp. "It's hard to see in here," he said. "I like to see what I'm doing." And then he returned to the foot of the bed. Sliding his hands up and down her calves, he gently pressed her knees farther open.

Her mouth went dry. She looked up at him.

His hands rose to his shirt. But instead of taking it off, he began slowly rolling up the cuffs.

Her eyes flew to his face. For the first time, she saw the amusement lurking at the corner of his mouth.

"You're doing this on purpose," she gasped.

"I think," he said, "that no one has ever taken enough time with you."

Paige lived through a thousand glorious lives that night. Yank had been trained in the lessons of patience, and he believed in careful craftsmanship. He liked to form hypotheses and then test them. For example, if he used his tongue here and his hand there . . .

He was an engineer, an absolute genius when it came to working with small parts. And every one of her small parts surrendered to his intricate inspection and exploded under his skillful manipulation.

Who could have imagined he would actually have to smother her cries of fulfillment with his mouth? Who could have imagined that this absent-minded genius could bring her the satisfaction that had been eluding her all her life?

When he finally came to her, his eyes were glazed and his breathing as heavy as her own. She was hardly capable of rational thought, but she dimly realized what his patience was costing him and loved him all the more for it.

Even as he poised himself to enter her, he took care. He was her husband, her lover. But above all, he was an engineer. And good engineers never forced parts together that were of unequal size.

"All right?" he murmured.

"Oh, yes. Oh, yes," she gasped.

"My wife. My love."

She cried out with joy and passion as he entered her. He caught her cries in his mouth and they began to move together, rushing in harmony toward a place of perfect fulfillment.

As dawn streaked the sky, they lay satiated in each other's arms. "Why did you act like it would be okay if I went to bed with Mitch?" she whispered.

"Because I knew Mitch wouldn't go to bed with you."

"He would, too," she said indignantly. And then she smiled. "No, I guess he wouldn't have." Her fingers played with the textures of his chest. "I thought you loved Susannah."

He stroked her cheek. "I do. The same way you love her." He didn't see any need to tell her it hadn't always been that way, that there had been a time when he had been very much attracted to Susannah. She had been so different from the women he knew.

"Susannah's happiness is important to me," he went on.

"That's why I had to make Sam understand that he couldn't have her back. But in terms of physical attraction . . ."

When he didn't go on, Paige probed. "What? Tell me."

He looked troubled. "Please don't take offense at this, Paige. I love Susannah and I admire her. But don't you think she's a bit—plain?"

Paige gazed around her at the tacky wedding suite that Yank thought was so attractive. She giggled with delight and hugged him to her breasts. "Absolutely, Yank. Susannah is definitely too plain for you."

Everything about Mitch had begun to irritate Susannah. His clothes, for example. How many perfectly tailored navy-blue suits could a man own? How many navy and red rep ties? Couldn't he take a walk on the wild side just once and wear paisley?

And she hated the way he tapped his pen when he was annoyed, the way he leaned back in his chair and tugged on his necktie knot when he wanted to make a point. He took notes on absolutely everything—she hated that, too. What did he do with all those yellow legal pads once he filled them up? Did he rent a warehouse somewhere?

She fumed as she watched his gold pen scratch across the paper. He probably had one of those yellow legal pads on his bedside table so he could take notes on a woman's performance after they'd made love.

But she couldn't let herself think about that, and so she thought about how crazy he made her in meetings. They would be sitting around a conference table and he would be reading from his ten zillionth computer printout and talking about shipments and quotas and sales forecasts. Then, right in the middle of a sentence, he'd slip off those stupid horn-rimmed glasses and look over at her. Just a look. Just this macho-stud look like she was some sort of marked woman. God, it was irritating. It was so irritating, she would lose track of where she was and stumble around and then everyone would start looking at *her*.

"Susannah?"

She blinked her eyes. Jack Vaughan, their vice-president of Research and Development, was staring at her. *Everyone* was staring at her. She'd done it again. Mitch smiled and leaned back in his chair, making this stupid church steeple with his fingers.

"Susannah?" Vaughan repeated. "Do you have any questions about our figures?"

"No, no. They're fine." She suspected that everyone at the table knew she didn't have the slightest idea what figures they were talking about. A giant clock seemed to be ticking away in her head, marking this last week until her divorce was final. Why did Mitch have to be so stubborn? Why did he have to drive her crazy like this? She wasn't sleeping well at night. All of this waiting had worn her nerves to the breaking point.

The loudspeaker snapped on. "Attention unmarried females. Free gynecological exams are now being given in Building C. Ask for Ralph."

Susannah jumped out of her chair. "That does it! I'm going to have somebody's *ass!*"

Mitch looked pained.

Jack Vaughan closed his folder. "I think our meeting is adjourned," he said quietly.

She stomped toward the door. Mitch intercepted her before she could reach it with another one of his new tricks. He simply stepped in front of her and blocked her path with his body. It was nothing more than a macho power play, a completely juvenile way of reminding her that he was bigger and stronger than she was. Real tough-guy stuff.

"What do you want?" she growled, ignoring the fluttering in her stomach and the wonderful scent of his starched shirt.

He leaned down and whispered in her ear. "One more week, Hot Shot. Then I take what's mine."

She swallowed hard. He was getting to her. He was really getting to her.

Her divorce became final on a completely ordinary Wednesday. She sat through a session with her East Coast marketing people, and met with the management team that headed up their Singapore plant. Paige had called and asked if she could drop by in the afternoon, and Susannah had rescheduled a conference call to accommodate her.

She finished drafting a memo and looked at her watch. It was nearly time for Paige to arrive. She hadn't seen Mitch all day. Which was perfectly fine with her. He'd put her through hell this past month, and she planned to make him suffer for it. If he thought he could just jump in bed with her now that she was officially a free woman, she would very quickly set him straight. She might be free, but she had no intention of being easy.

Paige stuck her head in the door. "Hi."

It was so good to see her sister that some of Susannah's tension faded. Since her marriage, Paige's skin actually seemed to glow with contentment. And whenever Susannah saw Yank, he had this goofy smile on his face.

The honeymooners had settled in at Falcon Hill. The idea of Yank Yankowski serving as lord and master of Joel Faulconer's home made her smile. *You might actually have liked him, Daddy,* she thought. *Once you got over the initial shock, of course. He's the best there is, and he's made Paige so happy.*

Susannah took in her sister's pale raspberry suit, the pearls at her throat, the chignon, and the gray lizardskin pumps. "My, my. I'm impressed. Did you get all dressed up for me?"

"No. I did it for Paul. He gets nervous when board members wear blue jeans."

"Paul?"

Paige stepped aside, and Susannah saw that she wasn't alone. Paul Clemens, Cal's predecessor as FBT chairman, was with her. Susannah got up to greet him. They chatted awkwardly for a few minutes.

Realizing that this was to be more than a sisterly chat, Susannah directed them to the small conference table in the corner of her office. No sooner were they all seated than Mitch arrived.

Susannah's heart did one of those peculiar somersaults. He took the seat next to Paige.

"I didn't know this was going to be a formal meeting," she said coolly.

Paige fiddled with her pearls. "I'm the one who asked Mitch to be here. Look, Susannah, I'm sorry about this, but—"

"It's my fault," Paul Clemens interrupted. "Paige and I had a long talk yesterday and I asked her to set this up."

Susannah clasped her hands on the table. "Paul, you've been a friend for a long time, but if you're here in any sort of official capacity for FBT, I'm going to need one of our attorneys present."

"I'm retired, Susannah, although I still sit on the board. Let's just say I'm here in an unofficially official capacity."

"Hear him out, Suze," Paige said. "This is pretty important."

Susannah reluctantly agreed, and Paul began to outline the crisis FBT had been thrust into since the public revelations about Cal Theroux. The fact that a man who had been the chairman of FBT would soon have a prison term hanging over his head had made everything incredibly difficult. The more Susannah listened, the more alarmed she became. She had known that FBT was in trouble, but she had no idea their problems ran so deep. The giant corporation was, quite literally, on the verge of collapse.

Paul finished speaking, and she gazed at him with dismay. "I hope both of you understand that none of us at SysVal wanted to damage FBT. Our problem was with Cal, not the company."

"You've made that very clear in your public statements, and we all appreciate it," Paul replied. "But the fact is, the public perceives us as the bad guys in black hats, while you're Snow White. Companies don't want to do business with us anymore. It's as if we're tainted, and they're moving toward our competitors in droves. We've discontinued the Falcon 101, but that's had little effect. The price of our stock has become a sick joke. Every division of the corporation is in jeopardy."

Paige looked up from the pattern she had been tracing on the table with the tip of her finger. "Suze, this is my fault. I'm hopeless at managing my stock. When I attend FBT business meetings, my mind wanders; everything is so boring that I can't keep my thoughts focused. I never have the slightest idea how I'm supposed to vote. That's why I gave my proxy to Cal. And look what that led to."

"You didn't intend to hurt the company," Susannah said.

"But she did hurt it," Clemens interjected. "And neither

Paige nor I want that to happen again. FBT has nearly three hundred thousand employees. Entire communities depend upon us. Many of the small towns where we have plants couldn't continue to exist if we closed down. And we're losing, Susannah. Everything is slipping away."

Paige leaned forward. "I want to give you my permanent proxy, Susannah. I want you to vote my shares."

"Paige, I appreciate the vote of confidence, and I want to help you, but that's one thing I can't do. It would be a direct conflict of interest. My board of directors would never permit it."

"They would if you resigned," Paul said quietly. "If you left SysVal, put your own shares in trust, and took over as chairman and CEO of FBT."

Susannah sat stunned. They wanted her to take control of one of the biggest corporations in the United States, to take her father's old position. A hand grasped hers under the table and squeezed. The solid comfort of that big hand steadied her.

Paul studied her with great seriousness. "FBT must regain moral credibility if it's to survive. Right now, you're the only one who can give it back to us."

Susannah shook her head. "I'm sorry. Truly I am. I'll help you any other way I can, but leaving SysVal is absolutely out of the question."

For the first time since he had come in to join them, Mitch spoke. "Susannah needs a few days. Let her have some time to think it over."

"I don't want time, I—"

"I don't think a few days will hurt," he said smoothly.

She wasn't going to get into an argument with Mitch in front of Paul Clemens, and so she nodded. "Very well. A few days." But even as she spoke, she knew that nothing in the world would make her leave SysVal.

She had no sooner gotten home that night than Mitch appeared at her door. He was still wearing his business suit, and he hadn't even loosened his necktie. As much as she had been anticipating this moment, now that it had come, she wanted to postpone it. The past month had been nerve-wracking, but as she stared at him standing on her doorstep, she finally admitted to herself that she had loved that primitive feeling of being sexually stalked by the man she loved.

How could the reality ever match the expectation? Mitch would be a good lover, but in her heart of hearts, she didn't believe that he would be a great one. He was too neat, too proper. As she gazed into his face, her stomach began to feel queasy. What if she shocked him? What if he liked women who were more restrained in the bedroom?

"I—I'm sorry," she stammered. "I can't invite you in. I've got a bad headache."

"You've got a yellow streak," he replied.

She slammed the door on him and went into the living room, where her hands trembled as she snatched up a magazine she had no intention of reading from the glass-topped coffee table. Why did she have to be such a sex maniac? As passionately as she felt about him, she would never be able to hold herself back. When he found out what she was really like, he would probably run from the house in terror. Maybe he'd send her a memo. FROM: Mitchell Blaine TO: Susannah Faulconer SUBJECT: Inappropriate Bedroom Conduct . . .

He walked into the living room and pocketed the key she had given him when she'd moved into her new home in mid-August.

"I want that key back," she said.

"No, you don't."

She stared at the lushly printed draperies Paige had picked out for her. She loved him so much and she wanted everything to be perfect, but this was real life, not a fairy tale. Remembering that they had something other than sex to discuss, she took a seat on the couch. At least she could postpone the inevitable a bit longer. "I'm not leaving SysVal."

"I don't think you have a lot of choice, Susannah."

"Don't say that!"

He sat down next to her and leaned back into the soft cushions. How could he be so relaxed when she was so uptight? "Somehow I can't picture you living the rest of your life with the fate of three hundred thousand people on your conscience," he said. "Not to mention all those small towns."

"I don't belong at FBT. It's old and stodgy and conservative."

"True. And it's been badly mismanaged ever since your father's death."

"You know as well as I do that they only want me as a figurehead. They'll expect me to use Paige's proxy as a rubber stamp for the majority opinion. Those men don't have the slightest intention of giving me any real power."

Mitch chuckled. "And aren't you going to have a wonderful time showing them the error of their ways?"

She switched tactics. "I don't have a college degree."

"I've got three of them. You want one?"

She tried another path. "I want to have a baby."

His face softened. "Do you? That's great. That is really great. I hoped so, but we haven't talked about it."

"We haven't talked about anything!" She jumped up from the couch. "Don't you understand? The president of SysVal can definitely be pregnant. At SysVal anything is possible. But can you honestly, in your wildest imagination, see the chairman of FBT breastfeeding through a board meeting?"

"Not the old FBT." He smiled, rising to stand next to her. "But the new FBT? The one with an updated product line, a streamlined management structure. The one with on-premises child care. Ah, Susannah . . ."

For a moment they let the vision sweep over them. It was a vision of a new corporation, one with a strong moral center and a commitment to the world it served. A corporation for the twenty-first century.

He took her hand. "You're thirty-two now, practically an old lady, and I'm thirty-eight. SysVal is a company for kids. We have so many talented people working for us that we barely know what to do with them. Let's get out of their way and let them run with it for a while."

"We both can't just walk out. That's impossible. And I'm not going to FBT without you. Our relationship aside, you're the best marketing man in the business."

"I'll stay at SysVal until the new team is in place and the board members' nerves have steadied. Then I'll join you."

He tilted up her chin with his fingers, and his eyes were soft with the depth of his feelings for her. "I love you, Susannah. Oh, God, I love you so much. All those years, watching you married to Sam. Sometimes I thought I was going crazy."

"I know, Mitch. Oh, my darling, I love you, too."

He dipped his head. A warm, hard mouth settled over hers. His big hands splayed over her back, ran up along her spine, tangled in her hair. His mouth was open, his kiss deep and aggressive. It was a man's kiss, a kiss that gave as well as took. Her breasts crushed flat against his chest as he pulled her closer. She accepted his tongue and gave him her own while she wrapped her foot around the leg of his trousers. He clasped her head between his big hands. It felt so right to be kissing him, so perfect to be in this solid, respectable man's arms. Oh, yes, she had been absolutely right to put little boys behind her.

His hand slid down over her breast. "Time's up, sweetheart," he said hoarsely. "I've been going crazy. I can't wait any longer."

At the touch of his hand on her breast, her nervousness came back in a rush. He was a good kisser, but kissing was only part of it. "Mitch, I'm not sure . . ."

He drew back and studied her for an agonizingly long moment. Then he tilted his head toward the hallway. "Upstairs, Susannah," he said quietly.

He didn't realize how important this was. He didn't understand that what happened next—or didn't happen—could put a shadow over everything. "Mitch, we may have some difficulty adjusting to—"

"Now."

She spun around and stalked away from him, marching toward the front staircase as if he held a gun at her back. Sometimes she hated engineers. She really did. Her shoes slapped on the carpeted treads. Since her fears weren't quantifiable, Mitch simply refused to recognize them. Everything had to be rational. The man didn't have one speck of intuitive power in his entire body.

She stomped into the bedroom and kicked off her heels. She could hear him behind her, moving at his customary unhurried pace, as if he were on his way to a staff meeting. As he came into the bedroom, she whirled around. "If this is a disaster, don't you dare blame me!"

He stared down at the carpet and shook his head. "I was

going to try to be a nice guy about this, but I can see that's not going to work." He lifted his head and glared at her. "Get out of those clothes, Susannah."

She was so tightly strung that her temper snapped. "You go to hell!"

"That does it." He reached for his necktie and yanked at the knot. "I was going to be a nice guy. Not come on too strong. A little moonlight. A few roses." He tossed his tie down on her pretty bedroom chair and threw his suit coat on top of it. Standing there in his shirt-sleeves, he splayed his hands on his hips and let his eyes roam over her as if she were a slave girl placed before him for his inspection. "Apparently, I have to remind you that you've been bought and paid for."

Her heart jumped into her throat. Oh, Lord, he was playing with her. The game wasn't over. A surge of love and desire rushed through her as she realized that he understood how she felt after all. Her tension dissolved. She lifted her chin and pursed her lips in disapproval. "I was not bought."

"Money exchanged hands," he said flatly, stripping off his shirt. "You were bought. Now get out of those clothes so I can get you warmed up."

The man had no shame. She walked over to the bed and slid down on it. Then she drew her legs beneath her and gave him her most smoldering look. "No need to warm up something that's already hot."

For a moment she thought she had him.

He recovered quickly.

"Coming from you, that kind of comment doesn't surprise me at all." His undershirt joined his shirt in a pile on the floor. She swallowed hard at the sight of his chest, already anticipating how it would feel beneath her hands. He kicked off his wing tips and removed his socks. "You may fool other people, Susannah, but don't forget that I have three college degrees and I'm not so easily misled. Beneath that prim exterior of yours, you like it wild. And that's exactly how you're going to get it." In one strong motion, he whipped his belt from the loops of his trousers and snapped it in the air. "You're going to get it wild."

Oh, Lord . . . And she had been afraid that he wouldn't be able to keep up with her.

"Get up on your knees and take that dress off right now," he ordered.

Yes, sir. Oh, yes, my very dear sir. She scrambled to her knees and began working feverishly at her buttons. While she worked, he actually had the nerve to slide the length of the belt back and forth in his hand. The sparkle in his eyes almost ruined the effect, but it was still wonderfully menacing, and she was going to kill him if he laughed. Imagine being tied to this incredible man for the next forty years. Her lover, her friend, the other half of herself.

Still, she knew it wasn't good for him to get too full of himself—especially after everything she'd let him get away with these past few weeks. She had a little surprise in store for Mr. Macho. No stuffed shirt in a pinstriped suit was going to call her prim and get away with it.

Opening the last of the buttons, she stripped the dress over her head, revealing the deliciously naughty undergarments she had put on that morning in a fit of nervous anticipation—the soft peach demi-bra and panties, the matching garter belt and stockings.

Mitch's black leather belt fell to the carpet. "That's more like it," he said huskily. He didn't take his eyes off her as he pulled down his trousers.

Susannah swept her gaze along his muscular thighs and then burst out laughing. Mitch was wearing the tiniest pair of black zebra-striped briefs she had ever seen on a man.

She fell back into the pillows and hooted. "How long have you been wearing underwear like that?"

"For a while."

"Do you mean to tell me that during all those endless presentations we've sat through together, all those boring budget sessions, you've been wearing underwear like that?"

"I could ask the same question." He lowered himself to the bed beside her and lightly snapped a peach-colored garter.

She wrapped her arms around his neck and slid her fingers into his hair, pulling him down beside her. "Sometimes I don't wear anything at all," she whispered.

He groaned and gathered her into his arms. His mouth opened over hers as he gave her a ferocious, demanding kiss. Before long, their naughty underwear dropped to the floor.

As they explored the secrets of each other's bodies, their skin grew sleek with sweat. But they had waited so long for this moment that neither wanted it to end too soon, and they prolonged it with gentle warfare.

"You'd better be good," he growled.

"They don't come any better."

"We'll see about that."

Each fought for supremacy—first one rolled on top, and then the other. She bit his shoulder; he retaliated with a nip at the curve of her bottom. She entangled him in the covers and ran from the bedroom. He caught her on the stairs and tossed her over his shoulder to carry her back. Their behavior was disgraceful, woefully inappropriate for people in their positions, but no one was around to point that fact out to them.

He dumped her on the bed and sprawled on top of her, catching handfuls of her hair in his fists. She arched her back and penetrated his mouth with her tongue. His hands roamed her body and found its secrets.

When they could stand their fierce love play no longer, she opened her legs and he cradled himself between them. As he poised to enter her, she looked up at him with her soft eyes.

"This is forever, isn't it, Mitch?"

All the laughter, all the mischief faded. He gazed down at her kiss-bruised mouth, and his face was young and tender with the depth of his emotion. "Oh, my love. My sweet, sweet love. This is till the end of the world."

They weren't children. They had lived through other loves and other lives, and so they knew the gift of their joining was precious. He entered her aggressively, possessing her with the boldness of a man who could only find happiness with a woman of daring spirit. She accepted him fearlessly, filled with the wild joy of a soul that had found its mate. Their bodies fit together as if they had been designed on the day of their creation to make a perfect match. And when they cried out at the very end, they were still gazing into each other's eyes.

EPILOGUE

• •

Ihe Northern California weather was chill and crisp the January morning Susannah took her place as Chairman of the Board and Chief Executive Officer of Falcon Business Technologies. She wore her most conservative gray suit, her lowest black pumps, her simplest earrings. The only other piece of jewelry she permitted herself was the heavy gold wedding ring on her left hand. It was a beautiful piece of jewelry, but the number of large diamonds that sparkled in the band made it a bit flashy for FBT tastes.

A small group of men greeted her at the entrance of the Castle. "Welcome to FBT, Mrs. Blaine."

"Good to have you on board."

"Wonderful to meet you, Mrs. Blaine."

"Ms. Faulconer," she said. "But please call me Susannah."

They beamed their pleasure at her—a dozen dark-suited executives who knew that her sister's proxy had given her control of the corporation's largest single block of stock. She searched their ranks for the sight of a female face, but then remembered that women at FBT rarely rose above the ranks of middle management.

The men were gracious tour guides, leading her through the building as if she had never been there. They chatted as they escorted her along the hushed hallways and into richly carpeted offices. They opened doors and cupped her elbow to guide her.

"We've planned a long orientation period for you, Susannah."

"No need to hit you with too much at the beginning."

"We have a complete staff set up to advise you. They'll answer any of your questions . . ."

". . . explain our policies."

". . . direct you so you don't misinterpret any of our procedures."

"They'll keep things running smoothly so you won't be bothered with too many details."

"We thought it best if you concentrated on public relations for the foreseeable future."

"Holding press conferences."

"Giving interviews."

"Being a woman, I'm certain you'll want to do some redecorating."

"Your assistants have a list of the charitable functions we'd like you and Mr. Blaine to attend in the next few weeks. Quite important."

She smiled her cool, inscrutable smile and envisioned the executive dining room as it would look when it was transformed into an employees' child care center. The precious speck of life already growing inside her would be one of its very first customers.

She desperately wished Mitch were with her today, but it would be at least six more months before they could turn SysVal over to that brilliant band they'd chosen to lead their young company into a mature, profitable adulthood. She was going to miss working with him. By the time he came on board at FBT, her pregnancy would be advanced. She smiled as she envisioned the macho strut that was going to put in his walk—the first man in history to impregnate the CEO of Falcon Business Technologies.

Her head lifted ever so slightly as the building's loudspeaker system emitted three gentle chimes. "Mr. Ames to security," a soft voice announced. She tried to imagine that voice warning of a Japanese invasion in the parking lot.

She endured another hour of polite admonitions and

veiled commands before she excused herself and headed to the offices of the chairman. As she walked into the reception area, an army of identically clad assistants snapped to attention. They began picking up leather folders and legal pads. And as they walked forward, their mouths moved.

"Mrs. Blaine, if I could brief you on your agenda for the week . . ."

"Mrs. Blaine, we've scheduled your first press conference for—"

She held up her hand. "My name is Faulconer. You may call me Susannah. And the next person who says a word to me will—I swear to God—be given permanent responsibility for cleaning out every coffeepot in this building."

Turning her back on all of them, she walked into the private office of the chairman of FBT and shut the door.

With the exception of the many sprays of flowers from well-wishers, the office looked much as it had when her father had occupied it. She toured the room slowly, touching familiar objects—the bookcases, side chairs, a brass lamp. The gold and blue draperies drawn back from the great wall of windows were exact reproductions of the ones she remembered. Her father's huge desk with its polished malachite top still dominated the room. The bronze FBT falcon hung on the wall behind it, its wings spread wide to encompass the globe on which it perched.

The awesome scope of the task she had set out for herself swept over her. "Oh, Daddy, what am I doing here?"

But her father wasn't talking to her today. Maybe he knew what she had in mind.

To steady herself, she began opening the cards propped in the various flower arrangements. One was from Paige and Yank. They were converting the old guest house at Falcon Hill into a state-of-the-art laboratory for Yank. He had decided to work independently, dividing his time between projects for SysVal, Sam, and whoever else managed to capture his imagination. It amused Susannah to watch the man who had once been so involved in his work that a nuclear explosion couldn't distract him now shoot up his head at the faintest echo of Paige's footsteps. She could only imagine what he would be like when they had a child.

A dozen roses had arrived from Mitch's children. Their

thoughtfulness touched her, even though she suspected their father had been behind it. Still, they were wonderful kids, and the cheerful acceptance with which they had greeted her marriage to their father had been a blessing.

Angela had sent a splashy display of carnations, snapdragons, and daisies. So far, she was the only one Susannah and Mitch had told about their baby, and she had immediately announced that the child was to call her "Na Na."

"Not 'Granny,'" she had insisted, adjusting the silver-studded sleeves on her new red leather jacket. "I'm too young for that. But 'Na Na' has a nice ring."

Mitch and Susannah were touched by Angela's offer. Both suspected she would prove to be a first-rate grandmother, regardless of what she chose to call herself.

Susannah's eyes teared as she read the card from her former mother-in-law. "You'll always be my daughter. Knock 'em dead, kiddo!"

She walked over to the malachite desk, and after a moment's hesitation, took her place in the great leather chair that had once belonged to her father. The panel of switches that controlled the FBT fountains was still there. She jotted down a note to have it removed. That sort of power held no interest for her.

As she pushed her notepad aside, she spotted a small package wrapped in silver foil. It couldn't be from Mitch; his present had been on her night table when she had awakened that morning. While he had looked on, she had unwrapped a week's supply of naughty black underwear imprinted with the FBT logo.

"Dress for success," Mitch had said, and then he'd kissed her until she could hardly breathe and dragged her into the shower, where they'd made love.

After turning the silver box about in her hand, she opened the envelope that accompanied it and pulled out the card. In big block letters were the words REMEMBER YOUR ROOTS. It was signed, "Sam."

Inside the package she found a small gold charm, a perfect replica of the Blaze. She cupped it in her hand and told herself that a wise executive understood changes couldn't be made overnight. Adjustments had to be implemented slowly. Upheaval threatened people, made them feel insecure.

The wise executive understood the value of tact and patience.

And then she gazed about the spacious office and remembered that this was the place where her father had humiliated Sam.

"You were wrong, Daddy," she whispered. "You should have listened to him."

Taking the charm with her, she got up from the desk and went over to investigate the walnut cabinets. In one of them, she found the equipment that tied the executive office into the building's loudspeaker system. In the next cabinet was the elaborate stereo system that Cal had installed. She pulled a tape she had brought with her from her purse and slipped it into the cassette deck.

Looking down at the little Blaze charm in her hand, she smiled to herself and whispered, "This one's for the kids in the garage." She picked up the microphone and switched on FBT's loudspeaker system.

"Listen up, everybody. This is Susannah Faulconer speaking. Beginning in exactly one hour, my door is open. Everybody in this company who wants to talk to me, start lining up. Rank doesn't count. First come, first served. My door stays open until we're done. And you'd better be ready to strut your stuff, because starting right now, I'm throwing this corporation into chaos. All official policies are suspended. All normal procedures are up for grabs. We're going to rediscover who we are. And when we're done—if we're very smart and very lucky—we'll be ready to dazzle the world." And then she hit the button on the cassette recorder.

While the hallowed halls of FBT filled with the music of the Rolling Stones, she settled back at her desk, propped up her feet, and waited for the screams to start.